Shadows in the Aftermath

2nd Edition

A DRAKER SERIES THRILLER

MARIANNE SCOTT

crowecreations.ca
Ottawa Canada

Shadows in the Aftermath © 2022 by Marianne Scott

1st Edition FriesenPress 2022
2nd Edition Crowe Creations June 2023

Edited by Jenna Kalinsky
Designed by Crowe Creations
Text set in Times New Roman; headings set in Beatnik SF

Cover photo needpix.com
Cover design © 2023 by Crowe Creations

Crowe Creations
ISBN: 978-1-998831-15-9

This book is dedicated to the memory of my wonderful husband. I love you and hold you in my heart forever.

Everything is unique. Every person, place and thing interacts in an endless combination of circumstances.

One

Roscoe drew back the string of his bow, let his arrow fly, and ended the fear we'd been living beneath for so long. I watched the arrow as it slowly arced through the air and found its mark in Felix's heart. I can still hear with perfect recall all these months later the sound of it, the metal tip penetrating his flesh, moving through bone and muscle, until it found purchase in his evil, callused heart.

True to form, Felix didn't die right away. He swayed a moment, hovering between life and death, as if he could choose whether to die or not, before the Draker Dobermans Rune and Riemes attacked him, snarling. Their paws landing forcefully on his chest caused Felix to fall backward over the edge of the villa's stone wall and plunge thousands of feet to the dark waters of the Mediterranean below.

Roscoe was only a boy, but as he stood on the path at the bottom of the garden, I saw a man's rage etched into his face.

Felix's death ended the torment the vengeful and demented madman had inflicted on us, but the cost was high. The fourteen-year-old boy, in defending everything he loved—all he had left—had to throw away the last of the beauty that was his childhood. I saw it in his eyes the moment he lowered the bow. For him, killing Felix changed his soul the same

1

way Felix had changed me when he set the fire that killed my family and erased my former life.

Flashes of my old self, Kathleen Jones, the girl I used to be, sprang to my mind. I'd been able to make myself forget about the fire, the clinic where they changed me from Kathleen Jones—straight "A" psychology student at NYU just on her way home from her last-ever university exam—to Ruby Draker, someone she'd never met who bore no resemblance to the girl she'd always been. Like a butterfly emerging from a cocoon, over time, Kathleen knew she had to die so Ruby Draker could live—and live to fight those who had murdered her family.

All of us who'd gone through similar fates caused by the same Felix Szabo were now Drakers. We didn't share blood, but we were in every sense a family. Through our mutual tragedies, we found one another and held tight. Reinhardt, the first of Felix's victims, made it his mission to save as many of us as he could from Felix's list and brought us to his adopted home of Fairhaven in Nice, France, under new identities to let Felix continue to believe we were dead.

Reinhardt's, and our, good fortune that he owned the villa was due to a most peculiar turn of fate. In France, after his wife and son were murdered, he lifted the name "Reinhardt Draker" from a tombstone before departing for Monaco where he would start a new life. He had always felt a pull to Europe, and he figured Monte Carlo would be a beautiful place to mourn and start a new life. He found a menial job in a casino and kept a low profile.

One afternoon, after several rounds of drinks, the casino workers went out on a lark to answer a newspaper classified ad. State lawyers were looking for the heir to the Rothschild estate, the at-large illegitimate offspring of Beatrice de Rothschild. Beatrice had been the daughter of a prominent banking scion and her family had forced her to give up her baby at birth to protect the family reputation. Before her death, she'd bequeathed her entire estate and unbelievable wealth to this child—wherever he was—as an apology for what she had done.

The men's drink made them bawdy and stupid, and one after the other they egged each other on and staggered in to leave behind genetic samples. They left singing, staggering and slurring heady accounts of what it would be like to be the missing Rothschild.

A week later, Reinhardt got a call that his DNA was a match. He had been adopted, but he had grown up in the USA in very humble circumstances and could have never imagined that he belonged to such a lineage. But it was accurate, and once he learned the details, he began to see how things lined up. He gratefully accepted the inheritance and vowed that with the wealth and estate, he would go after Felix and avenge his family's murder. When he found out about more murders taking place, all for similar reasons as the one he'd suffered, and all caused by Felix, he used his means and circumstances to become the father to us all, grabbing us out of danger and saving our lives.

But vigilantism had its risks, and it eventually betrayed us. All eleven of us had been there that day the previous autumn when Felix Szabo—done with being thwarted by Reinhardt and the rest of us Drakers—brought a militia and descended on Fairhaven, determined to blast the estate and every last Draker into dust.

Our plan to exchange the hostages Szabo had taken went very wrong: we had secured his estranged father, who agreed to step back into Felix's life in exchange for the release of Ransom and two senior ex-CIA agents we had befriended while trying to best Felix in the U.S. It should have worked but Felix turned and in a blind fury, began shooting wildly. He wounded Reinhardt, killed his own father, and then killed our beloved Rosalind, Reinhardt's partner, lover, and the person who had helped him over the loss of his wife.

We should have known that Felix would not value life—not even the life of his own father. He had executed our Rose Draker only days earlier. He had been intent on killing every single one of us and destroying all we held dear.

When his goons, dressed in black, crawled up and over the cliff, dropped from helicopters and crashed the front gate, bent on killing us, it should have been clear that negotiating would be futile. We fought back as best as we could and our contact, James Hollinger, the head of the CIA, also showed up at the last minute to help. But in the end, Roscoe's arrow was what freed us.

Afterward, through the balmy Mediterranean winter and into the spring, we put our heads down and rebuilt the material things in our lives. Rachel, who had studied art history at the Sorbonne in Paris, took charge of the house and garden restoration and soon the mansion was buzzing with power tools and hammers as skilled craftsman painstakingly fixed the damaged structures and artifacts so lovingly installed by Reinhardt's birth mother, Beatrice de Rothschild, so many years before. Gardeners replanted everything from crawling, lime-green ground cover to arching plane trees and Cyprus. In the Japanese Garden, the red bridge that arched over the bubbling stream emptying into the pool of Koi below was rebuilt, and within days, it looked like the original. Within a few months, everything was back to normal. Those of us living inside, however, would never be.

Most nights, less than a handful of us gathered for dinner in the dining room, even though our cook certainly tried to tempt us out with homey, delicious meals. Mostly we didn't have an appetite, and the room contained too many ghosts: we left Rosalind's place empty and moved Rose's chair to rest against the wall.

In those months, Reinhardt didn't come out of his room for dinner even once.

Roscoe, too, rarely showed up, instead, eating straight out of the fridge at odd hours, staying in his room, or going straight to the living room to play video games. He'd even stopped playing with Rune and Riemes, who roamed freely, sniffing about without purpose. He didn't go to Reinhardt either, even though I knew him well enough to know he ached to and was so alone. His real parents had been murdered, and now his adopted mother, too. His adopted father was locked away holding her picture and withering. On the rare occasion I saw Roscoe, he was also thin and wan, as lackluster as an inmate. He had killed a madman to save us, but he was too late for Rosalind. At his age to lose two mothers was surely too much to bear. I left him alone to grieve. I wished he could accept what a hero he was, but I knew he felt the burden of what he'd done, and it ate at him from inside.

Those of us who did gather for dinner didn't speak much. It wasn't just Roscoe who needed love and care. We all did. We needed each other desperately, but no one made a move to open that door. I needed the others. If not their embraces, then at least their proximity, but the vacant chairs felt like tombstones, markers of who we once were. I shivered at the emptiness and worried we would never heal or come together as a family again.

***

One cool May day, I went for a run and ended by standing quietly on the second-story veranda that overlooked the gardens. I was startled to see Reinhardt outside. My heart opened for him with love, a far cry from when we'd first met and I'd taken him for an abductor and captor rather than a savior.

He sat on a stone bench, looking numbly into the horizon. Before the shootout, I'd occasionally witnessed a hint of melancholy in his eyes, but now it was a sadness so thick and dark it looked to be over-taking his sight. Ours was a legacy of loss. To be a Draker, a person created out of nothing, meant that to love was to lose. Reinhardt had lost his first wife and two young boys to Felix's wrath, and now he had lost his Rosalind. He may have healed from the gunshot wounds from the altercation with Felix, but that was the extent of how far he'd come.

A chill ran through me. I wondered if his grief would, like Felix's, turn into bitterness satisfied only by revenge and become the only way to soothe his pain. Would his grief overtake him? With all its unpleasant qualities?

Felix hadn't always been a monster. He'd grown up in an orphanage because his father was serving a life sentence for murdering Felix's mother who had been a hopeless alcoholic and addict. But the state educated him and gave him opportunities and he rose to prominence in the CIA. His ability to make decisions without the complications of emotion or empathy at a time when the world was threatened by nuclear annihilation, and when feelings were seen as a liability, was his asset; and the work he did was valuable to the institution and to the country. During the Cold War, Felix was in charge of foreign intelligence with a team of undercover agents in his command, people from whom he demanded complete loyalty. Rubbing shoulders with the President and Heads of State, he thrived on the power of his position.

When the Cold War ended in 1991, the government disbanded his department and offered all the agents lucrative retirement packages that the agents—who neither respected Felix nor liked working under him—gratefully took. Felix was no longer needed but he refused to retire and was therefore given a token government position in charge of Cold War records.

The fall from power was what broke him. He still considered the Russians a virulent threat, and those who "abandoned" him by taking the retirement package, traitors he vowed to punish. And thus his murderous raids began and one by one, he took to wiping out not just his ex-agents, but also their entire families. He was addled, but still shrewd and was able to cover up their deaths as accidents. In Felix's mind, these "casualties" were a small price to pay to protect national security.

When Reinhardt began rescuing the victims of these attacks—Rosalind being his first—Rosalind immediately became his partner and undertook the task of not only keeping us secret but creating a family out of us by giving us all names that began with "R" and with the last name Draker. When messages had to be sent by BBM or text, using RD maintained our cover and kept us non-entities. Rosalind organized us into a hierarchy of father, mother, brothers, sisters, uncles and an aunt, giving us both a structure and something that vaguely resembled the families we each had lost. Her nurturing made our personal losses less painful to bear.

I thought back to my outrage and fury when on my first day at

Fairhaven following my "abduction" and surgery, she introduced Renegade and Ransom to me as my brothers. Roscoe, whom I had met earlier, was a little boy and could pretend such nonsense without guile, but grown men buying into it seemed ridiculous to me at the time.

But now, these people, all victims of one man's wrath, were my only family and the love I felt for them was fierce. I felt the loss of Rosalind almost as acutely as the loss I felt for my own mother. I wasn't alone. When we gathered at dinner, with each passing day, Rosalind's chair haunted us. The memory of her bloody body had embedded itself into our minds and tore at everything left of our humanity. Without her to hold us together, her artificial family she made real, the holes standing between us seemed too vast for us to ever be able to close them again.

My sweat from my run had dampened my clothes so although the breeze was warm, I began to tremble. I wrapped my arms around myself. I'd run hard, harder than I'd thought I had energy for, and needed a shower. But I couldn't move. I watched Reinhardt, watched the now-restored gardens, and felt as if we were all part of a still life.

Even though the devil had claimed his disciple, Felix still had us in his grip. It sickened me. Even in death, Felix had us in his carefully orchestrated clutch of fear. He'd changed every one of us. Ruby Draker was hard and pragmatic and carried a gun and wore black; my old self as Kathleen liked to write bad romance novels with friends, and wear ten-hole Doc Martins and floral sundresses. I missed my cat, Misty. I missed my room. But the hardened shell I wore now was permanently etched onto me like a second skin. My past hurt too much to consider. Kathleen periodically would creep through and whisper, *Remember your humanity.* Since the attack, she'd been getting in more and more, her whispers louder as vengeance flared in the men around me, the men who were now my father and brothers. I prayed that they, too, had voices inside them that called for compassion—if not for a dead enemy, then at least for each other—and that soon we could find our way back to each other.

During the restoration, Renegade, our resident computer geek, handled the installation of the new front gate. Rachel had her opinions about how it should look, but he took care of the tech that ran through it. Because money was no object, she thought it a fitting tribute to Rose to have metal smiths create a single giant intricate rose intertwined with thorny metal vines on the front, while Renegade designed the heavy, gauged rods using the latest NASA technology.

Still, I knew no barrier was ever truly impenetrable. Even after the new motion detection equipment and cameras were calibrated and installed, a gnawing feeling of impending danger continued to churn inside me. Rosalind had taught me to trust my instincts, and my instincts told me to stay alert and keep my guard up. The fact that Felix was dead should've quelled my fears, but the psychologist in me understood the aftermath effects of PTSD all too well. If only I could have kept my life. My parents. My brother. The internship I had been about to start at University Hospital. All of it.

Hot tears sprang to my eyes and I turned away from the view as if it had turned sour. Kathleen was gone. But Ruby knew what Kathleen had learned. And Ruby, I, had had a mentor and teacher in Rosalind who had helped me reinvent myself. Her tutelage made our relationship strong in a way I'd never felt with another woman, not even my own mother, both of us bonding to each other in a need to fill the void, for Rosalind that of a lost daughter, for me a lost mother.

My stomach lurched and I took off again. I was stiff and cold and thirsty, but instead of going back to the house, I ran down the stairs back out into the garden and headed straight for where we had built a special grotto dedicated to Rosalind.

I arrived at the base of the marble temple structure that marked the end of the garden peninsula, breathing hard. The new roses had grown fat and full and gave off a rich scent. The ocean breeze toyed with my hair and lifted the chestnut strands around my shoulders. I thought back to that first morning the previous spring when the Drakers had surprised me on my morning run, how they joined me in sequence along my planned route, and how I tried so hard to ignore them, hating every last one for kidnapping me and imprisoning me in some random European estate, denying them entry into my heart. They knew I would figure it all out in my own time and remained by my side until I did.

I plunked down onto the marble bench in front of Rosalind's grotto that curved around the pedestal where her urn stood. The urn was only a symbol; we had set her ashes free over the Mediterranean. I wanted to talk to her. I ached to hear her voice and have her guidance. But when I squeezed my eyes shut and tried to connect with her spirit, it wasn't Rosalind who answered my troubled heart. It was Kathleen.

It jolted me to hear my own former voice, so clear, so distinct and real, I almost fell off the bench. It sounded much lighter and bubblier than my voice had become.

Ruby, she said. *It's time to do something. Everyone has mourned long enough. Rosalind would have never allowed this to go on so long. Take the lead. She's counting on you.*

I wanted to argue with Kathleen. She had no idea what I was going through. Then I paused and bent over laughing. How far removed I'd become from my real self. I laughed so hard, I couldn't catch my breath, and then my gut and body turned on me, and the anger and frustration I'd been carrying around burst like a dam inside and I began to sob.

After my tears spent themselves, I lifted my head to look at Rosalind's urn again. I shakily stood up, wiped my slimy hands on my shorts, and swiped at my face with the back of my hands. My voice out loud startled me.

"OK, Kathleen," I said as if the former me were standing there. "You're right. It's time." I started down the path back to the mansion, the crunch of my sneakers on the pea gravel seeming to chant a message back to me.

Or maybe it wasn't Kathleen anymore. She belonged to the past where she was safe. Perhaps the voice was actually Rosalind's. The thought made me stop and turn back to look at the grotto.

I spoke again, quietly. "Rosalind, I promise. The Drakers will always be a family—my family." The gentle winds played with my hair and I knew her spirit was still out there. Comforted, I went back to the house with a lighter heart.

Without Rosalind, the Draker family was floundering. It was her determination that had brought order and structure to our unrelated cross-generational colony of orphans and reorganized us, the accidental strays, into a loyal family, each with our own roles as we branded ourselves into the new identities of our pseudo lives. She was the glue, the substance around which everything made sense. Without her, our roles and purpose were scattered and disorganized. For now, perhaps, that's how we wanted it. We clung to the memory of her perfect orchestration. We missed her so much that reorganizing the family in any other meaningful way would seem to dishonor her. So we wallowed in our sadness, each of us isolated in our own grief. But it was time to move forward.

Rune and Riemes bounded toward me happily as I approached the west terrace and nearly knocked me over. "Easy, guys," I laughed. On the terrace, Cook was setting up breakfast and turned to wave at me. I waved back and went up the steps to her.

"*Bonjour, Ruby,*" she said. "Such a beautiful day, *n'est-ce pas?*" She smiled, but her smile fell when she saw my face.

I probably looked horrible. After two runs and a good cry, I was dehydrated and boiled-eyed, like a blue-eyed zombie in a ponytail.

She came over and gave me a warm hug and a sympathetic smile. "Come. We have breakfast outside this lovely morning. I made fresh *crème* puffs. All that hibernating inside when the sun is shining, terrible." She waved her hand and lumbered to the table while ushering me into one of the cushioned chairs at the long table. "I get it for you. You sit."

I ran my finger over the glass. This was the patio table where Rosalind had introduced me to my new brothers that first day. It was only a year before when my new life happened, but it felt like a lifetime ago.

The table seemed enormous with no one else there. I felt terribly alone.

Cook came out, balancing two cappuccinos, a plate of her delicate pastries, and a bowl heaped with berries. She laid it all out for us and plopped down into the chair beside me. She leaned back comfortably and breathed in deeply, relaxing as she looked out over the sparkling waters of the Mediterranean, slowly sipping her cappuccino.

"Each morning I set up breakfast either in the solarium or here on this splendid terrace. Each day I prepare the food, and the food is eaten. But the family does not eat together anymore." She shrugged and sighed. "But you, *chérie*, are outside, and I'm so happy. Even the air is delicious, *n'est ce pas?*" She placed her hand on mine and looked tenderly into my face.

My eyes filled again. "I was at the grotto this morning," I murmured. "I... Rosalind..." I looked at her helplessly. "I don't know how to convince them to start anew. "

"Ah, *chérie*, perhaps it's as easy as asking them to join you for dinner tonight..," Cook's voice was soft and kind. "Tell them I prepare something very special."

I looked at her. I hadn't ever realized how in tune she was with what we were all feeling. But then again, anyone who nourishes a family would be perceptive.

"Rosalind always called you Cook," I said. "*Mais, quel est ton nom?*" I tried, surprising myself. I had been so resentful in the early days, I hadn't so much as said "bonjour" to a soul, and then we were flying all over the place to target Felix so there wasn't exactly the time to learn how to conjugate French verbs. But over this summer, I'd decided it was time to open my ears a bit.

Still, I knew I hadn't said it right, and we both giggled.

"*Très bien, chérie,*" Cook said. I knew "chérie" meant darling. That made my heart hurt; that was what Rosalind called us.

Cook reached over and gave me another hug and kissed both my cheeks. "*Enchanté, mademoiselle. Je m'appelle Sophie.*" She clapped her doughy hands to her thighs and stood. "So what do you think about having a little dinner tonight, *hein*? What can I do to make it too irresistible to refuse?" Her grin was infectious.

Suddenly, more than anything, I missed the smells of New York: burned chestnuts in Central Park at Christmas time, Chinese food floating out over the street on a warm night, big slices of pizza as fat as shoe boxes covered in pepperoni and mushrooms. My stomach constricted. "Pizza?" I whispered, not able to get the whole word out. I took a deep breath and tried to imagine how I was going to get everyone down to dinner.

As if they understood a party was coming, Rune and Riemes yelped and sprinted to the newly fortified gate, returning with a stick for me to throw in a game of fetch.

The gate. That was it.

The craftsmen had just put the final touches on the rose the day before.

"We can celebrate the completion of the gate. It may not be a special occasion like a birthday or anniversary but, well, it means we're safe, and Rose is…" Rosalind loved roses and Rose… surely it would remind everyone that we loved each other and were still a family. That we needed each other now more than ever.

"*C'est brilliant,*" Sophie said. "*But only pizza? Pas de coq au vin ou—*"

I found my voice. And my hunger. "Pizza. Nice and casual. No fuss. No pressure," I said. "And I've never met a person who didn't like it."

I felt the weight of decision lift. The wind swirled around me then and I swore I heard Rosalind whisper her approval.

The dogs danced at my feet and dropped the stick closer.

"OK, go fetch!" I threw the stick down the path and both dogs tore across the grass to wrangle over it, returning in what seemed like seconds, yelping and dancing for more.

"Good, *chérie,*" Sophie said. "Roscoe didn't play with them like that for a long time. You stay here, and I will go make everything perfect for tonight."

"Nothing fancy, OK?"

"Mmm," she said. "Indulge me a bit, *s'il te plaît*. I promise. I will not disappoint." Sophie clapped her hands and returned to the house with a cheerful energy in her step.

I knew immediately that tonight's pizza wouldn't be even close to a New York slice. I smiled sadly. But then, nothing was the same. But it would be just right for what I—for what we—were now.

Two

AFTER A FEW THROWS WITH THE DOGS, I purposefully tossed the stick toward the Fairhaven gate. I hadn't gone over to inspect it—as if seeing it made real the two women's deaths—but if at dinner we were going to celebrate our security and survival, I needed to see this technological marvel for myself.

Yet this time, out of all the tosses, the dogs didn't go after the stick and instead ran together straight down the long driveway to the entrance. Rune and Riemes had a keen sense of when things weren't right and when they opted to check things out instead of keeping up our game, I immediately felt my stomach tighten. The summer before, they had a near flesh-ripping frenzy when unauthorized gardeners tried to gain entry to the estate.

The dogs got to the new gate and sniffed around with curiosity. They weren't snarling or barking, but were clearly on alert. As I got closer, I noticed people doing work at the guard's hut off to the side, and heard Renegade arguing with a workman in an indigo jumpsuit, who was perched precariously on the top rung of a ladder to adjust the camera.

"I thought everything was finished," I said, coming up to Renegade's elbow.

"Morning, Ruby," he answered. His full cheeks were flushed scarlet as he pointed angrily at a surveillance camera just out of the workman's reach.

One would think Cook wasn't feeding us more than lettuce for all the collective weight we'd lost, and Renegade's normally average frame—with some muffin top, the mark of his sitting too much—was now too lean to keep his khakis up. He used one hand to yank on his pants and the other to direct the workman to move the camera more to the right, waving to indicate how far it should angle toward the house until finally, he decided it was fine. "Fine, that should do it."

The squat worker looked not at all pleased that some American with bed-head and a Hawaiian shirt was telling him how to do his job. The man exhaled a disgusted grunt and rolled his eyes as he dismounted the ladder and started packing up his tools. "*Des riches sont bâtards stupides,*" he muttered under his breath.

Normally, I would have chuckled, but these days, I worried that anyone mad at us could be a potential threat.

"I think you just made an enemy," I said, raising a cautionary eyebrow at Renegade to clam up before this guy turned on us.

Renegade rolled his eyes. "That's just the point," he said. "No one is ever going to catch us off guard again. This is the latest security technology. This gate and the camera equipment will set off all kinds of alarms in the control center." He looked at the technician and sneered.

I felt bad for the man but didn't say anything about Renegade's behavior. I knew he felt terrible that Felix and his team had managed to best his security. He blamed himself for everything. No wonder he'd grown so thin.

Yet, being a Draker, I understood. We were all in this together, and we all felt responsible. But to get past it, we were going to have to wrestle our inner demons into submission. I was at least glad he'd come out of the computer cave where he'd been hibernating. This was, at least, progress.

"So hey," I said, balancing on the balls of my feet, "Cook is making a special dinner for us tonight! I don't think we've sat down to eat together since... You know. What? Seven months ago? So I thought it was time we... It would be nice to eat together as a family again. We can celebrate—"

"Celebrate?" he scoffed. He glared at me and took a step back.

The technician looked up sympathetically at me and said "Pshh," as he waved his arm at Renegade to dismiss his foul temper.

"Yes. Let's celebrate security as an art form instead of a defense strategy." I ran my hand over the exquisite iron-work vines and shrugged. "I asked Sophie to make pizza," I sang as I tickled his arm. "Come as you are. Maybe afterward we can christen the gate."

"Who's Sophie?" he said.

"Cook. She's concerned about us and I'm concerned too. It's time."

Renegade paused and I wondered if he'd yell again, but his face softened. He nodded and reached for my hand, pulling me close into a hug.

"Oh, right. Sophie." He nodded. "You got her to make pizza? You know she was one of the top graduates in her class at Le Cordon Bleu, right?"

I shook my head. He knew the pedigree of the woman who fed us but didn't have a clue what her name was. I cuffed him on the shoulder. "You're hilarious," I said. "Anyway, if we're going to celebrate our new security, I thought I should check to make sure everything was finished."

"It is. Now that that bozo re-positioned the camera."He started to walk away, then turned around. "Come with me to the control room. I have to verify the surveillance range. "

"Bozo?" I said. That poor man. I hoped he didn't speak enough English to know what that meant. "OK, I'll come but only if you help me convince everyone to have dinner together." I folded my arms across my chest and threw back my head.

He looked at me for a long time, frown lines deepening in his fore-head. "Why are you looking at me so weird?"

"For a second there, you sounded exactly like Rosalind."

He gaped for another moment before brightening. "Fine. Deal." He stuck out his hand. "Everything has its price." Then he started to laugh.

It was wonderful to hear the sound. I began to regret not reaching out sooner, but I knew all things happened in their right time. I hoped also that it was time for the others.

We started to walk up the long driveway toward the house when I heard a truck. We turned as a cube-shaped lorry was getting clearance at the guardhouse then rumbled past us, coming to a stop directly under the portico by the front entrance.

The front entrance was very grand, not one we used every day, but it was the one I was brought through when my ambulance pulled up that first day at Fairhaven and Ransom came out to help me negotiate the steps and my new life.

I remembered his strong arms around my waist and how shaky my legs were. How frightened I was. Even so, drugged up with sedatives, I could still recall with instant clarity how terrified I was of these people. If only I'd known then that they'd saved my life. Or how deeply Ransom would eventually work his way into my heart.

I shook my head at the memory. Tinged with sorrow from having misjudged these people was how I'd misjudged Ransom most of all. My eyes welled up, but I shook my head and took a deep breath. Not everyone can love in return, I thought.

Just then, Rachel came clicking out from the vestibule, all heels, and Parisian efficiency, to greet the men stepping out of the cab.

One went around and opened the back of the cargo hold, the other approached Rachel with a clipboard and pen.

She signed the delivery manifest while issuing rapid-fire instructions, and he and his partner immediately took to unloading the van of what looked like—through its generous wrappings—a large dining table and chairs.

I knew right away the furniture was for the solarium where Felix's raiders had ruined the original antique table and everything else in the room. Rachel stood beside the van, her hands on her petite hips, to watch them.

I felt unkempt beside Rachel at the best of times; she was effortlessly chic, her auburn hair swept into a French roll, and her Tunisian-accented French coupled with her aristocratic upbringing ever clipped and perfect. Yet she was always warm and affectionate toward me, and when she spotted me and Renegade over the top of the van, she waited for us until we made our way to the entry.

We approached just as she was about to follow the men into the house.

She gave a little hop in her heels. "*Mes amis*, that was the last of the deliveries." She clasped her hands grinned. "Now, everything is complete."

"Can we break in the new table by having dinner in the solarium tonight?" I asked.

Rachel opened her brown eyes wide and started to squeak, "Break…?"

I realized she didn't know the expression. I laughed. "Sorry. To break something in means use it for the first time."

She twisted her mouth and I could tell she wanted to say no. She had restored the house like a museum curator and probably preferred we look and not touch, but she glanced back at me and smiled.

"We promise not to actually break them," Renegade offered.

"You say we have dinner together?" she asked, tilting her head. "*Bien oui*, I suppose I'll have to be there to make sure everyone respects the furniture." She smiled sadly.

That's when it hit me. I had counted only seven chairs coming in. There would be no empty seats for Rosalind and Rose.

"But how do we get Reinhardt to come out of his room?" Rachel asked. "He often doesn't even let the housekeeping staff in to clean. He barely eats. He's getting so thin. I'm really worried about him." A veil of despair fell over her face again. She searched our faces. "Now I must supervise the workmen to make sure that the dining set is properly positioned." She hurried off into the house.

"Still coming to help me check to see if the bozo got the camera positioning right?" Renegade asked.

"After you," I said.

As usual, all the computers were in full hum in the underground control center. I was surprised to see that Monitor 1 was still running the Facial Recognition Program; 2, 3, and 4 were sequencing the visuals from the security cameras.

Renegade punched away at the keyboard of 4.

"Bozo!" Renegade shouted. "It's still out of line. It should pan over another twenty feet. I'll have to go and fix it myself."

He was walked to the wall where a secret motion-sensor panel opened into the stairway that led up to the main floor, when Monitor 1 pinged and an alert flashed on the screen.

We both turned.

When I saw the name and the image, my body went cold. It was a photo with the identification and alias of another ex-agent.

We approached the terminal as though it were a ticking bomb.

I read the name in the recognition field again. I felt like a knife had pierced my heart.

It simply wasn't possible.

Three

"ROBERT DRAKER?" I WHISPERED IT AS THOUGH the name itself weren't possible. I skimmed the info the computer brought up. The photo had been taken at a rehab clinic in Portland, Maine. It showed a male physiotherapist, a woman in a white lab coat, and our Robert sitting in a wheelchair, grasping two parallel bars as if he were about to try to stand.

How could this be? Robert was dead. Felix had showered him with machine gunfire. A horrible flash of guilt and shame came into my body. I tried to remember what had happened. Could this really be our Robert? He'd been fatally shot... He couldn't have survived such an onslaught. The picture had to be doctored. I glanced over again. The man in the photo looked exactly like Robert: same shaved head, the same strong, tall carriage with cut biceps. Which then meant we'd left him at the farmhouse in Springfield, in the mud, still alive.

We'd abandoned him when he needed our help.

That dreadful day returned to me in an instant.

When we emerged from the barn, Felix, who was perched on the veranda roof of the Springfield farmhouse, Robert's family's home, began firing. I could still hear the rattle of the bullets from his Gatling gun that rained down on us. Myrtle, Robert's longtime companion, had tried to take Felix down, stepping out of the bushes with her treasured cougar gun. She was an excellent shot and never missed. But that night, in the dark, she tripped on a tree root, and in the second it took her to recover, Felix fired. He got her first and she fell face-first into the mud where, instantly, an inky red pool oozed out from underneath her. I could still hear the tortured echo of Robert yelling "No!" as he rushed to help her, even amid the flying bullets. Then his body jerked violently as several caught him. He fell directly on top of her, his own dark blood mixing with hers.

I couldn't breathe as I looked in disbelief at the computer screen. It was like my heart had been torn from my chest, the pain was so great. We'd left him there. We thought he was dead.

"I'll go get Ransom to help us verify the authenticity of this photo," Renegade said. His voice was trembling, his eyes almost popping out of his head.

He started for the door, but just then Ransom burst through. A sound was pulsing from the band he wore on his wrist. "My phone and Smart-Watch are going crazy," Ransom said. "What's going on?" He stared at Renegade.

Ransom had never disabled the facial recognition feature on all of his devices, even after the attack was long over. Felix may have died, but this was just another vestige of the legacy of fear he'd left behind.

Ransom looked at the monitors and lunged for them to get closer, knocking over a chair in his haste. He didn't say a word about the image on the screen as he frantically punched a code into the keyboard, paused to wait for results, then repeated for second verification, third and fourth.

The pinging kept on like a nightmare. He stared at the monitor for a long time then printed the screen image. When it came out, he held it in his shaking hands, horrified at the discovery. "The photo is unaltered," Ransom said. His eyes were open wide as he searched my face for a sign that perhaps this might have been some kind of terrible joke.

My knees went weak and I thought I might collapse, but Renegade took my arm and brought me over to the chair he had righted.

The words just fell out of me. "We left him there. He was alive and we didn't go back to help. How could he have survived? There was so much blood." I looked at Ransom with hot eyes. "Ransom, the photo—it can't be him, right?"

Ransom looked down, which confirmed it.

"We need to tell Reinhardt," Renegade said, glancing between us.

Part of me rejoiced that Robert might still be alive. Another part felt thick ugly shame for having left him. Unless... "Couldn't it be a trap? Felix operating from the grave? Or someone else?"

Renegade looked at me kindly and took me by the arm. Wordlessly, we went through the panel and up the stairs. "This photo wasn't sent by a dead man," he said gently.

Ransom and Renegade went off to talk—just the two of them—and I wandered back out into the garden. I knew I needed a shower and to start my campaign to get everyone to dinner, but I was in a fog. For some time, I half-heartedly wandered around the estate, played fetch with the dogs, stopping now and then to stare dumbly at the churning sea. I thought about eating or getting a drink of water, but I didn't make a move toward the house. I needed to see the ocean.

I walked to the end of the peninsula and climbed the temple steps, crossed the platform and leaned over the railing to look at the sea below. A gust of wind had whipped off the ocean. The spray teased my face. Gulls circled and jeered insults overhead. Below, jagged rocks sprang up like teeth where the water met the estate wall.

Of course, Felix was dead. Just because they didn't fish an intact body out of the sea didn't mean anything. The beautiful but violent waters housed all manner of hungry beasts that would have left no trace of the guileful human who had fallen off the cliff into the waves below.

It soon grew chilly, and I began to shake. I went in to shower and as I walked by the dining room, Sophie was there, humming as she was setting up our evening meal. The elegant antique dining table that had arrived that morning was craftily draped with mismatched expensive table linens. I suppose that was her idea of casual. She was humoring me. She mixed sterling silver serving dishes with rustic French crockery, and I felt her love in the care she'd taken to bring us together.

I wondered how much she knew about us—and the prison we lived inside, never again to be the people we once were. I knew it wouldn't matter to her. Maybe for security, Rosalind had convinced her that the Drakers were related by blood, but Sophie didn't strike me as that thick. One by one, newcomers arriving and being introduced as long-lost family? Come on.

She turned and smiled. "Where is everyone?"

"Last I left it, Rachel was going to coax Roscoe from his room," I said. "Shouldn't be too hard. What fourteen-year-old boy would turn down pizza? And Ransom and Renegade went to see if they could convince Reinhardt. Rowan? I saw him doing his perimeter walk and figured I'd wait until he was done with his rounds."

Even after all this time, Rowan had kept up his surveillance just as vigilantly as ever. Or—probably even more so. I paused and wondered if we'd ever feel fully safe again. I didn't mention the photo.

Rachel came clacking in with Rowan behind her. She sighed, her face awash in disappointment. "Roscoe says he's not hungry," she said. "When I told him it was pizza, he said he'd think about it. But I did manage to convince Rowan pretty easily." She laughed.

"What can I say, I love pizza," said Rowan. He shrugged and made a silly face. I appreciated that he was trying to lighten the mood. Everyone was uncomfortable.

Rachel's resting stance was her hands on her slim hips like a drill sergeant, making it easy for Rowan to hook his arm through hers and try to cajole her into coming into the room. He saw the table and laughed. "What's this?"

"*Un peu de* whimsy *ce soir,*" Sophie said, a bright smile on her face as she winked at me.

"So, Rowan. Are the flowers and bushes secured?" I teased. I realized though, I wasn't teasing. I was afraid.

Rowan wrinkled his forehead before staring me down. "Let's just say that caution is a sign of wisdom. Where's Renegade?" He had let go of Rachel's arm, easily forgetting about her and moving on to something else.

Rachel pursed her lips and raised a penciled eyebrow. She turned and went to the side buffet and poured some grounds into the espresso machine.

"Renegade and Ransom are upstairs trying to get Reinhardt to come down," I said. "We have some…" I struggled to find the right word, "news."

Ransom burst into the solarium, and I jumped. "No luck," he said. He threw his arms into the air, defeated.

We heard Renegade's footsteps. His cheeks were trembling with frustration. "We have to do something. His door is locked, and when I tried to talk to him, he just told me to go away. That he wasn't up for a chat." Renegade hiked up his pants. "He sounds terrible. We're going to need to do something rash. Maybe break down the door. "

"*Mon Dieu,*" Sophie said. She pulled a lace handkerchief from her apron pocket then raised both hands to her face, sniffing softly. "I try every day to make him foods he likes, to remind him to be a father to you all, to help him, but nothing," she murmured. "He has slipped away."

"Well, speaking of slipping," said Renegade. "I slipped the photo under his door, and if he looks at it, I think he'll come down here to ask for an explanation."

"You're right," I said. "Give him a few more minutes. The photo will get his attention."

Then Roscoe called out, surprising me. "Dad?" Roscoe shouted from the foyer. "Are you coming to get some pizza?"

We looked at each other before going out to see what would happen.

Roscoe had always called him Reinhardt. We stood beside the boy, our boy, and looked up toward Reinhardt's closed door. All of us seemed to hold our breath as we listened for a reply. It felt like an eternity, but soon, Reinhardt opened his door.

I gasped at Reinhardt's appearance. His clothes hung as loose as if on a skeleton and his normally robust olive face was pale with gaunt cheeks. The distinguished gray at his temples had spread throughout his dark brown hair, and his beard had become salt and pepper too. But all we cared about now was that he'd come out and was standing in front of us. I felt like crying, and when Roscoe burst away from the rest of us to run to Reinhardt, his father, and grab him tight, I had to turn and go into the dining room to wipe my streaming eyes.

The others followed me to give the two their privacy, and in a few minutes, they came into the solarium, Roscoe now almost as tall as Reinhardt, clutching him tightly around the shoulders, Reinhardt holding the printed photograph in his free hand. "Where did this come from?" Reinhardt asked.

We all looked at each other, but no one said a word.

Four

Sophie ran to Reinhardt and kissed him on both cheeks. "Come and eat. Come." She put her arm around the two and guided them into the room. "Our Ruby wanted a taste of home, and your French chef gave it to her!"

She tittered with excitement as she dashed up to the sideboard and began doling out salad onto plates.

I couldn't help but smile and caught Rachel's grin from across the room. Everyone took a seat and admired the innovative tablescape of grapes in crystal bowls, mixed with earthen urns and crockery butter dishes. She came around to Reinhardt who had paused in the doorway as though dumb, gently took the photo from his hand and pulled out the nearest chair.

"*This,*" she said, putting the paper on the buffet, "can wait until we thank the dear Lord for bringing us back to each other again." Sophie motioned that we should all put our heads down. "*Cher Dieu, s'il vous plaît, amenez-nous ensemble pour nous réconforter et nous fortifier encore.*"

Everyone together whispered, "Amen."

Our dear Sophie certainly knew her way around a thin crust pizza.

That was for sure. I ate at least five slices, though I lost count after about three. Everyone began talking again with each other, first about the food, but soon, about everything under the sun, rekindling our bond as friends and family—all of us except Roscoe, who hovered close to Reinhardt throughout the entire dinner.

Roscoe doted on Reinhardt like a worried mother, offering him slice after slice of pizza, stacking them like pancakes on his plate. While the rest of us chatted and laughed, so relieved to finally be together again, Roscoe's happiness was quieter and more like a slow burn. Every time I glanced over at him, I saw more and more color in his face, more delight in his eyes.

Reinhardt, too, borrowed on our energy and nibbled on a few slices, held hands with Roscoe, and looked around more than once as if deeply grateful for what was unfolding before him, but unable to say a word. I knew. I watched Roscoe and knew that if tonight weren't a fluke, but the start of our returning to one another, the two of them, father and son, would be OK.

The sun was setting and the familiar glow from the moon over the Mediterranean cast long shadows in the solarium. The moon had come in like this that night after my first shopping trip with the Draker clan.

What a day that had been. I smiled and shook my head at the memory.

Still believing they were out to get me, I'd been dragged into Nice to Frédéric's boutique to buy clothes because I had none. In reality, they were testing me, putting me alone with that slimy, womanizing sales-man to see if I could hold my own. I didn't know they were about to start my training as a Draker and first wanted to see what I did under pres-sure. Roscoe had been the only one who had wagered I'd be able to handle the jerk. I shuddered at the memory of Frédéric's hands crawling over me, and my delight in kneeing him so hard, I was sure he still remembered me to this day every time he sat down.

Once Rosalind, Rose and Rachel came into the dressing room, I enjoyed watching Rachel dig her stiletto into the palm of his outstretched hand. But I still thought most fondly of Roscoe for believing in me and for adopting me as a sister to replace the one he had lost. I filled a void in his life and he in mine.

I glanced over at him. He looked alone and a little lost beside Reinhardt. My heart ached for him.

The evening light from the Mediterranean washed the solarium dining room in sultry colors and shadows, which were mysterious yet comforting. It was clear in everyone in the room that we were all feeling better, lighter, somehow a layer removed from the crippling grief that had paralyzed our lives for the past several months and kept us apart. We started as Drakers broken and losing Rosalind and Rose drove our pain in deeper, but it was a start and I knew things would get fairly close back to being normal.

"Coffee is ready," sang Sophie, bringing out a tarte Tatin to the buffet where the luscious smell of freshly brewed coffee wafted over. Roscoe loved her apple pie.

I got up to get us both a wedge and brought Roscoe his.

He looked up at me with tears in his eyes. "I want coffee too," he announced. "Rosalind, my mother," the words were saturated with loss, "said I was old enough and let me have one that one time. Remember?"

A thick lump formed in my throat. I couldn't speak. Just like Roscoe, I still couldn't handle the mention of Rosalind's name. I missed her so very much.

Reinhardt stared at Roscoe for a moment and then he stood slowly. He ruffled Roscoe's hair. "I'll get it for you, son."

He walked over to the buffet and prepared Roscoe a coffee made of mostly milk and sugar. Before he returned to the table, his eye caught the photo Sophie had put on the buffet. Coffee in one hand and the photo in the other, Reinhardt returned to the table, placed the cup lovingly in front of Roscoe, and gave him a tender smile and his hair another gentle tussle before sitting down beside him.

His hands shook. He hesitated, then turned the photo around to show it to us. "If this is real, I'll have the plane waiting for an early morning takeoff." Reinhardt's voice was sure and even.

I was surprised and so relieved. He sounded like himself, his old self. Was he back? I dared to hope.

"It's real, Reinhardt," Ransom said. "I ran it through all the verification programs and the article has a date and time signature on it, though there's no way of telling exactly when the photo was taken. The date feature was turned off in the camera. But of this I'm sure. Robert is alive and was seen fairly recently in Portland at Portland Physio at 1467 Elm Street."

Reinhardt turned the photo back around and studied it for a while. "Why hasn't he tried to contact us?" Reinhardt asked. "Something about this doesn't seem right."

"A more-important question is why is this coming through our facial recognition program six months after." I hesitated, not wanting to say, *after we left him there.* "He would have known someone was taking his picture, and he would know we'd see it. It feels tactical." I paused and studied the image. We couldn't have known what he went through in the last six months or how or why he allowed himself to be found now, or why he was putting himself in a position to ask us to find him now. "I agree with Reinhardt. Something about it feels odd. Like Felix, or someone, is baiting us."

Roscoe's eyes widened and his lip curled as if the tarte in his mouth had turned. "Maybe Felix isn't dead," Roscoe said. He leaned back in his chair.

His voice was tinged with darkness. It was foreign, full of hatred, remorse and so many other conflicting emotions I knew he had no way of handling or could even begin to understand. The anger he had been carrying around in his tall, thin frame vibrated visibly from his body. His nubile basketball player's hands were taut like spiders.

"Felix is gone," Reinhardt said. He put a reassuring hand on Roscoe's shoulder. "He'll never bother us again. No one could have survived such a fall, especially after an…" Reinhardt stopped short. He had been alone in his room grieving, but he knew of Roscoe's anguish for having killed someone, regardless that he had done it to save his family.

"So what do we do now?" I asked.

"We find out the truth," Reinhardt said. "If Robert is alive, we will bring him home to Fairhaven."

"Right," I said. I didn't say it, but I felt Felix's clutch. Something wasn't right about how this was turning out.

"Renegade," Ransom said, "we'll start with the Portland clinic, although he probably isn't there anymore."

"The photo was published in the *Portland Herald*. I'll make some phone calls and get the background on the story."

We'd all been too much in shock at seeing Robert to begin any digging, but now, from the firm way Renegade strode to the door, I knew he'd go into the computer center, hack into the security footage at the facility, and do what he did best: sleuth out information. It wouldn't be long before we knew everything we needed.

"I'm going to Portland with you," Roscoe said.

Reinhardt was shaking his head before Roscoe had finished speaking. "Son, it could be dangerous," he said. "I won't risk your safety."

"I'm going… to protect you," Roscoe replied, his chin high. There was nothing childlike in his tone.

Reinhardt knew what he meant. If he was old enough to save his father's life, he was old enough to be part of rescuing another Draker family member. Reinhardt had no rebuttal.

"I'll pack some stuff and be ready whenever you decide to move." Roscoe headed out to the stair silo back to his room.

Rachel leaned in, "But it's not safe to let him…" she trailed off at seeing Reinhardt's expression.

I was touched that she cared—she had always had a soft spot for Roscoe. Tonight, her defense of him pulled on my heart. She was so caring and always thinking about others, making the house feel like a home, not only because she loved art and décor, but because she wanted us to feel comfortable and safe. I wondered whether she had wanted children before her husband was killed. She was still young. It wasn't too late.

I wondered what all of us had wanted in our former lives that we might now never have the chance to experience. "Well, at least he's out of his room and talking with us again," I said.

Reinhardt looked both fearful and proud of his young son. "Let's get Hollinger in on this. He'll want to know who's behind it. Maybe he's got another rogue agent running loose. He can give us extra cover."

"Hollinger messes up everything he touches," I said. James T. Hollinger, formerly part of Felix's army of foreign agents, and now head of the U.S. Department of Defense, the DoD, effectively should have been in control over catching Felix, a madman, who was systematically stalking and taking down former agents, but instead, somehow he bungled the whole affair, and when we were in Washington, wired and poised to catch Felix and put him away for good, he lost control of the situation, causing Ransom to get shot. Then to add salt to the wound, he was late arriving at the mooring docks in Nice, which resulted in Rose being murdered by Felix's mercenaries. And, if he had trusted us and come to Fairhaven where we knew Felix would raid the grounds rather than follow his hunch and go into Nice where he'd thought he'd find Felix, Rosalind might still be alive. Despite his title, I didn't have any good feelings for the man.

No, if Robert were in fact still alive, the thought of Hollinger possibly bungling the mission—again—and putting Robert at risk was something I didn't want.

"Couldn't we see what's going on first before we get him involved? We can go under the pretense of visiting the seniors at the farmhouse. Kind of like a family visit. I'll bet Amos and the gang would love to see us. And once they know about this photo, there's no way we'll be able to stop them from helping. And, they're very fond of Roscoe. They'd also be able to help keep an eye on him."

The "seniors" as we called them—Amos, Hannah, Norm and

Alice—had become like family to us. The foursome, a meddling bunch of busybodies we'd met in Springfield, Maine, the summer before, turned out to be much more than we'd imagined. Unknown to us when we first met, they had also worked as agents under Felix during the Cold War. They were long since retired, but spying was in their blood. When Felix invaded the sleepy, uneventful town of Springfield, it didn't take them long to smell a rat and come to our aid.

Renegade rushed back into the dining room waving two other printed photos. "OK, the photo was taken at the Portland Physio Center and a therapist by the name of Maggie Spenser sent in the photo to the *Herald* to promote the opening of their new clinic."

He put the pictures on the table. One was of the building where the shadow of the outside sign reflected in the therapy room mirror, and the other was of Maggie, a short, ample-bosomed woman probably in her late fifties, with tight cheeks.

Rowan grimaced. "That's one heck of a discounted facelift," he muttered.

I examined the woman more carefully. One side of her face bore deep scars. Something about the shape of her body and her eyes looked familiar.

"I think Ruby's idea is a good one," Ransom said. "We could keep a low profile at the farm and drive up to Portland. We should easily be able to check things out at the clinic, find Robert, and get him back to Fairhaven before anyone even knows he's missing from there. Renegade, how long will it take to get Robert a passport with an alias?"

Renegade waved his hand dismissively. "Already got our documents expert…" He winked. "… on it. It will be waiting for us at the airport, which we should get to since our charter is ready and waiting. Who's going?"

"Reinhardt, me, Ransom and Roscoe, I said without thinking. "Are we flying into Portland or Westport?"

"Westport," Reinhardt said. "I'll grab my bag and be in the foyer in three." We stared at him. "You don't honestly think I haven't been waiting for this exact moment?" His eyes darkened. "Rosalind would have expected nothing less." I noticed Reinhardt's voice broke at her name, but he quickly composed himself as he stood and went to his room.

Ransom came over to me from where he'd been standing at the buffet nursing an espresso and leaned down. We hadn't stood beside each other in a very long time, and immediately I was aware of the heat coming off of him.

"Just like old times, right, Ruby?" he whispered in my ear.

I turned and looked at him, his face a few inches from mine. My heart thumped as he looked into my eyes.

He flashed his charming seductive smile, the one he knew melted me.

I don't make the same mistake twice, Romeo, I thought. I glared at him for a second before I leaped up and rushed upstairs after Reinhardt to pack.

Half an hour later, the four of us stood in the foyer waiting for Rowan to pull up with the SUV to take us to Cote d'Azur International, with me avoiding Ransom's eyes.

When Rowan squealed to a stop in front of us, Roscoe jumped into the front passenger seat, clutching his travel bag to his chest, eyes focused straight ahead as if in a trance, looking stern and determined. He acted like he'd done this a hundred times. The gritty look on his young face was disturbing, like he had a vendetta to settle.

I thought it amusing that the youngest of us took the front seat without a thought to age as rank, and smiling gently and saying nothing, Reinhardt, Ransom and I climbed into the middle and back rows.

This was feeling very familiar, bearing a distinct similarity to how we'd gone to save ex-agents the year before from one of Felix's attacks. But this time, I had to remind myself, over and over: Felix was dead. I said it, but a part of me didn't believe it. Not at all. A shiver ran up my spine as I pictured Felix, now a malevolent phantom covered in seaweed, continuing his murderous raids. The horror movie image creeped me out. But what gnawed at me most was that Robert ought not to have survived. It was seared in my mind: the image of two bodies lying, one on top of the other, in a muddy pool of blood. Who could survive that?

I glanced diagonally up at Roscoe as we sped along the coast.

His chin was set so I knew he was ready to do whatever he had to do to destroy whatever might be threatening us again.

Guard him carefully, Ruby, Rosalind whispered.

Five

AFTER AN EIGHT-HOUR FLIGHT, we landed at Westport under the cover of darkness. I was tired and anxious; uncertainty and nerves had prevented me from getting any sleep during the flight. I noticed the same restlessness in the others. I remembered how Robert had never seemed to need any sleep, yet he always seemed sturdy and stable. Perhaps the surge of adrenaline that pulsed in me now was the same thing that had kept him so constantly alert and able to respond.

As soon as we landed, we unclicked our seat-belts, grabbed our jackets and travel bags, and readied ourselves to deplane.

"Norm and Amos will be waiting for us in the terminal," Reinhardt said. "Renegade notified them we were coming."

I wondered if Norm and Amos were still maintaining their cover as genteel old country bumpkins, which seemed to give them free rein to do all kinds of things, including a routine pickup of some family members from the airport. Their disguise had served them well. On the outside, they looked simple and easygoing, but in truth, they were keen observers and not only spotted the smallest inconsistencies when things were out of the ordinary, but could smell them in the air like a pair of hunting dogs.

The co-pilot unhinged the door hatch. It opened with a loud thump.

Single file, we met the humid June night as we exited the plane down the stairs onto the tarmac. The air stank of petroleum and hot asphalt. I shuddered. The last time we were here in Westport, we had subdued two of Felix's hired killers by knocking them unconscious and sprinting for the terminal. From Ransom and Reinhardt's stiff postures, I sensed they were remembering this as well. My body seized up as I scanned the airfield for any signs of ambush. I hated that feeling, the one I acquired as a new Draker, a sort of sixth sense that nudged me to be on alert to an imminent threat when in a second, someone could endanger my life or the lives of this family I'd come to care so much about.

Walking down the stairs, I tried to shake off the feeling that we were walking into a trap. Apart from Amos and Norm, no one should have known we were here. I reminded myself that Felix was dead and that my fears were unwarranted. Still, it was conceivable that someone had planted that photo of Robert and made sure we'd see it. If it was true that Robert was alive, something peculiar was going on, and we had to find out the truth.

When we were all on the ground, Reinhardt drew Roscoe close beside him. Ransom's jaw was set. I could tell he was counting the number of steps it would be to the terminal.

The four of us in our black pants and jackets maneuvered cautiously through the darkness and into the terminal.

An attendant waiting there opened the door and escorted us to a private immigration clearance room Renegade had arranged, probably by paying off border security to make sure our arrival would be uneventful and discreet. Exiting and entering the U.S. without being entered into the computer system was the mark of Draker travel. I chuckled at how things like this had become normal and rubbed the back of my neck to find it was tight, the muscles strained so much to their limits, I was sure they could snap.

Reinhardt, looking very much himself again, tall and authoritative, approached the counter where a heavyset woman whose uniform strained at the seams took his passport without a word. Her ponytail was pulled so tight her eyes could only open halfway, giving her a haughty look. We took turns handing over our passports in silence, but when she got to Roscoe she put her head back to get a look at him.

"What is the purpose of your stay here in Westport?" she asked.

My heart stopped. Why was she asking questions? We were not supposed to be asked anything when the "details" had already been looked after. I glanced at Roscoe. We hadn't briefed him on how to respond to questions.

"We're visiting my aunt and uncle," Roscoe said, smiling sweetly.

"Any particular reason for the visit?" she asked.

A stout, bald man, also in uniform, scurried over from the hallway when he saw what was happening. He laughed. "Michelle, the Drakers are regular New York Charter Service customers. I know them personally. Don't bother asking any questions. They're all cleared." He took the passports from her computer counter and handed them back to Reinhardt with a sweep of graciousness.

"Thank you, Alex," Reinhardt said. They smiled cordially at each other before Reinhardt turned to leave.

A quick look at Michelle's face told me something more than her ponytail wasn't right. She watched Alex closely as he went to the other computer and began typing. Her lips were pursed, and her eyes narrowed even further. I knew it was a short lunge for the phone between our going to prison and our freedom, and second-guessed my decision to keep our trip from Hollinger.

We filed out after Reinhardt through the automatic terminal doors and out past the cars and directly into the parking lot. Ransom and Roscoe scooted ahead of me. I wasn't as eager to plunge into the unknown.

After we were outside under the airport lights, we looked around for familiar faces. Two men dressed in camo hunting jackets, plaid shirts, and khaki pants were leaning against a dark-blue SUV in the front row of cars in the parking lot immediately beyond the airport's pick-up area.

The two gray-haired men looked relaxed as they ambled over to us, but I could tell from their eyes and posture that our two seniors were in high surveillance mode.

They weren't looking toward the terminal doors where I'd thought the danger would lurk; instead, they were preoccupied with another sedan circling the parking lot.

Norm's familiar beat-up, white pickup was parked beside the blue SUV.

"Amos," Ransom called quietly.

Amos studied the sedan as it drove out of the parking lot, looked around cautiously, and then with a quick lunge and sweep of his arm waved us over and opened the back door of the SUV.

"Get in," Amos said. "I don't like it when I see the same car more than once. This one, I've seen three times now. Put your bags in the back of the pickup. Ransom, you ride with Norm. The rest of you ride with me."

Amos had good instincts. I knew that car was potentially serious; he was only this abrupt when he was in work-mode and smelled something amiss.

The old truck rumbled to life beside them, and Norm revved the engine.

"We're taking separate, scenic routes back to the farmhouse," Amos said.

"You think you're being followed?" I asked. I nervously scanned the area Amos had just finished scrutinizing.

"Guess we'll see if they follow us when we leave," Amos said. We hopped into the van, Roscoe in front again, Reinhardt and I in the middle row. Amos slammed the driver's door, took a sharp turn and screeched out of the airport parking lot onto the highway, leaving Norm's pickup to follow in the rear—I assumed as back-up if we were followed. We all yelped from the lurch of the car.

"Nothing like trying to make a suspicious getaway," Reinhardt said, righting himself.

"Of course," Amos said. "If the sedan is checking us out, it'll be right on our tail."

Sure enough, a burgundy sedan screeched out onto the highway several cars behind us.

Amos floored it, his SUV ripping up the pavement. We rocked side to side as he sped ahead, frequently changing lanes to put more distance between the sedan and us before taking the exit onto County Road 86. Amos could look older than his years when he wasn't in action mode, one shoulder higher than the other, a jerky amble, but here, he was in perfect agile form. Amos slowed his speed, and two minutes later there it was again, the burgundy sedan in our rearview.

I hadn't been wrong to feel nervous.

"Well, looky there," Amos cackled, putting on his old fogey country accent. He turned sharply off the highway onto a graveled crescent in a rest area, thick with tall spruces, and came to a stop in front of a picnic table still littered with the last visitor's lunch debris.

The sedan, now in plain view, easily pulled up and parked about a hundred feet behind us and stopped.

"Oh, come on. This is ridiculous," I said.

We stayed inside, listening to the hum of the air conditioner, and waited for Norm.

When his white pickup pulled in behind the sedan, Ransom opened his door. "This has to stop," he said. He walked up to the sedan, everything in shadow from the dark night against the bright moonlight. As he approached, the sedan passenger door opened, and a tall man, dressed in a dark suit, and with short spiky hair, stepped out in front of Ransom.

My heart was beating so fast, I thought I might be having a heart attack. What if he had a gun? My stomach tightened with panic. The shootout at the Weston in Washington was running through my mind. I felt the urge to run out and throw myself in front of Ransom so I could take the bullets this time.

Reinhardt had one hand on his Glock and put down the window with the other. His face was taut.

I touched my chest where my pistol rested at my left breast in its holster.

"I see you've recovered nicely," the man said. His voice was small with the distance, but something about it was familiar.

"How the hell did you know we were here?" Ransom said, dropping his hand.

I wanted to shout, "No! It could be a trap!" but I waited, tense and ready. Maybe Ransom was baiting him.

"It's my business to know," the man said. "You're kind of cocky stepping out in front of an unknown follower. Why would you do that?"

Ransom laughed. "Come on. The DoD has registered license numbers. Not easy to get a hold of, but our Renegade is particularly talented." He held up his cell phone to show Renegade's text. The man shook his head and the two men grasped hands. That's when I realized who it was.

"It's Hollinger," I said, feeling both relieved and annoyed.

"I wondered if it was him," said Amos as we all piled out. He called over, "You know there, Hollinger, Norm and I spotted you two seconds after we pulled into the airport. You might want to work on that."

Hollinger glared at him and snorted.

"How about we talk about it back at the farmhouse," said Amos. "Just follow me.

"Amos, I know where you, your cousins, and your cousins' cousins live," said Hollinger. "Maybe I felt it was best we chat out here, away from any other wandering eyes."

I wondered if that were true, or if he might have been just covering that he'd been caught.

We all returned to our vehicles and our motorcade of three spent the next twenty minutes being escorted to Springfield.

After they returned from Fairhaven, the four elders had made Robert's farmhouse their new home and base of operations. When Myrtle, Robert's companion and longtime friend, had taken care of the place, it had been spotless and organized; I wondered how it'd look now, especially after the shootout with all the explosions and gunfire tearing up the grounds.

I squeezed my eyes against the memory of it, of Robert and Myrtle slumped atop one another, their blood pooling thickly beneath them. I had called out to Robert for him to stop, to not go out there, but it was in vain. Robert had thrown himself on top of Myrtle to protect her and they'd both been shot.

A thick and painful lump formed in my throat. The reason we were here weighed heavily on me. I hoped desperately for Robert to be alive, but something I would never admit was that, in a way, I hoped he wasn't. The thought that we'd abandoned him was almost too much to bear. We'd done what we thought was right. He'd been dead. We saw that with our own eyes.

I tried to take deep breaths so the others wouldn't see I was close to panicking.

When we pulled up to the farmhouse, I couldn't believe what I saw. The exterior was manicured and landscaped. The clapboard siding and front door were new, the porch was freshly painted, and four Adirondack chairs were arranged around a small table at the end. Beyond the porch lay a pleasant and serene view of the forest, the spruces rustling gently in the breeze. Solar lights had been planted on the new stone walkway leading to the house. No one would have ever suspected that several months ago, this pretty country farmhouse had been riddled with bullets, trees torn up, and everything in disarray.

We got out, and I was grateful for the cool forest air. When we were nearly at the front door, I heard the scuffling of footsteps. We hadn't seen Alice and Hannah since they left Fairhaven after the horrible events that had taken place. I wondered if they had, like their husbands, returned to their Springfield disguises, living as two country ladies, frumpy in elastic-waist pants, intrusive and nosy. I chuckled when I remembered my first time meeting them: how did four people of retirement age manage to keep themselves looking so fit and trim when all they seemed to do was sit in the local café having coffee and donuts and keeping their fingers on the pulse of the town?

When the door flew open, the screen door smacked against the clapboard and sounded like a gunshot. I yelped but recovered quickly at the enthusiasm and warmth of the two women who rushed out.

Hannah threw her arms around me in a tight clutch. Alice ran straight to Roscoe, someone she had taken a strong shine to as he had to her, but as she approached him, he stiffened up and looked at the ground.

My heart hurt for him just then. What he needed more than anything was a grandmotherly embrace, someone who cared for him unconditionally, someone to whisper that he was going to be OK. But he was too afraid to love. I could see that in his tense shoulders and how he turned away from her.

Fortunately, Alice hadn't come so far in her career without being able to accurately assess a situation and stopped short, put her hands in her jeans pockets, and came to stand beside him instead. "Looks like you've grown," she said. She turned, and smiling, she stared into his face waiting for a response. I could see she knew what was happening. "You guys must be exhausted. Come in and we'll get you fed and settled. We can talk more after you get some rest."

Hannah began to pull me inside when I realized my bag had dropped. I turned and saw Ransom picking it up. He followed me inside, his eyes on mine.

Being here wasn't easy on any of us, and each of us had our way of coping. He hovered closely, but I wasn't ready to acknowledge him in any way other than at arm's length. He'd created that, and now he couldn't up and arbitrarily rescind it just because he was feeling vulnerable.

Reinhardt clapped his hand on Roscoe's shoulder, and they walked in with Alice leading the way. I'd been so deep in my thoughts, I'd forgotten about Hollinger, who was standing in the doorway. He let us file past him into the house, then he looked back at the sedan and held up his hand to indicate to his driver to stay outside before he turned and came in behind us.

The interior was equally as well-kept as the exterior. It was like Myrtle had never left. "Hannah," I said. "The place looks… great!"

Hannah gave me a questioning stare, her forehead wrinkling, but her face flushing in embarrassment. "We hired a cook who also does house-work," she said, shrugging. "Hey, Alice and I can sleuth a ferret out of its hole, but housework just isn't our thing." She smiled. "Lola, however, is a great cook, very health-minded, and keeps us from eating too many donuts. We don't go to the diner nearly as often."

That started Alice laughing.

A big grin on her face, Hannah lifted her over-sized plaid shirt draped over her jeans to point at her trim waistline beneath a tank top, and then at Alice's, then dropped it again. "Shucks, y'all. Gotta keep up the girlish fig'r!"

A tiny woman emerged from the kitchen. Like the ladies, she also wore jeans and an untucked over-sized shirt, but her black hair laced with gray was twisted artfully into a Chinese cloisonne clip and she wore flip flops. Like Myrtle, but half the size, I thought.

"Welcome," she said. "There are sandwiches and coffee in the kit-chen, but you must be very tired. Your rooms are ready." She gestured up the stairs.

I looked over to Roscoe. He was already asleep, curled up in an overstuffed upholstered chair.

"I think he's not that interested in dinner. I'll get him to bed." I gently nudged him awake, guided him up the stairs, found him a bedroom, and let him plop onto the bed fully dressed, where he immediately fell back into a deep sleep.

Alice was right. He had grown. I chuckled at his childlike face on a body that was developing a man's muscular structure. Still, to me, he was just little. I wanted to give him a hug, maybe kiss his forehead, but instead covered him with a throw and went back downstairs.

In the kitchen, Ransom and Hollinger were in a heated discussion,

Ransom looking like he was ready to punch Hollinger. Reinhardt was leaning against the kitchen counter keeping a neutral silence, and the seniors were sipping coffee at the farmhouse table.

"We mishandled Ruby's extrication? Are you insane? How else were we supposed to get her out? Robert wasn't supposed to have run out after Myrtle. Myrtle took it upon herself to shoot at Felix. It wasn't a situation we could have planned for!" Hollinger's face was hard. "You didn't handle it well. Your incompetence caused too many casualties."

I stared at him while he was saying this. That's when it hit me: he knew about the photo and he was testing us to see what we knew. I wondered what he knew that he wasn't telling us. But forgetting about that for a second, I was furious. Did he really think we would have caused such a loss on purpose? I glanced at Ransom and half hoped he'd clock him.

I looked at Reinhardt. He remained calm and collected. Or maybe he was checked out. I wasn't sure if his old fire to keep the Drakers safe and secure was still in there, or if loss had colored his ability to feel whole forever. I watched him for a moment longer. No, he was in there. He was trying to get a read on Hollinger and why he was attacking us for something he'd know we already felt terrible about. He was overly keen for us to leave and go back to France, to be out of his hair. The question was why.

"Whatever," said Ransom. "That's in the past and we can't do it differently. But for now, we need to go to Portland and find out what the clinic knows about this photo. If it really is Robert. And if it is, who is holding him and why." A vein in his forehead throbbed as he spoke through gritted teeth.

I wondered why he'd let our agenda slip, but then I saw Hollinger gesture. He was holding the photo.

"Look," Hollinger said. "We knew about the photo before you gave it to me. I have undercover agents staking the place out. We started an investigation as soon as Felix's assistant went missing from Washington. The clinic says Robert was never there, and if you guys start asking more questions, you'll be playing right into the hands of whoever is in on this. Maybe someone else will be killed. I can't let you do that."

"And you think," said Reinhardt smoothly, "we're going to get in the way."

Hollinger's eyes shifted and he didn't answer. He didn't have to. We knew him well enough to know that there was more to this than he was letting on. Perhaps it had to do with an investigation for something bigger than Robert Draker being alive, and since he was with the U.S. government, that it might possibly be related to national security, which was why he was trying to talk us out of interfering. If he was involved, then whatever this was fell under the jurisdiction of the Department of Defense. Beneath his cross demeanor, Hollinger trusted and respected us, but we didn't have anywhere close to the clearance one needed to get involved in the matters he and his department handled.

"Michelle," I blurted out. "That immigration officer at the airport. She was one of yours, wasn't she?" I instantly regretted asking the question because I didn't want Hollinger to know we were aware he was watching us.

Hollinger sighed and rubbed his head. "Ruby, this is bigger than you can imagine. Get some rest tonight and go back to France in the morning. The DoD will handle this. Whatever is happening with Robert, we will get to the bottom of it." He stared at me with a mixture of pity and sorrow. "Haven't you already lost enough family?"

A lump formed in my throat as he said that. I understood why Hollinger didn't want us involved, especially if this was a much-wider-reaching issue, but he knew how important Robert was to us.

Beside me, Reinhardt and Ransom stiffened with feelings of guilt.

We were silent. I wondered what Hollinger thought our silence meant. Did he think that by telling us the DoD would handle it, we'd just go home? Glancing around, I noticed we all looked cooperative. Maybe that would make him think he'd made his point and we'd leave the matter to him. But of course, I knew that not one of us was planning to do as he'd requested. I didn't care anymore if this was a matter of universal security. Galaxy security. We were going to get Robert and bring him home. I smiled sweetly.

"Good," Hollinger said. "We'll escort you guys back to Westport in the morning."

We nodded and Hollinger and his man left in their car. We waited until the lights from the car disappeared down the driveway before we spoke.

"Exactly how are we going to convince him that we're going home?" I said. "Or are you intending to leave without Robert?"

Reinhardt was smiling slyly. "We'll just need to make him think we're leaving. He won't know that we didn't get on the plane. We'll use decoys."

I snorted out a laugh. I remembered how they had arranged for people to look like us the night Reinhardt, Rose and Robert sprang me from the plastic surgery clinic in New York where I'd been altered into Ruby Draker. The deception had gone without a flaw. Our look-alikes simply stepped into a twin of our car and led Felix's men in the wrong direction.

"And, for the hired decoys, they get an all-expenses-paid trip to France!" Reinhardt laughed.

It was good to see him embodying his old self. Like riding a bicycle, I supposed, you never really forgot how to play the game. And it sounded like this version of hide and seek was going to be a good one. Not only were we going to have to get around Hollinger and the entire Department of Defense, but around someone else who had drawn us here and was involved in some significant way. At least now we knew it was someone other than Hollinger who had sent us the photo. Here we go again, I thought.

"You guys need to get some sleep," Norm said, getting up from the table. "We'll get you back from the airport without Hollinger suspecting a thing."

As if on cue, Amos and Hannah went outside toward the barn, and Alice and Norm headed out the back kitchen door. They were up to something, but whatever it was, we had to leave it up to them. I was too tired to handle anything more.

I went upstairs, hoping this time all would be still. No helicopters or Felix's goons in black masks storming the farmhouse with guns. *Felix is dead. He's dead. Dead,* I repeated over and over in my head. The chant lulled me into a deep troubled sleep, my hand firmly around my gun in the holster.

***

While I was sleeping, a noise at the door woke me. I sat up and shook my head. My heart was racing. The sun was coming through the Priscilla curtains of the quaint little pink and cream cultured room.

The door opened a crack and Ransom peeked in. "Are you decent?"

"What time is it?" I asked. It looked late. I bolted out of the bed and ran my fingers through my hair. My shirt had come unbuttoned at the top.

He pushed the door open further and came in. "Don't think that I'm just trying to get another look at your reindeer underwear."

I glared at him. The previous summer, before the shoot-out, I had slept in my underwear in this same room and Ransom had come in and had seen me.

"Let's just say that experience has taught me a lesson. What's up?" I gave Ransom a stern look. There was no way I was going to send him signals that I liked his flirtation.

He smiled sweetly.

What was going on with him? Was his memory of our previous summer making him warm toward me again?

"Everyone's eating breakfast. We've got some plans to fill you in on."

"Why didn't you wake me earlier?" I demanded.

He was staring at me with that lusty smile that made him look so sexy. I felt my body get warm.

Stop it, Ruby, I scolded myself. *He never loved you.*

"It'll be a long day and Reinhardt wanted to let you sleep in. But it's almost ten and we need to get going." He turned, leaving the door ajar. "I do miss the reindeer," he called out from the hallway.

I threw my shoe at the door. I tried to tidy myself but instead of buttoning my shirt up to my neck like I had the last time, I unbuttoned it even more so the lace from my tank was visible. I sneered haughtily and left the room.

***

Lola was at the kitchen stove turning bacon in a cast iron pan. Beside that was a large pot. Everything smelled amazing. My mouth watered, and only then did I realize how hungry I was.

"Good morning, Ruby," Lola said. "Hope you like bacon. I made lots. Got some congee here, too, and do you like steamed greens? You need the vitamins." She ladled some into a bowl and put it on the table for me. "Help yourself to coffee."

An extra leaf had been put on the kitchen table so everyone could sit together. Hannah, Alice, Norm and Amos, sitting at the far end, had almost finished their breakfasts. Roscoe sat beside Alice where Lola was now refilling his bowl without asking, Ransom and Reinhardt were enjoying their breakfast, and I was sitting down to the steaming bowl of rice and chicken and coffee. It was so warm and fragrant, but when I remembered how much I had enjoyed Myrtle's breakfasts, tears came to my eyes. I sipped my coffee and waited for them to subside.

"OK," started Reinhardt, looking at me over his reading glasses and holding up his phone. "Renegade has arranged for a charter to leave Westport at 1 p.m. It's scheduled to fly directly to Nice with our doppelgangers onboard. Hollinger has his own people watching the airport and a special agent on the charter desk. But Renegade has outdone himself." He smiled. "The charter service has been adequately paid off to distract whoever might be there while we change places with our twins.

"Hannah and Alice have our disguises ready, and you know how good they are with disguises. We'll wait an hour in the charter's secure room and then make our way back to the parking lot where Amos will be waiting to scoop us up and drive us out of town.''

It was comforting to see the grin on Reinhardt's face.

And Ransom couldn't stop glancing at my unbuttoned shirt. It was as if he'd forgotten all about Rose, and how he'd chosen her over me.

"Where will we go when we leave the airport?" I asked.

"Erie," said Reinhardt. "There's a report of another one of Felix's ex-spies having been killed there. But this time, there's no cover-up. It's in the newspapers. And Amos saw it on the morning news." He sipped his coffee. "Someone other than Hollinger and the DoD is trying to get our attention. Anyway, Hollinger is watching the Portland clinic, so we need to stay away from there. I don't know how, but Robert is somehow the missing puzzle piece. I suggest we find out how it's all related."

"Are you sure it's one of your Cold War team members?" I asked.

Reinhardt nodded. "Norm said he recognized him immediately, and Renegade verified the identity. Sean Granger. He was stationed in East Berlin. I never worked with him, but he was under Felix's command."

"The signature on the crime is all wrong," I said. "And who else would have a vendetta with retired spies? That motive died with Felix. Right?" This wasn't doing my nerves any good. "He was the one who considered them traitors against the country for... 'colluding with the Russians and undermining the security of America,'" I said, making air quotes. "My parents included. He killed them all out of his own personal twisted reasons, but who else would want them dead? And for what?"

Now to have a murder but with no cover-up, whereas Felix's whole shtick was to make every last murder look like an accident, only bore a partial fingerprint. What was going on? Could it be possible that Felix survived and was trying a new tactic?

No, I shook my head. It could not be possible. But was someone trying to play with our minds? It wasn't a coincidence that Sean Granger was killed. First, the photo of Robert, then Hollinger being on the scene knowing more than we did, and now another ex-agent murdered? One thing was sure. Someone wanted the Drakers pulled back into the United States and was using Robert as the bait. I shivered. It was as if his murder, the whole shootout at the farmhouse, Myrtle's death—all of it—had been staged and we'd been played all this time.

"Reinhardt," I started, "what do you think this Sean Granger killing has to do with finding Robert?"

"If you remember, Felix had the bodies taken to Erie for post mortems," Reinhardt said. "It's like we're being drawn there to find clues about Robert. Why? I don't know yet. But Hollinger said that Robert isn't in Portland. The Erie coroner's office should have records that will give us some clues."

Alice had gone into Springfield earlier in the morning, I presumed for supplies, but when a gunmetal blue SUV pulled up in front of the farmhouse, Alice stepped out. I wondered why she had picked up another car. I watched her from the window checking around the back of the house, behind the barn, and doing a visual sweep of the forest. Amos, Hannah and Norm were nowhere to be seen.

She came in with some bags and approached Roscoe. "How's it going, Roscoe?" She tousled his hair and when he ducked his head and tried to glower at her, she made a *gotcha* face and he laughed.

I wondered if she and Norm had ever had children of their own. It was clear she had a special feeling for Roscoe and she seemed very aware of his fragile emotional state so tread carefully.

Roscoe sat at the kitchen table taking in all the information around him. He was as much involved in this as any of us, and we didn't shield him from any of it as if he were still a child. Roscoe got up to see what Alice had in the totes she'd put on the table.

"I've put together some travel bags with disguises inside," she said. "You're all going to age considerably by the time you leave the airport." She pulled out a gray wig and hunter's hat and held it up. "Roscoe, my love, try this on and practice walking like an old fogey."

He grinned, beside himself. He tried on the wig and the hat, but he looked like a kid playing dress-up.

"Keep your head hunched down and walk like your feet hurt. Maybe we can put something in your shoes to remind you to walk funny. Let me see your walk."

Roscoe walked across the kitchen, but it was evident he was acting. "Not quite, Roscoe," Alice said. "Here, do it like this." She demonstrated what a senior with sore feet would walk like. She corrected his gait a few more times.

Each practice made him smile a bit more until finally the two of them were giggling the way a young boy would with his grandmother.

Alice grabbed him for a hug, knowing this was exactly what he needed, and this time he stayed, but his smile faded. Perhaps he remembered Rosalind's motherly embraces. Alice pulled him off her and looked him in the eyes. "Just remember, like you have stones in your shoes."

"As for the rest of you oldies," she said, "we'll have two cars waiting outside the airport and we'll be watching for you," Alice said. "You just toddle out like you've just arrived from Florida or something. Amos and Hannah will be in one car, and Norm and I in the other. Hollinger won't know a thing: he'll see four people getting on your charter, and the rest will be up to us."

We got ready and arrived at Westport with only half an hour to spare. The less time we had at the airport, the better. We walked slowly to the New York Private Air Charter Service check-in counter where Maurice, a familiar face from past flights, greeted us with a wink. The stern-faced Michelle from the day before glared at us through half lids.

Maurice took our passports. "Everything looks good, Mr. Draker," he said.

"Sorry," said Michelle, her ponytail as tight as it had been the day before, as she grabbed them from his hand. "I'm just going to confirm your information." She scrutinized each one, looking up and down between the passports and our faces, to make sure we were the Drakers Hollinger wanted out of the country. She took a painfully long time before returning the travel documents to Maurice.

He shrugged at Reinhardt apologetically.

We walked to Gate B where our Challenger C Series 600 waited on the tarmac. I had to admit it was an elegant way to travel. Only a year earlier, when I was a psych student at NYU, eating mac and cheese late at night, and studying with friends in the library, I never imagined that my reality only one year later would be that I'd be living in an opulent estate in France, flying across the Atlantic in a private jet, and with a whole new identity. Or, that these flights would take me into and out of danger with as much regularity as was normal for the Drakers but completely bananas for a regular person.

We opened the door to go out to the plane, but as we started to leave, a distance from the counter, a loud commotion erupted, catching Maurice and Michelle's attention.

An indoor luggage carrier cart had taken a corner too quickly and tipped out several large suitcases and its passengers. Everything was on the floor in a terrible mess, and we heard one of the people call out, "Oh, my leg!"

As Maurice and Michelle ran over to help, a door behind the counter opened and four people dressed exactly like we were, took our place and walked calmly to the plane. We slipped silently into the secure room they had just left, the door locking behind us.

Although we couldn't see what was happening outside of the windowless room, we knew our decoys would board the plane long before the ruckus calmed. It would take time to clear up the mess and tend to the people.

Maurice must have secured the travel bags from Amos before the check-in procedure because they were waiting for us in the room. We put on our disguises: wigs, hats and orthopedic shoes, everything Alice had packed.

I had to admit, at a glance we were convincing. And fortunately, our gate wasn't far from the exit to the terminal, so even at a shuffling senior's pace, we'd be outside within a few minutes. We stood around in our outfits, trying to look elderly for what seemed a very long time.

Finally, Maurice knocked four times to signal that all was clear.

Not missing a beat, four elderly people shuffled out to the hallway and headed slowly to the exit doors.

Across in the parking lot, a tan and a steel-blue SUV were waiting. They opened their doors.

We pretended to struggle to get inside, and once we were seated and buckled in, Amos drove off, carefully, making sure we weren't being followed. It wasn't until we were miles away from the airport that he accelerated to normal speed.

"Were we followed?" Roscoe asked. His eyes were wide, and he was breathing heavily. He looked stimulated, not smiling or happy, but energized by our deception.

While I didn't like this situation, I was happy to see that his enthusiasm was starting to show again. Several minutes away from the airport, he pulled off his wig and hat while twisting around to check out the side and back windows for signs that we might have been followed. Reinhardt did the same.

"No, son," Reinhardt said, looking proud, a wide smile on his face as he beamed at Roscoe. "Our disguises seem to have worked. But stay sharp. Look for anything out of the ordinary. And we should keep our hats on just in case."

Good, I thought. It was so nice to see them connecting again.

Roscoe nodded and plunked his hat back on at a rakish angle.

Several miles down the road, Amos pulled into a gas station. Hannah, Alice, Amos and Norm got out of the SUVs and headed for the rest area where a massive luxury RV motor home was parked. We stared at them before getting out.

"No way," I said, taken aback. "Come on."

Norm was grinning from ear to ear. "Like it?" he asked.

The RV must have been thirty feet long, black with swirling stripes. It looked like a political campaign bus. Or something a rock star would take on tour. What happened to being under the radar? I looked helplessly at Amos, but he was grinning, too.

"She's a beaut!" He walked around and whistled a few times before climbing inside.

We had no choice but to follow. I had to admit, it was beautiful, a gleaming modern luxury house on wheels. I walked through, amazed at the luxurious finishings: creamy leather seats, a kitchenette with walnut cabinets, and a granite counter with a stove, refrigerator and more cabinets across, a large eating area, a bathroom, then further in was a living room with a pull-out sofa bed and recliners facing a giant screen TV, and then in the back was a bedroom with what looked like a king-size bed and full bath.

I whistled, "This is nicer than anywhere Robert had us stay." I laughed, then stopped myself. Until we were sure he was alive, it didn't feel right to talk about him.

"Exactly what we talked about, Reinhardt. Snug, but very comfortable," Norm said. "Thanks for covering the tab. He winked.

"Robert may have had us stay in more subtle accommodation," said Ransom, looking around, "but at least we can stretch our legs. How many people does this sleep exactly?" He paused and crossed his arms.

"We'll be harder to find if we keep moving," Norm said. "Don't worry. We have air mattresses for everyone. There's lots of floor space."

He winked at Ransom who looked over in my direction, his eyes smiling and serious both.

"We can take turns with the bed." Norm stopped short when he realized what he had said. "The married folks, I mean."

Norm looked at me and then Ransom and shrugged.

Six

FUELED UP AND READY TO GO, we pulled back onto I-476, Hannah and Amos in the lead with the SUV and the rest of us in the over-the-top motor coach following behind, Norm at the wheel looking like he had been driving one of these vehicles all his life, and Alice with her arm on top of the living room sofa looking out the window.

"I could really get used to this life," Alice said. She smiled as she watched the mountains pass by the wide windows of the RV.

"It feels like we're riding on a cloud. Or does this thing have turbo blasters so we are actually airborne?" I asked.

Reinhardt was in a recliner with his feet up, and Ransom was relaxing, staring out the window on the other side of the coach. In a moment of repose like that, I wanted to go to him and unearth the truth of his heart. What had happened between us was never made clear, and then faded without a word. I was still shaken by his turnaround, moving his passion from me to Rose without explanation. No, it would hurt too much to know the truth. Better it was left unsaid.

Traveling like this, it was hard to remember that we were on a mission. But our drive was going to be seven hours and even though we were traveling in style, rolling gently over the Alleghenies and through mountain tunnels, I knew we'd need to make some stops periodically and Norm picked the oness with breathtaking views of the Pennsylvania countryside: huge copses of trees, meadows, hawks sailing overhead. He said it was so we could stretch our legs and get some air, but I knew he and the other seniors truly enjoyed taking in the scenery. I enjoyed it as well.

While the drive was exceptionally pleasant, and we chatted and relaxed and listened to music, every so often, a weird, unsettled feeling moved into my stomach, and I remembered what we were on our way to do. I was haunted by the fact that Felix's body had never been recovered. That played with my insecurity. Was it even possible that Felix might have survived that fall? I couldn't see how. I again saw the arrow in his chest, his body propelling backward over the rock wall of the estate and down into the churning Mediterranean. Sean Granger's death was probably just a coincidence, some fluke that resembled Felix's style. But he was an ex-spy under Felix's command, and what if it weren't a coincidence at all? What if we were being set up worse than any of the murders that came before?

When I glanced over at Reinhardt and Ransom, I saw them ranging through similar thoughts. Roscoe, I couldn't read. He had fortified himself with thick protective walls he wasn't ready to take down. He was sitting up front with Norm, watching the countryside pass by and listening quietly to Norm's running geographic and historical commentary. The old Roscoe would have peppered him with questions. Maybe he was just tired. Or maybe he was processing the situation and its possible consequences.

"You know, Roscoe," Norm said, "we're driving through some of the most historical places in America. Pittsburgh has the Liberty Bell, and it's where the Declaration of Independence was signed by the Founding Fathers. Then a couple of hours down the road, there's Gettysburg, the site of the 1863 battle where forty-six thousand men lost their lives in the Civil War. "

"Too bad we're not exactly on a sightseeing trip across America.

Are we Norm?" Roscoe said.

Norm was silent for a moment, and I wondered if he felt stung. I smiled. At least Roscoe was showing some attitude, which meant he was still alive and kicking in there somewhere. But I felt bad for Norm; he was only trying to lift Roscoe's mood.

"No, but I thought you might find it interesting," Norm said. "What'd you think, Reinhardt? Maybe a short stop at Gettysburg? Could be interesting for the lad. Once in a lifetime opportunity. Take your mind off certain things."

Norm kept his eyes on the road, but he seemed to be serious about a side excursion. He knew how important it was for us to get to Robert, but perhaps he knew it would be good for us to take an hour to just be normal. I knew that Norm had seen his share of things. I trusted him.

I was all set to agree, but Reinhardt said gently, "Maybe we can fit it in after we find Robert."

"You mean if we find Robert," Roscoe said, searching Reinhardt's face for reassurance. I thought that might sway Reinhardt into agreeing to the side trip; after all, Roscoe needed normalcy more than anything, and none of what we were doing was anywhere close to normal.

"Don't be crazy," Ransom said. "The sooner we get in and out of here and back to France the better. Stopping at tourist attractions is just asking for trouble."

Roscoe's eyes darkened again before he turned his back and stared out the window. He moved his head back and forth as if he were scanning the highway for danger.

I wondered if he thought we might be ensnared en route, armed attackers jumping out of the forest to ambush us as Felix had done at Fairhaven. Those experiences were printed on his psyche forever. And even though I'd never seen Gettysburg and would've loved to just be a tourist for an afternoon, Ransom was right. It would be unwise to linger in one spot for too long where we could be spotted. And, we all knew we'd been manipulated into coming here. I think Roscoe knew it, too.

So he remained silent and guarded sitting vigilantly in the passenger seat with his back to the people I knew he wanted to reach out to most.

It was almost 10 p.m. when we pulled into the Erie Haven RV Park. Norm deftly drove past a thicket of coniferous trees to our site, which was well back from the other campers in a secluded area near the lake.

It had been a long day of driving, and I felt not only tired but drained, like my body didn't have enough energy to sit up anymore.

Alice and Hannah bustled around and soon had sub sandwiches and freshly brewed coffee ready. "You two are turning into quite the chefs," I teased.

They chuckled. "Don't get spoiled. Breakfast is toast and day-old donuts," said Alice.

"Our specialty of the house," said Hannah, laughing.

Reinhardt was examining his phone, not eating. "Renegade emailed the police report," he announced. "Sean lived just outside Erie, twenty minutes from here. His neighbors reported several gunshots and saw two people drive away in a truck shortly after. No descriptive particulars or make and model or license number. Police came to the scene, but Sean was dead when they arrived. Shot several times in the torso. He lived alone and kept to himself. Neighbors said they rarely saw anyone coming or going."

"Where did they take the body?" I asked.

"The Erie County Coroner's Office," Reinhardt said, twisting his mouth. "Is this sounding contrived to anyone else?"

"Contrived like Felix was managing the sting," Roscoe said.

Everyone stopped and stared at him. "Sting" was not a word a fourteen-year-old person would know, let alone use seriously in a sentence. But we were all feeling nervous; I felt a chill run through the RV.

"What if my arrow missed his heart?" Roscoe said. "What if he's alive?"

I looked into my lap. I wasn't the only one who'd thought it.

"Roscoe," Reinhardt said, "that's impossible. No one could have survived that fall. It's a thousand-foot drop to the ocean."

"But his body was never found," Roscoe said.

"Now look here," Amos said. "There's a reasonable explanation for everything. There's no such thing as vampires or a supernatural boogeyman, so stop thinking the worst. That man is dead. D-E-A-D. I know all of you have been wondering whether he's rising like a ghost or he had some magic power that swept him into the wind and turned him into a bird or whatever, but trust me. He was human. You shot him. And he plunged one thousand feet into the ocean. That guy is finito. What we also know is that Felix had people working for him and his tentacles reached wide and broad. So clearly, someone else is carrying on his legacy and trying to spook the hell out of us. "

Amos got down on one knee at the coffee table with a huff and grabbed some paper and a pen from the drawer. "So let's concentrate on the facts. In the morning, you guys go to the Erie coroner's office and check the records there. Tell them you're family—which you are—and you're looking for a missing relative. Hannah and I will find out what we can about the Sean Granger incident. The murder was committed yesterday so the police are probably still doing investigations at the scene. You guys leave that to us."

"Amos and I still have our CIA ID from when Hollinger gave us clearance in Washington last summer to hunt down Felix," Hannah said. "He thought it would make it easier for us to access records. I just happened to 'forget' to give them back." She smiled coyly. "No one in Erie will know that they've been invalidated."

"When Amos and Hannah are done at the murder scene and you folks have finished at the coroner's office," Norm said, "I'll have the coach parked at the Millcreek Mall. Get back here right away and we'll get out of town. We're only a few minutes away from the Interstate. I've booked another campsite in Grove City under a false name."

I had come so far as an independent woman, carrying a gun, making important decisions—even ones that were life and death—but sometimes, I still felt young and inexperienced so it was reassuring to just be told what to do. I liked that we had a solid plan, knew our roles, and had a way to get out of town. Whatever answers we got would lead us to whatever was next.

When the conversation turned to sleep and everyone started to jokingly bicker over who'd get the king-size bed, I ducked out, found an air mattress, laid it out in the kitchenette, and was asleep in minutes.

When I woke up from a noise in the morning, it felt like the night had been a blink. I wanted to lie there at Alice's feet while she ground coffee for what seemed like forever. The day before had seemed relaxing but getting out of the airport had zapped my energy. Everyone got up and wordlessly took cups of hot coffee to our corners to get ready for the day.

An hour later, we left for Erie. Amos and Hannah took the SUV to the crime scene and Norm brought us to the coroner's office in the center of Erie, located in a cluster of municipal buildings.

"I'm parking at the Millcreek Mall about two blocks from here," Norm reminded us when he let us off.

"I need more coffee for this place," I mumbled.

Reinhardt patted my shoulder. The building was a one-story square structure with a gray brick front and a sign that read DELIVERY IN BACK. We knew what kind of deliveries they got. I shivered. The four of us went inside to the front counter.

A heavy-set woman with dark-rimmed glasses was sitting on a high stool behind a glass enclosure, muttering obscenities as she looked down at a paper. She squinted, and tried to type in what she'd read into the computer in front of her. She was so engrossed, she didn't even see the four of us entering the office.

"Excuse me, Miss…" Reinhardt tapped on the glass and glanced around for her nameplate or a badge. "I'm looking for the death record of my brother. I was told that he was brought here for examination last July. His name was Robert Draker."

"It's Ms. Granger," she said. She sighed and shoved the offending document to the side and glared at us.

Granger?

Reinhardt and Ransom looked at me.

She took a drink from her tattered coffee thermos. "Your brother has been dead since last year and now, a year later, you want a copy of the coroner's report?" she hissed.

"Yes. You see, we live in France and only recently learned of his passing," Reinhardt said. He looked sad and upset.

Ms. Granger's eyes moved over each one of us. "I need a subpoena to release the records to you."

"Please, ma'am," Reinhardt said. "This is upsetting enough…"

I stifled a giggle. I hadn't known what a great actor he was. All those months of grief gave him a lot to work with.

"Actually, the subpoena was emailed to your office," Ransom said from behind us. "Can you kindly check? It was sent from our home abroad, and our attorney assured us you'd have it today."

I glanced over at Ransom, who had just been texting Renegade. I felt a warm flush for how resourceful he was.

He caught me looking at him and smiled.

"You'll have to wait until I finish this report I'm working on. It's needed for the courts today," she huffed. "Come back in half an hour… No. An hour. And I'll look for it."

I felt that dark fear nudge into my gut again. In half an hour we wanted to be far away from this place.

Reinhardt reached into his pocket and pulled out a hundred-dollar bill. "Please, Ms. Granger, I don't have much, but I would just be so grateful." He said this humbly as he handed her the cash.

"I can't possibly…" she said, looking at him sideways.

Reinhardt pulled out a second hundred-dollar bill, which she looked at hungrily. "That's all I have. Won't you please help me?"

She snatched the money and slipped the bills into her bra. "What name did you say you were looking for and approximately what time frame?"

"Robert Draker, July 2015," Reinhardt said. "D-r-a-k-e-r."

She typed quickly, scanned her screen, and shook her head. "There's nothing in our records. Are you sure he was brought here?"

"Here's a copy of the news report," Reinhardt said.

She took the copied document from Reinhardt and typed again on the computer. She tried several times, shaking her head. "No. The deceased was never brought to this office."

"Well, that is odd," Reinhardt said, looking sideways at us. "I just don't know what to do. Myrtle Hamilton and Christian Slade were also on the report. Would you please check their names?"

She typed some more, looking very annoyed. "I see what the news story says, but they are not in the system. I've checked the entire data record going back over one year. Maybe there's some mistake with the story. Check with the newspaper. "

Reinhardt wasn't acting anymore. His look of shock was real. If not one of the three had been brought here as reported, had Felix manufactured the story? Perhaps Robert really was alive. And what of Myrtle and Christian?

"Are you absolutely sure, Ms. Granger?" Reinhardt asked.

"Look," she said. "I've been doing this job for twenty years. Don't you think I'd know how to look up records? If they'd been brought here, I'd know it. I suppose you want your money back?"

"You can keep the money," Reinhardt said. "But I don't know where to check now."

"Check with the hospitals," she said. "They usually go there first to confirm... Well... You know."

"By the way," Reinhardt said. "I don't mean to pry, but I saw in the paper that someone with your same last name was... deceased recently here in Erie. I hope he wasn't a family member because... Well. He'd be here for examination, wouldn't he? Oh, I'm sorry."

Ms. Granger's face went white and her lip quivered. "I saw the news, and that Mr. Granger and I are not related," she said. "Just a name coincidence. Now," she smiled unprettily, "I'm quite busy. Is there anything else you need?"

"Thank you for your help, Ms. Granger. I should have thought about checking at the hospital." Reinhardt turned to us abruptly and signaled with his head that we should follow him out.

Reinhardt's energy shifted, and he seemed extremely uncomfortable as he moved hastily to the door. Once we were outside, he motioned that we should pick up the pace. Reinhardt and Roscoe broke into a run. Ransom and I followed, running with them for the two blocks to where Norm had parked the motor home. Once in the parking lot, we slowed the pace to a brisk walk.

"Why the hell did we get out of there so fast," Ransom asked, breathing hard.

Reinhardt said nothing, but Roscoe turned to me. "Didn't you notice the man behind the blinds in the office behind that woman? It looked just like Felix."

I could see from Reinhardt's face that he'd seen him too.

"That's impossible, Roscoe," I said. "He's dead. He has to be."

"We could only see his shadow because he turned the blinds at an angle so we couldn't see his features," said Reinhardt. "I know it's nearly impossible that Felix is alive, but I saw someone of Felix's height, the same buzz-cut hair and wiry body. I didn't get a clear look at his face, but I didn't want to take any chances."

Seven

WE KEPT UP OUR PACE UNTIL we got to the RV. Ransom pounded on the door and Amos opened it and looked at us with surprise as we all piled in looking unnerved. The seniors were sitting at the fancy little table in the kitchenette, with donuts and coffee. Amos and Hannah must have had an efficient trip because it looked like they'd been back for a while.

"Norm, not to be an alarmist, but I think we should get moving," said Reinhardt. He leaned over Amos to look out the windows and Ransom and I, on the other side, did the same. Roscoe stood with his back to the door, his face ashen.

Without a word, Norm jumped into the captain's chair and started the motor home. Our companions didn't need explanations; they knew when to react first and ask questions later. Norm pulled the motor home onto the highway and headed north up Peach Street to Interstate 90. Roscoe made his way to the passenger seat, looking as keenly as the rest of us for signs that we were being followed.

"I need everyone to be on the lookout," Reinhardt said. "I'll explain when we're safely out of town."

"But we need to get the SUV," Amos said, clutching the armrest as Norm took a turn at high speed.

"No, I'm sorry. We can't risk it. If the police or possibly someone else is looking for it…" Reinhardt said. "We'll get a rental in Grove City. If this all turns out to be a misunderstanding, we can go back for it."

An hour later, Norm pulled "Beulah the Behemoth," as I had nicknamed it, into another campground, The Emerald Woodland Conservation Park. It was early in the day and mostly still empty. Norm asked for a remote spot, and within minutes the motor home was safely concealed behind a thick grove of trees. Norm turned off the engine and rotated his driver's chair to face us.

"OK, Reinhardt," Norm said. "What's got you guys so spooked?"

Roscoe began to tremble. "Felix was there," he whispered, "in the coroner's office."

"Now, Roscoe," said Reinhardt. "Let's not jump to conclusions. Whoever was there looked like him, but we didn't see his face clearly."

"You saw a Felix double?" Alice screeched. She moved in closer to hear the story. "Tell us what happened."

"First of all, the name of the clerk at the coroner's office is Ms. Granger."

"No, seriously?" Amos asked.

Amos and Hannah's eyes moved as if they were trying to fit this woman into the murder reports.

"Why do you suppose the newspaper reported that Sean had no living relatives?" Hannah said to Amos. "Maybe she's a sister or wife"

Reinhardt shrugged as he continued. "She was preoccupied with a report that she seemed desperate to finish. Two hundred dollars from me encouraged her to look up the records from last summer.

But the whole thing seemed off. She's worked there for many years, and she seemed to have a hold on what went on there, which to my mind means she'd remember who is coming in and going out. She certainly looked like she was looking hard through her records, but she couldn't find any record of three bodies coming to the office for autopsies. She looked back over the entire year just to make sure there weren't any mistakes in the date or late entries."

Roscoe jumped in, "And while she was typing away, I saw a man lift the slats of the blinds on the chief coroner's office door." His eyes were wide as he sat stiff and tense in the passenger seat. "He must have overheard us, but he didn't come out. In fact, he changed the position on the blinds so we couldn't see him, but his shadow still showed through. It was Felix. I just know it. I'd recognize the shape of his body and head anywhere."

"What about you, Reinhardt?" Amos asked. "You saw him, too?"

"Yes," Reinhardt said. "It was just too odd. I know it can't be Felix, but someone is trying to make us think it's him. All in all, it seems we're being played, and I thought it best to get out of there."

"OK, wait a second," said Hannah. "If none of the bodies arrived for autopsy, then where are they? Could they all be alive?"

I gasped at the thought and felt sick. Not only Robert, but possibly Myrtle and Christian as well? This was starting to feel like the zombie apocalypse. They were dead; we saw them dead. But where were they?

"We need to find out," I said. "This is getting ridiculous. That Granger woman said we might be able to get some information at the hospital. Is there a hospital in Erie or someplace where they'd verify that they were actually dead? Like, we all thought they were dead, but what if they weren't?" I started to cry. I hated this. I hated the thought that we might have left them lying in the mud while we saved ourselves.

Ransom scooted over to me and rubbed my back.

I felt a warmth invade me then. I sat up straighter and wiped my face. I looked Ransom in the eyes, gently took his hand and put it back in his lap.

You can do this, Ruby. Think through the situation. Use your logic, Rosalind whispered.

I felt so relieved to hear her in my thoughts I nearly wept again. But I cleared my throat. "OK," I said. I took the paper on the coffee table and began jotting down notes. "We know Felix had a cleanup crew at every one of his murders, so maybe he had one at the farmhouse to remove

Robert, Myrtle and Christian. Or he had the local police do it for him. If they were on his payroll, that would make sense. It was reported as a gas leak explosion and the television news reports did say that the bodies were taken to Erie for autopsies. So that means Ms. Granger was actually searching her computer and didn't have a record. Her suggestion was probably right. The bodies would have been taken to a hospital for examination first."

"I assume that people from neighboring farmhouses would have notified the Springfield police," Alice said. "They probably dispatched cruisers and emergency vehicles to the farm. Springfield only has an emergency walk-in clinic, but they might have been taken there first. I'll make some phone calls. I have a friend at the local clinic. Clara is a real busybody and she loves snooping."

"But since someone knows we're asking questions…" Ransom said. "we can't exactly just show up at the Erie hospital."

"Could we get a doctor in the Erie area to make the inquiries for us?" I asked.

"Good idea," said Reinhardt. "I'll send a message to Renegade to look up the backgrounds of doctors in the area. You're absolutely right. A local doctor might have specific reasons for wanting to know and, I hope, wouldn't arouse suspicions." He typed into his smartphone and hit send. "Amos. We never talked about what you learned at the Granger murder scene."

Amos chuckled. "Let's just say we weren't entirely welcome. An inspector by the name of Larking didn't take kindly to FBI poking around his crime scene. We asked about the body but apparently, it's already been moved to the coroner's office. Or at least that's what he wanted us to believe."

"And yet," Reinhardt said, raising an eyebrow, "Ms. Granger was adamant that no one with the name of Granger was there."

"Larking also said the police report hadn't been filed yet, but they'd notify me when it was," Amos said. "Normally, that would mean they'd check out my FBI ID. However, I noticed Larking didn't write down my badge number, which means he had every intention of letting me know squat. I'd bet money that Felix also had the Erie police involved in his cover-up."

"If the Erie police did have your ID number and ran your badge, would Hollinger cover up for you?" I asked.

"Or…" said Ransom, jumping up, "Hollinger is already involved. He doesn't want us in the U.S. because he knows this thing has something to do with Robert being alive. I feel like we're being deliberately manipulated…"

He trailed off and went into his thoughts then, and the RV became unusually quiet.

"Do you remember last year?" Ransom blurted out. "Hollinger suspected that Felix was involved with a Corsican crime ring. Remember the photo with the ferry in the background that had the name *Corsican Ferry Lines* on it? No one ever tied that knot, did they? Hollinger dropped it after Felix died."

"I wouldn't even know where to start with that as a lead, Ransom," said Reinhardt. He furrowed his brow, and I could tell that what Ransom had said was making him think. "But whether those people are involved or it's something else, why is someone trying to get us to interfere now? That's the question."

He pulled the photo of Robert out of his pocket and stared at it as if it might contain answers.

"Whoever this is and whatever the motive," I said, "the Drakers are already part of the plan."

"That's the part I don't understand," said Reinhardt. "We are safe behind our code name. RD is a non-entity, and all our correspondence is in code known only by the Drakers. I developed all this with Rosalind to keep us safe."

I felt sad and sorry that we were under attack like this. Again. I could see the helplessness written on Reinhardt's face. He'd been sturdy and sure before but now, he'd been through too much. Too many parts of him were broken.

"Why don't we just admit it," Roscoe said angrily. "Felix is still alive. Who else would know how to get to us like this?"

"Or Felix had an accomplice who wants us to think that Felix is still alive," I said. "We'll get to the bottom of this, Roscoe. We have to stay strong and united." I went over to him and put my arm around him. He was trembling hard. What kind of monster would do this to a child?

"On another note, we should get ourselves another car," Norm said quietly. "Can't drive a motor home all over the city."

"I'll make inquires with the owners of the park," Ransom said. "I'm sure if I ask very nicely, they can accept a delivery at the gate."

"No need to buy," Hannah said. "We can get a rental in Grove City. I'll use a disguise and a *borrowed* driver's license." She whispered the word "borrowed" then laughed as she pulled it from her purse and waved it around proudly. "As I like to say: an alias a day keeps the doctor away!" She laughed. "Leave the rental to me. I assume we want a family-sized SUV again." Hannah bent over Amos and gave him a quick kiss. "Maybe I'll pick up a few things at the outlet mall too. Never know when you might need a new look." She went to the closet and found her hat and sunglasses.

"In that case, Hannah," Alice said, "Hope you don't mind if I join you. How about you, Ruby?"

"Thanks, ladies, but I think I might have a walk if that's OK."

They smiled and headed off.

I was glad to stay back. Spending some quiet time with the trees sounded much nicer than a florescent-lit mall. But I couldn't move. My thoughts were moving faster than storm clouds. "I'm still wondering why Robert hasn't tried to contact us or escape."

"The photo did show that he was in a wheelchair," Ransom said. "He may not be mobile on his own. And if he's being held against his will, he wouldn't be hard to restrain."

Of course that was a probable explanation, but it made me feel sad. Robert had been so capable, always a step ahead of everyone else. I blinked quickly. I needed to put aside my pity for him. What Robert needed from us was a Draker-style rescue.

"Of more concern to me," Ransom said, "is why Hollinger is being so secretive. He's not usually this evasive about details. After what we went through with Felix, and how pivotal our help was, there has to be a really good reason why he doesn't want us to get involved."

"Maybe it truly is a matter of national security," I said. "It might not be that he doesn't want us to get involved because he doesn't trust us. It might be because he's trying to protect us. But the question is, why? And from what?"

"Yeah, I'm sure it's like someone's building a nuclear bomb and targeting the U.S. and it's going to be heading straight for... us!" Ransom said, making an exploding sound and jumping on Roscoe to tickle him.

Roscoe pushed him away, a scowl on his face. "Not funny!"

"Roscoe," I said. "Come on. Your brother's just joking." Still, I glared at Ransom to get off the boy and stop it.

He threw up his hands and backed off but his grin indicated that he was not apologetic in the least. The poor kid had enough to worry about. He didn't need to add someone dropping a nuke and wiping out an entire U.S. city on top of it.

Reinhardt looked at me curiously.

"What?" I said. I heard my voice and then I realized. I had done it again. I sounded just like Rosalind.

"That's not a bad point to consider," Reinhardt said. "Felix wouldn't have thought twice about making a deal with organized crime to fund his murders. Imagine how expensive killing people and making it all look like an accident can be. I'm sure there are people out there with their fingers on a dark pulse, looking for weapons to sell to insurgents."

"I'm lost. Why would that involve us?" Roscoe asked.

"For now, our only mission is to find Robert and bring him home," Reinhardt said. "Whatever national security issue Hollinger may or may not be facing, I'm more than happy to leave it in Hollinger's capable hands."

Our eyebrows collectively rose when he said "capable," until Ransom barked out, "Ha!"

A shiver rippled down my spine as I thought of Hollinger being responsible for the safety of millions of people. Under his protection, we had lost two family members and Ransom had nearly died of gunshot wounds. I looked at Ransom and remembered how he had barely hung on to life, how he'd jumped in my way to take Felix's bullets that day last summer in Washington. I owed him my life. I'd thought he'd risked his life because he loved me. I fought back the memory. He'd done what anyone would have done. We were Drakers. We stood up for each other. It didn't mean he loved me. He'd loved Rose. Hadn't he?

I let myself ruminate further until my thoughts began to come together. "Felix had a network of accomplices." I stood up. "Oh my God. What if he had debts to these people. An unfulfilled arms deal? Those guys don't care if their point person is dead. A deal's a deal. So then if that guy's dead, who would they go after for delivery?" I began to pace, thinking out loud. "Felix had a full-time assistant at the Archives Department in Washington. I wonder what Hollinger has done with him. What if he were in on it!"

"Easy, tiger," said Ransom, "He's probably still under very tight surveillance. It's still a good idea, but I doubt he'd be involved in any of Felix's outstanding munitions deals if, in fact, he even had outstanding munitions deals. Hollinger would have him on a very tight string I'm sure."

"That's not to say he wouldn't be involved," I said. "Guilty until proven innocent!" A strange feeling gripped me. I felt resolute inner confidence.

Now, all three of the guys looked at me almost in horror. I had to admit that what had just come out of my mouth had startled me as well.

I straightened my back and returned a strong confident stare. I wasn't sure who was saying those words. It was like Rosalind had entered me, made me whole and strong again. I couldn't brush away the feeling. But also, I didn't want to. I liked it. No. I loved it.

"What?" I said. "We should investigate him. Now."

"This is all valuable, Ruby," said Reinhardt. "But let's wait until we hear from the clinic in Springfield. Stepping back a bit, we can wait to find out about the bodies, where they were taken, what the records show. We'll let that be the start of our trail."

We had been so busy talking that we hadn't noticed Amos and Norm had been sitting off to the side just listening. "Gathering intelligence" is the way they would have put it. I'm sure their brains were churning and processing. They had an uncanny knack for unscrambling facts from suspicions. Although they didn't add anything to our speculative diatribe, I could see them exchanging knowing looks. I knew they always did like to have a Plan B, a little something up their sleeves in case of unforeseen circumstances.

"The ladies will be at least a couple of hours," Amos said. "Why don't you guys get some fresh air? Check out the campsite. Pretend you're on vacation. Or at least trying to be recreational. Or something." He grinned at me. "You know how to do that, don't you?"

I wasn't sure if he was being sarcastic or if he was just fed up with our obsessive rantings.

Norm nodded. "Go on. Shoo."

"A bit of fresh air sounds great." I nodded toward the door that the guys should come with me. "I think Amos and Norm want to talk privately. Maybe we're making them uncomfortable."

"Why would they be uncomfortable with what we were talking about?" Ransom asked.

I rolled my eyes at him. "Because," I said, "it probably sounded like we were getting them involved in another very dangerous situation. Maybe what they want to do is live a good retired life. Tour around in the RV. Have some fun. They worked long and hard and this is their time to relax. Back near Gettysburg, I know they would have liked to stop and take in some important American history and be tourists for a while. Come on, Roscoe," I said. "This place is pretty fancy. Let's see if they have a rec center. Maybe there's an arcade."

I knew I'd said the magic word when Roscoe's eyes sparkled. He took off ahead of me while I darted back and got some money from Reinhardt, just in case. I caught up with Roscoe on the dirt roadway that led to a couple of rustic buildings, leaving Reinhardt and Ransom to explore on their own.

***

Three white clapboard buildings were clustered near the entrance to the RV Park, close enough to the highway that I could hear the steady swish of cars driving past. The sign over the shop nearest the highway read *Emerald Woodland Variety.* Going inside, I felt nearly assaulted by the musty smells of old merchandise and bathroom deodorant. I had the same edgy feeling I'd had when Felix had tried to trap us at the gas station convenience store a year before in Springfield.

Roscoe ran ahead inside. I followed, but stopped at the entrance to have a good look around to make sure no one was watching us. When I went in, I saw Roscoe already at a video game in the rear of the store, joystick in hand, gleefully shooting lasers at an alien spacecraft on a large screen.

"Morning, dear," said someone to my right.

I jumped and turned to see who it was.

A gray-haired woman in a faded Gap T-shirt was standing behind a cash register, smiling pleasantly at me.

I cursed myself. I'd been so intent on watching out for Roscoe that I hadn't even noticed her.

If it had been a poisonous snake, it would have bit you, I could hear Rosalind say.

I almost lost my breath. She was so much in my head, my thoughts were getting crowded with the various personnel occupying it. I wondered how Kathleen felt about her, whether they made good roommates.

The woman laughed. "I see your brother has already found the games. It's like the kids are pulled by magnets!"

I didn't respond.

"So where you in from? I'm Rose. I only work here part-time." She beamed at me, probably hoping I'd rescue her from abject boredom. The place was empty.

On hearing her name, my body seized up. *Seriously,* I thought, *of all the names in the world?* Maybe our Rose was haunting me, too, and this was her sadistic way of getting in a good dig.

I decided Roscoe and I needed to get out of there and nearly called out to him that we should go, but he was hooting and having so much fun, I stopped myself.

"Morning," I said. "How do I pay for the video games?"

She wrinkled her forehead and looked at me strangely. Why was she looking at me like that?

"Oh," she said. "Our machines aren't automatic. But the boy dropped a twenty on the counter, so I gave him tokens. He should have enough to last him at least an hour."

While I tried to think about where Roscoe would've gotten a twenty, she said, "Oh, maybe you didn't know that he had money." She paused, looking suspicious. "Did he steal it from you? Sometimes kids do that you know?"

"Of course he didn't," I said. This whole thing was going badly. I felt so worn and thin and now some woman was accusing Roscoe of stealing.

"I'm so sorry," she said. Her face turned red as she spoke. "I didn't mean to accuse him of anything. I was just... Well. Really. I was just trying to make conversation." She laughed and scratched under her ample bosom. "But is everything, OK? You seem... Well. I'm not so bad to talk to. Gum?" she offered me a pack.

I shook my head and returned a tight smile before going over to keep Roscoe company, though I doubted he'd even know I was there.

I leaned against the wall to watch Roscoe play. I felt better watching how much fun he was having shooting down enemies and getting to the next level.

The bells on the front door dinged, and I strained to hear who had come in.

"Do you know where I can get a cup of coffee?" A man asked.

"The building next door," Rose said.

I peeked around the machines.

The man was wearing sunglasses and a dark suit with a white shirt. People didn't dress like that in campgrounds. He pulled open his jacket to put his wallet away, and I thought I saw something silver glint from underneath. My throat closed up. He had to be either CIA or DoD.

I leaned in close to Roscoe and whispered, "Keep doing what you're doing, but there's a man at the counter who is probably with Hollinger."

That jolted Roscoe back from outer space. He glanced at me but kept his head trained on the screen and continued to fire lasers.

"Door," he said under his breath. He pointed the joystick toward a side door propped open with a chair only a few feet away. Roscoe kept his composure and continued to play, only now, I could tell it was just to maintain the status quo until we could sneak out.

The front door bells dinged again.

A second later, Roscoe whispered, "Let's go."

We slipped outside and down the wooden steps and peered around to the front of the store where an unmarked black sedan was parked, and another man dressed similarly to the man at the counter, was sitting in the driver's seat.

I pulled out my phone and took a photo of the car and license plate. We waited behind a cedar hedge until we saw the man who'd come inside return to the car with two Styrofoam cups and a small paper bag. The SUV started and they drove off onto the highway.

"We need to get back to the motor home," I said.

"Do they know we're here?" Roscoe asked. "Why else would they be here?"

I put my arm around him and shrugged. My nerves were rattled, and I didn't trust myself to talk. I, too, wondered if he'd noticed us.

Perhaps Hollinger had figured out that we'd pulled a fast one on him and hadn't left the country.

Rosalind's voice inside of me was hissing, *Trust your instincts, Ruby.*

I needed to get us back to the motor home. I rolled my eyes at the thought of the discreet behemoth with the flashy paint job. Practically unnoticeable, I cursed. What on earth was Norm thinking when he decided to use that?

Eight

WE SPRINTED BACK TO OUR CAMPSITE. My heart was up in my mouth, I peered all around the motor home to see if there were any signs that someone had been snooping. Reinhardt and Ransom were nowhere to be seen, and the area appeared to be deserted. The quiet was unnerving. The only sounds were our footsteps on the pine needles and the birds chirping in the trees overhead. I didn't see anything that looked suspicious—for the moment at least.

Roscoe bounded up the steps, making two deep loud thuds. My footsteps echoed his. Expecting Roscoe to keep going, I knocked into him when he stopped cold.

"Ouch, what the…"

I looked up and stared at the scene in the kitchenette. The four men, Reinhardt, Ransom, Amos and Norm were sitting at the breakfast nook, two rifles and a couple of handguns spread out on the small tabletop. The men stared at us, bewildered by our frantic entrance.

"What's up, young'uns?" Norm asked. "You look like you're being chased by a bear. But not to worry. I have just the solution for that." He patted the rifle in front of him as he grunted out a chuckle.

"Men. Agents probably. They stopped at the variety by the camp entrance," I said. "I think they were either CIA or DoD. They asked Rose if there was somewhere they could get some coffee, and—"

"Rose?" Ransom blurted out, looking struck. He watched my face for an explanation.

I sighed. "The woman behind the cash register. She introduced herself. Yeah, Rose! What are the odds of that?" I let out an exasperated bark and waited to see what Ransom's reaction would be. I felt unhinged enough and whatever grief, loss, or guilt he would feel now would just be a kind of icing on the cake.

"What makes you think they're CIA?" Reinhardt asked.

I was glad he was so calm, a buffer for the hot emotion about to spark Ransom and me in an ugly way that I was sure nobody wanted. I showed him the photo on my phone.

Reinhardt took it from my hand and started to click away on his phone. "I'm sending it to Renegade. He'll verify them. "

Roscoe plunked down next to Reinhardt. "What's with the artillery?" he asked.

"Sit down, you two," Amos said. "Do you remember Hannah's brother in Springfield who owns the gun shop?"

We nodded.

"Seems he knows a local funeral director who has a contract with the government to take care of the bodies that come into the morgue and aren't claimed."

"Does he remember anything about three bodies last summer?" I asked. I felt like I was going to throw up, like invisible hands were pressing on my stomach.

Reinhardt looked over, took my hand, and squeezed it. But it only made the agitated upset feeling in me more intense.

A quick succession of flashbacks, not just the farm, but the fire at my New York State home where my parents and little brother had died were haunting me, and their ghosts would not leave me alone. So many people I loved, and Felix had torn them away from me.

"Nope," Amos said. "Or rather, yep. I asked specifically about the incident and he verified what your Ms. Granger told Reinhardt. The bodies never arrived there. " He paused a moment to let the information sink in.

"Sit down, Ruby," Reinhardt said. "There's more. "

Amos went on, "Furthermore," he said, leaning back and spreading his arms wide across the banquette, "your Ms. Granger lied to you, or half lied to you. In fact, she knows Sean—quite well—because he's her husband, but his body didn't come into her coroner's office." He paused dramatically. "Because he's probably not dead." Amos held up a photo of Granger and his wife. He had buzz-cut hair and a similar wiry body type as Felix.

"So we can rest a little easier and assume this was probably the man we saw behind the blinds in the chief coroner's office," Reinhardt said.

I was lost. "But then why are the newspapers reporting that he's been murdered?" I asked.

"Because someone is trying to make us think another ex-CIA agent has been murdered, Felix style. My guess is, to draw us into their specific agenda. Who would do that? Do you think it's Hollinger?"

Ransom said, "I don't think that's Hollinger's style. Also, why would he do that? No. I think someone else wants us to think Felix is alive."

"All we want to do is find Robert," I said. "Someone is going to a lot of trouble to make us think Felix is still out there, but what would that accomplish?"

"Whoever is behind this seems to want something from the Drakers," Norm said, his pleasant expression darkening.

"Then why don't they just ask us?" Roscoe said. "We'd give them money if that's what they were after, wouldn't we?" Roscoe looked at Reinhardt for reassurance. "What could they want? We don't have anything else. They've taken everything else." His eyes were filling with tears.

"It's far beyond a simple ransom scheme, Roscoe," Reinhardt said. "I think Ruby's theory about Felix having unfinished business has merit.

It could very easily be that Felix left behind a debt—he was a man who had his fingers in a lot of pies—and certainly, he would have died before he could make good on everything he was involved in.

The room was quiet.

Reinhardt continued. "I'm not saying that's it, but I'm trying to put together the pieces of how Felix paid for all his killings and covered them without ever arousing suspicion. All that had to cost a bundle. Secrecy doesn't come cheap and neither does loyalty. His pension and the money he stole from his ex-agents wouldn't have paid for yachts and the elaborate cleanup efforts that made his executions look like accidents."

"Fine, but that was Felix's problem," I said. "His unpaid debts wouldn't have anything to do with us and none of this explains why Hollinger wants us to stay away."

"Well, OK, let's think about this for a moment," Norm said. "Here's what we know. There's Hollinger who is in charge of national defense who doesn't want us here. We have reason to suspect that Felix was involved with an organized crime group only based on that photographic tip with the yacht. But the fact that Robert is likely out there and hasn't contacted us makes me think that there's someone else who has a sideline motive."

"Organized crime! Mafia!" I yelped. "That's all we need. As if we haven't been through enough. " I jumped up from my seat and wished I could pace but there was no room. Instead, I just threw up my hands in frustration. This was all starting to sound like some bad Hollywood movie, not to mention very dangerous. Sideline motive or not, I wasn't interested in seeing anyone else in our family get killed.

There was a noise outside. The men grabbed the weapons on the table and pointed them toward the coach entrance. Two strange women clomped up the steps.

"Yoohoo, dearies," called a hippie with long brunette hair braided with beads and ribbons. She climbed up with her hands on her hips and a wide smile on her face, but when she saw all the guns pointed at her, she dropped her smile. "What the hell?" She threw her canvas tote down onto the ground and put her hands up. "It's just us, you old poops. Guess our disguises are damn good. " She looked at the other woman who ws one step lower.

"Alice?" Norm asked. He started to laugh.

"Of course, it's me, Norm," Alice said, laughing, too, but she stopped laughing and became serious almost instantly. "What happened? Why are you pointing guns at us?" She pulled off the very convincing wig. "But, before you answer, Hannah and I have things to share as well."

The men laid their guns back on the table and she and Hannah came in and sat down in the living room area.

"Grove City is crawling with government vehicles," Hannah said. "When we walked in to the car rental place, two men in suits were grilling the poor teenagers behind the counter for a list of everyone who had rented today. We turned right around, hightailed it out of there, and walked to the outlet mall for a quick fashion makeover." Hannah pointed to the bags she had dropped when they came in. "We picked up some things for you guys as well. We took our time, so it was several hours later when we went back. Luckily, this time, we were the only ones there and still managed to get two cars." She put her arms around her husband. "Norm, honey, I know you love this motor home, but I don't think we can drive around in it anymore."

"Where did you leave the cars?" Roscoe asked. He was looking out of a side window to see what they'd rented.

"Down the road in a parking lot," Hannah said. "We didn't want to be followed here."

"Ruby said agents were snooping around the RV park variety store as well," Reinhardt said.

"Well," I said, "I'm not sure whether they were looking for anyone or whether they just stopped to get a coffee. But Roscoe and I slipped out the back door of the variety so they wouldn't see us."

"Did your friend Clara get in touch with you about what happened last summer at the Springfield clinic?" Ransom asked.

"I phoned her to tell her about a 'sale at my brother's gun shop,'" Hannah said doing her air quotes. "She feels the same about the first amendment as we do, so of course, that led perfectly to a conversation about what happened last summer at the farmhouse. When I asked her if the three bodies came into the clinic, she said yes, but they were in such bad shape, they were transferred by air ambulance to a trauma hospital in New York."

That was all I could take. I ran to the washroom and vomited, the sour distaste of what we had done overcoming me.

Roscoe came in behind me and wet a washcloth in the sink.

When I lifted my head from the toilet, he handed it to me. I rubbed it hard over my face, but the tears kept streaming down my cheeks.

He knelt in front of me. "You can't blame yourself for what happened. Felix would have killed you all. How were you to know that anyone could survive that kind of thing?" He was quiet a moment. Then he said, "But I know exactly how you feel." He leaned in and hugged me tenderly.

I cried softly onto the shoulder of my little brother who had taken over the role of both my real little brother and my parents. When I finally looked up, Reinhardt and Ransom were standing at the door.

Roscoe helped me to my feet and handed me off to Ransom who put his arm around me and brought me back to the living room. I didn't argue. We all sat numbly together.

A *ping* from Reinhardt's phone broke the silence.

"Seems Hollinger has been making inquiries about our arrival back in France," he said. "Renegade used voice manipulation software to return Hollinger's calls as me so Hollinger would think we were happily eating croissants on the Fairhaven terrace."

"He's right not to trust us," guffawed Ransom. "And we've been encountering people right and left. All it'd take is for someone to tip him off that we're here, sniffing around with questions at the coroner's office. Maybe Ms. Granger was in touch…" He trailed off and shrugged.

"There's something else in the mix," Reinhardt said, raising one eyebrow. "I asked Renegade to get information about Felix's assistant at the Archives in Washington. It seems that the assistant is missing. But you won't believe what his name is: Oscar Worchenski." Reinhardt held his phone out for us to see. "Rings a bell?"

"As in Magda Worchenski?" Or otherwise known as Margaret Warren, the woman Rosalind brought to the farm to help us bring down Felix after he found us in Springfield, and the same woman who died in the helicopter explosion? I thought for a moment, trying to bring the threads together. "She hadn't been married and said she didn't have any family. But if she was lying, was Oscar her brother? Or son?"

"It could be a coincidence that they had the same last name—" I started.

"Come on, Ruby," sneered Ransom. "What are the odds of that? No. Felix was a cold, calculating bastard. Back at the farmhouse last year it was clear that Magda and Felix didn't like each other. He could've hired her son just to control her, to have something she held dear in his possession." He stared at me. "Look at how he hired Christian, his son, that he had with your mother after he raped her. Do you think he did that to be nice?"

I felt another rise of nausea at the mention of what that monster had done to my mother while she was married to my father. I hadn't even known about Christian until that night at the farmhouse. And he never knew I was his sister, not even as he stepped forward in the last minutes and tried to save my life before his own father shot him and left him to die.

I was shaking. "Did he... rape Magda too? Is Oscar his son?"

Ransom looked down.

Reinhardt's phone pinged again. He looked at it, closed his eyes, and held out the phone for us to see. It was a photo of a younger man bearing an uncanny resemblance to Felix Szabo.

"This is Oscar Worchenski," said Reinhardt. "I don't think we need a DNA test." Scowling, he continued. "I'd never wished death on another human being until I met Szabo."

I tried to clear my head against the fury building in my core. "OK. Magda's body was never found after the helicopter crash. Right? Could she somehow have jumped out of the helicopter before it took off or before it exploded? We were busy trying to save the rest of you and I didn't see the helicopter as it lifted off." I fought against the memory of Christian, riddled with bullets, the glow of moonlight on the blood. The horrible sounds, the helicopter thwacking against the trees.

"Maybe that's how that chunk of fabric got ripped off her jeans," Ransom said.

When we found the wreck of the helicopter at the junkyard, that patch of her jeans was the evidence we gave to Hollinger so he could verify the possible causalities.

"So how are we going to find these 'not so dead' people?" Roscoe asked.

I stared at him. This was hardly a conversation a boy of fourteen should be having. He was losing his childhood, his innocence. He'd never have the chance to get that back.

"Roscoe, the only thing we are going to do is find Robert and bring him home," Reinhardt said firmly. "I have no intention of getting involved any further than that. I don't care what Magda, Hollinger, and the Grangers are up to. It's their business and we're staying out of it."

"Dad," Roscoe said. It was still new to hear him call Reinhardt "Dad." He wasn't just trapped between childhood and adulthood, he was straddling an identity of a boy who'd lost his real parents, and then watched his second mother die as well. His calling Reinhardt "Dad" was his last chance at being loved in the particular way only a parent could. It sounded so wanting, so vulnerable.

"I suspect if we're going to find Robert, we're going to have to find Margaret first," I said.

"Not even Hollinger was able to find her, Ruby—" Reinhardt started.

"Then we'll just have to find Oscar," I said. "If anyone knows where she's hiding, it'd be him, don't you think?"

Reinhardt typed a message into his phone. "That's a job for Renegade."

"Somehow," Hannah said, "all these loose ends must be connected. Our best option is to start questioning the people we have access to. Let's find out where Ms. Granger likes to hang out or what places she frequents. We can bump into her, make some idle conversation and see if we can get her to reveal something. Gossip is an amazing tool, you know."

Our seniors had already stood and were preparing to go back into Erie to do just that.

"Can I come?" Roscoe said. "Maybe I can help make her talk. Why would she worry about saying stuff to a kid?" He smirked cutely.

"Roscoe, son, we don't know what we're up against," Reinhardt said. "I don't want you going off to do something that could be dangerous without us there."

"Well, that settles it," Amos said.

Roscoe's face fell.

"Then we all have to go."

Roscoe lit up again.

Alice threw some bags in our direction. "Here, catch!"

We rummaged through and began dressing. As we transformed into biker people with leather pants, black shirts, and vests with chains dangling from belt loops and pockets, we had to admit the women had outdone themselves.

Roscoe was dressed in a T-shirt with knee and elbow pads and a nice skateboard. "I'll need to rough this up," he said, whistling as he eyed the board.

"What about the motor home?" I asked.

"The campsite is paid for four nights," Norm said. "We can leave it here while we come and go. It'll be OK."

"Hollinger probably knows we're here since he has men all over the area," I said.

"Now Ruby, I don't think you need to worry about that. We've blended in, and there's nothing here that will give us away."

That made me laugh. There was enough ammo and guns in this RV to protect a small country.

So there we were: four hippies, three bikers, and a skateboard kid. What a strange group, I thought as we walked to where Alice and Hannah had left the rental cars. So strange, in fact, that we should have turned heads, but every manner of person seemed to be in residence in this campsite, and no one even looked our way. Maybe the more you stood out, the more invisible you became, I thought.

Meanwhile, good old Renegade found out some important intel. Ms. Granger's name was Elizabeth. She'd been married to Sean for twenty-five years. One would have imagined she would be distraught by the murder of her husband, but she went to her job in the coroner's office every day without fail as if nothing had happened. This was, of course, because nothing did happen. The "murder" was a ploy to lure us into town. The question was who had set it up and why, and further, how Sean and Elizabeth were in on this Felix-style plan.

Renegade said they seemed like normal people and couldn't figure out how they'd have gotten involved in this. He suspected they were being used as pawns, and uncovering why would help us find Magda who, we determined, could lead us to Robert.

We parked across the street from the coroner's office and waited. We lucked out after an hour when Elizabeth came out the front door and walked down the street to a coffee shop. Once she was inside, we split into two groups, each group going into the coffee shop after the other was settled.

Roscoe played his part like a pro, chatting and teasing his grandparents and aunt and uncle, spouting skateboard lingo, and having a great time while they were led to their table.

Ransom, Reinhardt and I lingered at the free newspapers while we waited to be seated. I was glad it wasn't crowded so we could hear everything.

"I'm telling you, Oscar," Norm said. "We should video you when you do that move. It'll go viral, man."

I was impressed by Norm's quick decision to name Roscoe "Oscar." I looked over at Elizabeth, who was at a nearby table, to see her reaction. The menu was in front of her, but I could see she was eavesdropping and not reading it.

"Aw, Gramps!" Roscoe said. "It's nothing special. Any serious boarder can do it."

Norm and the others chuckled and sipped the coffee that had just arrived.

"Kids these days," Alice leaned over and said to Elizabeth amicably. "There's nothing they can't do. Do your kids show off like that too?"

"My husband and I don't have kids," Elizabeth said. "But yours is certainly sprightly." She smiled and glanced at the door.

"He is," Alice said effusively. "Our grandson Oscar here is the joy of our lives, the joy of his great aunt and uncle as well. He's always doing jumps and spins and acrobatic stuff with that board. Makes us all so proud of his ability."

"You and your husband could come down to the skate park and watch me," Roscoe said.

Inside, I cringed, hoping she wouldn't take him up on his offer. I didn't even know if he could skateboard, let alone put on a demonstration at the level he was talking about.

"Thank you, but we have somewhere we have to be," Elizabeth said. She smiled at him briefly and looked at her watch.

"Oh, that's too bad," Roscoe said. "Maybe you could ask him if he'd like to see some really awesome moves. I know you guys would love it. Is he meeting you here?" Roscoe was playing his role with the perfect enthusiasm of a fourteen-year-old. His innocent energy started her laughing. We chuckled under our disguises now a few tables away. He was adorably charming.

"We're going out of town and have to leave as soon as he gets here," Elizabeth said.

Bingo!

Elizabeth glanced again at the door.

"Gramps?" Roscoe said. "Are you done with your coffee yet?"

"OK, kid," Norm said, taking the last sip and clapping his cup down on the table. "Let's get over there and see what you've got."

They got up and followed Roscoe who had already bounded out the door.

"Always in a hurry," said Alice. "Have yourself a good trip." Alice beamed a proud grandma smile and waved goodbye as she walked out.

We remained behind to see if Sean would indeed arrive.

About five minutes later, a stocky man with buzz-cut hair and a day's growth of stubble on his chin, and wearing a dark T-shirt and jeans, walked over to the counter and ordered a coffee to go. He looked cautiously around the coffee shop and nodded discreetly to Elizabeth before leaving with the coffee.

Elizabeth waited a few minutes before scuttling out the door. From our table by the window, we watched the two of them get into a shiny blue sedan with rental tags on the license plates. They seemed to be arguing with their cell phones in their hands. Then Sean put the phone to his ear, said what looked like "OK," and put his phone away.

We paid for our coffees and hurried back across the street where we had parked our car and waited for them to drive away.

A moment later, Norm, Alice, Amos, Hannah and Roscoe did the same.

Minutes passed. We watched and waited. Finally, the blue sedan pulled out onto the street and headed north.

We followed them north on Peach Street toward the Interstate. Reinhardt kept a safe distance, though the traffic was heavy so they wouldn't have noticed us anyway.

Before we got to the Interstate, they turned off. The only thing just before the Interstate was a row of hotels marking the outskirts of Erie.

They pulled into the parking lot of a Marriott and again waited in the car. Sean looked around cautiously before getting out of the car, closed the door behind him, and the two of them walked briskly to the hotel entrance.

Just before they reached the hotel doors, a muscular man wearing dark sunglasses and an ill-fitting brown suit came around from the side of the building and barreled right up behind Sean. The man's hand was in his pocket and he was pressing his pocket up to Sean's back.

I couldn't believe the audacity. Sean was being mugged or something in broad daylight! I looked around and wished someone would see this and call the police, but no one was outside. There was nothing we could do. Sean and Elizabeth would recognize us from the coffee shop and wonder why we were following them, and that could be a "bad scene," as one of our hippies would've said.

Alice texted Reinhardt from their car. "Time to change our appearance again." They were parked on the other side of the hotel lot.

Alice got out, walked around the SUV and pulled out several bags from the open hatch and brought them over to us.

Ransom opened the window and she threw the bags inside before turning around and going back to their car, scanning the parking lot the whole time.

In their SUV, all I could see was a bunch of arms pulling on new shirts. I'd have laughed if this whole thing weren't so serious.

We changed, too, me with my head down so I couldn't see if Ransom were looking over or not, and moments later, Reinhardt, Ransom and I entered the hotel in khaki pants, T-shirts, jean jackets, and sneakers.

I spotted Sean and Elizabeth in the bar, sitting stiff as boards. Two fit and good-looking men in beautiful suits hovered over them while the man who had brought them inside was sitting beside Sean with another guy.

We took seats in the lounge area where we hoped we could overhear what was going on.

Their voices were low and menacing. "Sean," the taller of the two men said. He shook his head and tsk'd three times. "Mateo is very disappointed. After all he's done for you? Come on now. Surely you don't want to get on his bad side." He patted Sean's face with an open hand.

Sean's head bounced from the impact. "I've done my part, Vince. I've pretended to be dead and complicated the hell out of my life just to draw them here. I've paid my debt. We're even."

"You're not even until Mateo says you're even," Vince said. "It looks like you might need some extra persuasion."

He nodded to his friend, the same thug who had brought them inside at gunpoint, who then grabbed Sean's arm, pulled him to his feet, guided him down a short walkway and out the side door.

Vince gallantly offered Elizabeth his arm as if they were on a date and followed. Poor Elizabeth's eyes were wide, but she said nothing and complied.

"Damn it," muttered Reinhardt as the four of them walked away then narrated a text to Amos, "Watch what goes on at the side of the hotel."

He waited, and then told us, "Amos says OK."

The two men who stayed back at the bar turned and scanned the lobby and restaurant, looking fidgety and nervous.

The three of us sat in the lobby trying to appear happy and engrossed in our affairs but kept a close eye on their every move.

One of them pulled a phone out, dialed someone, and didn't say a word, only motioned with his head to his companion, then hung up.

The two moved past us and walked to the elevators.

Once they were inside and the doors had shut, Reinhardt walked over to where they had been sitting at the bar. He stealthily pulled a notepad and pen out of his pocket and looked around for the bartender.

Seeing none, he went to the reception desk. "There were two men at the bar, and it looks like one of them left his notepad and pen," Reinhardt said. He leaned on his elbows and smiled up at the woman. "I know for me, I'd be lost if I left my notes behind."

"Thank you. Yes. I saw them there. I can give the paper and pen back to him, sir." She reached out for them.

"Oh, it's no trouble. I can do that for you. You must be very busy and I'm on my way upstairs anyway," Reinhardt said.

I shook my head. He certainly knew how to put on the charm. His voice was so syrupy it was giving me diabetes.

"Sorry, but I can't give out guest information," she said.

"Oh, I'm sorry, I wasn't clear. I know Vince. It's just that he checked in after us, and I don't know his room number," Reinhardt said.

She looked at him skeptically.

"His wife gave him this pen on their last anniversary. See, it's engraved."

She nodded and smiled. "Of course. I didn't realize. Mr. d'Angelo is in room 624. The suite at the end of the hall."

"Thank you, Miss," Reinhardt said.

She nodded and excused herself to go answer the ringing phone.

Reinhardt started toward the elevators where after a moment, Ransom and I joined him. But instead of going up, we went outside through the back door that led to the parking lot.

"I'll send the name to Renegade," Reinhardt said. He shook his head. "Oh, boy. I've heard of the d'Angelos. They're an infamous crime family. Mafia. And do you want to guess from what country?" His eyes were dark.

Ransom and I looked blankly at him.

"Corsica," he said.

I blinked, racking my brain. We'd talked about Corsica recently. But where—

"The yacht!" exclaimed Ransom. He groaned and turned to me. "Felix standing in front of a yacht in Corsica? Remember?"

Now I remembered, and my blood ran cold. "But why would they be after Sean and Elizabeth? That doesn't make any sense!"

Reinhardt dictated another text to Amos. "What did you guys see?"

Amos came over to our SUV. "They roughed up Sean good and left him squirming on the ground," Amos said. "Just before the thug and guy in the bad suit left, they threw a fat envelope on top of Sean and said something, but I couldn't hear what it was."

"Where are Sean and Elizabeth now?" Ransom asked.

"When the guys left, Elizabeth helped him up and into their car. Then they drove off toward the Interstate."

"I guess they're too far ahead for us to follow now," Ransom said.

Nine

ELIZABETH HAD BEEN OUR ONLY LEAD, our only way of trying to find out the truth behind all the strange things that pointed to Robert still being alive. Maybe Myrtle and Christian were alive, too. Maybe nothing was as it had seemed. Was paranoia taking over my mind?

But by now, the Grangers were already a long distance down the Interstate. I wondered if they knew we had followed them. Did Vince and his companions also know we were here? It didn't seem plausible we had eluded these people entirely yet DoD agents were swarming Grove City and now Vince and his people—probably Corsican Mafia—were here as well. Did they know who we were? If they did, I still didn't understand why they were seeking us out. No. Our extraordinary luck didn't feel right. I could feel my inner Rosalind warning me.

"Listen, I'm starving," said Ransom. "Lunch?"

Reinhardt and I nodded, and I texted the five in the SUV up ahead.

Ransom pulled off at the next exit and parked at a strip mall in front of a little restaurant called The Underground. It was a dark little place with British paraphernalia on the walls and a blinking Guinness sign in the window.

We took the waitress's suggestion and ordered fish and chips, and sat, each of us thinking until Reinhardt's phone pinged several times in a row.

Reinhardt read the messages to us in a low voice. "OK. It's confirmed. The d'Angelos are a Corsican family from Bastia, a town with a ferry service between Bastia and Nice. They run and control everything there. Corsica is an offshore refuge for organized crime. Drug sales are a front for larger activities like…" He nodded and grimaced. "Like munitions sales to insurrectionaries. That's probably how they found Felix, knowing he had such an ax to grind with the government authorities who removed him from his powerful position."

Reinhardt put down his phone and added, "Also, perhaps he did a trade with them for when they helped him explode Fairhaven."

He nodded at Roscoe, whose look darkened at the mention of that day.

I thought about Felix's fall from grace, to go from being head of the CIA during the Cold War days, with teams of undercover agents spying on Russian activities, and so powerful, the President relied on him personally to keep the U.S. secure, and then once the Cold War ended in 1991, to being suddenly head of nothing: his department disbanded and his agents given retirement and identity protection packages. I tried to understand the mentality of the man who considered them all traitors, committers of treason, and who then went on to make it his mission to kill them all, one after the other, for their disloyalty.

The next message had a photo attached. It was of Oscar at the ferry landing in Bastia being shoved into the back seat of a limo by two muscular men. Vince and Luciano, dressed in elegant suits, were standing behind them, talking.

In the last message, Renegade confirmed that Sean had borrowed and lost a large sum of money in Atlantic City at one of the d'Angelo casinos.

"This is a bit confusing," Norm said. "Sean pays off his gambling debt by agreeing to play dead? How does that benefit the d'Angelos?"

"And the envelope they threw on him," Amos said. "What do you suppose was in it? Money? That wouldn't make any sense. Not only do they forgive a large debt but pay him for doing it? If it was money, they must really want something. Bad!"

"Well, what else could it be?" I said. "If they work in drugs and weapons—and it doesn't appear to have anything to do with drugs—do you think Felix promised them weapons?" Still, even with this conversation, or especially with this conversation, I couldn't see the connection between anyone needing the Drakers to think that Felix was still alive and all the rest of it. "Like, if Felix did promise them some grenades, or whatever Mafia people use on each other, what did that have to do with us?"

"It has to be something more important than a small shipment of weapons," Norm said. "Ruby's right. Further to that, while shipments of guns or other weapons are serious, that'd be a more localized issue and not one of national security. So even if Hollinger knew about what these creeps were up to, someone else would be handling this."

Another message pinged on Reinhardt's phone. He read it to us: "Magda Worchenski took a leave from Cold Force about the same time Patricia took leave."

The mention of my real mother's name stabbed my heart. In an instant, I could nearly feel on my skin the scorch of the fire that killed her, my dad, and Johnny. The day that ended my life as Kathleen, and when all of this started.

'Records exist that prove both women were patients at a private maternity hospital in Washington in the same year." Reinhardt read quietly for a second then put down his phone. "So it's confirmed. Magda had a son. There's a birth certificate with the name Oscar Worchenski and between that and the photo we have, it seems clear he is Magda and Felix's son. Renegade found his school and medical records going right up to the time that he started working for the Archives. She kept him and raised him."

"And she never exposed Szabo as a rapist," Alice said. She shook her head in disgust.

"I'm sure that was tactical on her part," Hannah said. "She knew it would ruin him so she probably made sure she got what she needed to give the child the best life possible, which I'm also sure didn't sit well with old Felix. And after the government closed the department down and she left, he likely felt even keener for Magda to be dead."

"And when Oscar was old enough, Felix probably hired him to manipulate her," Ransom said. "Look at what he did with Christian. The guy never even knew Felix was his father. Good thing, too. Imagine knowing your father was fine with shooting you and leaving you for dead."

Reinhardt got another text and interrupted him. "Renegade checked emergency air ambulance flight records and found one dispatched to Springfield last June. Three people were airlifted to New York City Kings County Trauma Center. Two men and one woman." His voice cracked as he read that. He shook his head and looked up to see our reactions.

My body went weak all over again. I thought I should run to the bathroom, but Alice calmly pushed a glass of water toward me and held my arm until I had taken several sips and was breathing evenly again.

It stood to reason that the three trauma patients were Myrtle, Christian and Robert. If they were, then we were monsters for leaving them there.

Reinhardt put his head in his hands. Ransom examined his nails. I could see they shared my anguish. No one spoke for several minutes.

Another text came in. I wished Renegade would just call. Every time I heard the phone ping, I jumped.

"How curious!" Reinhardt read, his voice thick with sarcasm. "It seems that Kings County Trauma Center had a fire that destroyed both computer and paper records for the month of June."

Naturally, I thought.

Then that's when our food arrived, and we all gratefully tucked in.

"Guess we're headed to Kings County?" I asked Reinhardt.

He nodded.

"That's good. We'll get some answers there. I'm sure a doctor or nurse who'd been on duty that night would remember what happened."

Norm grinned. "Now, before you get uppity with me about this, hear me out. The RV might be a bullhorn on wheels, but it would keep us moving, which is less of an easy target than stopping all the time in hotels and restaurants. If the DoD and these d'Angelos or whoever it is who wants us in on their oddball plan haven't found us in it yet, I say we use it until we have to lose it."

I looked around the table. He had a good point.

Norm polished off the rest of his—and my—fries and we went back into the bright sunshine. It was 3:30 p.m. , and it would take us an hour to get from Erie back to the campground. It had been a long day, and Norm decided he'd rather we get a good night's sleep and head out first thing in the morning for the five-hour drive to Kings County. I felt gutted. I doubted I'd sleep at all.

Our seniors and Roscoe drove ahead. Alice said she'd get us some pizza and salads for dinner, which made me long for Sophie and her warmth and gourmet touch. Then I remembered Myrtle, Robert's trusted companion, or maybe she'd been more to him than that. Their relationship was a mystery, but it was clear they had a bond that ran deep. I thought about how gruff and plain she was but how she could touch a tin of soup and some bread and soon have a delicious meal for all of us. The thought of what we did to her made my heart ache again.

"Since the Marriott is on our way,"Ransom asked, "should we go back and risk trying to find out more about what Vince and his brother are doing in Erie?"

"That's a good idea," I said without looking at him.

Throughout the day, I could see he was softening, thinking more from his heart in a way he hadn't in a long time. Out of the corner of my eye, I caught him smiling tenderly at me.

My old feelings for him were rising, feelings I hadn't even known existed—until he'd thrown himself in the way of bullets meant for me—and then they'd come in furiously. He'd been willing to give up his own life to save mine. Surely that meant he cared for me.

I kept my eyes on the road. It wasn't likely the d'Angelos would have stuck around after they finished roughing up Sean. I assumed they would have gone after the Grangers to make sure they did whatever they were being blackmailed into doing. But maybe someone in the hotel had seen something.

***

The hotel parking lot was full, and patrons were shuffling bags and suitcases from their vehicles to the hotel lobby. I didn't see the black limo anywhere, but we went inside to see what we could find anyway. The place was crowded with people waiting to check in.

We stepped up to the counter when there was a break in the check-in line. A different woman was at the reception desk this time. She could have been a model with her dark hair in a perfect bun at the nape of her neck, and her hotel uniform fitted tightly to her slender body.

"Good afternoon, Miss…" Reinhardt read her name tag,

"Martin," she said efficiently. "Jillian is fine. How can I help you? Do you have a reservation?"

"I'm looking for my friend Vince d'Angelo," Reinhardt said. "We met him here this morning, but I think he's checked out."

She looked at her computer. "Do you know which room he was in?

"Room 624. I think?"

"I'm very sorry. He checked out about an hour ago."

"Oh no," Reinhardt said. "I'm quite late for our appointment. I guess he couldn't wait any longer. I'll give him a call on his cell. Thank you, Jillian. You've been a big help." Reinhardt slipped her a hundred-dollar bill.

Jillian's eyes widened and she smiled graciously, took a cautious look around the desk area and lobby, and seeing no supervisors or other staff, she slipped the bill into her jacket pocket.

"Y'all have a nice day," she said as we left, still looking at us curiously.

Even though the d'Angelos had left, we walked briskly out to the cars, each of us scanning the area for signs that we were being watched. There was no way of telling who might be keeping track of us, local police, CIA, DoD—or the Corsican Mafia. Our situation was bizarre and unsettling. But why go to such secretive means? If they were all acting in ways that were designed to get our attention, it was working, though bewildering. My mind was churning with possible scenarios of what Sean Granger or the d'Angelos would want from us.

***

The Interstate was busy and the line of cars waiting to get off at the exit for the Grove City discount mall snaked about a mile down the highway. The Outlet Mall was where Magda, or rather Margaret Warren, as she had called herself then, had taken a job to stay incognito and live a quiet life. Rosalind had ruined it for her—she had abducted her from the mall, and brought her to the farmhouse to lure Felix out into the open.

The thought of chic Rosalind in her Dolce & Gabbanas and Alexander McQueens going into a discount mall among all the people in T-shirts and sneakers running from one sale bin to the next made me laugh. I felt good then; like Rosalind was letting me poke fun at her in my head. Plus, I felt closer to her, knowing I'd started dressing like she dressed and liked it.

An hour later, Reinhardt pulled off the county road into Emerald Woodland Park. My skin prickled as we drove past the little clapboard variety store where Roscoe and I had run into the DoD agents. The campsite didn't feel safe anymore. It was like we were driving into the center of a hornet's nest. I scoffed at my frailty. When did the Drakers ever feel safe while we were on a rescue mission? We were like magnets that attracted all things weird, all things dangerous and all things deadly. It was good that we'd be leaving in the morning.

A hissing sensation in my ears suggested that Rosalind was warning me again. *Stay alert, Ruby. Trust your instincts.*

Roscoe ran out to greet us as we drove up to our behemoth which, even in the short time we were away from it, looked bigger than ever.

Norm and Amos were walking around its perimeter checking the holding tanks, propane, and kicking tires. They seemed content and relaxed, in their element. I knew that in any other circumstance, our beloved seniors would have loved to use this home on wheels to tour America. Their sacrifice was so dear. They had become as special to the Draker family as one of our own.

"What took you so long?" Roscoe demanded. His face was strained, and his arms were crossed over his chest, a far cry from the confident skateboarder he'd been that morning. "Did you find the d'Angelos?" He hugged Reinhardt who had gotten out of the car and was trying to straighten his legs out from the long drive.

Reinhardt chuckled and hugged him back. He tousled his hair. "No," Reinhardt said. "They'd already checked out."

Roscoe looked at him tentatively, his brow furrowed. "Alice just came back with pizza." He pulled away from his father and leaped up the steps into the coach.

Reinhardt and I followed.

The bus smelled deliciously of spicy pepperoni, tomato sauce and cheese. Two piles of two large boxes cluttered the short counter space. Roscoe opened one and pulled a stringy wedge onto a paper plate.

"How's dinner?" Alice asked. "I made my specialty." Alice and Hannah laughed heartily as they served Norm and Amos.

I looked over at Roscoe. The question seemed to have caught him off guard. I thought I saw his eyes start to glisten, changing his hungry enthusiasm to a look of sadness. "It's… It's good." His face crumpled. "When Sophie made hers, she served it on silver pedestaled platters. My dad made me a café au lait." He paused, his voice cracking with emotion. "Rosalind…" He got up and took his paper plate to the living room area to be alone. I knew he was thinking about the first time Rosalind had served him coffee, saying, "I think he's old enough."

Reinhardt cast a sympathetic look his way. His heart was broken, too. I could see it in his face. He didn't say anything.

I wanted to throw my arms around Roscoe to comfort and protect him. I hoped he could feel all of our love from the kitchenette just a few feet away. He'd stopped eating and was angrily wiping his face. Everyone tried to make small talk to give him his privacy.

The sound of a car pulling up paused our conversation. Everyone sat alert, wondering what was happening.

Roscoe leaned over to look out the window. "It's a blue car," he whispered.

I glanced over in disbelief. Sure enough, Sean and Elizabeth Granger got out of the car, walked up to the coach door, and knocked.

We all looked at one another, shocked. What on earth? How did they find us?

They knocked again.

Norm went to the front door.

Elizabeth came up the steps first, followed by Sean. "We're supposed to deliver a message to you," she said. Her eyes were wild, and she seemed disoriented.

Holding onto the handrail, Sean lunged inside then collapsed. He was breathing heavily, and he was clutching his side. Ransom and Amos rushed to help him up and brought him to a recliner in the living room.

Roscoe's mouth dropped open.

"I'm so sorry," Sean said. His voice was thin as he struggled to catch his breath. "I think Bruno, Vince's bodyguard, broke one of my ribs."

Elizabeth came to his side and took his hand.

"All I have is some extra strength Tylenol," Hannah said as she darted to the bathroom. Then she started peppering him with questions. "Do you need a doctor? Should we take you to a hospital?"

Alice got him a glass of water.

"Hospital? I'm supposed to be dead. Remember?" He glanced at his wife guiltily.

Elizabeth looked at the floor.

Hannah handed him two capsules and Alice steadied his hand on the glass as he swallowed. He coughed and wretched in pain for several moments before settling back into the recliner, completely exhausted.

"Elizabeth," Reinhardt said. "I think you need to explain what's going on."

She sighed, her face tense. "About a week ago, these two slick-looking young men came to our door. They said that someone named Mateo is looking for the money Sean owed him. Sean has a gambling problem. He ate up our savings then, like an idiot, he borrowed from a loan shark. That's the man who beat him up this afternoon. Anyway, I told them he wasn't home but they pushed their way into the house and held Sean at gunpoint." She paused, trembling, on the verge of tears.

"Go on, Elizabeth," Alice said, putting her hand on Elizabeth's shoulder. "We suspect that Vince and his brother are involved in all kinds of illegal business."

"Sean and I didn't have the cash to pay them," she said. "So Vince made him an offer to absolve the debt."

Sean hung his head.

"He asked Sean if he remembered Felix Szabo. Oh, that name! We want to forget it ever existed! Szabo was Sean's boss while he was an agent for the CIA. He was a horrible person. Sean practically spit at Vince for even bringing up the name in our house."

"What was the offer?" Reinhardt asked. His voice was flat and grim. We gathered tightly around his chair.

"He told Sean to fake his death," Elizabeth said. "Said they'd arrange the whole thing and give us money to relocate. They needed the news story to attract someone's attention, Vince said. When you came to the coroner's office, sniffing around, I figured it was you people they were after. Your story about your brother lined up, but something didn't seem right." She looked at Reinhardt with watery blue eyes. "And we couldn't figure out how Szabo was connected to any of this."

"You say that you're supposed to deliver a message?"

She pulled a folded piece of paper out of her back pocket. "This note was in the envelope of money Vince paid us to leave Erie and not come back," Elizabeth handed the note to Reinhardt. "It doesn't make any sense. How would Felix Szabo have been connected to these people?

And why do they think Sean has anything to do with him anymore?"

Reinhardt read the note aloud. "Find Szabo's munitions dealer and have him deliver the plutonium or all of you and Magda will be dead."

This was getting very tangled. And scary. Plutonium? We'd thought it might be guns, but this was beyond what we'd imagined.

I looked up at the others, but everyone was in his own world, thinking. And Magda… Of course. Sean would have known her. They worked together in the agency during the Cold War days under Felix. I started feeling very nervous. But this couldn't be real; who had access to plutonium? Maybe it was a code word or something.

Sean sat up a bit. "Hadn't heard Magda's name in a long time. After our department was disbanded, she went as close to underground as she could, taking some terrible little job at a clothing store in the mall." He shook his head. "What an unfair hand in life she was dealt. I always felt sorry for her. But she was tough. Hung in there, raised her bastard kid from Felix by herself… And after she disappeared, he never stopped trying to find her. We'd kept in touch with her, but we kept it easy, didn't want anyone to realize we knew each other. Then one day… Yeah, about a year ago… she disappeared. I figured either she moved again to stay under the radar or Felix found her."

"So you haven't seen her or heard from her since then?" Ransom asked.

"Not directly," Sean said. "But you know Felix was working in the Archives, doing dead-end God knows what. They only kept him on out of guilt. Felix hired their son, Oscar, to work for him. The boy never knew Felix was his father even though he's a dead ringer for him." Sean shook his head. The Tylenol must have kicked in because he was talking a mile a minute. "So this spring, Elizabeth and I were in Washington—cherry blossoms, you know—and we happened to run into Oscar. I asked how his mother was and he said he was going to have coffee with her that afternoon."

"This spring? As in just a few months ago?" I asked. "Did you see her?"

"We went to the same restaurant and sat a ways away. We didn't talk to her. And she looked different. The side of her face was wrecked like she'd had an accident or a tumor removed, but it was definitely her. I was glad she was alive, in any case. She doesn't know Elizabeth, and I don't think she saw me. I thought it best not to speak to her in case it would blow her cover, and I don't know if Oscar ever mentioned that he had talked to us."

Sean leaned his head back on the recliner and closed his eyes. He'd spent his energy. He settled back into the chair and was asleep in minutes.

"We need a place to stay," Elizabeth said. "I have money. We can pay you."

"Stay as long as you need," Norm said. "We don't need your money."

"We're heading to New York tomorrow morning. To a hospital, in fact," Reinhardt said. "I can see to it that Sean gets the medical attention he needs while we undertake our investigation. We have reason to believe one of our family members was taken there."

Or three, I thought bitterly.

Elizabeth squinted. "Your brother?"

Reinhardt nodded and continued, "It is seeming very possible that Magda is involved in things on our end somehow as well."

"We just need to stay away from anyone who could turn us in to the d'Angelos," Elizabeth said.

"Don't worry," Reinhardt said. "I find money creates... memory loss. His smile was a tight line.

Elizabeth nodded that she understood.

I felt bad for her and Sean. They seemed like decent people who'd just gotten caught up in a snare.

***

It was a crowded motor home that night. Alice and Norm gave Sean their bed, but he kept waking to ask for more Tylenol. I hoped that once we got to Kings County Hospital, the doctors could do something for him. He seemed to be in an awful lot of pain, but we knew it was too risky to leave the campsite and go to a drugstore for anything stronger. Also, I hoped he and Elizabeth could find some refuge in New York. Once we got there, they'd have to be on their own. Our only mission was to find Robert.

Just after dawn, Ransom jumped into the driver's seat of one of the SUVs with the Draker family. Amos drove the other, with Hannah and Alice keeping him company. Sean and Elizabeth remained with the motor home where Sean could recline. He looked pretty ragged. We hadn't intended to take the RV, but Norm seemed happy to drive his prized motor home. I had been feeling guilty we'd up and hijacked our seniors from their easygoing lives, but I knew they thrived on being on a case. It was in their blood.

Just as we neared the variety store on our way to the highway, the store clerk, Rose, ran out into the middle of the road and frantically flagged us down.

"Oh, what now?" sighed Ransom.

He stopped our SUV in front of her and put down the window.

"Two men in fancy suits, were here last night looking for you folks," she said breathlessly.

"Who were they asking for?" Ransom askaed.

"They didn't give any names. Just that they were looking for a large group of people driving a very fancy motor home."

I leaned over. "I'm sure we're not the only motor home in the campsite."

"No," she said. "But you're the only one with a set-up this nice. And between that and the way you and your brother spirited out of the arcade that day, I figured it was you folks they were looking for." She looked at me with compassion. "I didn't tell them a thing, truly."

I believed her.

Reinhardt had rolled down the back window. "So what did you tell them then, Rose?"

"I asked them for identification, thinking they might be police or something, but they wouldn't show me anything. Just said never mind, they had the wrong place, and they drove off again." She shook her head. "Listen, are you guys in some kind of trouble? Maybe I can—"

"Thank you, Rose," Ransom said. "We appreciate that you didn't say anything. You take care." He put the window up and drove back onto the county road.

Great, I thought. Either Hollinger's people or the mafia was looking for us, or Sean, or both. We all pulled out onto the county road convoy style. If the d'Angelos were looking for us, we certainly wouldn't be hard to find.

Reinhardt sent a text to Amos to pull off at the first rest stop.

The next few minutes seemed like it was half an hour before we had an opportunity to pull off the road to discuss the new development.

The motor home loomed like a mountain in the parking area. *Hey-ho, stare at us!* If only Rosalind had been here. She'd have had some choice words about this.

Everyone except Sean and Elizabeth got out and stood in front of the coach to find out what was going on.

"The woman who stopped us in front of the campground store told us that two men came looking for some people in a big motor home yesterday evening. When she asked for their ID they said they had the wrong place and left."

Elizabeth must have overheard our conversation because she came out of the coach. "Vince and his brothers are keeping track of us," she said. "I know why they want Sean, but why do they want you?"

"We're not sure, Elizabeth," I said. "Felix was killed at our place in France. Maybe they think we know something about some arrangement Felix made with them. But we're only here to look for a family member and don't know anything about any of this." I didn't fill her in on the part of the story that spoke to said family member being someone we had left for dead in a shootout with Felix at the Springfield farmhouse because, quite frankly, she didn't need to know.

By the look on her face and the way she was shifting her gaze from one of us to the other as if trying to read our thoughts, I guessed there was a great deal more she knew on her end and was keeping from us.

"Look," Elizabeth said. Her tone was soft and apologetic. "We just need to get Sean to that hospital so he can be treated and then we'll be out of your hair. But I'm warning you. The d'Angelo brothers don't play nice. If they were looking for a motor home, this one certainly has a big target painted on it. I'd thought we'd be safer by leaving our car behind, but I think I was wrong."

"Did they tell you where to find us?" Ransom asked.

"Yeah. They gave us the name of the campground. That's how we knew where you were."

My heart almost stopped. The mafia knew where we were, but they didn't approach us. This was getting ridiculous. What the hell was going on?

But before we could ask Elizabeth any more questions, suddenly several cars came roaring up. Two black sedans screamed into the rest area and stopped behind us. Two more marked police cars came in directly after, coming to a stop on either side of the motor home. State troopers blocked the rest area from both exits.

Everyone got out with guns pointed.

We raised our arms and stood motionless and bewildered surrounded by officers who looked ready to shoot but said nothing. We hadn't done anything illegal, and they appeared to be American police, not mafia or CIA. I glanced at Elizabeth; we didn't know anything about them apart from what they'd told us. Maybe there were warrants out for their arrest.

A door opened on the black sedan closest to us. My heart sank. It was Hollinger. "I should have known that you guys wouldn't leave the matter to us," he shouted. "What the hell is wrong with you? Haven't you lost enough of your people?"

"Did you think we were going to just leave without knowing what happened to Robert?" Reinhardt said calmly.

Hollinger looked at the ground and jangled the keys in his pockets. "I am trying… to help you," he said through gritted teeth. "There's a whole lot more going on here—" Hollinger stopped himself. "Please, Drakers. If I asked you… nicely… to stay out of it, even more nicely than I asked the last time, would you please trust me and go home?"

"We know Robert is still alive," I blurted out. "We're not leaving without him, so if you know anything about it, it would make things easier if you helped us."

Reinhardt put his hands out. "That's all we want, Hollinger. Once we have him safe in our protection, we'll be out of the U.S. in a matter of hours. You understand, don't you?"

"The truth is that I don't know where he is," Hollinger said. "I know about as much as you do. That there's a photo of him at a rehab clinic in Portland and it's recent and undoctored." He glared at Elizabeth. "What I do know, however, is that Elizabeth and Sean Granger have been seen with members of a family known for organized crime and that Sean—who is supposed to be dead—has been ID'd as having been walking around in the Grove City area."

Elizabeth looked alarmed and horrified. "Sean's had—"

"Elizabeth," Sean called. His voice was high, full of panic.

"Let me guess," Hollinger said and grimaced at Norm who shrugged.

"We don't know anything," said Norm. "Except that they came to us at the campground last night with a message from the d'Angelos, who seemed to know where we were." He sighed and gestured to Beulah. "May as well go on board and debrief. Everyone seems to know every-thing except where we can find Robert. And I need more coffee."

Norm held out his hand to show Elizabeth that she should go first into the motor home, and he followed.

Inside we found Sean lying on the bathroom floor bleeding from the mouth. We ran to him. I wondered if his broken rib had punctured something. Hollinger briefly assessed the scene and left the coach to make a call, then came back inside two minutes later.

The men lifted Sean as carefully as they could and placed him on the bed. He cried out in pain. Elizabeth hung back in the doorway paralyzed with fear.

"I've had the troopers radio for an air ambulance," Hollinger said. "It should be here in a few minutes."

The RV became very quiet. Sean had stopped screaming. In fact, no sound came from him at all. His chest was still rising and falling, though barely, and the blood streamed profusely. I hoped he could hang on until the paramedics could get him to a hospital.

Alice and Hannah put towels on either side of his head to soak up the blood as Sean lay motionless and deathly pale in front of us.

It seemed like hours, but finally, the whapping sound of helicopter blades shattered our silence. The time, which had been held in suspension, suddenly warped into chaos as two paramedics raced on board, each carrying large black totes of portable equipment.

"Everyone out," one called as they got onto the bed to work on Sean.

Everyone except for Elizabeth stepped out of the motor home to wait.

"What the hell happened to him?" Hollinger asked.

"Vince d'Angelo had his thug beat Sean up when he refused to cooperate," Ransom said.

"Cooperate?" Hollinger said.

"Playing dead was supposed to absolve his gambling debt but then Vince made him deliver this to us."

Reinhardt pulled the note from his pocket and handed it to Hollinger.

"Find Felix's munitions dealer and have him deliver the plutonium or all of you and Magda will be dead," Hollinger read out loud. "What do you make of this, Reinhardt?"

"As far as we can figure out, Felix got the d'Angelos' protection and their help to find us last summer. All the extra troops that descended on Fairhaven had to be mafia connections, or local police paid off by the d'Angelos. What it looks like is they expected bomb-making material out of the deal." Reinhardt nodded at the note in Hollinger's hand. "It's certainly something I couldn't have expected he could provide." Reinhardt shook his head, suddenly furious. "How on earth would Felix have access to nuclear stores of plutonium?" he yelled.

Hollinger shook his head too, almost with admiration, I thought. "That bastard had connections to everything during the Cold War days. Hell, he was best friends with all the military and national defense generals. And if they were decommissioned the way he was, I can see where they'd have axes to grind as well."

Ransom put up a hand. "But I still have to wonder what this has to do with Robert."

I stood and stared at the three men. It was all coming together from somewhere deep in my subconscious mind, from a place that the old me wouldn't have ever been able to access, but that my new me, Ruby Draker, knew all about and derived power from. "Don't you see!" I exclaimed. "Whoever is keeping Robert alive and holding him hostage is insuring that we help whoever Felix manipulated to complete the deal in case he couldn't do it himself. Felix may have been cracked, but he was also smart." I started to laugh. "He hated us so much. He must have set this up as an insurance policy. As another way to keep torturing us and getting back at the U.S. government for taking all of his power away."

Amos shook his head. "I knew he was a rotten apple, but arranging a weapons deal of this proportion could jeopardize America. No. The world. This isn't something to mess around with. And now, with all this stuff going on, they must have a buyer who is getting impatient."

Without looking at one another, he, Hannah, Alice, and Norm, all in sync, started for various parts of the RV as if symbiotically preparing to jump into action. When they used to go on about their patriotic duty, I'd originally thought it was just an act they put on to ensure anonymity, but I could see on their faces that they were taking this personally.

"The DoD is keeping an eye on a new faction of radicals who have been raising concerns in Saudi Arabia," Hollinger said. "These people would pay millions, maybe billions, to get their hands on nuclear material for a bomb. Also," he paused, "there has been a report of security leaks at… a major nuclear plant."

The paramedics came down the stairs with Sean on a basket stretcher and moved swiftly to the waiting helicopter.

Elizabeth ran after them, a paramedic helping her on board once they had secured Sean in place. Then without a word, they lifted into the morning sky, the loud whapping sound diminishing as it flew northward to New York.

"Reinhardt," Hollinger said in the quiet, "it seems clear that all your snooping around is stirring up a lot of dust. These people are damn interested in what you're doing and what you might know. If everything comes down to someone smuggling weapons-grade plutonium out of the country, it becomes a matter of national security. So even though it may jeopardize the life of a Draker, you're not going to be facilitating any unfulfilled weapons deal. You'd better tell me about your leads on Robert."

"So far we have nothing," Reinhardt said. "Elizabeth led us to Sean. But while we know Sean was beholden to the d'Angelos for gambling money, all things are pointing toward the d'Angelos' being associated with Felix and the plutonium deal we just found out about yesterday. And, no, we have no leads on where to find Robert."

Hollinger stared into Reinhardt's eyes.

Reinhardt's expression was calm.

Of course we weren't going to just back down and Hollinger could see this. He ran his fingers through his hair and his right eye started to twitch. His face grew red and his nostrils flared. "I'll say it one last time. This is a matter of national security. You will leave things to me, or I'll have to arrest all of you." He sucked in a breath and forced it out. "If for no other reason than to protect you." I could tell he was trying hard to sound threatening, but after catching the alarmed look on my face he softened his glare.

Amos shrugged and put on his best country bumpkin expression.

"Oh now. You don't have nothing on us. We're just touring the country. Just a bunch of American RVers appreciating this wonderful land of ours. And we all know there's no law against that. Just a coincidence that we ran into some folks with a medical emergency. How about you stay out of our family affairs and we'll stay out of national security. Do we have a deal?"

Hollinger sneered hard again and started back to his car. "OK, Amos," he said. "But if you start investigating anything that has to do with power plants or people on our national watch list, you're going to need some very good attorneys." He turned and muttered under his breath as he got into the car. Before he slammed the door, he added, "Not that you people don't have the means to get the best representation money can buy. But I still wouldn't want to be you."

The DoD vehicles all roared to life simultaneously. They backed out of their parking spaces. The State Troopers followed Hollinger's vehicle out of the rest area's parking lot northbound, probably to follow the helicopter to the hospital where they could interrogate Elizabeth some more.

Reinhardt pulled his phone out of his pocket.

"What are you doing?" I asked.

"Texting Renegade," Reinhardt said. "He might be able to find out who these so-called friends of Felix are. His old military and defense chums."

"Wait. Hollinger will see…" Ransom caught himself. "Right. Never mind."

Reinhardt's lips formed a guarded smirk and he raised his eyebrows as he held up the phone with the text message. "Of course, Ransom. I only asked him to 'Send flowers o… x… o…'"

"That sounds so vague," I whispered, even though we were now alone in the rest stop. "You're sure Renegade will know what that means?"

"Ruby." Reinhardt smiled. "He's the one who invented the code. 'Flowers' means people he knows. The hugs and kisses mean everyone he was associated with in the Cold War Era. It's going to take Renegade a while, but we have time. New York is still a long drive from here."

Alice joined Norm in the coach. Roscoe teamed up in the SUV with Amos and Hannah. Roscoe was loving how the seniors doted on him, like both sets of grandparents long lost from a previous life. I loved seeing him smile and enjoy their attention, which I could see was helping him feel more normal and happier. The tortured look hadn't left his eye, but it was fading.

As they got into the car and shut the doors, I stood alone in the sun. I'd never known my grandparents. I'd been told they were deceased, and my mom and dad never spoke of them. I realized I knew very little about the true stories of my family, and now I never would. The emptiness throbbed like an open wound.

**

Our time at the rest stop had been exciting and disruptive, and in the chaos, we hadn't discussed the implications of the d'Angelos knowing where we were. Did they know that Sean was taken to a hospital? They probably had eyes everywhere. Were they always closer than we anticipated? Rosalind's messages buzzed inside of me. *Don't take anything for granted, Ruby.* Did they know where we were headed? And most importantly, why were they not showing their hand? What did they want from us? I didn't want to admit it, but I knew we had an important role in all of this. It was never going to be so simple as merely finding Robert and getting out. The note, the plutonium, and Hollinger's rant about national security complicated everything horribly.

For the next hour, we drove in silence, I was sure each of us rolled the different possibilities around in our heads.

Finally, I blurted out, "And anyway, how would Felix get his hands on plutonium? It only comes from nuclear power plants. He may have been powerful, but that had to be beyond his security clearance. Right?"

"Right, Ruby," said Norm. "During the Cold War, the U.S. produced hundreds of tons of plutonium. Even today it's produced as a by-product in the nuclear power industry. Storage locations for stockpiles are secret and stored several miles underground. It's dangerous stuff and requires very specialized handling."

"So what you're saying is that Felix didn't have direct access to it, but if he had any friends or allies who were military and industrial leaders during that time, he could get his hands on a supply for a special deal like the one he probably made with the d'Angelos?" I felt like I was digging a hole we were all going to fall into just by saying it aloud.

"Absolutely," Amos said. "He probably had a personal stash of the stuff hidden somewhere. I wouldn't put anything like that past him."

"And he was nuts enough, and had enough of a vendetta against the government, he'd make double sure to have a backup plan." Another thought came to me. "Someone else also knows where this stash is located. And putting the United States in danger from foreign powers would be the final payback for how they'd demoted him."

Ransom asked, "But why wouldn't this person just pay off Felix's debt and be done with the whole thing?"

I had to admit it was a good question. This Felix ally had to have a powerful reason for holding back. It would have to be a pretty big trump card.

"Oscar Worchenski was in Bastia being held by the d'Angelos," I said. "So that's it! They must be holding Oscar as a ransom for the plutonium in case Felix's backup person had a resurgence of conscience. And Magda is holding Robert because she knew we would come for him. And before she gives him back to us, she can make us help her negotiate the plutonium pay-off for the release of Oscar."

Ransom was staring at me. He whistled long and low. "Damn, not bad for a Psych major," he said.

I felt my face go hot and I looked down.

"Everything you said makes complete sense, Ruby," Reinhardt said. "Now all we have to do is find Magda—Margaret. I hope someone at the Kings County hospital will remember to whom Robert was released and where he was taken."

"But why is she being so elusive?" Ransom said.

"She's probably in hiding because Robert is her only insurance. Maybe the d'Angelos don't know where she is either. But they know we're here to find Robert. Maybe they're looking for him, too, to de-leverage Margaret. Do you think Margaret is the munitions dealer that the note was talking about? She must have taken Robert for a reason and that's what we need to find out next."

Ransom nodded and pursed his lips. "Right. Got it. That's why they're following us. They want us to lead them to Magda—or Margaret—whatever her name is now. They don't know where—or maybe who—this Felix ally is."

Reinhardt's cell phone rang. "Reinhardt here." He listened intently, his eyes moving side to side. He was almost holding his breath.

A shiver rippled down my back.

He finished quickly and hung up. "That was Hollinger." His voice was heavy. "The helicopter crashed just as it was landing on the helipad at the hospital. He said it looked like a direct hit from a rocket launcher.They're investigating the wreckage now. The pilot, paramedics and Sean and Elizabeth are dead."

I was in shock. Something like that had to be planned. But why would the d'Angelos want to kill the Grangers? And the others in the helicopter? My heart sank. Were they collateral damage?

"But the Grangers did what Vince asked them to do," Ransom said.

Reinhardt shook his head. "It wasn't about them. It's a message to us. That if we don't cooperate, they'll kill us too." He lifted his eyes to meet ours. "Our mission just got more complicated."

"Are we sure it was the d'Angelos?" I asked. "Maybe Sean owed someone…"

"Come on, Ruby, who else would it be?" Ransom said. He looked over at Reinhardt and almost swerved off the highway. Ransom hated being manipulated. I could see how angry he was by the vein pulsing in his neck. "What did Hollinger say about the crash?"

"Nothing, but he wants to put us into protective custody. I think that might be a euphemism for a jail cell."

Ransom nodded. "He's right to distance himself from us," he said. "Otherwise Vince will know that the Feds are involved, and that would complicate things."

"I can't see Vince being that stupid," I said. "He'll stay in the background and keep an eye on things. What he needs to do is let us find Magda. Then, once we lead him to her and the plutonium is released, I'm sure it'd be easy for him to arrange for a Felix-style accident for Robert, and quite possibly for all of us."

"Great," Ransom said. His mood was dark and foul. "We're going to have to let Hollinger think we're happy about the protection, and pretend we don't know that Vince is following us, all while trying to find Magda who wants to play cat and mouse." Ransom's lips were forming the letter *F* but he just banged on the steering wheel. "F-aaah! Peachy! Just peachy." He looked in the rearview mirror to see my reaction.

"Peachy?" I said. I was laughing, but it was an ironic, annoying laughter. Everything was just so screwed up at the moment and getting worse. "Is that the best you can do?" My mood had turned as sour as Ransom's.

"Well, actually, Ruby, I was trying to be sensitive as I know your delicateness prefers we all not use swear words."

I shrugged. What could I say? My parents had raised me to find alternative ways to express myself. I looked at him in angry confusion. What was he saying? Was he trying to be nice? His eyes in the mirror softened and somehow reflected compassion or hurt, or maybe something else.

One thing I knew for sure about Ransom was that he certainly wasn't open about his feelings. Maybe squashing his emotions was something he'd learned to do from the time he worked with Felix at the Archives. Maybe it went further back into his life before any of this.

Anyway, even if he were being nice, I was more infuriated than before. I was ready to shout the lewdest string of obscenities I could think of back at him, but just then Reinhardt's phone rang again.

He put it on speaker mode and held it up.

"The chopper crash site is at Kings County Hospital," Hollinger said. "I assume that's where you're headed? We need to find a way to make you less conspicuous. You're a pretty big target. Norm's motor home has to disappear, and you'll need different vehicles again. I'll make arrangements. These guys aren't going to get their hands on you."

"We don't want to get involved in this," Reinhardt said. "All we want is to find Robert and then go home."

"You're already involved," Hollinger snapped back. Desperation was in his voice. "These guys will do anything to get what they're looking for. Sean and Elizabeth Granger knew too much so they were eliminated and they took innocent lives with them. Now meet me at the hospital and I'll fill you in." End of conversation.

"Norm's going to be heartbroken," I said.

"When this is over," Reinhardt said, "I'll buy him another. But you heard what Hollinger said. He wants the motor home to disappear." He cast a peculiar glance at Ransom. "Can't very well just abandon it on the side of the road."

I saw Ransom's acknowledging smirk in the rearview mirror. The two of them seemed to be reading each other's mind. They were planning something big, something big enough to get Hollinger off our trail.

"What do you mean?" I asked. I felt bad for Norm having to leave behind or put into hiding his RV, but more, I felt bad for Roscoe. He liked riding in that thing with Norm, and anything that helped him feel better, even normal, was a thing to hold on to, that is, if riding around with a bunch of people with violent pasts in a giant RV could be considered "normal."

"We're going to stage an accident," Ransom said. "A fatal accident, so Hollinger will think we're all dead. It may not fool him for long, but at least we'll have both Hollinger and the d'Angelos off our backs for a while."

My ears started to buzz.

Kathleen and Rosalind were chattering with each other in my head. My Rosalind side told me to trust that the men and I would know what to do to keep us all safe. Still, I'd only been at this Draker stuff for about a year; nothing in my old life biking around my cul de sac and singing into hairbrushes in my room had prepared me for staging fatal accidents with RVs to fool government officials.

"So we're resorting to Felix's methods now?" I said petulantly. I had to admit I was giving in to my Kathleen self more than I should have. The boys were scaring me. What if something went wrong? "What's your plan for making an enormous motor home disappear? Magic?"

Reinhardt gave me a wry look. "No. We're going to drive it off the road and let it tumble down a steep embankment so it explodes when it hits the bottom of the ravine. Most of it will melt so it will take a forensics team days to figure out that no bodies were in it. The recovery operation and subsequent investigation will take additional days, which buys us plenty of time for us to grab Robert and be long gone." Reinhardt grinned. "It's messy but should work. Who knows, maybe Vince and his brother will be convinced that we're dead enough to slink back to Corsica. It should also buy us a window of time inside of which Magda can contact us without leading the mafia to her."

Reinhardt got on the phone to let the seniors know to pull off the highway. We all gathered at the next service center and collected in the motor home to discuss the developments.

Reinhardt started in. "First, the Grangers are dead. Helicopter explosion. Imagine that." Reinhardt shook his head while everyone else was still. "Hollinger wants to put us under DoD protection."

"What does that mean? I don't want to be locked up," Roscoe said. He was smart enough to know that protection meant we would be restricted as to where we could go and what we could do. "What are we going to do?"

"We're going to crash the motor home," Ransom said.

Roscoe's face registered shock. He looked to me as if to say, *What the heck?*

Ransom continued in a bossy tone like he'd said this a thousand times before, "That way, both the DoD and the mafia should be off our backs. Or at least until they figure it out." Ransom glanced at me, I think to see if I were impressed by his bravado. I wasn't. But the fact that he checked was a little cute. I sensed that he wasn't filled with the confidence he was pretending to feel.

"Wait a damn minute," Norm said, standing up. "You want to crash my motor home? I'm pretty sure that purposefully driving this thing off a mountain is not covered under my insurance plan."

"Don't worry about that," Reinhardt said. "I'll take care of it."

Norm squirmed nervously but said nothing.

"When are we supposed to do this... crash?" Amos asked.

"It has to be done before we get to Kings County," Ransom said. "Hollinger expects us to cooperate." He semi-laughed. "He utters the words 'national security' and we're supposed to comply or something."

But Amos and Norm weren't listening. They'd already put their heads together to start to plan how the accident could be done without anyone being on board.

Amos got up and went for a notepad and pen, then he went back for the map. He plunked down and Norm took the pen and began sketching and looking at a map.

Roscoe chimed in, "Why don't you operate the gears and gas with a remote control? We could jam an RCV on top of the gas pedal and use a remote to dislodge it after everyone is out."

I snickered. A young life of video games and electronics and this is where it got him? Damn. I could almost hear Rosalind cheer, *That's my boy.*

The men both nodded at his suggestion. "Good." Amos pointed to the map. "Looks like there's a cliff about twenty-five miles ahead. It's the perfect spot."

"Where will we go after that?" Hannah asked.

Reinhardt looked at her. "Nothing's changed. We're still going to Kings County Hospital to try to find out about Magda. It's seeming more and more like she'd have been the one he was released to."

Everyone got back into their respective vehicles. Norm looked especially crestfallen to know he was about to lose his prized motor home. I felt bad for him. But if we were going to find Robert without getting involved in much, much bigger issues than we'd bargained for, this was going to be the best way to get Hollinger off our backs for long enough to let us do that. We needed Vince and his brothers to back off so Magda would feel comfortable enough to find us and reach out. But how was she going to know we'd given everyone the slip?

She wouldn't, I reasoned. There was no way she could know. I thought about this hard for a moment. But Robert would! All we had to do was leave some kind of message that could be picked up and reported in the news. Something Robert would catch; something that would allow him to help Magda contact us.

Minutes later, the motor home was parked precariously close to the edge of a breathtaking lookout point. A metal rail was installed to protect cars from going over the edge, but beyond the rail, only low guard rails stood between the shoulder and what could be a precipitous tumble into the ravine far below.

I'm sure my heart was as heavy as Norm's. Under different circumstances, that motor home would have been so much fun even with eight of us crowded into it. I couldn't imagine doing it with anyone else. We'd spent so much time nursing our pain in isolation at Fairhaven, being thrust together in this tiny space was actually comforting. That we had to destroy it was almost too much a metaphor to bear. Something, or someone, was always trying to destroy what little we had left.

The plan was to leave the coach in neutral and let gravity do the rest.

***

Norm's face was heavy as he bounded out of the coach, already starting its unstoppable roll toward the edge. He joined us at the SUVs parked fifty feet away.

It would not be out of the realm of possibility that Hollinger would have radioed for some of his people to follow us to Kings County, so we all bolted into the SUVs and drove off again. Less than a minute later a loud thunderous boom echoed into the air and we saw billowing smoke and the shadow of flame out of the rear windows. We drove on, knowing travelers coming up after us would report the accident.

"Will Hollinger think that the d'Angelos arranged our accident the same as they arranged the helicopter crash?" Roscoe asked. His voice cracked, but I could tell he was in the game of things and it was more puberty than emotion. I wanted to ruffle his hair and hug him and then push him away with a punch in the shoulder, sibling style, but I wasn't sure if he were ready, so just smiled at him.

"Good thinking, kid. It's the same kind of signature," Ransom said. "Hollinger will probably think the mafia did the same thing to us as they did to the Grangers."

"Good," Reinhardt said. A broad smile filled his face. "Poor Norm. We're going to have to do something nice for him and Alice, and for Amos and Hannah, too. After we get information from the hospital, we'll find a nice place to stay, and maybe..." He started to laugh. "Maybe hold our own wake."

Ransom burst out with a contagious laugh that started Roscoe going, and though I tried to hold back because this wasn't funny, I cracked up, too.

***

Even from the parking lot, we could see the hospital was swarming with FBI, DoD and local police. We couldn't all go in, so Alice used her disguise talents and dressed in a lab coat, over-sized glasses, and her hair severely pulled back in a bun. She went inside to the hospital records area. We waited while she did her thing. I had to pee like crazy, but we couldn't leave.

An hour later she strode efficiently back to the car and we sped off. Amos had found a roadside motel just outside city limits where we would spend the night. When we arrived, I realized it was very similar in layout to the Springfield Motor Inn where we'd hidden the year before. I hoped their restaurant was as good as Helen's was in Springfield. But unlike Springfield—which had been weirdly vacant—this motel had other guests, and about five cars were parked in front of doors to rooms that lined parallel to the road. We checked in to our two rooms that we'd share, and then after I dashed off to the bathroom, we met in our room for a debriefing.

We sat huddled together, anxious to hear what Alice had learned.

"I told them I was the sister of a man—a trauma case that would have been admitted about August twenty-fifth last year. I gave them a fake name and explained that he'd probably come in as a John Doe. I explained that he was missing, and I just recently found out that he was brought there for treatment." She paused to make eye contact with all of us. "Then the clerk said something really strange. She confirmed that the records were destroyed in a freak fire late in August, but then she leaned forward and whispered that she remembered the file.

"The man's name was Robert Warren, she said, and his wife Margaret had already had him transferred to a private care hospital. She also said that I was the third person asking about this guy. She laughed and said he must have been either a celebrity or wanted by the authorities. I think she was hoping I would tell her which one!" She laughed.

"Who else was looking for his information?" I asked.

"Two men who didn't give their name. Nicely dressed, she said, and she said just yesterday, another woman came in saying she needed a copy of the records for his doctor. The records clerk explained that the records had been destroyed. But without batting an eye, the woman then said an affidavit from the hospital would suffice. One saying that he was there and what he was treated for, his procedures and meds—if anyone could recall. No name on her either, of course."

Alice took a deep breath. "The best part," she said giddily, "was before I could ask any other questions about the woman, the clerk was called away from the counter, and lo and behold, the folder with the form in it requesting Robert's file was still in the rack on her desk. I pulled the file and look what was stuck to it."

Alice handed Reinhardt a handwritten paper with a Post-it attached. The name M. Warren was scribbled at the top but the Post-it read, Dr. Draker l'Hôtel Dieu, Quebec City.

"Clever!" Ransom said. He paused then added, "I wonder if anyone else has seen this."

"If we get there quickly, it won't matter," Amos said. "I say we leave immediately."

"Come on, Amos!" Hannah said. "We can start fresh in the morning. Let's check out the restaurant here. I'm sure we all could use a hot meal."

Hannah had a point, and my stomach rumbled just then as if to punctuate it. Amos's did, too. We had no idea who was with Hollinger, or with Vince. I volleyed the argument around in my head. Hunger won out first. But I knew, sitting in a very public restaurant, even in the middle of nowhere, was too great a risk. I was right to be concerned: when we walked back outside, the motel parking lot was full. I guessed the on-site restaurant would be packed. I knew our seniors wanted to sit and have a several-course meal with coffee and dessert, and I felt bad suggesting we just get something quick and eat in our rooms. It was just that everyone we saw or came into contact with could be a possible point of danger. Our fiery crash would probably keep our enemies otherwise engaged. Well… I caught myself. Hollinger was more an annoyance than an enemy, so with them off our scent, it was probably not risky to have dinner. Or maybe we could start out for Quebec in the middle of the night after a few hours of sleep instead of in the morning.

I really wanted Hannah to be right. I was tormented with worry, hunger, and tired all at the same time. I wanted to eat and curl up in bed and to be normal. But of course, we were anything but normal. I needed advice. Rosalind, where are you when I need you? I thought. Bless her. She was right there. *Trust your instincts,* she quipped. I sighed and tensed up. My instincts, or Rosalind's, or whoever was tickling cautionary vibrations in my head, told me this was a bad idea. But we were now walking to the restaurant across the parking lot, and I kept my mental vibrations to myself.

A harried woman in an apron, striped shirt and black pants huffed as she counted the people in our group.

"Eight?" She rolled her eyes. "Where are all you guys coming from? The restaurant has been slow for days and now all of a sudden the place is swarming. I won't be able to seat you together. Hope you don't mind."

I did mind. We couldn't be separated. The universe was talking to me. It said, *Get the hell outta here.*

"That's fine, ma'am," Amos said. "We're just looking for a quick meal. Do you have a special tonight?"

"Everyone's looking for a quick meal," she said. Her lips were pursed so tightly that one might have thought he was threatening her. "The special is barbecued ribs, but it's not going to be quick." She started moving toward an empty table still littered with dirty dishes from the previous customers.

I scanned the room, noting a few people glance furtively over at us. Everyone looked normal, like regular, ordinary people. Not like government, not like mafia, not like maniacs wanting us dead. But looks were deceiving.

I felt a hot and cold chill race up my spine. "Reinhardt, "I whispered. "Please. Let's get out of here."

Ransom picked up on my unease immediately and took me by the elbow. We started for the door.

Roscoe was quick to whisper that it had been years since his last Big Mac.

"OK. I get what you mean. I think I saw a golden arches about ten minutes back down the road," Norm said. "But I was looking forward to the special..." he trailed off.

Offer them donuts, Rosalind suggested. I wondered if she was being snide, but I said, "There's probably a donut shop close by as well." I tried to sound authentically helpful, but I heard my own voice and it was sarcastic. The ladies squinted, nodded, and abruptly turned and walked toward the door.

"Donuts are always fine with me," Hannah said.

"Me too," Alice said.

Norm and Amos followed obediently behind.

"We should get our things from the room. In case we change our mind while we're out. And decide to keep going toward Quebec." I tried to say it lightly, but for some reason, my instincts were shouting *MOVE!* The boys noticed my agitation but didn't question what was going on with me.

It took us only minutes to grab our few things from our rooms. None of us had packed much, and I was grateful when we got out of there and onto the road. I didn't want to rest on the laurels of the RV explosion. The further away we got from here, the harder it would be for Vince or Hollinger to pick up our trail.

My nerves must have infected the group because we didn't stop at the nearest McDonald's or the next ten McDonald's. Only after several hours of driving did we finally pull in at a truck stop along the Interstate.

We got out and stretched the kinks that hours of driving had put into our joints, all the while keeping a careful eye on our surroundings.

A warm breeze blew the hair into my eyes. For a moment everything seemed safe, like we were nowhere. The pungent smell of French fries permeated the air, making my mouth water. My stomach had been growling since the motel, and I was lightheaded from hunger. We all had a bathroom break and bought some terrible sandwiches and snacks at the takeout counter and piled back into the car, hoping to reach Quebec City before dark.

Ten

THE HILLS OF PENNSYLVANIA eventually turned into green fields and patches of rock along the highway. Luckily, we crossed into Canada with no problem, though we did get the fish eye at the border. I suspected they taught all the border guards to do that to everyone who crossed into or out of the country.

The hours dragged on, mile after mile, giving me lots of time to think and worry. I worried that the deception of our staged motor home crash would be discovered and figured out as a ruse sooner than we hoped, and that Vince's group would get right back on our trail, only this time, they'd be quite pissed off. At least Hollinger—while his plan would be irritating, to say the least—wouldn't pose the risk of us dying. I started to think that maybe we should have taken him up on his offer to put us into protective custody.

Once we crossed into Canada, we let out the breath we'd been holding, and Reinhardt decided we could afford the time to sleep in one of the small towns along the way. The GPS showed it would still be about six hours before we got into Quebec City, and none of us was in any shape to keep going. I hoped that we were far enough away now to be able to risk stopping at a hotel. Surely an unplanned hotel stop, out of all the random hotels that lined the highway, would be safe. Truthfully, our energies were spent so we had no choice. It would give us time to discuss our planned strategy for when we got there.

I was so happy to stop and finally put my head on a pillow. Even though I knew we were likely walking into a dangerous situation, I fell off to sleep in minutes. Something big was about to happen once we arrived. I knew that much. We would get a few hours of sleep and get a very early start in the morning.

***

We pulled into Quebec City just after 7 a.m. I was rested but remained guarded as we entered what felt like a seventeenth-century European village with stone buildings and cobbled streets. Its distinct charm did not soothe my worry.

As we neared l'Hôtel Dieu, I shook my head and tried to focus on our plan. We needed to learn where Magda's clue would lead us. I wished we could go to the hospital straight away, but it was too early in the morning. We'd have to wait until they opened to go to the records department to learn about Robert being admitted the year before. We didn't have any reservations, but when we arrived at the Manoir Victoria, Ransom just pulled over and we piled out. The seniors in the other SUV did the same.

The receptionist insisted that the hotel was fully booked, but when Reinhardt silently held out two one-hundred-dollar bills, two rooms surprisingly became available. Funny how that worked, I thought grimly.

Each of us scanned the empty lobby just to be sure we weren't missing any signs that someone might be watching out for us. It was second habit for all of us to be suspicious. As we got into the elevator to go up to our rooms, the others looked comfortable, but I felt prickly. Rosalind whispered her cautionary words in my ear, *Don't take anything for granted.*

We ordered room service for breakfast. Pancakes with lots of French Canadian maple syrup. It would still be a couple of hours until 9 a.m.

when administrative services opened at l'Hôtel Dieu, so we had ample time to shower and re-energize with coffee and the buttery sugary carb-loaded *petit déjeuner*.

The short reprieve calmed my nerves somewhat. Fortunately, the hospital was directly across the street, so on the dot of 9, we wandered over, leaving the seniors and Roscoe in the waiting area at the entrance.

"*Bonjour. Comment puis-je vous aider?*" asked the woman behind the glass enclosure.

"*Où puis-je trouver le service des dossiers, s'il vous plaît,*" I said in my most authoritative French accent.

The receptionist smiled at us. "It's on the first floor," she said. "I'll get a volunteer to take you there."

I was offended that she'd switched to English and annoyed that I'd scooted to the front to do the talking when Reinhardt could've certainly buttered her up in French more effectively.

She called over to a man sitting at a desk in the corner of the office.

When he stood, I was taken aback by his looks. He was tall and swarthy with a perfectly chiseled chin and Roman nose. Maybe late twenties, I couldn't tell. He came around the doorway to lead us inside. He had the commanding presence of someone in charge. This guy could have been a model or an actor or probably anything with a face and body like that. Weren't volunteers people who couldn't get a job?

Glances of concern between Ransom and Reinhardt made me realize that they also thought something was off.

"Please, come this way," he said. Without asking any further questions he turned and walked briskly to a hallway across from the entrance waiting area.

As the three of us followed him, Reinhardt turned and motioned for the others to remain in their seats.

We followed the man down a long hallway and then turned down another running perpendicular to the one we had just left. It was clear that this man was not taking us to the records department.

I lightly touched my gun in its holster.

We finally arrived at a glass door that led outdoors. He opened it and we all walked through into a sunny courtyard. I noticed it was enclosed. My throat tightened.

"I think you've made a mistake," Ransom said. His hand went directly to his holster.

The man smiled gently at Ransom's hand. "There is no mistake. I believe you are looking for Dr. Draker?"

We looked at him in surprise. I tried to figure out what was happening. We were the only people in the courtyard. Obviously, no records were stored here, and there was no Dr. Draker. Magda had planted that as a code for us.

"Tell us what you know about… Dr. Draker," I said.

He turned to me and bowed cordially, a reassuring smile on his face, his eyes moving from my face to my breasts and then back again to my face. "My name is Serge," he said. "You need to come with me. There is someone who has to talk with you."

"And who would that person be?" Reinhardt asked as Serge began to walk back to the door. He sounded annoyed. This guy was being deliberately evasive. Was he toying with us? Was he one of Vince's goons?

Ransom stopped. "Sorry, pal. We're not going anywhere until you give us more information." He eyed Serge and glanced at me as if I had something to do with how this guy was checking me out.

I hadn't even brushed my hair. It was up in a messy bun. I might have dropped a pound or two from not eating enough in the last few days, but I was hardly the stuff of someone's fantasies. I licked my lower lip and looked back at Ransom, then at Serge. The way the guy was staring at me was hot, I had to say. I didn't mind how naked I felt under his gaze.

"That's OK," Serge said, chuckling. "Margaret warned me you'd be difficult." He shrugged and grinned without taking his eyes off me. Then his gaze shifted so he looked curiously at Reinhardt and Ransom to see how they'd react to the name he had just dropped.

Rosalind poked me in the side as if to snap me out of a reverie. I took a deep breath and considered that while this guy might be extremely good-looking, he could as easily be an enemy. After all, why did he bring us to a lonely courtyard whose only door leading back into the hospital was the one he was standing in the way of?

"Sorry. Who is Margaret?" I asked, widening my eyes.

"Yes," he sighed charmingly. "Margaret said if I told you the helicopter left without her that you would understand."

"OK, where is she?" Ransom said. His nostrils flared and he growled as he spoke. He looked ready to grab this man by the throat.

Serge smiled at Ransom tolerantly. "That's why I'm here. And so now that we are both sure that we have the right people, I'll take you to her."

I looked at Reinhardt and he met my eyes. What were we going to do about Roscoe and the seniors?

"And don't worry about your companions. Elaina at the reception desk has delivered them a note that they should meet us at the rendezvous point. It's all arranged."

"Is Elaina your girlfriend?" Ransom asked mockingly.

I felt bad for him; he wasn't accustomed to exploring his feelings and now he was acting like a petulant teenager. Ransom shot me a sideways glance, a sort of a *don't be fooled by this pretty boy* warning.

Of course, I wasn't. We'd just met him, and I had no idea who he was, or what he was up to. But I had to admit, I was enjoying how uncomfortable Ransom was. I hadn't realized he still had feelings for me. Or was he just reminded of what he used to feel for me? I couldn't tell. Whatever. It wasn't my problem. I'd let him wallow for a bit.

I looked back at Serge. For a brief moment, I didn't care whether he was out to kill us or not. He was tall, had well-defined biceps; he clearly had a six-pack under his shirt; thick wavy hair; and he smelled spicy and exotic but just enough scent that made me want to lean in, not like Ransom with his cloud of cologne that walked into rooms before he did. I sneered inwardly. That had been Rose's doing. She liked it intense.

Maybe her olfactory senses were damaged or something.

"Elaina is a nurse who also works for Margaret," said Serge. "The real receptionist was told she was needed in administration upstairs. Elaina was 'the temp' sent down to relieve her from her desk duties." He snickered and waved to us that we should follow him to an idling car parked just beyond an iron gate.

The gate opened to an upper, tiered road protected from a precipitous drop down to the St. Lawrence River by a low stone wall. From up here, I could see that Old Quebec City was divided into upper and lower town areas, which was cute and charming but probably hard to get around in a hurry.

Serge offered me his arm, and once our arms were entwined, he placed his hand on top of mine. He led me around to the front passenger door, held it open for me and then proceeded to buckle me in, which I normally would have thought ridiculous, but as he leaned over me to pull the seat belt across my shoulder and lap, his face inches from mine as he clicked it in, I felt my entire body heat up and had to hold my breath. After he closed the door, I could feel the daggers from Ransom's eyes as he stared at me before he and Reinhardt got into the back.

Serge drove the car easily through the narrow streets of Old Town. After about fifteen minutes of twists and turns, we arrived at the Fairmont Le Château Frontenac, a posh and historic hotel. I was surprised Margaret would choose something so out in the open.

He pulled into the hotel drop-off area and a doorman came to the car. Serge came around and offered me his arm again as we went inside. Reinhardt and a seething Ransom followed.

Serge took us directly down to the lower hotel level where the floor-to-ceiling windows exposed the restaurant to a panoramic marine view overlooking the St. Lawrence, cargo vessels, ferry and sundry pleasure craft constantly on the move, sandwiched between the deep waters of the river and the billowing white clouds overhead.

Without a word, the hostess at the front guided us to a large table where Roscoe and our seniors were having coffee and Margaret Warren a shot of something. They watched us as we walked up to join them.

"Well, Margaret Warren," Reinhardt said with admiration and a neutral voice. "Or do you prefer Magda Worchenski? We are very happy to see you alive and well." He kissed her on both cheeks.

She gave out a loud and boisterous laugh, the shot of whiskey in her hand almost empty. "Interchangeable at will," she said. Her cheeks were flushed, and she slurred her words a bit.

I shrank back at this. How did she think she could orchestrate an important negotiation half in the bag? I remembered our first meeting at the farmhouse when Myrtle had poured her two extra-large glasses and she'd passed out in a drunken stupor. She'd said she needed it for the pain from her badly injured leg and ankle. Or had she been pretending?

Hannah and Alice were poised in spy mode, listening intently, "gathering intelligence," I think they would have called it, their eyes following Serge and the rest of us as we entered. It probably took them all of two seconds to assess the little triangle between me, Serge, and Ransom, though I'm sure it wasn't hard to gauge the dynamic from our expressions.

Norm and Amos did the same as they sipped their drinks, but slowly.

Roscoe looked like he was taking everything in, watching all the players intently: studying, listening, learning. While I worried about his being involved, I could see that he was learning to read people and situations. He would grow up to be a good spy. I shuddered. I hoped he would have the chance to grow up normally and never have to do anything like this again. Our eyes met and he smiled then made a grotesque face. He could tell I was proud of him.

"So. Margaret," Reinhardt said, putting his hands on the table and leaning forward in his chair. "Let's discuss why we're here. Where is Robert and why didn't you let us know sooner that he's still alive?" Reinhardt would have made a good poker player: his question was posed calmly and straight to the point with no emotion, just asking for the facts.

Margaret snorted at him and slammed back the rest of her drink. She waved at the server and held her empty glass in the air, then slouched comfortably in her chair, smiling like a Cheshire cat. "My dear Reinhardt. You didn't think I was just going to hand him over to you." She pursed her lips into a contented smirk.

Reinhardt turned away then back to face her with a sympathetic smile. Then mimicking her subtle faux endearment, he said, "My dear Margaret, I know you too well. If you want our help, you'll have to give up some details. Why are the Drakers so important to you? And what was your motive for keeping Robert's survival hidden from us?"

The server delivered Margaret's drink from which she took a long slug, then slammed the tumbler on the glass table top, precariously close to the edge.

Serge took the glass and moved it out of her reach, then unfolded her linen napkin and placed it on her lap like a parent tending to a child. When he'd done the same to me in the car, it had seemed sexy, but now seeing him do the same to her, it just seemed maternal.

"Felix was always a bastard," Margaret said. "Always had something to hold over your head to make you do what he wanted. Even now that he's dead, he's reaching out from the bowels of Hell to torture all of us. Trust me, I understand your annoyance. I'm damn annoyed, too." She reached for her whiskey that was now across the table out of her reach.

"Madame," Serge said. "The Frontenac has excellent coffee. Let me order you one, s'il vous plaît." Serge raised his hand to catch the server's attention. The server, understanding his gesture, immediately brought over a steaming carafe, its delectable aroma wafting over the whole table. I hoped she wouldn't want any so I could steal some.

Margaret wrinkled her forehead but then acquiesced. "Always looking after me," Margaret said. She patted Serge's thigh as he poured her a cup of coffee and steadied it in her grasp as she raised it to her lips.

Serge glanced apologetically at Reinhardt.

She took a short sip and winced. Serge steadied the cup back to the table. Margaret's hands trembled and now it seemed she was the one at a disadvantage. She folded her arms across her ample bosom, took a long drawn-in breath, and leaned back in her chair.

"Felix had an assistant at the archives," she said. "Named Oscar. He's my son. Mine and Felix's son." She looked down, shame and fury radiating over her expression. "Had to keep the boss happy, you know," she spat out, her voice thin and hard. Pausing for a moment, she looked up defiantly as if she expected to see us judging her. However, all we felt was compassion for the woman. She wasn't a saint, but she was only doing what she had to.

Margaret looked tortured, a twisted expression on her face. "It wasn't like I was his only conquest either, you know. He got Patricia, too, but she gave up her son for adoption. Felix arranged the whole thing. Never even saw the baby. But I couldn't do that. After I held my baby, I just couldn't. Or rather, I wouldn't." Her face soured even more. "To tell you the truth, I don't know if part of me did it just to spite him. But it worked. He was furious, threatened to bring breach-of-government-security charges against me. But since I had evidence that he was the father, I told him I'd lay rape charges and go to the press, and the scandal would ruin him. He had tons of money, and I made him support me and Oscar while I kept my job. I wasn't going to quit! I loved seeing him squirm as he knew he'd better not make conditions rough or uncomfortable for me. I guess I stooped to his level. But Oscar had the best of everything: professional nannies, best schools, college. He never knew his father and that was perfectly fine with me.

"But when Oscar graduated from Harvard and looked for work, Felix…" Her guttural laugh made me cringe. "Good old Felix. He got back at me good. He hired him. I was horrified, but Oscar was thrilled that he had a great government job. You'd think there'd be some bio-logical connection that would make a person inclined to want to protect, as opposed to harm, his child, but Felix, of course, didn't have that. Some father! He corrupted Oscar, making him do illegal things and then threatened to turn him in if he didn't do as he said. When the retirement package was offered to me, I grabbed it, changed my name to Warren, and went into hiding. Felix nearly found me a number of times but I kept moving and somehow managed to evade him." She paused. "Well," she said bitterly, "until you people showed up and brought me to see him at the farmhouse last year."

Hannah clasped her hand around Margaret's. "He tried to get into my pants, too, but I told him I had the big H and he backed right off."

"Wish I'd thought of that," Margaret said. "When Rosalind and Robert snatched me to bring me to the farmhouse, I didn't realize that I wasn't the only one Felix was trying to kill. I couldn't believe your... you people were trying to stop him. I nearly shit myself when I found out what horrible things he'd been up to. Killing all those innocent people. My friends for years. And their children and families..."

She cleared her throat. "All I know is, after my little confrontation with him at the farmhouse, I regained consciousness while the helicopter was still on the ground. I was alone. I guessed the pilot had gone inside or into the bush to pee, so I just slipped off into the forest to try to get away, but I fell and hit my face on some rocks and passed out again. Still have the scars from that one." She pointed to the right side of her face where there was an indentation and the corner of her mouth drooped slightly. "I only barely recall the explosion. After I came to, I somehow got out to the road and someone picked me up and brought me to the clinic."

"But what happened to your son?" I asked.

"I guess Felix ran out of cash killing people and needed money to escape Washington last summer to look for you guys. He made a deal with a wealthy crime family in Corsica using the only collateral he had access to. But they weren't stupid. They wanted insurance that they'd get what Felix promised even if something happened to him. So Felix implicated Oscar. He arranged that Oscar would deliver the goods in the event that he was killed. And..." She smiled wryly. "It seems that's exactly what happened. I guess you guys and Hollinger had him sufficiently occupied in Washington last year, and in his hasty disappearance, he left a special envelope in his office, one that Oscar was meant to find when going through Felix's desk. Hollinger had set up surveillance cameras in the Archives office and at Oscar's apartment, which Felix had accounted for. Since Hollinger was monitoring Oscar's communications and watching his every move, Felix needed to find a way to get the information to Oscar without Hollinger finding out." She fished around in her pocket and brought out a thin USB key. "I found this thumb drive in the post office box we used for his child support payments. I check it every once in a while. Sometimes Felix likes to flaunt his power over me."

"Have you examined the files on it?" Ransom said.

"You bet," Margaret said. She was really having difficulty forming her words now. Serge fed her another slug of the strong black coffee. But it was too late. Margaret bent over. Her head thumped on the glass table top. Serge gently brought her back up to a sitting position and shrugged.

"She hasn't told us yet what she wants of us," I said to him.

"Madame is in need of a nap," Serge said. "We will be in touch again. "

"But you know where she's keeping Robert, don't you," Ransom said. "Come on, man. That's all we want. We'll take the whole thing off your hands if you just tell us. "

"There is a great deal more involved than you know," said Serge. *"Tout n'est pas si facile."*

"What do you mean it's not all that easy?" Roscoe asked. His fists were in a ball like he was ready to throw a punch. He narrowed his eyes and tightened his lips. "It's like Felix all over again." I could feel the determination coming off him.

"It's OK, my son," Reinhardt said. "We'll let Ms. Warren sleep it off and then she'll tell us where Robert is. *N'est-ce pas*, Serge?" Reinhardt spoke firmly, looking Serge in the eye. "We're not playing games here."

"My apologies, monsieur," Serge said. It was clear there wasn't anything he could do. It wasn't even lunchtime and Margaret was already drunk and passed out.

Then I thought perhaps her choice of beverage could be used to our advantage. I looked pointedly at Ransom and motioned with my head that he should offer to help.

"Right. Ccan we help you take Ms. Warren to her room?" Ransom said, smiling magnanimously.

Serge studied our faces momentarily but shook his head. "We," Serge said, "are staying at an... undisclosed location. We will contact you at a more convenient time."

"But you don't know where we're..." Ransom started.

"The dignitaries suites 1201 and 1202 at Le Manoir Victoria," Serge said with a raised eyebrow at our upgraded accommodation. He signaled for the server to assist him with the incapacitated Margaret.

"Perhaps a wheelchair, monsieur?" the waiter asked.

"*Merci,* that would be most helpful. And please have the concierge bring my car around front."

The server returned shortly with a wheelchair and the two of them struggled to lift her in. She wasn't very tall, maybe five foot five, but she had some heft to her, and passed out like that, she was dead weight. Once they'd piled her into the chair, Serge nodded to us then wheeled her out the front entrance and was gone.

"How on earth did Serge know where we were staying?" I said. "Unless... They're staying there too and saw us?"

"That would make sense," Reinhardt said. "Margaret's note directed us to Hôtel Dieu. Since it's close by, I guess they figured we'd stay there, too. My bet is we'll be hearing from her soon."

Since we were there anyway, and our earlier pancake breakfast had long since worn off, we decided to order brunch. The breakfast room was cozy, but the tables were spaced far enough apart for privacy. Also, the view from the windows over the boardwalk and beyond to the river was breathtaking. I was keen to get outside in the sunshine to do a bit of sightseeing. It would be better than waiting in our rooms to be summoned again. I'd swiped a brochure from the lobby and Lower Town had quaint little shops and historic buildings I wanted to check out. I didn't know much about drunken stupors, but Margaret didn't seem like someone who would be moving and shaking any time soon.

I was staring out the window, but when I felt the others' eyes on me, I smiled. "We'll buy postcards!"

That cracked Roscoe up. "And fridge magnets!"

Of course, it was a risk to go out. It was a risk to do anything. But I ached to stop feeling hunted if only for an hour. To do something like normal people. Although the word "normal" was as far fetched an adjective as could be when it came to us.

Everyone at the table ordered omelets, but Roscoe decided he wanted to try some crazy concoction called poutine, which was French fries smothered in thick dark gravy and topped with cheese curds and bacon.

"Gross!" I said when it arrived, and he shoveled a huge melty, gluey bite into his mouth. We laughed at the satisfaction on his fourteen-year-old face. Sophie would've been horrified.

After we finished, we strolled out onto the boardwalk. I saw Ransom and Reinhardt out of the corner of my eye keeping watch for anything suspicious, and I decided to let them be the ones who did it. I wanted a few minutes off.

A cool breeze blew in from the river, but the sun had warmed the air enough to make it pleasant. I noticed on a small building standing close to the protective railing, just before the cliff drop, a sign that read "Funiculaire." It was a trolley car on lines that took the car up and down the cliff-side like an elevator. It looked fun.

We got in and I gasped. The view from the one-hundred-and-ninety-five-foot drop was amazing. We watched as the rooftops to the town came ever closer and the St. Lawrence River brimmed with ship traffic. The Funiculaire exited into a historic building, the Louis Jolliet House. When we exited, I briefly felt free, like someone on vacation.

For the next little while, we wandered in and out of the small boutique shops, enjoying ourselves, checking out the touristy treasures. Cheap items like T-shirts and hats were mixed in with the handcrafted and specialty items on display. One treasure we didn't want to find, however, was a man in a white shirt and cutoff shorts who kept appearing wherever we went. I suppose he thought he was being discreet, but it was our habit to always keep half an eye open for anything that seemed slightly "off." Certainly, there were coincidences in life, and not everything that crossed our path more than once meant danger was lurking. I could also rationalize chance encounters for one or two sightings. After all, he could've been on the same path of going from store to store as we were, but when we encountered him the third time, that was to me no longer a coincidence. After the fifth, it was clear we'd have to take evasive maneuvers, which was not going to be easy given that there were eight of us.

We doubled back quite conspicuously to the Funicularie, pausing to take pictures of each other with our phones, chatting loudly, but instead of taking the lift back up to Upper Town, we ducked behind an aisle of merchandise where we couldn't be seen. Fortunately, as soon as the lift door closed, he was in line waiting for the next car. Who was this person? Why was he following us? More importantly, was he with the d'Angelos or with Hollinger? And would either have just one schlumpy guy tailing us? And badly at that?

"Let's just ask him," I said. "The place is full of people. He won't try anything here."

"Ruby, you don't know that," cautioned Ransom.

He tried to grab my arm, but I ducked away. "Look at him. He's not going to open fire in a crowd. He doesn't have it in him. You know that."

Ransom rolled his eyes but didn't disagree. I left our group to approach Mr. Cuttoffs.

As I got closer to him, I realized he was taller than I'd thought. I steeled myself and tapped him on the shoulder. He turned with a start and stared at me in disbelief.

"Hi," I said cutely. "So you've been following us for an hour. I'd like to know why." I turned off my cute act. "Who are you and what's going on?"

He turned red, obviously embarrassed that he had so easily been spotted.

"I'm just looking out for your best interests," he said. "Serge assigned me to tail your group and be ready in case you encountered an unfortunate situation."

The others came out from behind the aisle.

"You're a lousy detective," Norm said. "A kid would have noticed that you were following us."

"Monsieur," he said, "Madam Warren knows you have enemies who mean you harm. She only wanted to offer some extra protection. "

"You mean she wanted to make sure we didn't get away," Ransom said scornfully. "We have no intention of leaving. Ms. Warren has something we want."

The man nodded. I wondered how much he knew about what it was we were after. Did he also know about the plutonium?

"*Comment vous appelez-vous, monsieur?*" Reinhardt asked. He stared at the man deliberately and waited.

The man hesitated but smiled. "*Marcel, monsieur. Serge est mon frère.*"

We had no way of verifying this but how would he know about Serge and Margaret Warren? Also, it seemed likely that neither Hollinger nor the d'Angelos would have used such a budget detective. Yet if Margaret and Serge felt the need to have us followed, they must have had their reasons.

"Would you prefer that we go back to the hotel and stay out of sight?" I asked pointedly.

He turned and scanned the Louis Jolliet House for a moment then shrugged. "Perhaps you can continue with your visit of our charming little village," he said. "I will stay in the background and complete my assignment. Serge and I have a third brother who is a police officer. He knows we have guests from out of town."

I couldn't believe my ears. Serge and Marcel had a connection with local police? There must be a reason why this guy shared that with us.

"The restaurant by the river is particularly pleasant, though you probably don't need lunch just yet," Marcel said, smiling at Roscoe. "And it's well patrolled."

"Patrolled for what?" I asked.

"Mademoiselle, this city is practically run by crime families," Marcel said in a low whisper. "Madame Warren is wise to be guarded. But go and have a pleasant afternoon." We considered his offer suspiciously and started back for the town and its shops. I felt Rosalind prodding me from the inside, reminding me to stay on guard and stop acting like a happy tourist. I sensed that Rosalind wouldn't have thought that wandering around in plain sight was such a good idea. Quite frankly, neither did I.

I looked at Marcel. He seemed older than Serge, solidly built and still handsome with flashing gray eyes, and the same mussy hair though not nearly as muscular as his brother. It wouldn't have surprised me if he were an undercover cop, perhaps with CSIS, the Canadian equivalent of the CIA, and maybe his amateur behavior at tailing us was an act. Or he wasn't with them because he looked like he was trying too hard to blend in. His clothes didn't match his body, which didn't match his being alone and browsing tourist shops. Nope. Something about him was off.

But we had no choice but to continue wandering even as he frequently appeared quite conspicuously a short distance away from our every step.

We all managed to carry on as if all were normal, or normal-ish, but for some reason, Alice was noticeably unnerved by him. While she appeared to be enthusiastically shopping and enjoying Lower Town, she was constantly looking out for him. Maybe she felt that if she knew where he was, our situation was controlled. There were a few times when she lost sight of him and turned around and around until she found him. Hannah also kept her guard up, though I assessed that her focus was on noting whether there were other eyes among the hordes of tourists in the streets. Norm and Amos were uncharacteristically quiet, not at all their usual animated country bumpkins of Springfield selves.

We kept this up until late in the afternoon, when in an instant, Norm grabbed Reinhardt's arm, motioning with an almost imperceptible sideways nod of his head that we all needed to leave. Roscoe was enthralled by a whirly gadget he was examining, so I bumped him gently and gestured with my eyes. He understood and all of us moved into a shop and went through their side door that opened up to a lower side alley.

"What's up, Norm?" Reinhardt asked.

"Marcel is chatting it up with some buddies," Norm said. "Two men in plaid shirts tucked into unmatching plaid shorts with cameras hanging from their necks. "

"Mafia or police?" Ransom asked.

"Can't tell," Norm said. "But something isn't right here."

"Do you think they saw us?" Roscoe said.

"Always err on the side of caution," I said sharply. The others looked at me strangely. "What? Don't look at me like that. It's true!"

There wasn't any more time to grill me as to whether I'd been possessed or not. And sorry, but whatever they were hearing was me, just me. Whoever I was, or was becoming, they'd have to accept and stop staring at me like I was a ghost.

We slipped into the shop directly across from us, using their back door the same as we had done in the previous shop. That exit landed us on the lowest street by the river where we hailed two taxis to take us back to Manoir Victoria. There, we could hide out and wait for Margaret to explain what was going on.

Around 6 p.m. the room phone rang. Reinhardt answered it. His answers were brief: yes, no, fine, etc. and then he hung up. "That was Serge inviting us to dinner, and not in the casual restaurant that opened up onto Rue Saint-Jean but," he said, putting on a pretend affected accent, "in the grand dining room." I'd poked my head into the dining room earlier. The tables were luxuriously draped with linens and heavily accented with silver service. My guess was the formal setting was less about impressing us than being dimly lit and quieter, something

Margaret's pounding head would appreciate. We were to meet at eight.

The maître d' gave us a disapproving look as Reinhardt announced we were meeting the St. Claire party, the name Serge said the reservation was under. We'd all bought some tourist shirts and were still wearing jeans. Nobody had brought anything more elegant, so we just stared back at the maître d' and waited.

"I'm sorry, sir, but…" he began to say, turning his nose up and beginning to greet the party behind us.

Reinhardt slipped him a Canadian one-hundred-dollar note. "We will go to our table now," he said firmly.

The man's lips curled into the implication of a smile. He nodded. "This way, *messieurs et mesdames.*"

We barely noticed Serge and Margaret in the far corner of the dining room. Our table was behind a half wall on which artificial roses, fashioned of silk, climbed heavily over latticing. Serge stood as the server pulled out the chairs for the ladies.

"Bon soir," Serge said. "I trust you had a pleasant afternoon in the Lower Village."

"It was rather crowded with prying eyes," I said, Rosalind's tenor echoing in my voice. I caught a glint in Reinhardt's eye confirming he found it appropriate, perhaps comforting.

"Marcel told me you gave him the slip," Margaret said. Her voice was raspy and her hand shook as she raised a glass of water to her lips.

"It wasn't Marcel we were worried about," Norm said. "Seems he has helpers."

"Friends from the local police force," Margaret said. "They were wondering what he was doing. Marcel isn't in the habit of mingling with tourists. They knew he was up to something and they were curious."

"So what did he tell them?" Reinhardt asked.

"He told them he was hired by a Canadian celebrity," Serge said. "One who wanted to remain incognito and whom he wasn't at liberty to name. They believed him."

"Marcel said the town is owned mostly by crime families," Roscoe said. His head was down, and he spoke in a whisper.

"Don't you worry about that," Margaret said. She reached over and patted his hand but couldn't manage a smile. "You weren't noticed, and we'll be out of here tomorrow. I have a place outside town that you will be happy to visit."

"Is that where you're keeping Robert?" Ransom asked.

"No," Margaret answered. She folded her arms over her chest. "And you won't get him back or know where he is until you help me."

"We won't get involved with anything that will put our family in further danger," Reinhardt said. He also crossed his arms and leveled a hard gaze at Margaret.

"I understand your reluctance, Reinhardt," Margaret said. "But they're going to kill Oscar if I don't deliver Felix's order."

"Then why don't you just deliver it?" Amos said. "You said you have the information in the files on the thumb drive Felix left for you."

"Because the storage site has been decommissioned as a weapons manufacturing facility," Margaret said. "It's just a bunch of abandoned off-limits government buildings now. Felix was in the process of relocating the delivery when he disappeared last summer. If I tell the d'Angelos that Felix created a deception, Oscar will be the one who pays for it."

"So what exactly do you want from us?" Reinhardt said. "Felix didn't tell us anything about his deal. We don't know anything. We're of no help."

"You probably knew Felix better than anyone else," Margaret said. She sat up straighter and folded her arms tighter. "The truth is, I don't know where Felix stashed the plutonium. I need your help to find it. Reinhardt, I'm sorry but my hands are tied." She steeled her face, and her cheeks quivered. "If you want to see Robert again, you'll have to help me find the location of the plutonium and arrange its delivery. Or, if we can't do that, you'll need to help me find some other way to rescue Oscar." She looked down at her fingers. "You're my only hope. "

"And if we refuse?" Reinhardt asked.

Margaret looked back up at him, a light sneer forming on her lips. "Then Robert will become a permanent fixture in my household."

"Margaret," Ransom said, leaning forward with his arms out. "You're not thinking clearly. What you're proposing is that you want to just hand plutonium to these people?"

Reinhardt shot Ransom a look. "Margaret, we can't let that happen. We have to take every precaution that these people don't get the nuclear material. Margaret, you must understand that."

"I didn't set the terms of Felix's deal with the d'Angelos," Margaret said. "I don't want to risk national security either. But Felix offered Oscar to them as an insurance policy. And when they found out that Oscar didn't know anything, Oscar suggested that his mother, I, might know." She chuckled ruefully. "My boy outed me. Now they know I'm alive, but they don't know where I am." She paused and softened. "You've done several rescues. I want you to rescue Oscar, and however, you have to do that, I don't care. Then you get Robert."

"Margaret," I said. "Robert has nothing to do with this. We'll help you however we can, but can't you just let him go? Why make him pay for what Felix did?"

I'd thought it was a reasonable thing to say, but Margaret turned on me with flashing eyes. In them, I saw someone who was no longer able to be reasonable. Whether it was the drink or the desperation, there was feral wildness there. "You're a good one to talk about suffering. You left him to die!"

I felt like she'd slapped me. I looked back at her and her sneer grew into a smug grin. I stole a glance at the others and they were also looking dark and chagrined. We'd gone over this in our minds and repented, replayed, with no explanation. But of course, we would have to do whatever it took to get him back. We weren't going to abandon him a second time.

Now the only thing we could do was to find a way to rescue Oscar without giving an extremist faction the means to unleash whatever wrath they had on innocent people. I had no idea how we were supposed to accomplish this, but as I looked over at Margaret, who was eyeing the server, probably to try to get another drink, I felt sorry for her. Her life had not been easy, and now she just needed to do the one thing that made sense to her: get her son back.

The server came over to our table and took our orders.

I'd lost my appetite, but at Serge's urging, we all ordered meals.

Sophie would have approved of the sole meunière, stuffed pork and tuna tartare. When they came, fragrant and beautifully plated, Margaret only picked at her roast chicken looking at it queasily, but when the server inquired about what she wanted to drink, she surprisingly declined, even wine. I noticed that her hands trembled as she ate, giving away her hangover, or maybe it was her nerves as she waited for us to answer.

Serge broke the silence on that front first by assuming we were on board. He wasn't wrong, it was just with very mixed emotions that we would comply. "We can start for the country house in Mont Tremblant in the morning," he said. "We can make plans when we get there. In the interim, tonight we will simply enjoy the pleasures of a fine meal and some pleasant company." He raised his wine glass toward me and smiled graciously. "We do want to remain out of sight, but perhaps a small stroll through Old Town wouldn't hurt?" He was staring right at me. "At night, with the lights and street musicians, it is a lovely way to spend an evening."

Ransom interrupted him. "No use wishing for something impossible. It would be ill-advised to take an evening walk. We were out like clay pigeons all day, and it's only a matter of time before we're found. I say the longer we can prevent that, the better our chance of finding a solution to both our problems."

Ransom didn't look at me, but it was clear he was jealous. I wondered if Rose lived in his brain as Rosalind and Kathleen lived in mine, chastising him, petting him, still trying to keep him to herself. He ran hot and cold like a broken shower. I couldn't keep up.

"It does sound wonderful, Serge," I said, lowering my lids, "but

Ransom is right. Plus, we need to turn in early so we can get an early start. "

Serge looked disappointed.

Ransom looked relieved.

I looked at my wine glass wishing there was more in it.

Eleven

I WAS GLAD TO LEAVE THE HOTEL. Being on the move made me feel oddly safe as if somehow we had more power by being less of a sitting target. But safety generally was something of an ephemeral concept for the Drakers. I felt like we had already been in one place for too long, and the ease with which Marcel had found us, made me realize that we needed to stay ahead of people who also had an interest in our affairs.

I was glad when we arose in the dark, got dressed, and prepared to leave the pretty little city before much of the morning activity started.

We picked up some coffees and piled into our SUVs.

As we drove, I admired the scenery. Rural Quebec had a rugged quality about it, different from the landscapes of the U.S. The European charm of Old Town faded into a French-Canadian countryside flavor all its own, each little town with a steepled church, a little business strip of shops, a gas station, a supermarket. But mostly we sped past modest homes, some probably centuries old, barns caving in on themselves. The mixture of sun and clouds left mottled shadows across the land-scape and highways as we drove past these sweet little settlements. I didn't know where we were going. Serge had merely said, "Follow us."

It seemed prudent to comply as it was clear that doing so was the only way we'd get Robert back. And it wasn't a terrible situation. Serge seemed thoughtful and caring, and while I couldn't help but feel attracted to his tall, strong body and handsome features, he was tight-lipped about what his and Marcel's interest in Margaret was. *Yes, Rosalind, I noticed, too.*

"Reinhardt?" I said, leaning up to rest my chin on the seat back. "Can Renegade get us background information on Serge and Marcel and whoever their third brother is? The one on the Quebec City police force?" It seemed odd that a third brother was with the police and his two siblings were… otherwise engaged, whatever that would turn out to be.

"Renegade is already working on that," Ransom said. "I sent him a text before we left." He hadn't given Reinhardt a chance to reply.

Reinhardt looked over his shoulder at me, sitting comfortably in the back seat with Roscoe. His knowing smile told me he had noticed Ransom's objection to Serge.

"I'm wondering about what Serge and Marcel's interest in Margaret's dilemma is as well," Reinhardt said. "They are overly protective of her."

"Serge likes Ru-by," Roscoe sang. He glanced up at us impishly from his game of Minecraft on his phone.

Reinhardt grinned widely at Roscoe and then winked at Ransom.

Ransom huffed and kept his eyes on the road. "Where the heck is he taking us?" He growled. We'd been on the road for over two hours. He hunched over the steering wheel to see any developing situation ahead on the road.

I had to admit that I felt the same. It was unnerving to be led blindly down unfamiliar roads. The sun had gone behind a cloud and I couldn't even tell which direction we were going in anymore.

But then, a few minutes later, Serge's SUV turned and came to a stop in a narrow roadway where he got out and walked back to the seniors' car.

"What's happening?" I whispered.

"Serge is talking to Norm," Ransom said. "What's that bastard up to?"

Reinhardt got out and walked up to the seniors. Norm had already stepped out. He looked back with an anxious expression as Reinhardt approached.

"Is there a problem?" Reinhardt asked. I saw his hand creep to his gun. Ransom, Roscoe and I sat still for a second but then we also hopped out of the car.

"Marcel wants us to walk onto the property," Serge explained when we got there. "He's arranged for your vehicles to be kept off-site. It's for security. We'll explain once we're settled inside."

"Fuck that," Ransom exploded. "You drive us on a wild goose chase and now this? You'd better explain now or we're turning around. I've had enough of this bullshit."

Margaret stepped out of the passenger seat of Serge's vehicle and called over. "Now you know how I felt when Robert and Rosalind abducted me last year." She looked vindicated yet compassionate at the same time. "You're not in any danger from us, Reinhardt. Now let's get out of the hot sun." She winced and rubbed her temples and then, noticing our stares, turned away quickly.

I watched her walk down the roadway that turned sharply to the right, leading into a grove of trees. At times, I couldn't tell if Margaret was orchestrating things, or if she were, like us, being held by someone else. Serge followed and within seconds, they both had disappeared completely from sight. Had Serge and Margaret vanished into thin air? What the hell just happened? Where were they?

"Well," Amos said. "That ain't polite."

Norm was already edging toward the turn in the gravel pathway. His curiosity was getting the better of him. He took a few more steps into the shadow of the trees, and then he, too, was gone.

"Norm," Alice called. "Where the hell are you?" Worried, she examined the spot where he had disappeared. She looked back at us, a puzzled look on her face, and waved us over.

Leaving the vehicles at the side of the road, we joined her, just as confused. The roadway just stopped! A grove of loose scrub was all that we saw. But then Alice pushed the wispy branches aside and inched into the vegetation. The branches closed instantly behind her with a rustle and swallowed her.

Her voice came from a short distance beyond the shrubbery. "You guys have to see this."

We pressed through the branches as Alice had done, and it was as if we had stepped into another dimension. We were standing at the top of a manicured roadway about a hundred feet from an ornate wooden gate. High wire fencing was attached to the brick pillars on either side of the gate and extended into the distance where it blended into the trees and disappeared. We walked closer and passed through the wooden gate that had been left open. There we were on another short road bordered by high bushes of the same variety as we had walked through. The road turned sharply to the left and opened into a clearing that lay before an enormous cottage. It was purposefully rustic with flourishes that called attention to the wealth that had built it.

Norm was nowhere to be seen but the front door was open. We stood on the grass, dumbfounded.

Amos shrugged, wearing a bemused expression. "Nothing bad ever happens in mansions in the middle of nowhere," he said with a laugh and started inside. We had no choice but to follow.

The foyer was easily two stories high with a gleaming hardwood floor and overhead was a chandelier made completely of antlers. It was Canadian chic, with black and red flannel pillows on a bench made of what looked like reclaimed wood, and all around was the feeling that the house had been designed and curated and was very well cared for. We stood for a moment, smelling the sweet pine air, when someone in another room spoke. It was Margaret.

"Are you going to take all day?" Margaret called. Her voice was raspy, but she sounded sprightly.

We walked into the dining room where Norm and Margaret were

sitting at an intricately carved wooden dining table laden with platters of sandwiches, salads and fruit. Norm's plate was full, and he waved "hello" with a carrot in one hand and a sandwich in the other.

"Please help yourselves," Marcel said, standing off to the side. "It was a long drive and you are likely very hungry."

"Good stuff," Norm said with his mouth full.

Margaret turned. "Marcel, dear," she said sweetly, "Do you have any Scotch? I'm quite thirsty."

I remembered this tone; it was the same one she'd used when Rosalind and Robert had brought her to the farmhouse. Or abducted her, more like it, though it had been our only recourse. When she'd sat back on the farmhouse sofa, her swollen injured leg up, she had brusquely demanded a whiskey in a way that made it clear, that despite being in a vulnerable situation, she was in control and this was her way of asserting it. Myrtle's expression had been very similar to Marcel's right now.

Before Marcel could say anything, Serge came in from the kitchen with a tall glass and a bottle of Perrier and put it in front of her. "We agreed," Serge said.

"Yeah, yeah..." Margaret took a long drink, burped delicately, and gave him a threatening look.

"This is not your ordinary cottage," said Reinhardt, smiling in an accusing sort of way.

"Let's just say we have a special benefactor," Serge said. "You will be quite comfortable while you're here."

"Margaret," Reinhardt said, putting his hand on her shoulder. "I expect you're not at liberty to tell us who this 'benefactor' is, but can you at least give us some information on Robert?"

Margaret looked at Reinhardt with a bit of longing on her face. I guessed she was trying hard not to divulge information, which seemed as hard as not having the Scotch she wanted. "He's in a lot better situation than my Oscar. That's all I can tell you." Her hands were shaking. "Serge, please..."

Serge came to her side and laid his hand on her shoulder. "It's a lovely day. Perhaps a walk down by the lake will clear your head." He helped her to her feet.

Putting both hands on the table and with some effort, Margaret pushed herself to a standing position. She awkwardly moved away from the table with her arm in his, and like a much older person, she blew out a long breath and toddled beside him to the French doors that led out to a stone patio. A few seconds later, they disappeared down a path that led to a blue lake sparkling in the noonday sun.

Amos was shoving a pastry into his mouth, with a different colored cream than the last one I'd seen him eat. "You're right, Norm," he said. "The food here is first class."

"Hmpf," Alice said, snortling at the delicate pastries. "But no donuts. Who doesn't have donuts?"

I chuckled at her. That was my Alice! She loved her sugar-glazed, jelly-filled lumps of fried dough. American to the core.

"And also, no information," Ransom said. "This place... Serge... Marcel... There's stuff going on here I want to know. And wasn't it so convenient how Pretty Boy chose to accompany Margaret on a nature walk now just when we started asking questions?"

"How about you, Marcel?" Hannah said. "Care to share some details about your so-called 'benefactor'?"

Marcel grinned but shook his head. "Please feel free to select a bedroom," he said. "There are many, so please pick any one you like. We've provided for anything you might need. And we also have new clothes in different sizes you can choose from. A debriefing is planned for after dinner, so until then, get some rest or explore the grounds if you wish." He motioned to the cottage wing on the right. "Through there, when you're ready. Enjoy your afternoon." He walked out to the patio and down to the lake where I assumed he would join Serge and Margaret.

"Come on, Roscoe," Norm said. "Let's see what's so special down there."

Roscoe jumped at the chance to explore. They broke away from the table, still laden with food, and hurried out in the same direction as Margaret and Serge had gone. Amos, Hannah, and Alice followed, but their much more leisurely pace suggested they were gathering intelligence. If anyone could figure out what this place was, it'd be them.

The room was suddenly quiet. "It's going to get crowded down there," I said, my voice sounding lonely in the giant space. I stared out to the lake, wondering all the while what was being said, what was going on. I tried poking at my alter egos to see if they had any advice, but they were quiet for a change. I turned to Reinhardt and Ransom, glad to finally have some privacy so we could discuss the situation.

"Well, what's your opinion?" Ransom said. He waved his hand.

I glanced into the corners up by the ceiling to see if there were any cameras trained on us. I didn't see any out in the open, but that didn't mean they weren't there. Catching my eye, Ransom lowered his voice to a near whisper. "Another mafia faction? Or government security?"

"It certainly does look like she's being abetted by someone significant," Reinhardt said, raising an eyebrow at the silver service on the table.

"It doesn't feel like Hollinger's style either," I said. "Moreover, if Hollinger knew we were alive, he'd have just accompanied us to the airport, onto the plane, and only rested easy after he saw us back at Fairhaven himself." I turned around in my chair and looked at everything closely. Then I recalled the fencing and gate. "Maybe Canadians have more discretion about matters of national defense. But then a nuclear bomb could have both the U.S. and Canada working together. Mutual interests could be why we're all here?"

Reinhardt and Ransom remained quiet but shrugged.

Startling us, two women entered the dining room. They giggled at my gasp and started to clear the table. I hadn't heard them coming. What if they'd overheard our conversation? We should have realized that a house this large and lunch this lavish would involve additional personnel.

The waif-like woman with dark hair pulled back in a loose ponytail turned to Reinhardt. "You finish here? I clean now?" she said and began clearing the dishes onto a silver tray.

"Yes, of course," he said. She said something to the other woman in a language I didn't recognize, and they worked quickly in silence.

We stood and went out to the patio. We did a quick survey of the garden for anyone who could be eavesdropping then sat in some brightly colored Adirondack chairs beside a bubbling fish pond. I figured if anyone were lurking around, the sound of the gurgling water might help to muffle our conversation.

"Are we in agreement that Margaret is completely incapable of handling this deal?" I said, trying to process everything. "Maybe when she learned that Oscar had been taken hostage, she hired Serge and Marcel to help her. But they don't act like they were hired by her. Or maybe she hired them to babysit her? Still, if she didn't hire them and someone else did, to make sure someone was watching over her, the next question is who are they working for?"

"She does appear to have a bit of a drinking problem," Ransom said, pinching his fingers together with the smallest of a gap. "Maybe she let the cat out of the bag in some drunken rant and the wrong people overheard and now she has more than the kidnapping of her son to deal with."

"No," Reinhardt said carefully. "Back during the Cold War days, Magda could carry out a sting under duress even with truth serum pumped into her veins. I'm wondering if Felix prearranged this all."

"You think Felix was working with organized crime in Canada?" Ransom asked.

"Maybe, given the way Rosalind's family was targeted," Reinhardt said. "Rosalind was one of Felix's top agents and even while he was busy impregnating his other female agents, he never stopped trying to seduce her, too. When she took the retirement package, he openly threatened her and said she'd regret her decision to retire. Sure enough, he managed to find her and kill her husband and daughter. It was extreme luck that I was able to rescue her and bring her back to Fairhaven. The explosion at her husband's newspaper office was very poorly investigated, and she was reported as having perished along with her husband and daughter, even though she hadn't been in the building. It stands to reason the local police were under mafia influence as well. It would fit perfectly into Felix's hit profile."

Serge and Margaret returned from their walk and came over to our spot by the fish pond. Margaret sat down with us. We looked at her in silence.

"I'm OK now, Serge," she said.

"Then I have some things to attend to," Serge said. "I will leave you with your friends." Serge patted her on the shoulder, glanced suspiciously at us, his gaze softening briefly when his eyes met mine, and he went inside the cottage.

I looked at Margaret. She wasn't our friend but I hoped she would level with us. Or was she working with Serge and he was hoping we'd ask her candid questions?

"Quite a place you have here, Margaret," Reinhardt said. "Have you won the New York State lottery?" Reinhardt let out a laugh and sat back in the wooden Adirondack chair. He was always so adept at reading people. Now he was acting nonchalant to get her to open up.

"You know very well that I'm as much a guest in this house as you are," Margaret said archly. "Between us 'guests,' there are lots of people interested in Felix's botched deal. The one he left for us to clean up." She shook her head and sighed. "He still has a way of manipulating every side. What we have to do now is figure out how to satisfy each of these people and keep all of us alive at the same time." Margaret was sober and clear-headed and staring directly at Reinhardt.

"Then who owns this place?" Ransom asked.

"Someone who trusts Serge and Marcel with a lot of money," Margaret said. "They won't even tell me. But they treat me well and they're doing what they can to keep me from falling off the wagon."

"Won't you tell us where Robert is being kept? We'll still help you, but we'd rest easier if we knew where he was," Reinhardt's voice was even, but it was clear he was losing patience.

"And all I want is to get Oscar back," she said. "I need your help and so do our hosts. Until we find the plutonium that Felix has so cleverly hidden, we have no negotiating power. Can you see that I'm at as much of a disadvantage as you are?"

I exploded. "Wait a second. You don't even have Robert? Serge and Marcel are holding him? Why would you lie?" Tears sprang to my eyes. It felt so unjust and dehumanizing to treat Robert like a bargaining chip. This was all my fault.

"No," Margaret said. She shrugged. "And Serge and Marcel don't have him either. But they're looking for the people who do."

"I don't get any of this," Ransom said. "We want Robert. You want Oscar. What is it that Serge and Marcel want?"

Margaret hesitated and shrugged again. "They want to help me." She rolled her eyes and pursed her lips tightly in anger.

"Come on!" Ransom said. "Even I know they aren't what they want us to believe they are. How did they even know who you are or that you had a problem?"

Margaret scowled at Ransom. "You ninny. I'm the one who found *them*." Her frown turned into a devilish grin as she looked from one of us to the other. "They're undercover police officers working with a special division assigned to control the crime families in the province."

It took me a second to process what she'd said, but when I realized what was happening, my throat closed up. She'd forced us to work with the police who were working undercover with the mafia, and the only way we'd get Robert back was to help them. I looked at Ransom. His face was impassive, but the vein in his neck was pulsing.

"Margaret," Reinhardt said quietly. "Why have you chosen to make us your allies?"

"More than anyone, you have resources and experience with Felix's disgusting, underhanded ways. It's good that the d'Angelos think they have us at their mercy. But I know that between us, we can make this work. Somehow."

"And what about the missing plutonium?" Ransom asked. "Everything—or should I say everyone's *lives*—depends on that delivery. Are we going to orchestrate a delivery that potentially puts the entire world in danger?"

"Why don't we leave that to Serge and his people to figure out," Margaret said. "Their job is keeping the world safe, and frankly, if it wasn't us handing the stuff over, it'd be someone else. All we can do is worry about our people, getting them back, and keeping them safe. So you help me find where Felix stashed the material, and when they release Oscar and the deal is done, the Feds can figure out the rest."

I looked at Margaret. For someone whose life's work was to protect and serve her country, it seemed a complete turnaround for her to be so apathetic about delivering nuclear materials to bad people. But how hard her life had been was still unfolding and becoming apparent, and perhaps now, in her later years, she'd come to see the futility of caring about a world that was hell-bent on destroying itself. It also seemed a little too easy and naive, which I couldn't understand. She was assuming everyone would cooperate. Would the person holding Robert release him and let us go on our way? I doubted that very much.

Margaret sat uncomfortably quiet and avoided our eyes. Rosalind was buzzing around inside my head like a trapped bee. *This smells very bad,* she warned me. I closed my eyes and tried to hear my thoughts, or Kathleen's, but it was as though Rosalind's fury had taken over my whole brain. I wanted to grab Margaret by the throat for keeping important information from us regarding her plan.

"Well, Margaret," Reinhardt said, clapping his hands on his thighs and standing. "We're not doing anything until we know Robert is all right. For all we know, he's dead, has been dead this whole time, and you and your *comrades*," he said archly, "are playing us."

Margaret furrowed her brow and waved him back into his chair. "Cool off, Reinhardt. You'll see Robert tonight after dinner. We have a Skype call set up and Serge and Marcel plan to give us all a debriefing on how this is going to go down." She got up and slowly walked back to the house. I hoped the cottage didn't have any Scotch stored for visitors. I trusted Margaret less than before, but now that I knew Serge and Marcel were cops, she was our only hope for any accurate information regarding Robert. We needed her sober and awake for that call.

Coming up to the stone patio from the lake path were the seniors with Roscoe bounding ahead of them. "There's an awesome boat dock at the lake," Roscoe said. "But I didn't see a boat."

"Probably so we can't get away," Amos said. His eyes met Reinhardt's with a questioning stare. Roscoe's tone had amplified what we were all thinking, I was sure. Who had a dock with no boat? "And the property is fenced right up to the lake."

"So the question is whether they are trying to keep the bad guys out…" I started.

"… or keep us in," Norm said.

No one spoke. My senses prickled and my ears buzzed. Yes, Rosalind, I said in my head. I know.

We split up to synchronize the time it took to move around the property. We made it appear as if we were settling into our rooms, but we were assessing our environment for the purpose of timing a quick escape. We needed to know it took exactly a minute and a half to walk from the bedrooms in the south wing to the garden patio. A part of me wished we could stay and treat this like a holiday. It was such a serene, restful place. The south wing bedrooms were cool, shaded by maples growing around the perimeter. Each room had an open screen window that let in the sounds of nature. Mine had a beautiful view of the lake. Marcel was right, everything had been provided for. Aveda body and hair products, Lululemon tops, and yoga pants. Even new running shoes. I yearned to lie down for even a minute on the soft duvet and listen to the birds, but we were in custody, and I knew we needed to keep our guard up.

I finished scoping out my room then walked back to the stone patio where the pathway seemed to call me down to the lake. I had to see this boat dock for myself.

The warm breeze tickled my skin. I squinted against the sun glinting fiercely off the lake and wished I'd grabbed my sunglasses. I walked down the sloping path, its stone steps spaced about every ten feet. A sand beach opened up just at the water's edge, fringed by grass on either side. I looked out over the large dock at more Adirondack chairs and low tables artfully arranged like they were in a magazine photo-shoot, and stood still. Apart from the call of the birds and the buzzing of insects over the water's surface, and a sweet breeze tossing in some cooler air, it was completely silent. I squinted again and looked out on the water for other cottages or boats. Nothing.

"Peaceful down here, isn't it?"

I turned sharply, startled. It was Serge with a drink in each hand.

"How did you know I was here?" I demanded.

Serge smiled gently. "I didn't mean to startle you, but when I was on the upper patio, I noticed you coming down here. This is my favorite spot. I hope you don't mind if I join you." He held out one of the drinks. "Do you like lemonade?" He pointed to the deck chairs, motioning for me to join him. "Please come and sit."

I took the tall glass and our fingers accidentally touched. He caught my eye, and an electric jolt ran through my fingers, wet with condensation. I turned quickly and sat.

"I wish we could share a glass of wine," he said, "but we don't keep alcohol at the cottage. And Margaret... Well. You know." He shrugged but he seemed to consider her drinking more a quirk than a legitimate problem. I guessed the French were more cavalier about drinking than we were.

The wind caught his hair, and I caught a waft of his cologne. I wanted to look at him, but I didn't dare. He was so casually hot. Maybe he was some kind of vampire, I mused. I sipped the sweet and tangy lemonade and kept my gaze out on the late afternoon sun shimmering over the ripples of the lake. A cicada started to chirp, then a second, then several more. *Don't let your guard down,* Rosalind hissed. I felt Serge's eyes on me, and my skin prickled. I wondered if we were alone here or if any of the others were watching us. I didn't trust my voice. Also, I didn't trust him. I wasn't going to start the conversation. He had come down here for a reason, and I was interested to see what that was.

"What do you think of our… little place?" He put his drink on the side table and waved his hand in a circle. He was trying to lead me into a conversation. He wanted to disarm me. Or was he sincere? I hated not knowing.

"I'm very fond of the fencing," I said.

He leaned in and looked me in the eyes. "Ruby, it's a secure location for everyone's protection."

I raised an eyebrow and met his eyes. I couldn't wait to hear what he meant by that. It occurred to me that I was in a particular position to possibly disarm him into disclosing who we needed protection from. I lowered my lids and softened my face. I could try to make this go in a new direction.

"We all have an important mission," Serge said, shutting down. This time he looked out onto the lake.

Darn, I thought. He knew what I was up to.

"Margaret said you'd give us a debriefing after dinner tonight," I said. I kept my tone even, trying not to frame it as a question. I was worried now that he could wield a certain power if he wanted.

He turned and put his hand on mine. His grip was soft and I tingled from his touch. My body rose and I leaned in, holding my breath. But I soon realized that he wasn't moving in on me, he had a look of deep concern on his face. He was communicating something.

I chuckled inwardly. This guy was good, but I could tell he was also a good guy. He knew I was waiting for information that would reveal Robert's location, but he also knew if we were going to help them find Oscar and deliver a dangerous shipment to overseas criminals who intended to sell the deadly prize to terrorists, that he had to play this very carefully.

"It's a shame our circumstances aren't different," he whispered.

He drew closer.

Rosalind pinched me, waking me up. I shook my head. "I have to go," I said, standing up.

Serge stood as well and grabbed my arm. "Please, don't go yet." He looked apologetic, yet his hold was oddly firm.

"Let go of her." Ransom was standing at the top of the path. The sun silhouetted his form as he descended the stone steps two at a time. He strode onto the dock and pushed Serge's shoulder, hard, knocking him backward.

"Ruby, are you all right?" Ransom asked, taking both my hands in his, a concerned look in his eyes.

"Of course, she's all right," Serge said brusquely. "We were only talking. And I would certainly never hurt her." Serge must have known how it would have looked with his hand gripping my arm, especially to Ransom who had already decided Serge was trouble.

The air between them was as tense as a thunderstorm and I couldn't help but feel a little flattered and, I realized, sad. Even though they were both baring their egos, it wasn't about me. It was about everything but me. Serge was police or mafia or who knew, but he wasn't trustworthy and what if we did hook up, then what? What would that look like if he had been deceiving me all along? And Ransom had made his loyalty to Rose very clear and had punted me to the side. If things were different now because she was dead and not around anymore, I didn't want to be anybody's second choice.

"Why don't we all go up to the cottage," I suggested. I was grateful that Ransom had showed up when he did, but I was angry and hot. I threw my hair over a shoulder and stalked up the path, swinging my hips. We needed to keep Serge interested in me, or at least as an ally, just in case he was a sympathetic person and could side with us. I sneered at how it felt so terrible to consider this a tactical situation. As I walked away, I could feel both their eyes on my back.

Twelve

WHEN I GOT INSIDE, I heard someone doing a lot of banging. Ransom had caught up with me and we went in search of the noise. We found Margaret on her knees in the dining room looking through cabinets and the side buffet, opening and slamming the doors shut. She looked frantic.

"Damn that Serge," she said.

Marcel walked into the room. "What is...?" He sighed, came to her, and took her roughly by the elbow to help her stand. "*Merde,* Margaret. We told you already. There's no alcohol here. You have to be stronger. We can't have you drunk and passing out all the time if we want to get Oscar back." I was taken aback by his harsh tone. He pulled her away from the empty liquor cabinet.

Margaret wrapped her arms tightly around her torso. She didn't look well. Her eyes glistened like someone with a fever, and her breaths were coming in short gasps.

"I can get you some coffee," I said. She looked lost. I felt sorry for her. I knew what it was like to lose my family, except, in my case, there was no chance to find them again. In some ways, her situation was worse. At least I could grieve. She had only her imagination. And what she'd seen during her career probably meant she was imagining the worst. "I'll see if I can ask the ladies who look after the meals here."

She looked at me with gratitude.

"Dinner is almost ready," Marcel said. "I'm sure I could get her a coffee." He huffed and left the room.

Roscoe came into the room just as Marcel disappeared into the kitchen. He had seen the altercation between Marcel and Margaret. Roscoe had a sixth sense about when someone needed support. He knew what it felt like to want love from the people he needed most and to not be able to get it. He didn't ask any questions but walked up to Margaret and hugged her.

She looked surprised and wooden, but then relaxed into holding him until she was hugging him with her whole heart and tears came to her eyes.

"Nothing stops the worry," Roscoe said quietly. "You just have to find a way to live with things. I haven't figured that out either, but I'm trying. But we all know what you're going through."

Tears came to my eyes, too, at these wise words. His youthful sincerity pierced my soul.

Margaret pulled away, wiped her face, and tried to laugh off the fact that she was crying.

"Roscoe, what a beautiful thing to say," she said. She took a deep breath.

Roscoe wheeled around. "Do you know if this place has Wii? I could teach you to play. It's fun and keeps my mind off all the bad stuff. Maybe it'll help you too."

Serge, who had come up from the lake in time to see the tender moment, interjected, "We do have it, but I'm pretty sure Margaret doesn't play video games."

"Shut up, Serge," she said. "If Roscoe wants to play Wii with me, then I'm going to do it. Now be a good man and set it up for us." She put her arm around Roscoe and they followed Serge to a room off in another wing.

My heart hurt from that episode. For the last year, Roscoe had been carrying around with him the burden of believing he was a bad person for having killed Felix, yet he was able to extend an extraordinary empathy for others, in his way giving them what they needed when they were suffering. I'd always remember how he helped me when I first came to Fairhaven, struggling with the death of my family and the loss of my own identity. His gentle kindness meant everything to me and helped heal my open wound.

Marcel came back into the room with a coffee cup. "Now where did she go?" He put the coffee down on the table. "It doesn't matter anyway. Dinner is ready in the dining room. I'll let the others know."

***

The homey smell of pasta was wonderful, but I could hardly make myself eat. I wanted this dinner to be over with so we could hear what Serge and Marcel had to tell us. I wondered if Serge and Marcel would be honest and transparent, or if this were just another layer of smoke and mirrors. But it was decided: no Robert, no help from the Drakers. On this, we wouldn't budge.

Margaret didn't eat much either and fidgeted quite a bit. I figured she knew the plan or at least part of it. Throughout the meal, all the Drakers eyed our hosts who ate and chatted about politics and books they'd recently read, but gave no indication as to what they were planning.

After dinner, we gathered in a large den. A rustic desk with a leather chair was the centerpiece of the room. On the desk sat a computer with the monitor turned around to face us on the sofa. Serge and Marcel waited until we were all seated. My nerves felt like they might snap.

"As you all know, we have a serious dilemma and a difficult decision to make," Marcel said. He spoke slowly, searching our faces for a reaction.

"All right, Marcel," Ransom said, jumping up like he was about to grab Marcel. "That's enough of this bullshit."

Norm put his hand on Ransom's arm.

"You're both being somewhat indirect," Norm said to the two Frenchmen. "Can you blame us for wanting to know what exactly is going on?" Norm smiled knowingly and calmly sat back in his chair.

I looked at the four seniors—and Reinhardt—and was impressed by how reserved they all were in body and energy. Their composure seemed to unsettle Serge, who glanced repeatedly at Marcel.

"I don't understand," I said. "You know what we want. You know what Margaret wants. What we don't know is what *you* want. Why are you interested in us at all? We don't even know who you're working with. For all we know you're buddies with the d'Angelos."

Serge caught my eye and I stood up and went over to Ransom. We stood together, both of us with our arms crossed, staring at Serge and Marcel. I wanted it to be very clear to Serge where I stood. He could be as sexy as he wanted to be. It wouldn't matter. I surprised myself by thinking this.

"Our obvious dilemma is that we can't allow a shipment of plutonium to get into the hands of terrorists," Serge said. "While we're pleased that Margaret doesn't know where Felix Szabo hid the materials, our job is to prevent you from helping her find it and arranging shipment."

"Well, then," Reinhardt said, smiling. "We do indeed have a dilemma. No plutonium? No Oscar. No Oscar? No Robert. But now it's clear why we're here and why we're locked behind a fence." He leveled a steady gaze at Serge. "Or is something else happening in the background that you don't want us interfering with?"

"I wouldn't exactly call this a prison," Marcel said, sneering. "But I can assure you that your Robert is alive. Margaret, I can also assure you that we know where Oscar is being held and that he is also alive and being well-treated. But you have to let us handle this."

Those words sounded familiar. That's exactly the way Hollinger had put it.

"And why the hell should we trust you?" Ransom yelled. "In our experience, what we don't know always comes around to hurt us. We have no intention of doing anything other than finding Robert. So just give us Robert and we're no longer a problem."

"I wish it were that easy," Serge said. His eyes met Marcel's, who shook his head.

"Damn you," Ransom exploded. He stepped forward and grabbed Serge by the collar. "Why won't you just tell us?"

Amos and Norm sprang to get Ransom off Serge.

"Come on, Ransom. Let him go," Amos said. "This isn't helping anyone." He turned on Serge. "But you said you'd brief us on details, and so far, you haven't given us anything."

"The less you know the better," Marcel said. "I can tell you that both men are alive, that we know where they are, and that the d'Angelos have very specific demands for the delivery of the nuclear material Szabo promised. I can also tell you that you are safe here and all your needs will be looked after."

"But…" Serge blurted out, "we are not with the mafia here in Quebec or in Corsica."

"Shut up, Serge," Marcel said through gritted teeth. Marcel's face was tight as he glared at his brother.

I wanted to smile but controlled myself. It seemed Serge had said more than he should have. He looked apologetically at me, and I cocked my head wishing I could ask what was really happening. I felt Ransom's eyes moving back and forth between us, missing nothing. I wanted to telepathically tell him I was handling this my way, and I might even be able to work Serge into telling me more. But of course, that only happens in the movies.

I stared at the two brothers, wondering why on earth it would be problematic for us to know that they were with national security forces. But under whose jurisdiction was the question. Then my mouth fell open. All of Rosalind's nudging made sense, and where I'd doubted this thought earlier, now it was confirmed. Hollinger. Of course. He knew. He'd known all along. We were stupid to think he hadn't tailed us and had seen through our little explosion decoy. Smart of him to do it this way, I decided. Well played.

"What if we told you that we don't believe you?" Hannah said. "That Oscar and Robert are as alive as you say. You might think that just because you've brought us to this big house and given us good food and new clothes we're going to roll over and believe you. We old folks don't just take people's word for things. We need proof."

"Show them," Margaret said. She was fidgeting again, looking around the room like she was figuring out how to escape.

Serge turned on the computer and switched on the monitor. He logged in and got onto Skype. After a moment of ringing, a blurry face appeared on the screen. Margaret let out a gasp and sat up straight.

The pixels of the computer were sorted out and we saw who, I supposed by Margaret's reaction, was Oscar.

He was sitting under an umbrella on a sunny terrace. He held up a piece of paper and hesitated before speaking. "I have a message from Mateo d'Angelo," he said. "Deliver the shipment or they—"

A tall man with dark hair and wearing a Hawaiian shirt, pushed Oscar out of the frame.

"Mateo, what—?" Oscar started to say.

The man laughed a curt laugh and took a seat in the chair. He leaned back and smiled cordially. "Margaret, dear Margaret," he said. "Your son is such a delight to have as a guest. However, his father has been very rude. By the way, my deepest condolences." Mateo's smile momentarily turned to a frown. He came closer to the camera, his face filling the screen. "It seems that I must impose on you to fulfill a business arrangement Felix left uncompleted." He whispered the last part of his sentence before resting back again against the cushions. "At least Felix was honorable enough to leave a guarantee of delivery." He let out three low, controlled chuckles and nodded off camera.

The camera panned over to another chair where Oscar was now sitting, with his knees together and drawn in.

The camera came back to Mateo who nodded. "Margaret, Felix had such confidence in your abilities to carry out his last wishes. Now I anxiously wait for you to take care of it."

He pointed off camera and it panned out again to look out at a large expanse of water. Tiny water skiers zoomed past.

"Did you know that your Oscar is very fond of water sports?" Mateo said. "But he is so very reckless! I tell him all the time 'Oscar, be careful. You will kill yourself with those stunts you perform.'" Mateo made tsking noises. "Ah, but young people... You know how they are. They never listen." He paused. "I hope that we can bring him safely home and in one piece." He laughed again. "So you see, it would be wise of you to be quick about the delivery. And Margaret, it's of no use to involve your government. It would be... How shall I say? Unwise?"

He waved his hand, his face turning into a stone mask before the screen went black. None of us moved because sound was still coming from the computer: muffled voices and shuffling. Within a few seconds, there was another click and there was Robert.

"Hi, guys," Robert said. His voice sounded raspy and weak. He was sitting in a wheelchair so that answered that for me. It hadn't just been for the original photo that he'd been in the chair. He'd sustained some significant injury and was confined to it.

My heart sank even though it was so exciting to see him alive.

"I know this comes as a surprise to you. Trust me, it surprised me as well." He huffed, or was it a sniff?

I wondered if he were in pain or just very uncomfortable, most likely under duress, or maybe he was irritated to finally be in touch with the people who abandoned him. I couldn't blame him.

"I'm sorry I can't help you find Felix's... delivery." That made me smile. Robert was the same, as dedicated and charming as he'd always been.

He looked over to the side. He was clearly under someone's watchful eye. I wondered where he was. Behind him was only a white wall.

"I'm still a bit, well, incapacitated," he said, gesturing to the chair, "so I have to depend on you to wrap this up. I'd love to get out of here. Please, don't let me—"

At that, the screen went black. I knew if he'd had more time, he'd have used some Draker code words to indicate where he was, but his captors may have known he'd try to do that. But at least we had our proof. Robert was alive. But the guilt I felt when I first saw him had turned into a hot rage. I could feel Rosalind rolling around my head in a fury.

"Is that what you wanted?" Marcel said. "Have we convinced you that we're telling you the truth?"

"We can help you with this," Ransom said. "So can Robert. Just help us find him. Bring him here if you want. He's a master at making things work out."

Marcel shook his head.

Our group looked exasperated.

Margaret shifted in her seat, and I got the feeling that she was still withholding something that we might use as leverage to get us out of here and help her find Oscar.

One thing was clear. Our plan to rescue Robert had just taken on a complication that we had not intended. What we needed was to escape from our gracious hosts and drag Margaret along with us. I wondered just how secure this fenced-in facility really was.

"Tell me, Marcel," Norm said. "What are you expecting us to do while we're here? Do you think we'll just sit around and trust you and whoever you're in cahoots with to resolve this?" He waited patiently for Marcel to answer.

"Yes. It would make it easy for us if you did." And with that, he and Serge left the room, Ransom's eyes throwing daggers as he followed behind.

Reinhardt turned to Margaret who looked like she was sitting on a chair made of pins. "You know more, don't you?"

I also felt she knew where Robert was being held. I hoped Robert might be somewhere close by. The room was silent as we waited for her to speak. I could tell she wanted to come clean. There was something in her expression that looked confessional. After all, she was in no better position than we were. She played with her cuticles. I wondered what hold those men had on her to stop her from telling us.

"Damn it," she said. "They must keep some vodka or something in this place. I'm sure they have a stash for themselves. Maybe I should search their rooms. Bastards!" She stood up and started to walk out, turned hesitantly to look back at us but thought better of it, and continued to another room.

"So that was interesting. But not exactly informative," I said. "They want us to just wait and do nothing."

"Where do you suppose they took our cars?" Amos asked. He had that look on his face, that sneaky satisfied look that I'd come to recognize as that of someone about to come up with a plan.

Norm, Alice and Hannah wore the same expression.

"Well, heck," said Hannah. "If Margaret can snoop around looking for booze, I suppose I can look around for donuts. I have a bit of an addiction of my own, you know, and I'm having a powerful sugar and dough craving right now."

I smiled. Our elder ex-spies knew every trick in the book. At the farmhouse in Springfield, Amos and Norm had been the ones who had found the helicopter crash site. Little escaped their seasoned eyes.

"Lots of trees and scrub around here, too," Amos said. "I bet they have some mighty good huntin'. Maybe we'll even bag us a cougar."

I stifled a laugh. That had been Myrtle's word for a bad guy.

Amos shared that twinkle and he'd put on his country accent, which always meant trouble, and I couldn't have been happier to hear it. It meant they were going to find a way out of here.

Reinhardt, Ransom and I shrugged and grinned as we left the room.

Thirteen

FOR THE NEXT COUPLE OF DAYS, we wandered around trying to find ways to amuse ourselves while thinking tactically about escape. Hannah and Alice made several requests for donuts and other American-style foods to be delivered. Serge and Marcel seemed not only happy to look after our creature needs, but relieved we were having them, as if they somehow signified we were settling in and accepting our lot.

On our end, we knew that deliveries meant vehicles going in and out, which were key to our getting out of here. Norm and Amos entertained themselves with "huntin'," which Marcel found hilarious. Of course, our weapons had mysteriously disappeared from our rooms but he agreed to pellet guns and even went out with the men and took up their challenge to see who could bag the most critters.

I thought it wise to befriend the two cooks, or housekeepers, or whatever they were. I told them I loved cleaning and offered to help them just to give me something to do, which made them laugh cutely behind their hands.

Marcel and Serge had hidden our guns somewhere and I intended to find them.

I also preoccupied Serge while Ransom sneaked into the study, disabled the surveillance camera in the den, used the computer to send a coded message to Renegade, then deleted all traces of what he had done and turned the camera back on without being seen.

I asked Serge about his hobbies, and when he mentioned fly fishing, I gushed about how much I'd loved *A River Runs Through It* with Brad Pitt, which I'd only heard of but never seen, and he delighted in telling me story after story about his mastery of the sport and the many fish he'd caught. I leaned in and let my hand graze his as we stood overlooking the water. He inched closer and closer, and while I knew I was in service and playing a part, my heart still raced to have him beside me, his heat radiating out onto my skin. I was glad Ransom was busy and couldn't see this. Then I rolled my eyes. So what if he did.

"I wonder what the others are up to," Serge said, putting his hands down to leave the dock.

I panicked and took his arm. "Leave them," I said quietly.

He stared at me for a second, then held my chin. My breath caught in my throat as he began to lean in. I was in service. I was doing this for all of us. I was so glad Ransom couldn't see. I let my eyes shut. It had been so long since I had been kissed.

The door slammed up at the house. I jerked away. Serge also pulled back, but more slowly.

"I will go see what Marcel is doing," he said, his voice a mixture of regret and annoyance. "He doesn't even like hunting. He is a vegetarian." Serge laughed, and I laughed, too, and we both walked up to the house.

I went inside to make myself scarce for a while and to cool off.

"What's with you," asked Roscoe, who came trotting up to me in the hall. "You look weird."

"Overheated is all," I said and turned into my room.

***

Later that afternoon, I was back with Ransom, Reinhardt and Alice making iced coffee in the kitchen when a vehicle pulled up outside. I went to the window and saw a grocery delivery van and what I guessed was a donut delivery car with the sign Tim Hortons on its side, parked just outside the kitchen side door.

"There must be a hidden driveway," I whispered to the others. "How else would they have gotten here?"

We all waited and didn't speak, to see if we could hear anything. I didn't hear Marcel or Serge, just what sounded like a delivery guy speaking French to someone. There must have been other guards we hadn't even seen patrolling the perimeter. I hadn't thought about it, but it made sense, given how badly they didn't want us to leave. We would have to find out how many guards surrounded the property, so we'd be prepared when we finally made our move.

We left our vantage point with a plan. I went to the cottage's office and found Serge. He was wearing reading glasses and typing something. I broke out into a light sweat. "Hi," I said.

He smiled and whipped off his glasses. "Hi."

"I'm going back down to the dock?"

He glanced at the computer then clicked his mouse around a few times. "That sounds nice." He got up and came to the door.

"Why don't I meet you there? Maybe you can bring some lemonade?" I hated how coquettish I sounded, but he didn't seem to notice. I turned and darted to the kitchen and motioned to Ransom to go quickly. He left out the back door to where the vans had been parked to find their hidden entrance. I was glad it had rained briefly that morning and the ground was still soft. With luck, he'd be able to follow their tracks and not be seen by any of the detail.

I was also glad he was gone. Serge arrived a minute later and when I saw him stride in, I didn't wait. I went to him, pushed him up against the wall, and kissed him.

"Ruby. No…" He pulled back and whispered into my mouth.

"I don't care," I said.

After we broke apart from hearing someone coming, I avoided everyone all afternoon until dinner. I tried to make myself eat and engage like a normal person even though inside, Rosalind was scolding me, Kathleen was cheering, and I was a mess. I'd made out with Serge and should've felt horrible, but I felt incredible, heady. Yet the whole time while he had one hand wrapped in my hair and the other holding the back of my neck in his warm strong palm, my thoughts kept going to Ransom. But Ransom was no help. I could feel him stealing looks at me throughout dinner that evening, and every time I saw him glance my way, I felt more and more like a rock had settled in my stomach. It wasn't like anything serious had happened—I mean a little bit, but not enough to say it was serious. Still, I knew in my heart I'd betrayed Ransom.

Afterward, we went outside, and Ransom lit a fire in the stone fire pit on the patio. We sat around it in the Adirondack chairs with the firelight playing over our faces. I purposefully plunked myself between Alice and Hannah so I didn't have to deal with knowing one or the other of my men was beside me.

Margaret was scratching her arms and getting distraught. "I need to go for a walk," she said, standing abruptly.

Marcel and Serge exchanged glances and followed her inside to calm her down. As she walked away, I thought I saw her smile. Had she planned this? Perhaps she was engaging in manipulations of her own.

Ransom waited until they were gone and then he told us what he'd found that afternoon. I felt regret—or maybe shame—flush through me, but I cleared my throat and tried to concentrate.

"Here's what I found out," he said, tracing his palm with a finger.

I stared at the gesture and remembered with shock how I'd done that exact thing to him after he'd been shot. Sitting by his side while he slept, I'd made hearts in his hand so he could feel me there. I shook the thought out of my head.

"The van comes at 10 a.m.," Ransom was saying. "Only one guard mans and opens a hedged gate at the west end. The road is just twenty feet beyond that, and because of the dense foliage, it disappears from view in seconds."

"OK," said Norm, "that means we could lose Marcel in the brush on the south end. We've spotted a fox skulking around the property and Marcel's pretty intent on being the one to pellet it. He sure loves a dare. Didn't take a rocket scientist to figure that one out." Norm laughed.

"And once Serge mentioned how much he loves fly fishing," I said. "I told him about my deep love for trout. Coincidentally, he told me the lake is full of rainbow trout and that he would catch some for us to enjoy at dinner tomorrow!" I'd seen the fish shimmering in the water earlier and was very proud of myself for my acting ability when I told him how it was my favorite dinner. I hated fish.

"And the household ladies will be busy putting away the food delivery, so that takes care of them," Reinhardt said.

"And what about Margaret?" I asked.

"She's totally into Wii tennis," Roscoe said. "Plus, she seems to like hanging out with me. What can I say? I have a certain charm."

We all laughed.

"I'll tell her I want to show her a new move, and when she goes to follow me, we'll pass by the entry where you guys grab her and put her in the van."

"I don't think we'll have to grab her," Hannah said slowly. "My guess is Margaret's not so far gone as she seems. Right now, for my money, I'd say she's in the cottage keeping the boys occupied so we can talk in private."

"Did she tell you she's in on this?" I asked.

"Didn't have to," Alice said. "We worked with her a long time ago and remember how to read her. She's made it clear she wants us to kidnap her."

Alice chuckled. "It's a smart move. This way if we get caught, she still has their trust. No, I don't think she will give us any trouble at all."

"Then ten tomorrow morning it is," Amos said.

Just then, Margaret came out of the house with Marcel and Serge on each arm. "These gentlemen don't trust me inside the cottage on my own," Margaret said. "All I wanted was some Perrier." She patted her chest. "Have a bit of indigestion." She glanced at Alice. "Well, I guess I appreciate their trying to keep me on the wagon."

They returned to their seats by the fire and Reinhardt smoothly brought the conversation around to fishing and the lake. That started Marcel and Serge reminiscing about one of the times their father had brought all three of the boys fishing when they were young. The third brother, who was on special assignment with the Quebec police force, was named James. We still didn't know their last name. I longed for my phone: so many unanswered questions could be cleared up in a second. Then, as I thought further, Rosalind stuck her finger out and tickled my sense of humor. Wouldn't it be a hoot if it were James, as in James P. Hollinger? Though, of course, they'd pronounce it Hollingiere or something. I stopped myself. That was nuts. It would be too much of a coincidence.

"You never told us what your last name is," I said. I looked straight at Serge.

Ransom, a few seats over, sneered.

Serge didn't notice. He was looking over at Marcel who frowned.

"We go by our Christian names only," Serge said. His voice was soft and gentle like he was apologizing for being evasive.

Ransom and Reinhardt glanced over at me, their eyes darting over to the seniors. I guessed their names would have clued us in to who they were associated with. *Mafia,* Rosalind whispered, *definitely mafia.* I shut down that thought. I didn't like the thought that I'd made out earlier with someone involved with people who killed people. Then again, I had to laugh at myself. So was I. But that was different.

Reinhardt looked at his watch. "I think I'll turn in early tonight. Goodnight, everybody." He stood and went inside.

That was our cue.

One by one, we all excused ourselves leaving Margaret, Serge and Marcel by the fire.

I wondered if Margaret suspected anything, or worse yet, tell our hosts slash wardens what we were up to. Once inside, I held back behind the curtains by the French doors that led to the patio, to see if they would follow as well.

"Well," I heard Margaret say, "if you're not going to get me a whiskey, I'm turning in too." She stood in front of them for a moment, head high and hands on her hips as if to say, *and there's nothing you can do about it.* They waved her off with unadorned "*bonne nuits*," but stayed back by the fire pit.

I pulled back further into the darkness of the room so I wouldn't be seen. Margaret went directly to her room.

Serge and Marcel watched Margaret leave and waited to speak until they were sure she was out of earshot. "*Ils planifient quelque chose,*" Marcel murmured to Serge.

"*Ils ne passeront pas notre sécurité,*" Serge said. "Et d'ailleurs, ils ne connaissent pas la sortie."

Marcel snorted at Serge. "Your feelings for the girl are making you sloppy," he said.

Serge said nothing.

That's all I needed to know. I stole quickly to Reinhardt's room and knocked as discreetly as I could. He opened the door and waved me in as if he'd been expecting me.

"They know we're planning an escape," I started. I paused, surprised to see Ransom and Roscoe in the room as well.

"Of course they do," Reinhardt answered, "which is why we're going to create a diversion for them, to keep them occupied."

"Norm happened to notice this afternoon that the two domestic ladies are not too keen on snakes," Ransom said.

He turned and grinned at me. He had teased me mercilessly at the cabin in upstate New York for the same reason. I shuddered at the memory. It had only been a garter snake, but it didn't matter.

"When they're busy putting the food supplies away, they're going to notice some unwelcome visitors. Serge and Marcel will come to check out what's wrong, which is when we'll hijack the van and slip away. The security detail won't even know what happened."

"Snakes? It has to be snakes?" I said.

Ransom grinned widely and wiggled his fingers over my arms.

I pushed him away. It wasn't my fault. When I was ten and had been camping with my parents and my brother Johnny, one had gotten into my sleeping bag, and I was a hopeless ophidiophobe from then on. And it didn't matter whether they were harmless garden snakes or giant pythons. I didn't care. But more, I hated that Ransom knew about it so he could tease me.

"Really," Ransom said in a sarcastic tone. "You don't seem to mind Serge. He's a snake. Even his name sounds like one. *Ssserge.*"

I rolled my eyes and turned away from Ransom's jeering. *Ignore him,* Rosalind hummed. *Don't you see? He's jealous.*

"Alice and Hannah have collected a few specimens," Roscoe said. A boyish enthusiasm had returned to his face, something I hadn't seen in a long time. It appeared to me that he thought the whole diversion was brilliant and also very funny. "They'll be in a box and they'll be let loose just before we hijack the van. Norm's got a plan for getting the butcher's knife that he can use on the driver and Amos is going to tie him up and gag him."

I felt bad for the driver, but business was business. "You forget one thing," I said. "We don't know where the exit is. Only the delivery driver knows the way out."

"Ruby," Ransom said condescendingly, "he'll have a giant knife at his throat. He'll tell us. After all, he won't know we have no interest in killing him." He sliced across his neck with his finger.

"But Marcel has probably put the security guards on alert. What if they search the van?" I asked.

"If the guard gives us any trouble, we'll just have to distract him."

At that moment, Norm, Alice, Hannah and Amos slipped into Reinhardt's room, Norm slapping a stick about two feet long into his palm. He'd probably found in the woods while pellet hunting.

"You guys won't believe what I found," Alice sang softly. "I know where those scoundrels hid our guns and phones. It pays to make friends with the hired help. But we'd best leave them where they are until just before we make our move."

"Damn, Alice! Nicely done!" Norm said. "How did you do that?"

"Lucy, the one who speaks a bit of English and is terrified of snakes, needed some toilet bowl cleaner. It seems that all the extra cleaning supplies are in the little shed down the path. But she doesn't like to go there apparently because of…" Alice did a waving motion with her right hand and said, "Ssss." She grinned. "That's how we found out she's afraid of snakes. But I'm a tough old bird and I offered to get it for her. I could see she was torn and glanced around to make sure no one was watching before she threw me her key for the padlock on the door. While I was in there snooping around, I found a box way in the back, and guess what was in it? When I left the shed, I made it look like I had re-locked the door but didn't click the padlock closed."

"Alice, you're amazing. That's going to give us a terrific advantage," Reinhardt said. "Is everyone clear on where they're supposed to go?"

"I'm keeping Margaret occupied in the games room," Roscoe said. "She loves *Call of Duty*. She's pretty good at it! I'll listen for the delivery truck and have her at the entrance to the wooden gate."

"I'll be in the kitchen with poor Lucy to leave her my… surprise," Hannah said. "Then hop into the van that Norm will take over."

"I'll collect our guns and phones and meet you at the gate where Roscoe is taking Margaret," Alice said.

"Ransom and I will be pellet shooting squirrels with Marcel," Reinhardt said. "When Marcel hears the screaming from the kitchen—which invariably he will—he'll run to the cottage, which is when we'll bolt to the gate."

"Ruby," Amos said, looking at me with concern. "Are you sure you can get away from Serge?"

I smiled. "No problem. Serge will be fishing for our trout dinner that he's planned for tomorrow night. He'll be in the water in hip waders with his line out, and I'll be watching from the dock with a lemonade.

Of course, I'll have had a few glasses by then and will need to excuse myself to go back up to the house. Guaranteed, in all his gear, from his spot in the water, by the time he gets up to the cottage after he hears the commotion, I'll be long gone."

"OK then, it's all set up," Norm said. "Ten a.m. tomorrow."

With the details arranged, we all stole back to our rooms. The possibility of getting away from here left me feeling wide awake. I settled back onto some propped-up pillows on my bed to think, but I was aware of every noise, the snap of twigs, the hoot of the owl stationed in the big oak tree outside my room. My body was on alert, too, and I wondered about Ransom and whether he was awake as well, what he was lying in bed thinking about, whether he was thinking about me. At that, I heard Rosalind chime in, the loudest of all. *Be ready for things to go wrong, and don't get caught... don't get caught... don't get caught...*

Somehow, agitated, hot and tense, I drifted off to sleep. When I opened my eyes, the sun was already up, but everything else was still quiet. I looked at the clock on the nightstand, 7:32 a.m. I was still in my clothes from the night before. I was groggy and crumpled, but I shook my head. It was an important day and I didn't want to risk falling asleep again.

I got up, showered, and put on the fresh clothes I'd grabbed the day before. I opened the bedroom door a crack and peeked out down the long hallway to see if anyone else was up. No one was in sight so I cautiously made my way to the kitchen, walking on the balls of my feet. I wondered if Alice or Hannah had already put their surprise in place, their box of live contents. My skin broke out in goosebumps as I imagined the snakes slithering out before they were supposed to. *Don't be such a wimp. I trained you better than that.* Rosalind didn't have to scold me. I was embarrassed that my phobia was so readable.

"You awake early," said a woman from behind me.

I jumped and turned around.

"You want breakfast?" It was Lucy from behind the island counter, sorting berries.

"Oh, hi, good morning," I said. "Just some toast would be fine."

She smiled and called in her language to her companion, who nodded and took a loaf of bread from the side and sliced off two pieces for me.

"You sit at table." She motioned with her hand to the sunny dining room where a gentle breeze was blowing the sheer curtains out from the open windows.

I nodded and let them go about their work as I sat and listened to the sounds of the morning: a bird chirping, the leaves rustling, and waves from the lake breaking against the dock a short distance down the path. This would have been an idyllic and luxurious retreat, one a person would never want to leave if it weren't for the minor fact that we were prisoners. They'd been gracious to a fault, and I somehow felt ungrateful that we were planning an escape, one that could get violent and ugly if things went wrong.

Lucy came in with a cup of coffee and a tray with cream and sugar. She smiled, cordially, putting the things down in front of me, and bowed slightly as if I were some kind of royalty. I hated the thought that soon she would have a terrible fright.

"Is that you, Ruby?" Serge was coming in from the hallway. "I thought I heard your voice. Are you ready for some early morning fishing?"

I turned and watched him enter. He was dressed in dark jeans and a long sleeved jersey. "It's going to be over ninety degrees today," I said incredulously, nodding at his outfit.

"It's for the mosquitoes," he smiled. He bent down for a kiss, but I grabbed my coffee mug and held it in my hands in front of me. "I'm not going to join you in the water, but I'll come down and keep you company from the dock."

"Are you sure you wouldn't want to give it a try? We have extra waders. I was hoping to show you my famous arc, just like in the movie." He smiled hopefully.

"I'm a horrible fisherperson," I said, shrugging apologetically. "I don't like to touch the bait and… I'd get the line all tangled in a tree or something."

Serge grinned at me. "No worms in fly fishing."

His voice was so warm and full of affection I started to get a dreadful sinking feeling in my stomach. I tried to laugh.

"But after I have some toast, I'll come down. Promise." I smiled at him winningly.

Serge went out to the patio but instead of going straight down to the dock, I noticed that he made his way down to the shed instead. I held my breath. Why was he going there? Did he notice that Alice had been in there snooping around? He was inside the shed for a long time, but soon he came back out with dark green rubber hip waders draped over his forearm and a fishing pole in his hand, whistling.

I let out my breath slowly.

He walked over to the dock and put on his gear then descended the steps that went into a shallow part of the lake. He waded out further and started gently whipping his fishing line back and forth. It arced in the air like a dancer mid-flight. It was quite exciting to see someone do something so well, so deftly. I was also worried; we still had hours left to go, and if he were as good at catching fish as he was casting his line, we'd be in trouble. I needed him to still be in the water when the uproar started.

Delicious aromas began wafting from the kitchen. By this time, the others were coming into the dining room in various stages of readiness.

Ransom was the first to arrive in the dining room. He came around from behind me, stole my coffee cup, downed the last of it, gave it back to me, and went to the window where he held aside the curtain blowing delicately from the breeze.

"I see Pretty Boy is out there in his rubber pants. Hope they spring a leak."

For some reason, that made me laugh. "He's right where we want him to be," I said. "He needs to catch enough trout for everyone because, he told me—the me who claimed to love, absolutely love trout—that he would take care of it. But they're not biting this morning, thank goodness. He should be in there for a while." I did a big fake wink at Ransom, who broke into a broad smile.

Maybe he was melting toward me. That, or he was still imagining Serge with leaky rubber pants.

"Morning, my dears," Alice said as she came in. Hannah, Norm and Amos were right behind her, looking energized and eager. "What's for breakfast? Donuts, I hope." She giggled and winked. They also looked out at the lake and around the room, missing nothing.

"Anyone seen Marcel yet?" Amos asked as he began gathering cups for coffee.

"He's outside, coming up the driveway," Reinhardt said, pointing.

Roscoe trailed eagerly behind Reinhardt. "It smells like breakfast is ready!"

"I'll check things out in the kitchen," Alice said. A grin spread across Alice's face.

Not yet, Alice, I thought. I felt panic seize my heart. She needed to wait until we were sure the delivery van was here, or at least until I could make sure to be out of the room. A crawling feeling grabbed my back.

I finished the toast and marmalade Lucy had brought to the table. "I'm going down to the lake to watch Serge catch trout," I said.

Ransom glanced up but didn't say anything and the others were busy gathering their breakfasts. I quietly went outside onto the patio to start my way down to the dock.

***

"Have you caught anything yet?" I called out over the still water. Serge was now in knee-deep water, slinging his line back and forth. I chuckled at him. "You look nice, maestro, but I don't hear any music."

"Trout like it quiet," Serge whispered loudly, putting up his hand.

"OK," I whispered and perched on the Adirondack closest to the dock edge so Serge could see me. I looked back to the cottage. Would I be able to see what was going on up there?

Suddenly, Serge's line pulled, and he hooted and reeled in a sizable specimen. He whistled with delight.

"I thought you said the trout like it quiet." I stood up from the chair and applauded.

"Yeah, they do," he said. He was breathing hard with excitement, his muscular chest rising and falling, his eyes twinkling. He stared at me for several seconds, but when I motioned that he should turn around again, he raised an eyebrow, stashed the fish in the bag attached at his waist, and cast his line again.

I stared at him for a moment. Wow, I thought. He's quite a specimen himself. I wish I wanted him. In some ways, it would have been easier. The thought of that made me laugh. *Stay focused, Ruby,* Rosalind warned.

"I thought you'd like some lemonade." Ransom was coming down the walk. I turned and saw him carrying a tray with three glasses and a pitcher. The triangle we were in was getting weirder by the minute. "Mind if I watch the excitement? Looks like you're getting lucky," Ransom called out to Serge in the water, glaring at his back, his lips twisted in a sneer at the word "lucky."

Serge grinned back triumphantly, but the tension was sizzling between the two. If only Ransom knew how he felt about me, it would have been that much more exciting to know they were competing for me, but Ransom was only claiming territorial rights. Like a dog its hydrant.

I turned to let the wind blow the hair off my face. I grabbed Ransom's hand and turned his wrist so I could see his watch. Quarter to ten. Alice would be at the shed now.

I signaled with my eyes for Ransom to get back up to the cottage.

He nodded and turned but not before giving a final sneer in Serge's direction, Serge who was elegantly waving his line back and forth over his shoulder and out to the water. "Show off," Ransom said. "Damn show off."

He tapped at his watch and signaled *five* back at me with his hand low at his waist so Serge couldn't see before sprinting back up the stairs to the cottage to get to his position at the front door with Norm.

My stomach tightened as I waited for my cue. I needed to get up to the cottage as well, and supposedly be in the bathroom when Serge heard the screams coming from the kitchen.

To my left, I noticed Reinhardt walking to the wooden gate, leaving Marcel captivated by his pellet gun and squirrels darting from branches in the forested area a distance from the house.

"I'm going up to the cottage," I said. I held up the empty glass of lemonade and shrugged. "What can I say, you guys make excellent lemonade." I smiled at Serge who had waded out into deeper water. He saluted with his fishing pole before going back to his work.

Once inside, I waited at the foyer a few minutes before a white delivery van with Chez Monty and an old stone building painted on the side of it drove up the lane. It crunched over the coarse gravel driveway before stopping at the kitchen door. A paunchy man with a receding hairline plopped down from the driver's seat and waddled around to the back doors, grunting as he hefted out a big box.

Lucy opened the kitchen door for him and they both walked inside.

I heard Hannah's voice. "Did you bring my donuts? I'll be darned if I'm going to be trapped in this place a minute longer without a good ole-fashioned American-style donut."

There was a thud and a few seconds later, I heard heavy footsteps and an "*Au revoir, Lucy et Marie.*"

Norm and Ransom scurried out to the passenger side of the van, which was my signal to start for the gate.

I knocked on the window of the games room as I passed and immediately heard Roscoe tell Margaret, "You just have to come with me for a second. I want to show you something."

I was within feet of the open wooden gate when I heard a shrill series of frantic screams that shattered the quiet morning air, and a second after that, saw Hannah, who in her mid-sixties, run faster than some teenagers. I guessed she'd let the snakes loose and Lucy and Marie were probably up on the counter or chairs trying to get away from them. I wondered who would reach them first. Probably Marcel as Serge would be struggling through the water and freeing himself from his hip waders.

Within seconds, the van skidded to a stop at the gate and Roscoe and Margaret, who had just gotten there, and Hannah and I all hopped in. Norm was at the wheel and Ransom, holding the terrified driver, was down on the floor. Alice had collected our guns and phones from the hiding spot in the shed and quickly distributed them to us. With guns trained on the poor man's face, he didn't need any convincing.

Alice tossed the key to the shed's lock out the window. Hannah had noticed Serge going in there for his hip waders and rod and had managed to sneak it from Lucy to get it opened again.

Ransom sat up and rubbed the back of his neck. "Bumpy ride," he said.

Norm stopped the van in front of the thick wall of brush. "Well, how the heck do you…?" he started to say but Ransom leaned over and tooted the horn. "Ransom, don't do…"

The bushes parted like the red sea, just as neatly as they had when we'd first arrived at the cottage from the highway.

"Well, I'll be," Norm said and drove us out slowly so none of the security men would think anything was unusual.

I guessed the bushes were attached to some kind of sound-sensitive garage door opener because they opened just wide enough for the van to exit. Once we were through, the bushes closed behind us and that was it. We were out.

I didn't know how much time we'd have before they'd be coming after us, but we couldn't ditch the van, so we had to keep driving down the highway.

Why did we always have such huge getaway cars, I moaned. After ten minutes, I began to get nervous; it'd be any minute now. After twenty, I knew something was wrong. I glanced at Margaret, but her expression revealed nothing.

That's when I noticed a black SUV coming toward us from the long stretch of road ahead. I hoped it was just a random car, but it looked out of place here, and I had a feeling in the pit of my stomach that it was trouble.

As it came closer, it veered into our lane.

Norm swerved but it screeched to a stop, pinning us in, and four burly men jumped out of the vehicle with their guns high and walking toward the van.

Damn it! When I saw the man in the lead, I groaned. It was Hollinger. That confirmed my suspicions that he was working with Serge and Marcel. I shot Margaret a questioning accusatory look. Did she know? Was she in on this? This wasn't the time to confront her, but I couldn't wait to drill her for answers if we got out of this.

Ransom had thrown open his door and dragged the delivery man out with him. He still had a hold on him and continued to point his gun, but the fat man must have known we weren't going to shoot him. He jerked his arm out of Ransom's and ran off into the trees along the road. It was just as well. Having a hostage did complicate things. We all got out with our hands in the air.

"Reinhardt," Hollinger said angrily, "you just couldn't stay out of it, could you?"

"What's going on, Hollinger?" Reinhardt said wearily. "Same as before, we haven't done anything. What's with the guns?"

"How about theft and kidnapping," Hollinger said, pointing with his gun to both the van and the vanished driver. "That's enough for me to detain you."

"This isn't your jurisdiction," Amos said.

Hollinger sniffed in frustration. "Our Canadian friends understand mutual threats to North American security, and it doesn't help your case that you're not Canadian citizens. So they're not going to object to my detaining you all."

A noise in the sky interrupted their conversation and the stillness of the morning, growing louder and louder as we looked skyward trying to assess what it was. Then it was clear: helicopters. Two of them.

"Doesn't that seem like overkill to you?" Ransom said, crossing his arms. "You got us already. See?" But Hollinger and his men weren't paying attention; their eyes were trained on the helicopters as they got closer.

Within seconds, the still air erupted into gusts that assaulted us from the giant blades blowing us around with what seemed like hurricane force. I had assumed these were more of Hollinger's people, but something in the way Hollinger and his team were reacting to the choppers suggested they weren't.

I suddenly felt afraid. This couldn't be good. Nothing was on the sides of the helicopters to indicate who owned them. They came in so quickly none of us could dart back to the cars and drive off. Plus, I suspected Reinhardt didn't want us to try to run in case that would make our situation worse. I wondered if Serge had called them in, but before I could consider who was responsible for getting the helicopters on our case or who was inside, men in black bodysuits and covered faces stormed out of the whapping vessels, formed a circle around us, and pointed automatic rifles in our faces.

This was not the work of the U.S. government. Who the hell were these people? No police and military dressed or looked that way, and I tried further to see who owned the helicopters, but I couldn't see logos or markings to indicate whether they were with local authorities, police, CSIS, or other armed forces.

The men said nothing but seemed to be looking for someone. Could they have the wrong people? Even with a gun in my face that thought made Rosalind snicker.

"Over here," a thug with a richly accented voice said. He pointed to me with his automatic weapon.

My heart stopped.

Two other brutes came over to where I was standing, grabbed my arms so tightly it hurt, and began to pull me toward one of the helicopters. Me? Why me? I wanted to scream.

I twisted and kicked to wrench free, but they were too strong. I might have been able to land a kick at one of them, but the two men were much taller and stronger than I could ever hope to disable.

I looked desperately around for Hollinger until I finally spotted him behind his car with his gun trained on me. The helicopter men were firing at Hollinger and his men to hold them back. One of them fired at the car, bursting the front tire.

I looked back at the Drakers and the seniors, but the thugs had yanked their hands behind their backs and held gloved hands over their mouths. I could see in their eyes they were desperate and wild with fear for me, but they couldn't help. I was alone.

My two kidnappers dragged me to the helicopter where two other men reached down and lifted me into the chopper, pushed me into a seat where one belted me in and the other tied my hands.

I tried to lean forward while the door was still open and shrieked, "Ransom…" but they jumped in behind me, shut the door, and within seconds, we lifted off into the sky.

All I could do was look out of the wide window to my side. I watched Hollinger and his men, Reinhardt and the rest of our group still on the ground, their hands in the air as the remaining goons stood by with guns pointed at them, completely helpless to come to my aid. The chopper lifted higher and higher into the sky until I couldn't see what happened after that.

***

We flew over roads and the countryside in silence. The men sat stiff and motionless with their weapons in their laps. There were seven of them in total: a pilot, co-pilot, and five others of unknown identity. Other than having been a bit rough to get me into the helicopter and tying my hands, they didn't seem intent on harming me in any other way. But I didn't know what to feel. I wondered if I were in shock, but then again, I felt somehow fairly reasonable given my circumstances. Maybe I was getting good at being kidnapped. I wasn't even scared, just intently aware, assessing everything, every sound, every move of each black-clad body, and mostly listening to Rosalind talk me through. *Stay alert. Remember what I taught you.*

The world seemed to go by beneath us in slow motion, and my companions were oddly still. My brain was on high speed though as I tried to consider what might be happening and who would've orchestrated such an event.

After what I guessed to be about half an hour, we started descending. The chopper hit the ground with a heavy thump and the blades slowed. A minute passed and then in unison, the two men who had pulled me aboard uncurled from their seats. One undid my belt, and the other grabbed my arm to help me out of the helicopter's now-open door.

We were on a long tarmac runway, but it wasn't an airport with a control tower or service vehicles, more like a private strip. I was unsteady, but that didn't matter as my captors had my arms securely in their grip as they led me away from the chopper to the waiting golf cart.

Once we were seated, the driver took us along another paved path through some trees and flowerbeds until after about a quarter of a mile, a large estate came into view. The sun was high overhead and the wind blew warm over us. With my hands tied behind my back, my hair that kept blowing into my eyes made it hard to see, but the house was enormous. As we drove closer, I was able to catch glimpses of its white-stuccoed facade with turrets on both ends. On the second floor, I counted eight wide windows. Cement steps led to the wide polished platform, centered by a large heavy black door. The whole structure was flanked by pillars. I knew, as soon as we arrived, I'd find out who had arranged this expensive abduction.

None of the men surrounding me said a word. The driver pulled up to the front. I didn't see any other signs of civilization, no din from a highway or road, just the gentle breeze rustling through the trees and some birds chirping.

The golf cart stopped directly in front of the house and the one man who still had my arm in a tight grip nudged his head toward the door. He pulled me gently out of the golf cart and his companion picked up my other arm and both walked me to the entry like it was some kind of wayward wedding ceremony. Someone inside opened the door as we got there.

We entered a large foyer with a wide marble staircase. A muscular female dressed in black pants, with a white shirt and black blazer, met us and nodded at my two guards who undid the ties on my hands and let me walk ahead to the woman.

"Come with me," she said. She turned and walked past the staircase down a wide, dim hall. I followed her, along with my guards, passing several other rooms until we were at the back of the house. She opened double glass doors that led to a bright sun-room that contained three men in khakis and loose linen shirts, and a striking woman—probably in her fifties—wearing a pale pink sundress with narrow straps. She looked relaxed sitting at a glass table in front of wide windows that looked out over a large expanse of manicured grass hedged by forest.

"Monsieur d'Angelo," the guard on my right said, "we have brought the girl, as you requested." Both of them let go of my arms, which were smarting from their tight hold.

The eldest man, about Reinhardt's age, slowly slid his chair back, stood, and made his way to us in no hurry. He was strikingly handsome, with dark hair, swarthy skin and piercing blue eyes. His orange shirt fluttered easily as he approached me. With a gentle smile, he motioned with his chin that the guards should leave.

"Hello, Ruby," he said.

I realized with horror and fascination that this was Mateo d'Angelo. His voice in real life was much mellower than it had been on the Skype video, his accent not quite French, but I couldn't place it. "You've had an exciting morning, haven't you? Come join us for lunch. My family has been expecting you."

He reached to take my arm, and I jerked back. I knew the gesture was meant to be firm, or fatherly, or whatever, but I'd had enough of people grabbing my arms like I was a handbag.

His smile faded. He pulled his hand back and cocked his head to one side. After a short pause, his smile returned. This time he held out his arm, the palm of his hand open, toward the table. "Please," he said. "Won't you join us?"

I glanced over to the table and while the woman had a pleasant face, the two other men sitting there looked less than warm. But of course, it wasn't like I had a choice. I followed him and sat down in the chair he held out for me.

"This is my wife, Francine," he said, "and my sons Vincenzo and Luciano." I looked up at him as if to say, *No. Really?* I knew very well who they were.

They studied me with curiosity, a half-formed smile on their lips as their eyes flitted between their father and mother to me. They leaned back in their chairs, arms folded over their chests, and said nothing, just looking me over as if I were the next course being presented.

"We are all friends here, so please call me Mateo," he said. Mateo looked at everyone gathered at the table and smiled brightly. "Consider yourself one of the family now!"

Vince and Luciano stifled a laugh.

Francine leaned forward and touched her husband on the back of his hand. Her nails were painted tangerine, which complemented her perfectly bronzed skin. "Where are our manners, Mateo, darling. Ruby must be hungry."

Mateo clapped his hands and the same woman who had answered the door came to the table.

"Julia," Mateo said, "please prepare a plate for our... new family member."

Julia nodded and hurried out of the solarium.

Mateo laughed. I suppose he was trying to sound cordial, but to me, he just sounded sinister.

Fourteen

THE HOUSE WOMAN, SERVANT, SLAVE, WHATEVER she was, brought me an array of lunch foods: salad niçoise with fresh ahi tuna and quail egg, a glass of sparkling water with lemon, and a basket of baguette. The pretty sun-room had floor-to-ceiling windows that were propped open to let in the breeze. The over-sized palms waved back and forth in their pots. Between the beautifully presented food and the faux tropical setting, if it weren't for my being surrounded by hostile people staring at me like I were carrion, it would have been a wonderful lunch. I said nothing and revealed nothing, though I was sure they could hear my heart thumping. I'd been abducted before, several times now, and I have to say I'd gotten good at it. I had no intention of showing them any fear.

When we all had finished, Mateo suggested we adjourn to his study to discuss business. We followed him, Vince in the lead. Francine smiled at me and took my arm to accompany me to the door. I didn't resist, but I wondered what it was with these people and my arms. Luciano followed behind. I figured, at the very least, Mateo was about to give out some information. As in why they had taken only me. Out of everyone, why me? I also wanted to find out where Robert was being held and wondered if I could use anything I knew as a bargaining chip.

I thought about Reinhardt, Ransom and the others and wished I knew what they were doing. I knew they were probably sick with worry and I felt bad I couldn't tell them I was OK. Or that I was so far away. They were probably organizing a search.

The study was a few doors down the hall. I walked there with the d'Angelos encircling me. The room was much dimmer and cooler than the sun-room and had a hazy and sober feeling, like a picture I remembered of an antiquated library. A large lacquered desk and overstuffed leather chair sat in front of the window, and a whole wall was a bookshelf. Perhaps Mateo was a learned man. I didn't know anything about him other than he was extremely wealthy and the head of a powerful crime family. But what was he doing here? Wherever here was. Wasn't his home base in Corsica?

"Ruby," Mateo said, pouring himself a drink from a heavy crystal decanter sitting at a side table, "I hope you are enjoying our hospitality." He took his glass to the leather chair behind his desk and sat. The rest of us settled into the couch and armchairs in front, like school children waiting for him to start a lesson. A buzzing in my ears told me that Rosalind was listening as well. I let her silence guide me.

"It seems we have a mutual acquaintance," Mateo said. He sipped from his glass. "We each have something that the other wants."

There it was again, that misleading gentle smile. Did he think he could feign warmth and I'd melt? I wasn't butter and he wasn't a stove. Nor was he nice, trustworthy, or anyone I would reveal anything to.

He stood and went to the window behind him. The hiss in my head grew faint. Confident bastard! He was turning his back on me to show us who was in charge. This wasn't the time to challenge him. He was trying to lead me into disclosing what I knew—which was nothing, but he didn't need to know that.

He turned to face us. "You, my dear girl," he said, "are looking for a family member you and your family left…" He paused, which I could tell was to unnerve me. "Shall I say… at a disadvantage?" He paused again and smiled. "And…" His face shifted into a distorted snarl.

"Another friend is looking for a family member as well. Do you know whom I am talking about?"

I straightened up and imitated his wide but impartial smile. "You mean Margaret Warren? Yes, we've met." I remained calm, yet I hoped that my calmness wasn't interpreted as obstinacy. No use arousing his anger. I just had to be patient and let this little talk play out.

The smile returned to his face. "And what do you know of the family member she is looking for?"

I waited, knowing I needed to be very careful how I answered this question. I sat back and raised my eyebrows, wondering why he was asking me this. He certainly knew all about Margaret and Oscar, and I could only assume that the primary reason he'd be here—wherever here was—and not in Corsica, would be to be on U.S. soil where he could acquire the plutonium Felix owed him. I knew that as long as he still needed that information, I was his golden goose. *Not goose,* laughed Rosalind, *more like fowl!*

"Would you mind terribly if I were to have another glass of water?" I asked sweetly.

Mateo stifled a laugh and nodded. He knew I was playing his game. He motioned to Francine to get me a Perrier from the side table.

She stood smoothly and went over to the bar and did as Mateo wished, turning like a ballerina then handing me a glass filled with the sparkling liquid.

I smiled and nodded my thanks and took a long slow sip.

"Ru-by," Mateo said, drawing out my name into all two syllables. While not angry sounding, his voice had tightened up considerably. "What do you know of Margaret Warren's missing family member?"

I straightened again and looked directly and calmly at Mateo. "Enough to know that we can make a reciprocal agreement."

A jovial laugh escaped his lips. He held his glass up to me as a toast to my shrewdness. "Vince, Luciano. You'd do well to learn from our... newest family member."

It was alarming that he kept using this term. I realized, that practically speaking, he wasn't going to let me go, but that he also respected my courage.

Mateo pointed his glass at me and nodded to his sons who squirmed as though uncomfortable at the suggestion of "learning" from me. I guessed he was much harder on his sons who didn't always measure up to his expectations. Perhaps they were less than discreet about the family business. I filed that information away.

"Look," I said. "What do you want from me?"

Mateo turned back to look out the window. This guy was better than an actor. He liked his theatrics. Or was he buying time to consider how—or whether—to disclose the reason he had taken me and not the others?

"Margaret knows where our departed Felix has hidden a delivery of weapons-grade plutonium that I've paid dearly for. You need to convince Margaret to release it to me immediately. My buyers are becoming impatient."

Did that mean he intended to release me again to get Margaret to pay up and complete Felix's arrangement? That must have been the reason they took only me, an easy capture and perhaps an easy release.

"That sounds great. But you need to release Robert and Oscar to us before we agree to do that," I said.

He wrinkled his forehead and turned back to the window to stare out at the manicured grounds for several minutes before turning back to me. His neck was pulsing, and his face had taken on a darker hue. He still wore his smile but it was clear he was annoyed. Good. Unnerving him would give me more answers than if he were in complete control.

"Suppose I offer you a small concession?" Mateo said. He turned to his son sitting beside me, a well-dressed lug I'd done my best to scoot away from so our hips wouldn't touch. "Luciano, would you bring our other family member downstairs to join us?" Mateo leaned against the windowsill and took another long swallow of his drink while we waited.

I could hear my heartbeat and tried to tap dance a little on the floor so the others wouldn't hear it as well. Several minutes passed with no one saying a word. I wondered if they were always so quiet with each other. Super fun family, I thought.

Finally, Luciano came in and held the door open while a man in a wheelchair came into the room. The man had his head down and was concentrating on maneuvering through the narrow doorway. Once inside he lifted his head.

I stopped breathing. "Robert!"

Robert smiled cautiously, his eyes moving around the room from person to person. I wondered if he wasn't happy about seeing me, but soon realized his reaction was deliberately neutral. Typical of our Robert, he was trying to tell me something. He always knew what was going on. For now, we both needed to allow Mateo to finish his game of questions.

"Robert," I said again, this time, trying to moderate my enthusiasm. "We've been looking for you."

Mateo came over to me and put his hand on my shoulder, a serious caring expression on his face, one he had fixed in place for my benefit. "And so now that you see that Robert is alive, perhaps we will begin to negotiate an arrangement."

"Mateo. I've already told all of you that we know nothing of Felix's arrangements with you," Robert said calmly. He pursed his lips and looked over at me. Was he trying to tell me to keep my mouth shut?

"Yes, yes, yes," Mateo said benevolently. "But the Drakers have sought out Margaret Warren... Or was it Margaret who sought out your help? And Felix left specific assurances that she would complete the delivery if anything happened to him. And, as we all know, the Drakers killed him and therefore bear part of the responsibility. Since you now have made contact with Margaret..." He smiled as if he considered the deal as good as done. "We can discuss how to complete this very delicate operation."

"There's still one loose end," I said. "Where are you keeping Oscar and how do we know you will release him?"

Mateo glared at me.

I was glad he was annoyed because I wasn't sure how to answer him about the plutonium. It wasn't like Margaret knew where Felix had hidden it. But, of course, under no circumstances could we let Mateo know that. "Is Oscar here in this house as well?"

"My dear Ruby," Mateo said through pressed teeth. "I consider you and Robert members of my family and treat you with hospitality. You would do well to offer some respect in return." He turned and left the room, and to my surprise the rest of his family followed him, leaving Robert and me to talk on our own. A curious tactic, I thought.

"Robert." I embraced him gently. He looked like his old self, thinner and grayer, but I didn't know what his condition was and didn't want to hurt him. "I'm so sorry. We all thought... We thought you were dead." My voice cracked with that last word, and my eyes filled with tears.

Robert reached for my arms and pushed me away.

My stomach fell. Was he angry? Perhaps he had disowned me. Or all of us.

"Step back, Ruby," Robert said quietly.

Still thinking he wanted nothing to do with me, I numbly did as he asked.

He wheeled over to the far corner of the room that was empty of furniture or books and leaned forward in his wheelchair.

I turned away as the tears started to flow down my cheeks and looked out the window at the trees at the edge of the estate, so pure and untouched. I ached to be outside, away from all this.

"Psst," he whispered.

I turned to look at him and to my amazement, Robert stood from his chair. He looked wobbly, but he stood. Then he took a step toward me and beckoned me to come over.

I ran to him on he balls of my feet.

"It's coming, Ruby," Robert whispered. He was beaming with accomplishment. "About a month ago, I noticed some new feeling in my legs. Now I can actually stand for a while. And, as you see, I'm able to hold my weight."

"Do they know?"

Robert scrunched up his face. "Let's just say I don't advertise it." He glanced up at the cameras in the corners. "But Julia, my nurse, is helping me with a bit of therapy every day. It's not like we hide it from them but they don't know how far my rehab has come."

"Do you think they're worried you might run away?"

Robert chuckled. "I'm not anywhere near ready to make a run for it. I just thought it might make you feel better to know that there's hope for me to someday be back to my old self."

I grinned and threw my arms around his neck. He laughed and hugged me back, which started fresh tears, but I didn't care.

"How did you know I was alive?" he asked.

***

The whole story burbled out of me like water from a spring. I leaned in close and told him about how Renegade had found the photo of him and Margaret; how, when we came to Portland, we weren't able to find them at the physio center. I told him about how Hollinger, Serge and Marcel were working together to keep us out of what they considered government business. I told him that Felix had hidden the shipment and that Margaret didn't know where it was. I told him that both the CIA and CSIS had us on their radar, but that we had no interest in compromising national security and giving weapons to organized crime or radicals who could wreak havoc on the world.

"It seems that neither of us has anything real to bargain with unless the Drakers and our seniors can outwit the authorities, find the plutonium and turn it over to Mateo.

"But of course, that's a lot of 'ifs', and also isn't something anyone wants to do. Also, then if we *did* do it, unless we all went into hiding, we'd all be going to prison for treason or espionage and poor Oscar would probably be killed." I was biting a fingernail and my finger had started to bleed.

Just then, Mateo and his sons came back into the room.

Vince strode up to us. "Now that you and Robert have had a chance to talk…" He grinned as if he'd overheard every word. "… it's time to get your people busy with details." He was holding a cell phone. "Call them and explain."

My blood ran cold. Had he overheard us? Was the room bugged? Robert knew the layout of the place. That was why he'd chosen this corner away from their surveillance cameras. Or so I thought.

I glanced at Robert. "Explain what?" I demanded. "What exactly are you thinking our people will do? You don't think we can just turn over a shipment of dangerous nuclear material to you. Or maybe you don't know plutonium is radioactive and needs very special handling?" I said this part condescendingly. I pushed further, "Which means if anything were to happen, it would be a very delicate exchange." I knew I was playing with fire by saying this.

"You don't need to concern yourself with that," Luciano said. "We have people experienced in handling nuclear material." He kept looking over to his father who alternated between nodding and shaking his head. Interesting, I thought. Like a dog performing tricks for his owner, he was seeking his father's approval. Vince probably did as well. I wondered if Robert knew their dynamic. If he did, he would know how to play it to our advantage.

Luciano handed me the cell phone. "Make the call," he barked.

I took the phone out of his hand and held it. I needed to stall for time. We couldn't make the delivery and once the d'Angelos knew that, it would put Robert, Oscar and me in jeopardy.

"I've already told you," I said. "We're not bargaining with you until Oscar is released. Margaret is the key stakeholder and she will tell you where the storage location is only after everyone is released and safe. That's all we care about. Whatever you do after that is on your conscience."

Vince and Luciano frowned and looked at each other. I could see they were perplexed, which was great.

I handed the phone back to Luciano and smiled sweetly.

We were at an impasse. One of Mateo's cheeks was twitching, and Vince and Luciano looked like they knew they were in trouble with their father. Rosalind would have had some choice words about these insecure little boys in men's bodies who, no matter how they tried, couldn't live up to Daddy's expectations.

I looked over at Robert and noticed the slightest upturn of the corner of his mouth.

"Ruby," Mateo said. "I don't think you understand. Luciano's request was not... optional."

"On the contrary, Mateo," I said more breezily than I felt. "Until we have assurances of Oscar's whereabouts and safety, and the terms of his and our safe release, there will be no phone call." I stood as firmly as did he. "Now I'd like to go relax for a bit. It's been a long and somewhat... awkward day. We can talk again later when you have your end of this bargain arranged."

At first, with the look of threat on his face and by how tightly he clenched his fists, I thought Mateo might hit me. Then his face softened with a different sort of smile, the kind that a parent gives a child when they are proud, even though it was an act, a ruse to disarm me.

Vince and Luciano studied their father but obediently stood by waiting for his next cue.

"Julia," Mateo called.

The same woman in the black pants and blazer was at the door in only a few seconds. She must have been waiting directly outside the study. I wondered if she'd overheard the conversation. I also wondered if she were one of them or a hired servant.

"Would you kindly show Ruby to her room? She would like to rest for a while before dinner." Mateo turned to me and bowed his head respectfully. "We will discuss details tonight, then?" He asked it as if it were a genuine question, but I knew he was already planning something else, though I had no idea if that something else would include a safe release or a quick plan to just kill us.

"That's up to you," I said.

Julia went behind Robert's wheelchair and pushed him into the hallway. I followed, leaving Mateo, Vince and Luciano in the study to brood over their failure to bully me.

Julia pushed the wheelchair to a small lift at the far end of the stairway. She pushed him inside, carefully set the brake on his chair then closed the articulating wire door in front of him.

"You and I will take the stairs and meet him on the second floor," she said to me.

Julia was a sturdy woman, severe, with thick eyebrows and high cheekbones. She was tall, maybe close to the same height as Mateo. Away from her employer, she softened. I detected that Robert liked her and that she liked him, too, although I couldn't determine the extent of that mutual admiration. I recalled his particular fondness for, or perhaps love, that he and Myrtle shared, although what had gone on between them hadn't ever been clear either. It hadn't mattered. What one noticed right away, regardless of the extent, was that love was there. A cutting pain tore through my heart as I thought of her, but I forced the emotion away.

Julia and I climbed the steps quickly so we could help Robert from the lift, but as we reached the top of the stairs, I saw that he had already released himself from the elevator and was rolling his wheelchair along the open stairwell, heading to a wide hallway with doors on either side. We followed him.

Several doors down on the right, Robert stopped. "This is my room," he said. "Julia, I hope Ruby has the room across the hall."

Julia looked dubious. "Francine thought it would be better if Ruby's room were beside hers," she said. She looked gently at Robert and nodded. "I agree that it's better that way. I'll show her where it is."

I wondered if she was worried that Robert and I had something going on. I wished I could tell her that while I adored and admired Robert, he was all hers if she wanted him. I had enough man trouble as it was.

Julia opened Robert's bedroom door and he disappeared inside.

Then I revisited what Julia had said about "Francine's room." I guessed Francine and Mateo slept separately. Perhaps trouble could exist in paradise, too, I snickered to myself.

Julia led me down the hall to the opposite end. We passed uncountable doors on our way. Such a lot of bedrooms. Who occupied them? Did the d'Angelos have other guests as well? I would do some sleuthing once Julia left me alone.

She stopped at the last doorway on the left and opened the door. "You'll find everything you need inside. Make yourself comfortable. Dinner will be at nine." She watched me look around the room before she left.

I laughed at myself for noting that the room was small. Of this entire estate, it seemed like they had given me the closet. Of course, it was enormous by New York standards, but I was feeling petulant. It also had a cute bathroom with a claw-foot tub. The sliding door to a free-standing wardrobe was open so I peeked in and noticed the clothes inside: a dress, a few shirts, and some jeans with the price tags still on. I had been abducted and provided for by so many people. It was like some phantom mother picking out clothes for a child. Did they think I couldn't pick out my own damned clothes? At least these things were nice, though, from Saks even, and there was enough that showed they planned on keeping me for some time.

I went to the polished walnut dresser and just as I expected, the top drawer was filled with what looked like a burgled Victoria's Secret. I picked up a pair of underwear; they were exactly my size and a hundred percent cotton with a lace band, the exact kind I'd always bought before all of this happened. A chill slithered up my neck. Someone was working with them who knew much more about me than they were letting me know. I thought about Robert. Surely, he wouldn't have given them details like this. He'd never seen my underwear. Had he? My skin was crawling. I opened the door to my room a crack and peered out into the hallway. It was empty.

I darted out on my tiptoes, past the open staircase to the other wing, stopping briefly to look back and make sure no one saw me. I continued to Robert's room and whispered his name as I tapped lightly on the door.

He opened it immediately. To my surprise, he was standing. He grabbed me by the arm and pulled me inside, leaving the door slightly ajar. "What took you so long?" he said. He cracked the door just wide enough to poke his head out. "No one saw you?" He pulled his head back in and grinned at me.

"Wow," I said admiringly. "That's amazing! But I don't get it. How does it benefit you to make the d'Angelos think you are incapacitated and stuck in the wheelchair?"

"I have made considerable progress with Julia's help," Robert said. "There's so much I have to bring you up to speed on." He took a cautious and unsteady step then grabbed onto the wall to steady himself. "Sit down, Ruby. You can see I still have a way to go before I can walk normally. But it's getting better every day."

Robert made his way back over to his wheelchair near the window of his room, plopped into it heavily, and let out an exasperated sigh.

"Margaret Warren explained that she had managed to get out of the helicopter alive. She knew Felix was dangerous and after the shootout at the farmhouse, she decided to check out the casualties—or what she'd thought were casualties. When she found out I was alive, she made sure I was well looked after in Kings County, telling them I was her husband.

"As soon as I was released from the hospital, she took me into her Portland apartment and got me the best physio and rehab she could. I was minimally mobile for a long time, and it was months before I could take care of myself. As far as we know, Felix was still alive and well, creating his usual chaos. It seemed for the best to keep my survival a secret, so I continued to let people believe I was dead. I was starting to get some feeling back into my legs, but I still couldn't move them."

He paused and took a deep breath. "One day, several months ago, two men barged into the apartment and took me hostage. It was Vince and his brother. They knew Margaret and Felix had had a son together. She and I didn't understand what was going on, but it came out that they needed her for something. That's when I found out Felix had been killed at Fairhaven and he had left something with Margaret, a sort of insurance policy, or guarantee for the money that the d'Angelos had loaned Felix to carry out his so-called 'accidents.' The d'Angelos, in return, had promised a client of theirs what Felix had promised them. They never said who the client was, but it's likely a Middle East terrorist faction."

"I hope Margaret didn't tell them she doesn't know where Felix stashed the plutonium."

"Of course she didn't. She said she had no idea what they were talking about." He smiled a knowing smile. "But I guess they expected her to deny it. When she didn't change her story, they took me and let her go to make arrangements for the exchange. To keep her motivated, they gave her a convincing reason to cooperate by kidnapping her son—"

"An easy target because he was Felix's right-hand man at the archives," I finished.

Robert nodded. "So you know a good deal of the story. Anyway, I had recently told her about Fairhaven's computer system and the facial recognition program. We had purposefully stayed off the grid to avoid being picked up by the program, as even security footage on the street, or in a store, could give our identities away, but now we wanted to be seen. I explained, if the physio clinic did a promotional news release, Renegade would find us and get involved. So she arranged for the local newspaper to do a story about the clinic. I knew you guys would come. Have you made any progress yet?"

I shrugged and cringed simultaneously. "We were doing OK, but then we ran into a slight complication."

"Hollinger."

"Hollinger knows about the missing plutonium and Felix's deal. He's done everything he can to neutralize our involvement, including trying to hold us at a secure facility in Canada, some cottage on a lake. Very lovely actually. But which we escaped from yesterday. I guess the two Canadian men Hollinger engaged to contain us, Serge and Marcel, notified Hollinger, which was how he intercepted us on the highway yesterday morning…" I paused, thinking. "But now that I say it aloud, I wonder how the d'Angelos knew we got away from the house and where to find us?"

"Who else was at the secure house?"

"Only two housekeepers. And they barely spoke English."

"Could they have been Corsican?" Robert asked, raising an eyebrow high into his forehead.

"They had a thick accent from somewhere I couldn't place, so it's possible, I guess."

He cocked his head. "Rosalind always said, 'You can't trust anyone.' Or how did she put it?"

"Guilty until proven innocent." I squirmed as I felt Rosalind gloating. It would have pleased her that she had left such a strong imprint on the Drakers. Her cautionary, *See, I told you so,* stabbed at me because I'd never picked up on it. But Robert was right. It had to have been our cute sylph-like housekeepers. Who else could have notified Mateo that we were on the loose and available for pickup by their goons?

"I suppose Mateo thinks it's just a matter of intimidating us enough to get Margaret to release the location of the nuclear material."

"Ruby, when Mateo catches on that we don't know, he'll kill us."

"I don't think so," I said. "I suspect he won't kill anyone until he's sure who's dispensable. Any one of us could be his golden goose."

A pang of sadness went through me as I remembered Mom, my real mom, reading me The Brothers Grimm fairy tale.

"He's desperate to finalize the deal," I said. "His buyers must be pressuring him, maybe threatening his family. Anyway, our problem is the national security issue. Hollinger and the Canadian authorities will never allow the transaction to go through. Somehow, the Drakers are going to have to help Margaret find where Felix hid everything and then make it look like the shipment just sort of 'disappeared. ' But I mean, can you imagine if this did work out? And we ended up delivering it to the bad guys? Hollinger is right to be worried. Whoever is after the material wants to not only terrorize the Western world but maybe wipe it out. We really can't let that happen." The grainy image of a mushroom cloud erupting and its apocalyptic aftermath flashed through my head.

"But without the plutonium," Robert said, "Oscar, you and I are dead."

That statement upset Rosalind. *Like hell,* she scolded in my head, *over my dead body!* I rolled my eyes. Hey, Rosalind, you're already dead. *A small complication. No one is going to die. Play on their weakness.*

"Mateo is going to have to release one of us," I said. "I suggest that person be you. You're the best qualified to help Reinhardt and the others. We will bargain with Mateo. And either he does what we say or no deal!"

"Absolutely not. We both go free, or nothing."

"Robert, you're not fully mobile. At least for me, I can wait for an opportunity and make a run for it. Anyway, you knew Felix much better than I did. And I think the d'Angelos find me a valuable commodity." I looked him straight in the eyes. "And if I know you, you haven't let on what you know or how you'd be able to be twelve steps ahead of the situation in your head. Right?"

I must have worn that Rosalind look of determination because Robert put up his hands. "You got me there. They haven't heard much from me."

We decided then that at dinner that night, we'd make the bargain.

***

It was only 4 p.m. when I left Robert's room. My curiosity was getting the better of me. I had told the d'Angelos I needed to rest, but what I really needed was to check out the house.

Instead of heading back to my room, I decided to explore. Press my luck was more like it. I didn't know if I'd run into anyone who might stop me and I didn't care. The more acquainted I became with my surroundings, the more I might be able to find a way to escape.

I tiptoed back to the landing and peered over the railing. No one seemed to be around so I gingerly went downstairs. I listened, but still, no one. It was strange being held hostage with nobody minding me, particularly after such a vigorously attentive kidnapping. Then again, I knew the property would be well-guarded.

I stared at the front door, mere feet away. My heart raced as I considered making a run for it. But then I thought about how that might jeopardize Robert, so I decided to explore the house instead.

I went down the same hallway Julia had led me along earlier, eventually making my way back to the solarium where we'd had lunch. I stepped inside and enjoyed the calmness of the gentle breeze that tickled the indoor tropical plants.

The French doors were open, and I heard voices. I moved closer to see if I could hear better. As I neared the open door, I saw Francine lounging on a chaise and Mateo talking on his cell phone on the patio chair beside her.

"Is Margaret with them?" she heard Mateo ask. "The Drakers must not allow the authorities to interfere. Are the Drakers still there?" He listened to whoever was on the line, looking pensive and running his fingers nervously through his hair. I could tell, he was being updated on the location and circumstances of the other Drakers and probably the seniors. I burned to know who was on the other end of the call. Who was reporting on the Drakers' activity?

Then my heart stopped. Mateo had planted a mole in their midst. Was it Lucy and her companion? Marie? Not wanting to be seen, I slipped quietly back to the hallway to investigate more of the lower level of the mansion.

I took the hallway back to the foyer and entered an elegantly furnished living room. It had a rustic fireplace and was decorated with overstuffed furniture and a large, intricately carved antique table topped by a giant, fresh-flower arrangement. Just beyond was a formal dining area with at least ten chairs surrounding the long, burnished table. There was a door at the far end of the dining room. I walked over and listened. I didn't hear anything on the other side, so I pushed it open.

A stout woman with her wiry hair pulled into a ponytail, and wearing a black and white maid's uniform, was at the sink scrubbing potatoes. Savory smells of roasting meat wafted through the air.

I guess I wasn't discreet enough because she turned toward me. "Come in," she said. Her accent was similar to Lucy and Marie's at the cottage. I guessed Mateo brought in all his own people.

The uncomfortable buzz of suspicion tickled me.

"I make dinner. You like eat now? I make for you. What you hungry for?" She seemed cordial and kind, so I came in.

"I was hoping to get a cup of tea." I beamed a wide smile in her direction and she immediately started pouring water into a kettle.

"I make right away. You like sit in kitchen or I take where you want?"

Suddenly the door behind me flung open and there was Vince, looking strangely at us.

"Therese, I'd like a nice cup of tea myself," he said, staring at my eyes. Then his gaze left my face and traveled down to my chest. It lingered there, a smarmy smile forming on his lips.

What a pig. I went to turn away when Rosalind pinched me. *Stop it, Ruby. His weakness is your strength.* Come on, Rosalind. Seriously? She didn't answer, so I straightened my back and turned fully toward him with my chest stuck out as far as I could. Not like I was that large, but I gave it my all. He must not have seen many girls or had been working with his father and brother for a long time because he sucked in his breath seeing the button on my blouse strain.

"Yes, Mr. Vince. I make for you," Therese said. "Where you like sit?"

"Bring it to the dining room." He was ordering her around like he was the master of the castle.

What a jerk. I glanced in Therese's direction and while she smiled at me, she rolled her eyes after he turned to go back into the dining room. He held the door open for me, grinning like a Cheshire cat, and I followed him to the table where he pulled out a chair for me.

His hand brushed my shoulder and I shuddered, scooting the chair away from him as much as I could.

He was unmoved. He took the chair beside me and pulled up close so I could smell his cloyingly sweet aftershave. "I hope you found your room to your liking." His breath was warm on my face. He looked again down to my breasts.

"The room is fine."

"Excellent," he said.

The kitchen door thumped open as Therese brought in a tray with two steaming cups of tea and a small plate of tea biscuits.

"That will be all, Therese," Vince said, eyeing her until she left the room.

I knew I wasn't trapped, but at the same time, I also knew I had to play by Vince's rules or he might have the power to do something nasty to me. I hoped Therese was on my side just in case he tried anything.

He leaned in, and I picked up my mug of tea and scooted back my chair. "I'm having my tea on the patio," I said. I stood up tall and tried to eye him with disdain the way Rosalind would have.

He probably could have stopped me from going outside, but he just stared at me with his mouth open. It was the same look that had crossed his face when I'd refused to make the phone call. That's when I knew he was far more bark than bite. Still, he was the one who'd had Sean Granger beat up and also who later arranged the explosion of their helicopter.

He nodded and held his arm out in the direction of the hallway as if to say he would go first, and I should follow.

I waited until after he was in the foyer to call out, "I'm going out through the kitchen," before darting into the kitchen to be near Therese.

She was standing at the island. She pointed to the door and motioned that I should go quickly back to the dining room door to see if Vince had returned.

"Thank you," I whispered.

She nodded and fanned with the back of her hand vigorously in the direction of the door that opened out to the patio area.

"You sit with Missus—" she started to say.

"Ruby, we are waiting for you," Vince called.

I went out into the sun where Francine and Mateo were still seated.

"Ah, Ruby," Francine said. "How lovely you're joining us."

Mateo smiled but his eyes betrayed him as he shot dagger looks at his wife. "Come sit here beside me. We can chat."

A shadow moved across the stamped concrete and I felt Vince behind me.

Mateo turned his scowl on his son. "Come, Vince," Mateo hissed through clenched teeth. "I have some business I want to discuss with you in the study."

Vince looked nervously at his mother.

I snickered under my breath as I plunked down in Mateo's chair. Mateo strode back to the French doors that led to the solarium, and Vince following like a puppy who had piddled on the floor.

Therese had also followed me, bringing the tray with the biscuits, a pot of tea, and another cup, setting it on the patio table. She poured a cup for Francine and took it to her lounger, bowed, and returned to the kitchen without saying a word.

"I apologize for Vince," Francine said, not looking at me. "Corsican men think they are so entitled." She frowned in the direction of Mateo and Vince. "I hope he didn't make you feel too uncomfortable."

I shrugged, not wanting to offend her, and she knowingly acknowledged what I didn't say with a disgusted huff, shaking her head from side to side. I decided I wouldn't comment any further. She seemed sympathetic, but I wasn't about to confide in her in case she reported everything back to Mateo.

I looked around the patio and back up to the house. "This is an extraordinary place. Do you live here or in Corsica?" I knew I was pressing my luck, but I figured I had to try to get whatever information from her I could. I didn't want to get Francine in trouble with Mateo in case she revealed something she shouldn't, yet I sensed in her relaxed attitude that she didn't care.

"We live wherever Mateo decides is right for the circumstances. His business at the moment has taken us here. I'm not even sure where here is." She took a sip of her tea, pressed her lips together, then looked at me. "Don't worry about where we are. I would think that Mateo will relocate us shortly." She glanced back to the kitchen door. "And I see you've made friends with Therese." She smiled.

"Well, if you mean that she made me a cup of tea with biscuits, then yes," I said, returning her gentle grin. I wondered if Francine was playing a game with me or whether she was sincere.

"If Vince gives you any problems, Therese will know how to handle the situation," Francine said. "She's more than a good cook and will look out for you." Another strange comment with hidden meaning, I thought.

I felt my face tighten. There was something portentous in her words. "That's good to know," I said, although I didn't exactly know what "looking out for me" meant. I decided not to ask for clarification. Oh, Rosalind, I thought, There are some interesting relationships within this bunch.

Francine must have seen my confusion. "You'll drive yourself crazy trying to figure out the d'Angelo men," she said. "My sons think they're like their father, but Mateo keeps them in line by sending them mixed messages." Francine got up from her lounge chair and joined me at the patio table. She put her hand on my arm. "You see, they all rather like women. So let me warn you, it's purely lust, nothing to do with affection, admiration or bearing any honorable motivation. Lust. That's all."

She took a biscuit from the tray, shaking her shoulder-length blonde hair out in the breeze, then sat up and looked out over the broad expanse of grass to the evergreens bordering the property.

I followed her gaze. In the distance, I made out some barbed wire fencing interlaced in the trees. I hadn't noticed it until now.

"We all have our prisons," she said. "I often wonder if they are to keep our enemies out or to keep the criminals in." Her voice had undertones of deep-seated resentment. "For some of us, money comes at the expense of happiness." She turned and looked at me.

Therese leaned out of the kitchen door. "Missus, Monsieur d'Angelo say you come inside."

"Excuse me, my dear," Francine said. She sighed. Francine stood and walked slowly to the solarium door. She hesitated then disappeared inside.

Left alone, I wondered if I dare venture into the trees to explore the fence-line up close, but this place was humid and there were probably snakes or lizards or something slithery in there. Of course, not that there weren't vipers of another kind inside. I got up and followed Francine.

***

I had already explored most of the main floor but I wondered what I'd be able to see into the trees from upstairs. As I went back up, I tried to look like I was just going to my room.

The second floor branched off into two wings. I figured at least one of the rooms would afford a view. Since I couldn't go into each room to check it out, I thought I'd ask Robert to see if he knew something.

I went back to his room and knocked softly. "Robert," I whispered into the doorjamb.

I waited, but he didn't answer. I turned the handle, and with a soft click, the door opened, and I slipped inside. He was gone. His wheelchair was beside his bed. I hurried to his window, but his room looked out over the patio. I could see a portion of the fencing from up here more clearly, and I guessed it probably encircled the house and would make escape far less possible. I started to know what zoo animals felt like with all these fences. I turned around. Where was Robert? And without his chair?

I left Robert's room, stepping as lightly as I could. The upstairs hallway in the east wing was dim in the afternoon light and tomb quiet.

My nerves were jangled as I crept to the landing and stood at the balusters that opened to the foyer.

I didn't see or hear anyone below in the foyer. Again, I felt like I was alone in the house, but naturally, I knew better. I wondered why the d'Angelos wanted to make it seem like such liberal imprisonment. What was their tactic?

Not sure where to explore next, I continued back to my room past double doors on the left of the west wing hall.

As I got closer, I heard moans and thumping.

I cringed. It might have been sweet if only Francine hadn't been so reluctant to go in. She must have known what he wanted. I wondered what made him desire her mid-afternoon with a strange girl in their midst. That thought made me freeze all over. I didn't want to think what I was thinking. I also knew Francine had had the same thought.

I darted past to the end of the hallway where my room was. I was about to go in when I heard a noise from inside. Someone was in my room. A shiver of revulsion ran down my back at the thought that Vince might be in there waiting for me. I wished I had my gun. But whatever. I could take him down. He was big, but he also looked like the only weights he lifted were cannolis.

I wouldn't have been able to cower behind fear anyway. Rosalind was pulling me forward. She would never let me run from confronting someone who threatened me.

I turned the door handle, and when I thrust open the door, I burst into a nervous laugh. "Robert!" I exclaimed. "What are you doing here? You walked here?"

Robert's shocked face turned into a relieved smile. He put down the crystal vase he was holding. I guessed he was ready to clobber me if it had been Vince coming in.

"I had more to tell you," Robert said, looking down impishly. "And, I needed the exercise. The more walking I can do the better. Where did you go?"

"I went to the kitchen to get some tea. Vince followed me," I said, rolling my eyes and looking grim.

"I hope you made it clear that you don't appreciate his company." His words were light, but he looked concerned. I could see he knew what Vince was capable of.

"I did and now the cook and his mother also know he's trolling. I get the feeling they're on my side in all of this, weirdly."

Robert chortled. "That guy doesn't get subtlety. Next time, I hope you discourage him with a bit more persuasion. Like a knee to his manhood." His voice dripped with sarcasm. "That guy is a complete creep." He started to laugh but then his leg gave out. He caught himself on the dresser and steadied himself over to the bed where he plopped down awkwardly.

I positioned myself on the chair across and waited for him to get comfortable. "You said you had something else you wanted to tell me?"

Robert smiled slyly and leaned forward. "I think I know where Felix might have concealed the plutonium he stole."

I glanced at him with wide eyes before looking pointedly at the ceiling. I couldn't understand how Robert felt so comfortable speaking freely when the room could've been bugged.

"Oh, you don't have to worry about that," Robert said. "That's what I was doing when you came in. My room is clear, too. They're arrogant and think that with three hostages they're sure to get what they want, so they didn't bother rigging the house. If you can believe it." He chuckled. "A very novice move."

I grinned. Robert was still the same ingenious person he had always been. A near miss with death and now challenged with a disability and he was still more than able to think three steps ahead of everyone else.

"Well, I also think Margaret knows but isn't telling anyone because Hollinger is watching her," I said. "The real problem will be getting Oscar and executing that release to Mateo without the CIA or CSIS interfering. Hollinger will do everything he can to stop that from happening even if it means our lives." I sighed.

"Ruby, we're not delivering anything. Of course, we want Oscar back, and I'd be very happy to get out of here, for the most part." He blushed and cleared his throat. "But we have to find a way to make it look like we're handing over the real materials when, in fact, they're fakes."

"I don't think Margaret would agree with you about trying to pull a fast one on the d'Angelos. Her son's life depends on it."

Robert wagged his finger at me. "You underestimate Margaret. There's much, much more to her than she lets on."

"But Robert. She's a hopeless alcoholic…" I knew as soon as I said it, it wasn't true. We'd been played. I felt bad for sounding so full of judgment.

"Alcoholic, yes. But hopeless, definitely not." He could see I was questioning my judgment.

I blushed. Rosalind had trained me to know better. At that moment I felt ashamed. Weak. Vulnerable.

"Last summer, when Felix abducted you in Springfield, Margaret had been watching the farmhouse the entire time," Robert explained. "Afterwards, during the cleanup at the murder scene, she posed as a paramedic rescue worker. She realized that the rest of you had escaped, and she arranged my falsified death certificate. She is the one who had me moved to a trauma hospital in upstate New York under an alias and stayed by my side night and day until I recovered enough to be discharged into her care. She was also the one who concocted that newsworthy story about the physio center in Portland, and contacted all the media outlets until she got it picked up, knowing Renegade would get it on your computers, and the facial rec would ID me." He shook his head. "Drinks too much? Definitely. But not at all hopeless."

"But why did you wait so long to let us find you? It's been a year, and—"

"Ruby, don't."

I was getting upset, and he put out his hand to calm me.

"Listen. I was in critical condition in the hospital for a very long time. It wasn't until months later, when we found out that Felix had been killed, that things started to happen. When Margaret learned that Felix had implicated her in the delivery of nuclear material, we had a decision to make. We had no intention of honoring Felix's deal with the mafia. But then when Oscar was kidnapped, it changed everything."

"So Margaret told Hollinger? I was shocked that two former CIA agents would even consider the possibility. But then when family was involved, that changed everything. Hollinger would have no qualms about sacrificing Oscar in the name of national security. Between the buzzing in my head and the incredible details Robert was disclosing, my agitation rose to the point where I had to stand up and pace.

I walked over to the bureau and poured myself a glass of water from the carafe there, though I figured if ever there were a time to drink something stronger, now would be it. I suddenly realized Margaret's compulsion to numb herself. So much tension over time from every single decision you make having significant consequences would wear a person down mentally and physically.

"No, she didn't tell him directly," Robert said. "That would have been too risky. Organized crime has connections everywhere. But we led him to the right conclusion by letting him find out about a possible threat, starting with Oscar's kidnapping. But Hollinger, while sometimes careless, is also clever, and we knew he'd eventually put one and one together. Sorry, we're the ones who tipped him off that the Drakers had chartered a plane into Westgate. He doesn't know specific details, only that Felix may have stolen some hot material."

"Does Hollinger know you're alive?"

"Probably. They also monitor all the newspapers."

"And how did the d'Angelos find out about you?"

"Mateo has connections, and they did some snooping. Before Margaret and I caught on as to what was going on, they found us in Portland. It was probably after the news article was published. Things started to get very intense after that. We noticed men following us. Margaret and I tried to evade them by moving to another remote location, but a few days after we settled into a new apartment, two men barged in, knocked Margaret unconscious, and took me captive. Now here I am."

He looked defeated. Had Robert been able-bodied that would never have happened. He sat still and disheartened, his fists clenched, and his lips pulled thin and tight as he hung his head.

"It was kind of stupid of them to kidnap me too," I said. "But if you and Margaret didn't tell him about the nuclear material, how did Hollinger know? He already knew about it by the time we arrived at Westport. He wanted us to stay out of it. Said it was a matter of national security. He told Reinhardt to get us back to Fairhaven."

"I know Margaret didn't tell Hollinger initially, but she must have gotten him involved after they took me. She probably didn't know what else to do."

"You say you know where Felix stashed the plutonium?" I asked.

"Plutonium has to be stored in a very particular environment. There are only a few places that are not government secure spots. I'm sure that once we start in with our research, we will find it."

"But you can't do that from here." It occurred to me that for him to work his magic, he'd have to get out of here. I had inadvertently set up that negotiation earlier that day. Later at dinner, Robert and I would have to carefully control Mateo's desire to dominate. I guessed that he was under extreme pressure from his clients to make the delivery. We would use his desperation to our advantage.

"I'm sorry, Ruby. You have to remain a hostage. I'm the only one who can find the plutonium. And I doubt they'll remain here after they release me back to Margaret."

"We have to make the release look like Hollinger isn't in the picture. Any ideas on how we do that?"

"It would be best if the authorities are blindsided on this for now," Robert said. "I will convince them to drop me off at a neutral location, and you notify Reinhardt only. He'll know what to do."

"Hollinger and Serge will be watching them." I was feeling even more frustrated. "I need a phone. Then I could send Renegade a coded message so he can notify Reinhardt. Renegade can set up a ploy to steer the Feds off track and then you can join Margaret and our group to do what you have to. A little extra help with details will make it easier." I couldn't help but grin. "Tonight at dinner, I might have to absent-mindedly put someone's phone in my pocket," I said.

Robert grinned, too, then got up to go back to his room. After our conversation, he seemed to have renewed energy.

He reached for his cane and started for the door, leaving me with lots to think about. I would have to carefully consider our strategy.

Fifteen

I STRETCHED OUT ON THE PLUSH BED and wondered what progress the Drakers were making in their search for me. I found it entirely creepy that Felix could reach out from the afterlife to continue to menace the people of the country he once promised to serve. The thought of putting such dangerous material into the hands of our hosts whose only motive was to sell it to terrorists was tearing me apart. I had no way to contact Reinhardt. Further, even if I could nab someone's cell phone, I couldn't be sure to delete the call from the recent calls stored on the phone. It went without saying that the d'Angelos couldn't know we were working with the authorities, even though it wasn't by choice. I considered Therese. Would she have a cell phone? I wondered if she were sympathetic enough to let me make a secret call. She had to know her employers were despicable people. Well, I had to laugh at that. Case in point: both their guests were hostages. My head spun with thoughts, not only mine, but those of the party of influencers I had stored inside. Come on, Rosalind. How are we going to pull this off?' But she didn't answer. Maybe she didn't know either.

I stared at the ceiling and tried to calm myself but failed miserably. I was jittery with the agitation of planning an escape, or at a minimum, a release for Robert. Mateo was not a man to be pushed too far, yet I knew that to have any bargaining power at all, I would have to push his buttons to the very edge of what he would tolerate.

I decided, since lying still in the middle of the day only made me feel more agitated, and it was still hours before the evening meal when Mateo said "we would discuss the matter further," that I would get some fresh air. A walk would help me figure out how to get a message to Reinhardt. I wasn't even sure how I'd word those instructions in a message. No matter how I practiced it in my head the message seemed ludicrous. *Deliver the plutonium for Oscar's release and also rescue Robert and me.* I knew they were already working on it.

I wasn't stupid and Mateo knew it. It was only lip service that he talked about honoring his end of the deal. We all knew he'd kill me. The room around me suddenly felt oppressive. I got up to go to the outdoor patio. Perhaps Francine would be there again, and I could subtly quiz her on what made Mateo tick. Could I find out what might throw him off his game or maybe even make him cooperative?

At the bottom of the staircase, I saw the front door was open a foot or so as if someone were taunting me. I certainly was curious. No one was around—or at least that I could see—and it stood to reason I would have liked to see what was outside this house, especially with the opportunity presenting itself like this. I was equally curious to know why they were baiting me into going outside. I hadn't seen any fencing or security people when we arrived earlier. I'd been feigning more confidence than I felt, and as I gripped the door to open it further, my hand shook.

I was hit by a gust of wind as I stepped out onto the polished cement landing of the roofed portico. Parked in the driveway, where I'd been delivered by golf cart from the private airstrip, was a black limousine with its engine running and a uniformed driver behind the wheel.

I didn't see his eyes in the rearview mirror, but as soon as I appeared, he got out and went around to the back door of the car.

Shit, I thought, I'm supposed to get in? Where are they taking me now?

I felt someone behind me.

"What are you doing out here?" Vince demanded. "Listen, girl, just because we're allowing you your freedom in the house doesn't mean you get to leave." A hungry grin emerged on his face. His expression, his posture, his whole demeanor made me cringe. He was looking at my breasts again. At that moment, I would have rather encountered a real snake.

"I heard a car engine running and wondered what was going on," I said. I stared into his doughy face. "And, just so you know, I'd love to leave here and so would Robert."

He scowled then recovered. "Terms that can be discussed at dinner tonight." He flapped his hand and stared at me for a few seconds, perhaps looking for a reaction, and when I didn't give him one, he walked over to the limo. "I have some errands to run. Sorry, you are unable to join me, Ruby." He sniffed haughtily before getting into the back seat. The chauffeur closed his door.

The sound of my name on his lips made me want to vomit. I watched with repulsion as the car drove down the long drive to a gate, waited for it to open, then disappear down the road. The gate closed and watching it, I had confirmation that just like at the cottage, we were completely imprisoned here. I was furious.

I went back inside, slamming the door behind me. In the aftermath, I heard a buzzing sound. Either Rosalind was trying to get my attention, or the noise was real. It was coming from outside.

I waited, trying to place it, then when I recognized what it was, I tore open the door again.

The wind tossed my hair over my face, but I rushed out blindly onto the landing. I couldn't see the sky from beneath the portico roof, so I took a risk and went down the steps onto the driveway and followed the sound away from the house.

From out here, the sound ebbed and flowed and was less a buzz than a throaty hum. I peered into the sky, searching for what I hoped it was. It got louder, and then I recognized it. It was a drone. The same kind the

Drakers had used to locate me at the farmhouse in Springfield the previous summer after I had been abducted by Felix and Christian. I walked down the driveway, getting further and further away from the house. I worried that something bad would happen to me for straying so far, but no one came after me. I couldn't see the drone, but that didn't matter. I knew I'd been found, and my heart soared. I was delighted to be out in the open so the camera could get a good view. I turned around with my face to the sky.

Of course, soon, I wasn't the only one who'd heard it. A guard patrolling the area around the gate also had his face to the sky and a cell phone to his ear, probably notifying one of the d'Angelos. His eyes were fixed upward, but I still wondered if he had spotted me. I quickly darted back to the house. I needed to let Robert know.

I accidentally let the door bang behind me. Hoping no one had heard, I made for the stairs to race up to Robert's bedroom, but someone from the living room called to me.

"Ruby, come here."

I cringed.

It was a woman, but not Francine.

I detoured into the spacious room and there was Julia, standing behind Robert in his wheelchair. He looked knowingly at me, signaling with his eyes to "say nothing."

Julia looked at me inquisitively. "What were you doing outside?"

I couldn't tell if she was concerned or scolding, but based on Robert's face, I decided that the less she knew the better. "Just seeing Vince off," I said breezily as if Vince and I were tight.

The side of her mouth turned up in disapproval. *She's jealous,* Rosalind quipped. I understood now. Robert may have had feelings for her, but she had feelings for Vince.

"Robert wanted some coffee," she said brightly. "Care to join us?" She didn't wait for me to answer but continued through the door to the kitchen. I knew I was supposed to follow.

A delicate aroma of vanilla wafted through the kitchen. Therese was pulling trays from the wall oven. She smiled widely when she noticed Robert.

I studied Robert in his wheelchair. Seeing his solid, tall body crunched down in the chair looked so unnatural for him.

Therese placed the baking pan on a wooden platform on the counter and turned her attention directly to him as if Julia and I weren't even there.

"Meester Robert, you like something to eat?" She bent down and laid her hand on his arm.

"Would you be kind enough to make us some coffee, please?" His smile back at her said it all. They had become friends. Then again, why wouldn't she like him? He had a way of endearing himself to people. Or maybe Therese generally felt sorry for any seemingly normal sympathetic people brought into this unusual household and put in vulnerable positions. She went to the elegant espresso machine in the corner.

"We will have it on the patio, Therese," Julia said. My whole body tensed up. If we went out there, she might hear the drone if it did another fly by.

"Do you know," I said, "it's very windy out there? I got so much dust in my eyes earlier! Why don't we have our coffee in the dining room?"

Julia narrowed her eyes into a nasty stare. She didn't like my taking charge.

Robert noticed and turned to her with the same disarming smile he'd used on Therese. "Actually," Robert said, "if you don't mind, Julia, I'd prefer the dining room as well. I do have quite the dust allergy."

Julia's sneer softened. "Of course, Robert. Allergies are distressing, aren't they?"

I stared at Therese, the keeper of the house, and then at Robert's nurse. She seemed to have a complicated personality. I sensed that she liked to be in charge, but I also sensed that she liked the attention of men. *Love-starved bitch,* Rosalind warned. *Watch out for her, Ruby.*

"Oh, yes, I make it nice for you on dining table." She scurried around assembling accouterments on a serving tray and took everything to the dining room. We followed her. She removed a chair at the head of the table to accommodate Robert's wheelchair. It warmed my heart to see her fuss over him. She carefully pushed Robert's wheelchair to the table then returned to the kitchen and reappeared a few minutes later with a silver pot from which she poured rich pungent espresso into the tiny white cups.

As Julia surveyed the proceedings, and me, I sensed she was uncomfortable with my being there. I didn't know what her problem was, but I suspected she would have had a problem with any woman coming into the house. She was stern-faced and drawn, with thin, pale lips and her hair pulled severely into a low ponytail. I felt sorry for her. She was probably put into the position of having to be both warden and nurse, roles that were diametrically opposed. Even though I knew she was good to Robert, she was also very clearly on the side of the d'Angelos.

The three of us sat silently, the energy among us prickly at best.

"Julia has been a great help to me with my therapy," Robert effused to me. "If it weren't for her, I wouldn't be able to stand."

"You could make so much more progress if we had the proper facilities and equipment," Julia said. She looked at him with genuine sympathy and reached for his hand.

"Oh, so you're a registered therapist?" I tried to keep the conversation going to ensure we were talking over any hum from the drone. "That's exciting work. Where did you study? Your English is—"

"Do you think he'd have made such progress if I weren't?" she snapped.

Ha, I thought. Score one for Julia. If that was her real name. "Of course," I demurred. I could see there was no point in asking how she ended up being a domestic/therapist for a mafia boss, answering doors and serving her employers if she were such a qualified therapist. I smiled sweetly at her and took a deep breath, needing for us to keep talking.

Robert caught my eye and flashed me a *cool it*. "Well—"

"I have to attend to something," interrupted Julia. "I assume you can help Robert back to his room when he needs rest?"

I nodded and she went out.

I started to explain and apologize, but Robert put his finger to his lips and motioned with his head to the patio. He'd said the place wasn't bugged, but I wondered if there were a listening device in the dining room. I looked at him for an explanation, but he was already maneuvering his wheelchair through the kitchen to the back patio doors outside and further to an enclosed gazebo.

I got up and followed.

"So what were you doing outside the front door?" Robert asked when we were outside.

"Reinhardt's found us," I whispered.

Robert looked back at the house to see if anyone was watching us, gripped the railed side of the gazebo, and stood from his chair to stretch and steal a look at the sky.

"I saw a drone scouting the property," I said. "It sounded just like the one you guys used last summer at the farmhouse. I'll never forget the noise it made. Did you hear it from inside the house?"

"No," Robert answered, "but they have more than enough security around here and cameras at every corner of the compound. And unless their security detail is a bunch of incompetents, which I doubt, then you weren't the only one who noticed it. We should assume that by now Mateo has been alerted to the fact that he's been found."

"What will he do with us?"

"I'd guess he's making air transport arrangements as we speak." He looked resigned.

"But that won't give me time to bargain with him for your release," I said. "Also, Vince went out. Not like he'd leave without him."

"Mateo would sell his soul to the devil and then double-cross him. Don't ever attach emotion to him or underestimate him, Ruby. Let me put it to you like this: in comparison, Felix was an amateur."

"Then I don't understand his approach. Letting us roam around freely, even leaving the front door open, calling us 'family members.' I don't get it."

"There's only one reason he's being so magnanimous. If he doesn't deliver, he will have to deal with someone even more ruthless who wouldn't blink before killing Mateo, his wife and his entire family. Ruby, he knows the danger he's in, and that's why he is so determined to get the plutonium. He took a few steps as if to pace, out of habit, but he had to grab the rail for support.

"How much time do you think we have?"

"Maybe an hour."

"Then I have to go talk with him right now. Now or never. Where can I find him? I never see him around the house."

"I'd try his study where we were earlier," Robert said. "But I'm going with you." He lowered himself back into his wheelchair.

I slid in behind and pushed him toward the house.

The door to Mateo's study was closed, and we heard voices from inside. We listened for a few moments. It sounded like Luciano. Mateo was on a phone call talking in what I guessed was Corsican, but then after a pause, he yelled, "Get here within the hour," in English, and hung up.

I looked at Robert. He was right. We were going to be moved to another location. I didn't bother to knock but just flung the door open.

Mateo looked up smoothly, not at all surprised to see us. He looked at Luciano and held up his hand for him to do nothing.

We paused and waited to see who would speak first.

"We are arranging a... Shall we call it a vacation?" He snickered at us like we had been duped. "Which means our dinner discussion will take place elsewhere."

"I'm sorry," I said as firmly as I could, "but if you want my cooperation, that conversation will have to take place right now." I folded my arms over my chest, raised my chin, and drilled my eyes into his.

"My dear Ruby, you don't understand. You have no say in this."

"Suit yourself, but if we don't talk now, the plutonium Felix owes you is as good as lost." I started to wheel Robert out of the room.

"Do you think you can threaten me like a child?" Mateo screamed, waving his fist.

Bingo. I had to force myself not to smile. I'd hit a nerve. One that unsettled him and made him feel vulnerable. And one that put me in control. He was desperate. He knew I understood his arrangement more than he wanted me to. Fury sparked from his eyes.

I smiled sweetly. "Felix's deal with you has nothing to do with either me or Robert. If you want our help, then it will be on our terms."

Mateo grunted and moved to the back of his desk and sat down, trying to regain his authority. A tactical error on his part, I thought. I knew from school that physical proximity in a power situation had a good deal to do with who held the dominant position.

When he had to look up at me, I bit my lip to force my face to stay serious. I calmly moved to the front of his desk and peered down at him. He laced his fingers together and placed them almost as if in prayer on the desk.

"Are you ready to negotiate?" I asked.

Mateo slammed his hands on the desk and shot up from his chair.

He came up so close to my face, I could smell the Cognac on his breath. Rosalind was gloating. *He's off-balance, Ruby. You have the upper hand.* She was right. I wasn't about to let him intimidate me. I took a step back and glanced back and forth between Mateo and Luciano who had moved in closer, as if to defend his father.

"I am listening," he said.

I stood firm and waited for them both to calm down. "Here's the problem. Margaret is under surveillance by the authorities. She is high on the terrorist watch list. That means her ability to get the materials to you is limited. If the CIA even suspects that she is about to turn over nuclear material to insurgents, they will arrest her immediately and nobody gets anything. So you see, that to comply with your demands, she would be not only compromising herself, but also compromising the entire exchange. Of course, it is unfortunate that she is the only one who knows the exact storage location where Felix has hidden the materials. However…" I paused to smile winningly again. "As you know, Robert is a close friend and ally of hers. She trusts him. Also, Robert has the wherewithal to arrange the transfer. Of course, he wouldn't be able to do that from here. So to make sure all parties get what they need, I propose that you somehow make it look like he escaped. I believe it's the only way you'll be able to complete the deal."

At that, Mateo barked out a nervous laugh. He looked dubiously at Luciano and shook his head. Luciano was incredulous. I don't believe that he had ever encountered anyone who would dare stand up to his father. I had to admit, I was loving my position of power, towering over two extremely dangerous men who seemed to be buying my suggestion.

"So," Mateo said, "let me understand your reasoning. Either I release Robert or what happens?" He sat back down in his leather chair to stare me down.

I pretended to look concerned. "Oh, well, then, you wouldn't get your plutonium and your customers… might give you a bad delivery review on Google." I smirked to unsettle him again.

He drummed his fingers on the polished mahogany before throwing me another question. "And in such a situation, what makes you think that your safety wouldn't be jeopardized?"

"I'm fully aware of our tenuous circumstances, Mateo," I said. "But I would imagine, if you don't honor your customer's orders, the consequences for you and your family would be the same." I paused. "It does seem as if we're all in the same boat."

Just then, Julia burst into the study and started to say something until she noticed the expression on Mateo and Luciano's faces. When she noticed me and Robert, she looked shocked.

"What is it, Julia?" Mateo asked without looking at her.

"The plane is here."

Mateo nodded and waved her away. He stood and began pacing. "Luciano, it's time to leave. Get your mother."

"But Vince has not returned yet," Luciano said. He seemed uncomfortable, but I could see he didn't want to contradict his father.

"Now," Mateo shouted.

Luciano ran to the door.

"Both of you will come with me," he said to me and Robert.

I wheeled Robert out of the study and out the front door.

Julia left the two golf carts where she'd been standing to help me with Robert's chair. Together, we got him down and into one of the carts, and she went around and sat beside him.

In the distance, I heard the buzz of a small jet engine.

Luciano. and Francine with only her Fendi handbag. came down the steps and hopped into the first cart. Luciano glanced back at his father before taking off in the direction of the plane.

"Get in," Mateo shouted, pointing a gun at me.

I could see he wasn't going to honor my request to let Robert go before we were relocated. I looked back at Robert and then at Mateo in the driver's seat before getting in beside him.

He gunned the cart after his son.

Just then, a series of gunshots erupted from the entry gate.

A black SUV drove through the gate and was speeding right for us.

It didn't matter. Luciano had already helped his mother onto the plane and Mateo had just pulled up to the plane stairs. With his free hand, Mateo grabbed my arm and handed me off to Luciano who pulled me forcefully up the steps, and at the top, shoved me into the plane.

I landed sprawled out on my front on the plush cream carpet.

Mateo then scrambled up the narrow steps behind me.

Luciano looked back out at the golf carts. "What about Robert," he yelled over the noise of the engines.

"Leave him," Mateo said. "Get in and seal the door."

Luciano dutifully complied. The plane started moving and within seconds we were in the air.

I looked out the window and saw the golf cart with Julia and Robert still sitting in the back row, Robert waving to me and getting smaller and smaller as the black SUV reached him.

I recognized Ransom and Reinhardt leaping out of the SUV and running to Robert.

How I wished I could have been with them for the happy reunion.

Sixteen

I watched out of the window until the ground disappeared and was replaced by a barren white cloudscape. I sat back in my seat trying hard to look bored. My stomach bore the same knot it had when Reinhardt and Rose had—what I'd thought at the time—abducted me and whisked me away on their private charter. Back then I didn't know they were saving my life. I was drugged and frightened, but the memory was still strong. I'd just had surgery to change my face and we'd had to flee the plastic surgery clinic because Felix's hit men had found me. I hadn't understood anything that was happening, and the Drakers weren't in a position to explain. This time, however, I knew exactly what my circumstances were. This time I was a hostage. I held to the hope that Reinhardt and Robert would come through, and if not, then I was at least happy Robert was no longer in danger.

Then it occurred to me that if they did come through, that would mean that terrible nuclear materials would be surrendered to terrorists who would probably do unspeakable things to the world. Rosalind in my head was no help either. *Even if they get the materials, they could kill you,* she hissed, her familiar sarcasm elbowing me. Thanks, Rosalind, I thought. Super helpful. *Just saying the way it is.*

I wanted to hug my knees to my chest and shut out the world, but of course, I couldn't let myself do that, so I settled back into my seat.

Seated beside me, Francine must have sensed my tension because, without prompting or conversation, she reached over and put her hand on mine. Had she been through this before? Probably. She was a victim, too, though her circumstances were different. She was the wife of a notorious crime lord, and whose job it was to bear him sons who would carry on that legacy, having been forced into a lonely life of gated estates and illegal activity. Her only crime was being associated with the man by marriage. She would have to live this hell for the rest of her life. I did sort of wonder whether she was playing me, but the sadness in her eyes was too distinct for that to be possible.

There was nothing I could do but sit back and wait and see what would happen next. I couldn't have asked for a better outcome. Robert was safe now, back with the Drakers who would have managed to make it out of the compound, unscathed, if I knew them. I missed them all so much. And I didn't want to admit it, but when I saw Reinhardt and Ransom run for Robert, I longed for Ransom in a way that was not helpful to anyone. Fortunately, while he might not have wanted me in the way I wanted him, he was a Draker, and he wanted me back as much as the others did. I was sure they would already be busy formulating another plan to get me and Oscar released. The question was, would Mateo honor his end of the bargain? I recalled Robert's words: "Mateo would double-cross the devil." A shiver ran down my back.

Mateo sat like a king in his leather seat, facing us. He poured himself a drink from the crystal decanter at his side. Leaning back comfortably to savor his Cognac, he appeared calm and relaxed, all traces of his earlier stress gone. He looked at me for a long time as if to assess my reaction to being stared at. I was amazed he would do this in full view of his wife.

His arrogance bolstered my poise. I felt indignant on her behalf. "Where are we going?"

"Somewhere you cannot be found." Mateo raised his glass to me in a toast.

I wanted to slap that smug look off his face. He seemed to delight in taunting me with the uncertainty of what might happen to me. He took another sip of his Cognac and smiled at Francine, waving his snifter at her to give her permission to speak.

"You will like Corsica," Francine said. "Our villa there is beautiful this time of year." Her voice was gentle and her smile genuine. She spoke as though I were a guest of hers.

She seemed to like me, and perhaps I offered her some company from a place that only offered isolation to her. But I didn't know. I was making assumptions based on her emotional cues. I nodded and sat back, my mind a cacophony of questions.

Luciano had positioned himself as a co-pilot in the cockpit. He and his father had a truly interesting relationship. While I could see that he resented his position as second in line to the dynasty, he acquiesced to all his father's wishes. I chuckled inwardly. He was probably delighted to leave his brother behind to fend for himself—or quite possibly be killed by authorities so he would be first in line for the throne.

I wanted to better understand the power struggle between Mateo's sons. I knew it would help me if I could play each of them off the others' weaknesses. *That's my girl,* Rosalind said.

About forty minutes into the flight, my ears started to pop, and I realized we were descending. It made sense. The plane was probably too small to go nonstop to Corsica. But I then realized, with excitement, that this meant we would have to change planes. My heart leaped at the thought of the Drakers intercepting me once we were on the ground. I sat up. I needed to be ready in case the Drakers were there to ambush Mateo.

Don't be silly, Ruby, Rosalind scolded me. Of course. She was right. Reinhardt and the others would have needed to be in the air minutes after we took flight. I was stupid for letting myself hope. I blinked back tears and took deep breaths, trying not to appear upset. If Mateo was taking me to Corsica, I just had to accept the fact that the only thing I had now was me. I had to be ready in case an opportunity presented itself for me to escape.

The jet landed with a violent jolt. Mateo turned to the cockpit and cursed wildly at the pilot and then yelled at Luciano. He finally calmed down enough to demand, "Is everything set up here at the airport?"

"The transatlantic charter should be fueled and ready for takeoff as soon as we arrive," Luciano said. The scowling look that he directed back at his father showed his displeasure at the way Mateo was talking to him, shouting orders at him like he was the hired help.

Ten minutes later, the four of us deplaned and walked to a private lounge inside the terminal. Two men dressed in navy pants and jackets, white shirts and blue ties approached Mateo as we neared the door of the lounge beneath a sign that said, Welcome to St. John's, Newfoundland.

I almost laughed. We'd gone back up to Canada! He greeted them perfunctorily and walked off with them, maybe to look after some details.

When we got inside, Francine and Luciano took the comfortable chairs, leaving me to perch in a peeling vinyl chair by the window. No one spoke while we waited. I wondered how long we would be in this room while we prepared to board our next flight. I noted the layout of the room and kept my eyes on the exits. I got up and poured a cup of watery coffee from the tureen on a side table, then leaned against the table to look out the giant window that overlooked the airfield where a Challenger 600 Series sat a distance away from the terminal.

I shook my head. I missed the days when I didn't know a single damned thing about the model types of private planes. It was parked far away from the building enough so we'd be very exposed as we walked to it. An opportunity maybe? No, it wasn't. I had to stop thinking that.

I sat down and sipped the terrible coffee, feeling abandoned and forlorn. Mateo was taking a long time. I hoped the delay meant he had run into some issues with passports or something. I chuckled under my breath, delighted that things were not progressing as he had planned.

Not like it mattered. We weren't going anywhere without him.

The door opened and a cleaner entered the lounge, pushing a cart with supplies. Her uniform was wrinkled, and her gray hair hung limply over her dark-rimmed glasses. She casually wiped a few surfaces, stopping in front of me to reach over to the table where the coffee was set up. She hit my foot and stumbled, grabbing the arms of my chair to prevent herself from falling right on top of me. I reached out to grab her arms before she flattened me, looking right up at her face. I gasped.

She leaned in closer and I felt her place a hard rectangular object into my jacket pocket.

"Ay, almost squat ya dere, my love," she said and winked.

My eyes bulged as I looked at her face again. She was barely recognizable in her realistic disguise, and I had no idea what she'd said, but my heart leaped inside my chest. It was Hannah. My Drakers must have known somehow that the d'Angelos had ordered a chartered plane, and that it was going to fly out of St. John's. Hannah, always a master of disguise and a perfect sleuth, had inconspicuously managed to plop a cell phone in my pocket.

Luciano strode over to us. "Get out of here, you clumsy woman," he said. He grabbed her roughly by the arm, pulled her off of me, and shoved her back against the door.

She apologized again, then disappeared through the lounge door.

Luciano's mood was foul. I wondered if he'd done something wrong and that was why we were stuck here. He was probably anticipating his father's fury. He looked at me as if the entire incident were my fault. I shrugged, but he kept looking at me as if wondering something.

He continued to stare at me to the point where I began to feel very uncomfortable.

"I'm OK," I said, trying to get him away from me. The phone felt heavy in my pocket and I was anxious to look at it. I knew there would be a message. "I'm going to the ladies' room."

He grunted and shuffled ahead of me to the women's bathroom and pushed open the door to inspect it. Once he saw it was small and windowless, he grunted and walked back toward his mother. I went in, sneering when I knew he couldn't see me, and locked the door behind me.

I reached into my pocket and pulled out the phone. I swiped my finger across the screen and opened the top message.

As I suspected, it was from Hannah: *Make an excuse and stay back in the passenger carrier. We'll do the rest.*

I resisted yelping with happiness. It was a great plan: of course, they would drive us to the plane rather than make us walk, and that's when the Drakers would intercept me.

I returned the phone to my pocket, used the toilet so they'd hear what they were supposed to hear, and opened the door.

Sure enough, Luciano was still guarding the door, still looking cross and unhappy.

I walked back to my chair and stared out the window.

In a minute, a six-seater cart pulled up to our door to take us out onto the tarmac. Two men in navy jumpsuits, who could have as easily been the same two men who had brought Mateo inside from the plane, were sitting in the front row. They kept their ball caps pulled low on their foreheads and wore large reflective sunglasses, which was odd since evening was approaching.

As I stared, I suddenly realized who they were. The smaller of the two men had one shoulder slightly higher than the other and made somewhat jerky movements. It was Amos! I was unsure who the taller man was. It wasn't Norm. But of one thing I was sure. A rescue intervention was in play. The Drakers were here and my escape plan was in progress.

Just then, Mateo burst into the lounge, his eyes fiery with rage and his nostrils flaring. He looked like a mad dog ready to bite. I liked that he was out of control, but bit the inside of my cheek to make myself look scared. His fury meant that he was fully distracted by the complications of the charter flight to his home in Corsica.

Luciano got up from his chair, looking anxiously at his father.

Francine looked back and forth between them.

I could see they were bracing for an outburst of biblical proportions.

"You idiot," he screamed at Luciano. His voice shot like a bullet into my ears. "You think you can just order an international private charter plane like you order a domestic taxi?"

Luciano looked shaken, which surprised me. Surely he was used to this. He held his hands out toward his father. "But I assure you everything was in order. There was nothing to cause any kind of problem."

I caught a subtle glint in Luciano's eye that suggested he wondered whether something had gone purposefully amiss. His father had trained him well to be suspicious. "What happened? What are you so angry about?"

Mateo looked around the lounge before starting into him again. He continued to berate him despite Luciano's pleads that he had covered all the requirements.

"Never mind," Mateo said. He started toward Gate A. "We have to go now. Let's hurry." He turned and went outside, and the three of us followed him. We waited in front of the passenger carrier that would take us to the waiting plane.

The carrier driver amicably tipped his hat to him. Mateo growled in response as he took a seat in the second row directly behind two terminal personnel. He banged the seat beside him for his wife to sit. I hopped into the back row and Luciano piled in beside me, his bulky form crowding me tight against the scratchy side of his suit jacket.

"Go," Mateo ordered the driver, who pulled the cart onto the airfield at a snail's pace. Mateo leaned forward, "Why do you drive like somebody's grandmother. Drive faster!"

The driver nodded but only increased the speed by a hair.

Purple with irritation, Mateo scanned the area then jammed his sleeve back to check the time on his Rolex.

While Mateo raged and yelled to his wife about God knows what in Corsican, I purposely slipped my foot halfway out of my shoe.

While I did not doubt that Mateo felt the ride to the plane was interminable, it was probably only about two minutes.

When it stopped, Mateo bolted out and stood at the lowered steps of the plane, frantically waving Francine over.

She complied obediently, mounted the squatty steps, her shapely behind swaying, and disappeared into the cabin.

Luciano followed, but when he noticed I wasn't right behind him, he stopped at the foot of the steps and turned around. "What's the problem, girl?" he growled.

"Having a problem with my shoe. Just give me a second." I was bent over, my head down under the seat.

"Stay down, Ruby," Amos said.

I heard the clunk of metal on the pavement and then a puff of air as everything around us became dense fog. He or his partner had detonated a smoke bomb between us and the plane. Then to add to the chaos, I heard popping sounds, not gunshots, but sputters and small sparks and blasts. Amos had thrown a tangled string of lit firecrackers toward our mafia hosts.

"Hang on," the driver said.

The snail cart suddenly became turbocharged and raced back to the protection of the terminal. I hung on for dear life as we squealed away, veering right and left to avoid being shot. I grabbed the seat in front of me and turned to see what was happening on the tarmac. I didn't know what my Corsican kidnappers thought was happening, but as the smoke dissipated, I saw that the Challenger was heading down to the runway for takeoff. I wondered if it would even wait for clearance from the tower. I didn't care. Within minutes it would be in the air and not our problem anymore.

We got out of the cart and raced back inside the terminal where Hannah pointed us toward the parking lot.

The people in the airport looked confused as the four of us ran through and disappeared outside.

Amos pointed a key fob at a black SUV parked a few rows from the front door of the airport, to unlock the doors. He got into the passenger seat with his accomplice taking the wheel. Hannah and I piled in back.

The driver screeched out of the parking lot, all of us too tense to even say hello as if we were afraid to congratulate ourselves for a job well done until we were sure to be in the clear. Airports were never good places for the Drakers. We were always running from someone in or out, and today was no different. The driver raced our SUV out onto the highway where it blended in with the other cars leaving the airport. We drove at top speed for ten minutes, weaving in and out of traffic, until the driver slowed to the posted limit then pulled over to a stop on the shoulder.

When the SUV was parked, we all sat still for a few seconds in the quiet as if we couldn't believe we were here, safe, together again. Hannah didn't say anything as she finally grabbed me in a warm hug. It felt so good to have her arms around me. It was like, in her arms nothing could hurt me. Hot tears ran down my cheeks.

She held me a long time then she murmured, "Ruby, honey," and pushed me gently away from her. She looked me in the eyes and brushed my hair back. "Are you all right? You're not hurt, are you?"

"I'm fine, Hannah," I said, not caring anymore that I was crying. "I'm so happy to see you guys again. They were going to take me to Corsica, where I thought..." I hadn't wanted to admit to myself the truth. That once we got to Corsica and he'd gotten what he wanted, Mateo would have quickly and easily put a bullet through my head. But now I was safe. They'd found me. My voice grew strained. I knew I was very fond of my dear friends, but until now I didn't realize how very much I cared for them, how very much we cared for each other. They truly were my family.

"Come on, little girl," Amos said affectionately, turning around in his seat. "You know we'd never let anything happen to you." He reached his arm back and gripped our hands.

I was still feeling a bit numb but nodded at him gratefully with red eyes and a wet face. I had to fight out the words that lay behind a painful knot in my throat. "How did you know I was here?"

Then the driver spoke up. "A little computer hacking and I knew where every charter flight in the world was going. I put the dots together and realized that a flight from St. John's to Corsica was all about the d'Angelos." He turned around to face me. "So I flew in personally to make sure your rescue wouldn't fail." He grinned and took off his ball cap and sunglasses, his tousled brown curls falling around his ears as unkempt as ever.

"Renegade!" I shouted. I bolted forward, awkwardly grabbing him around the neck in an embrace so tight that if he'd been driving, the SUV would have swerved off the road. I was completely overcome, laughing and crying at the same time.

Renegade, my brother, well, not my real brother, but yes, my brother, had come to my rescue. He had come to my rescue because I was in trouble and that's what family did. They came through for you when you most needed help.

Renegade reached around his neck and loosened my vice-like hold, taking my hands in his and kissing both before he released them back to me. "I have some rooms for us at a hotel in town," he said. "Reinhardt is expecting us to call. You ready?" He grinned again, started the car, and pulled back out onto the road.

Seventeen

IT FELT GOOD TO BE SAFE IN THE ARMS of my family again, but once the initial glow had worn off, I realized, that in many ways, my rescue and escape from the d'Angelos had complicated everything else. Part of me wanted to be done with this whole stupid thing, to gather up my family and fly back home to Fairhaven—our refuge, our safe house—and be happy. We had every security measure installed there: high walls, and cameras wired to the local police, everything we needed to keep the outside world from dragging us back into situations we wanted nothing to do with. We'd started all this because we wanted to get Robert, and now we had him. What I wanted now was peace, to not feel like my life was in danger. We'd all had enough of that to last several lifetimes.

While I indulged in this wishful thinking, Rosalind rustled uneasily in my brain, putting yet another tight knot in my stomach. *Ruby, this is far from over.* Gee, thanks, Rosalind. I didn't need her to remind me of that.

I knew that until Mateo had collected Felix's debt, we would be threatened, pursued and hunted. His life and the lives of his family depended on the delivery and he wouldn't stop until he had it. Some-how, I suspected that even if the Drakers were able to make that happen, we would then have a whole other host of issues to deal with. Treason being first among them.

It was dark when Renegade pulled up to the Sheraton hotel downtown. "Here, everyone. I checked you in already." He handed out our room card keys.

I was so drained—physically, emotionally—I was happy he'd arranged everything.

We traipsed in and wordlessly took the elevator to the third floor where the hallway was quiet, the carpet plush, and the lights soft and diffuse.

He'd gotten me a separate room, and after I said goodnight to everyone, swiped my card and entered the comfortably appointed room with its queen-size bed looking like the place in which I wanted to be the most in the world, I felt instantly overwhelmed with fatigue.

I crossed the room to draw the curtains, first looking down at the parking lot and road that ran along the front of the hotel. I scanned the grounds for signs that someone might be there, watching, anyone who might be wandering, or looking for us, but nothing looked suspicious. I pulled them across and jumped when the room went pitch black. I laughed at myself and turned on the light on the nightstand.

I decided to have a shower before going to sleep and smiled when I saw an array of drugstore products on the counter with a little hand-written note from Hannah. "Happy homecoming," it said with a fatly drawn heart.

I teared up again, and when I stepped into the hot water, I stood still, not washing, just letting the soft spray and steam melt away the tension that gripped my shoulders. I felt guilty for how un-environmental I was being, but I consoled myself with the idea that it wasn't every day I was kidnapped and rescued and perhaps that could be my one gift to myself: every time I got back from being kidnapped, I could have an extra-long shower while hoping that Mother Earth would understand.

Finally, I got out and dried off with a thick, white towel, brushed my teeth, and slipped into the over-sized drugstore Toronto Blue Jays

T-shirt Hannah had probably found in the lobby gift shop, and climbed into bed. I propped myself up on several pillows, intending to sit and think for a while. Renegade had said to meet downstairs for breakfast at 8 a.m. He would have news from Reinhardt by then and we could discuss what needed to be done next. I leaned back and within seconds was in a deep, dreamless sleep.

I awoke from noise in the hallway. I sat up, confused, my heart racing, trying to orient myself. I looked over to the window where a narrow ribbon of light streamed in through the sides. It was morning, and I then remembered I was in a hotel with Renegade, Amos and Hannah, the d'Angelos had flown away, and for now, I was safe.

I settled back on the pillows, the bed soft and warm, and I lay blissfully there for a few more minutes before looking over to the side table where the clock read 6:53 a.m. I had an hour before we'd meet for breakfast. I flopped back, thinking how great it would be if I could doze off again for a bit, but the tension in my body began to rise, and that was it. I got up and had another shower.

Afterward, I put on the makeup Hannah had bought, dried my hair, and was ready to start the day. I was very interested in talking talk through our plans. It was only 7:45 a.m., but I figured I'd go early, get some coffee, and collect my bearings.

When the elevator I was in reached the lobby and pinged to signal the door was about to open, I broke out into a rash of sweat as I imagined Vince staring me in the face when the doors opened. Rosalind had been buzzing in my thoughts from the moment I'd gotten on the elevator. I readied my stance so I could disarm him if necessary, even though I knew it was silly.

When the doors opened, a woman was there with her toddler. They came in and rode down with me to the bottom. I tried to quiet my heart and ignore Rosalind. *Better safe than sorry,* she cautioned.

I walked out into the lobby, cheery morning sunlight coming in through the glass front of the hotel. Already, a few hotel guests were milling around, nobody paying me any mind. To my left was the restaurant, open to the lobby. I waited by the Please Wait To Be Seated sign, figuring, when I spotted Renegade, Hannah and Amos, I'd just head in, but they didn't seem to be there.

"Ruby." I heard Hannah's voice, but couldn't locate the direction it came from. I scanned the dining room several times.

"Over here."

This time, I looked to the right and noticed a private room.

Renegade appeared at the doorway and subtly waved me over. He was looking around, probably making sure we were alone. He was also dressed differently, wearing a white, button-down shirt untucked over dark jeans and not his signature Hawaiian print shirt and baggy shorts. If it weren't for his typical tumble of unruly dark curls, I might not have recognized him.

I hurried over, relieved to see him. He grabbed me and gave me a quick hug before guiding me to the table. "Did you sleep?" He asked, frowning at my face.

I smiled. "Like a dead rock."

He chuckled and elbowed me as we came to the table where Hannah and Amos were sipping coffee, a plate of sugary donuts between them.

"There's our girl," Hannah said. "Hope you don't mind we started without you?" She chuckled and shrugged to feign sheepishness.

"Old habits, you know," Amos said. He wiped the powdery sugar off his fingers, took another bite, and wiped his chin. My heart melted at the familiar sight. I did love my seniors and their love for their all-American coffee and donuts.

A waitress came over to the table and poured me coffee and passed out menus. While I was looking at the list of breakfast foods, my stomach growled loudly.

"Nice one, Ruby," laughed Amos.

"I haven't eaten since lunch yesterday when I was a hostage at a mafia boss's secret estate, thank you very much," I said in mock indignation before I ordered a three-egg omelet and a side of oatmeal.

"When will Reinhardt be calling?" I asked.

The two-second pause tickled at the uneasiness in me again.

"Well," Renegade said. "He won't be calling." He tried to look sad but I knew the look on my face changed his mind because he erupted into a huge grin. "They're going to meet us in Rocky Flats in Colorado later today instead. We'll be going back to the airport soon. I've arranged a flight."

"Where on earth is that? Why? Why Colorado?" My voice was louder than I'd expected it would be. I felt suddenly brittle. More running around? I wanted to go home.

"Ruby, listen," Renegade's voice was low and cautious. "Rocky Flats is a decommissioned nuclear weapons plant that was shut down in 1989. The government relocated all of the radioactive material, but Margaret has a contact who believes that Felix may have a reserve of material hidden somewhere on that site. If all goes smoothly, and this material does still exist, we can set up the exchange from there."

My stomach turned over but this time not from hunger. I took a deep breath. We had to do what we had to do. "When do we leave?" I tried to sound casual, but looking around the table, I could see how each of us was conflicted. Everyone's faces suggested the same discomfort I was feeling, but I had to trust that they had thought through the plan and put a contingency in place—just in case.

"I've arranged our charter to leave St. John's at three," Renegade said. "Reinhardt, Robert, Ransom and Margaret are already there. That gives them enough time to locate Felix's old acquaintance, George Nash. From what I understand, he's a bit of a character, but he worked closely with Felix and the Defense Department during the Cold War. If anyone can find Felix's stash, it will be him."

I struggled between excitement and apprehension. The Ruby part of me, spurred on by Rosalind, wanted to leave immediately to confront our enemy head on and take them down while doing it, but the Kathleen part of me wanted to run away and forget this whole thing, be safe and at home behind the protective walls of Fairhaven. I felt split in half by my various selves, and since I'd become Ruby Draker, I'd become some kind of mutant hybrid between the girl I once was and the woman I had become, dragging around a lifetime of memories mixed with recent experiences in one big confused suitcase and still trying to feel like one cohesive person with a "real" life who believed in real flesh and blood people and in the family that had become mine, however, invented it was.

I studied Renegade's face. I saw his resolve. He knew his role. When the Drakers were faced with a problem, they faced it head on. Amos and Hannah, too, were ready for taking care of our next steps. I admired how they took to these situations. They just considered them challenges to be overcome. They seemed to enjoy them.

"I'm not comfortable with this George person," I said. "I don't think we should be associating with anyone who might still have an allegiance to Felix."

Hannah and Amos nodded but Renegade's assured expression turned introspective. "You're right to be cautious," he said, "but my research shows he has firsthand knowledge about the Rocky Flats Facility. He was Felix's inside man during the days when the Flats still made nuclear bombs. He was indeed a favorite in Felix's clutch of conspirators but he has his own underhanded motives as well. And while that makes him dangerous, it also makes him vulnerable. Anyway..." Renegade shrugged. "He's the only chance we have for finding the plutonium. And luckily, Margaret knows him well and is well-versed on how he operates. I don't think she'd take chances with a Felix sympathizer and jeopardize her son's release."

The table went silent as our breakfasts arrived.

The waitress busied herself with arranging the plates and pouring more coffee, grabbing ketchup and salt, and fetching more napkins. We dove into our food.

After a few mouthfuls of warm sweet oatmeal, I felt everything come into perspective. I knew fate would run its course and events would unfold as they would. It was a situation where the unknown would guide our actions. Nothing unsettled me more than not knowing who I was dealing with. I had learned the hard way that no one was who he seemed. We had no choice but to play this game to the end.

It was still several hours before our charter would take us to our new destination. We leisurely finished our breakfasts and after Renegade paid, Hannah had the waitress put the remaining donuts in a bag. "No use wasting perfectly fresh donuts," she laughed.

We decided to get some fresh air and walk along the scenic maritime harbor front. The night before, it had been a forty-minute drive in from the airport with only a few rough and abandoned factories and derelict buildings to look at along the way. But the hotel backed a harbor, a boardwalk with touristy craft shops, and little eateries on one side, and fishing boats and large seagoing vessels moored on the other. Seagulls scavenged the walkway and screeched in flight overhead. It was a sunny morning, and the chilly, soft breeze coming off the ocean renewed me somehow.

Hannah and I walked arm in arm behind Renegade and Amos who may have looked like they were strolling leisurely, but I could tell they were at the ready should anyone try to surprise us on our pleasant morning constitutional. Were it not for the task that awaited us, in different circumstances this would've been a lovely vacation day.

We had to stop touring charming places this way, I thought ruefully. That thought spun me into feeling edgy.

Hannah noticed my shift in mood. "You get used to it, you know," she said gently. "Some of us jump back into service when it's needed. That's our job. Why we're here. We make the world a little bit safer." She wordlessly handed me a donut from the paper bag.

I laughed and hugged her from the side.

"That's OK, sweetie, I find that a donut can fix just about anything." She held hers up to mine and we bumped donuts as if toasting to our next adventure, our next caper, our next predicament, getting involved with matters of national security, matters we had no authority to engage in, and quite possibly could complicate things even more.

Just go with what happens, Ruby. You can handle this. I wasn't sure if those words came from Rosalind or if they were my own and I was giving myself a pep talk.

***

The rest of the day was a mathematical blur. Denver was three hours behind us, and the flight just over six hours. It was after 6 p.m. when we descended toward Denver. From the air, the airport—comprised of what looked like a series of circus tents—looked like it could have been a building on another planet, one to where the people of earth would have to evacuate to survive the contaminated atmosphere of the earth after a nuclear blast.

I realized I was shaking. The consequences of what we were about to do were suddenly hitting me. I was very happy when we landed and at least were back on solid ground.

Renegade had arranged for a car to take us to the hotel in Denver where, the following day, we would meet up with the rest of our people.

We would get some sleep before heading fifty miles west to Arvada, a few miles from Rocky Flats, America's most controversial and contaminated nuclear weapons facility; probably one of the most contaminated places in the world. At one time it had housed enough poisonous plutonium to kill everyone on earth.

In the morning, we met for a quick breakfast before leaving in a rented SUV—our signature black seven-seater—for the one-hour drive.

I tried not to feel too excited that soon we'd be reunited with Reinhardt, Robert and Ransom in case I jinxed it somehow. I'd tried not to think about Ransom this whole time, knowing it wasn't in my best interests to keep that ember glowing. But now it surged up into a little flame that licked my insides. I hated that I was so susceptible to the whims of my heart.

Among other things, on the drive to Arvada, my mind kept trying to conjure up images of Nash. Renegade had called him "quite the character." I wondered whether it was a reference to his appearance or that it meant dealing with him was going to be tricky. I knew we had to be ready for anything.

We arrived around 11 a.m. I had only been separated from Reinhardt, Robert and Ransom for a couple of days, but I was dying to see them. All of them. I needed to see them and hug them to convince myself that we were all still OK.

I got my wish within a couple of moments of walking into the hotel lobby. We spotted each other and ran into each other's arms.

Reinhardt bear-hugged me and kissed my cheek before examining my face to get a read on how I was feeling. He smiled at me knowingly and released me. He understood all I'd been through, and I could see how proud he was of me.

Ransom kept his arms around me for longer than I expected, and when I went to pull away after what would have been a fine hug for someone who had the role in my life of "brother," he kept me pressed to his chest.

"Ruby," he murmured into my hair.

He finally let me go but his arm stayed around my waist. A flood of feelings swirled within me. I wanted to think this meant something, but he was probably just relieved I hadn't been killed by Mateo. Yet his aftershave, musky and sexy, his broad arms, his chest, these things pressed against me, reminded me of how much I once loved him.

"Thank God you're OK," Ransom said. "I was so worried I might never see you again." His voice trembled with emotion, but at this moment when I could have believed he was feeling something for me, when I could have gotten lost in the sincerity in his eyes, I was only reminded of how he'd rejected me for Rose. I couldn't react. I had misread him before. I wouldn't do that again. It hurt too much.

Reinhardt, Amos and Hannah were talking off to the side when I saw Robert coming across the lobby. He was walking with a cane but seemed quite steady. So steady in fact, I thought the cane might only be for insurance. He was making remarkable improvements.

"Slow and steady wins the race," he laughed. He looked at me and came in for a hug. "No need to worry about our Ruby." He pulled back and smiled proudly at me. "She's the reason I was released." He kissed my cheek. "She's my hero."

"Well, what's the plan now?" Amos asked. "Because we sure as heck didn't come all this way for the scenery." He frowned and pointed out the hotel window at the mostly flat grassland with hazy mountains in the far distance.

"We're going to meet Nash here at the hotel in about an hour," Reinhardt said. "I booked a conference room."

Realizing not everyone was there, I looked around. "Where are Alice and Norm? And where's Roscoe? Or Margaret? They're all here, right?"

"Margaret is in her room still asleep," Reinhardt said. He shrugged, an understanding smile on his face.

I understood. She was locked in her own personal kind of prison.

"Then where's Roscoe?" I was worried. Why wasn't he here?

"It's OK, Ruby," Reinhardt said. "He wanted to be here, but he also understood the seriousness of what is about to happen and very sensibly agreed to go to the farmhouse with Norm and Alice. Norm and Alice will take good care of him. And as soon as we're finished here, we'll go back and get everyone. And fly home."

I knew it wouldn't be quite that easy. Home sounded so good to me, for a brief second, I wished I were there with Roscoe, playing catch at the farmhouse, making popcorn balls, not being worried and scared all the time. I wanted the Drakers, all of us, to be safe and secure. We deserved a break from all this craziness. If Hollinger did care about us, if he really didn't want us involved for safety reasons, he'd have to step in and make things turn out all right. None of us wanted to be involved in Felix's affairs, and certainly not in this. After all of Hollinger's bungling leading up to Felix's death, he owed us and needed to be the one to get us out of this.

But to bring this drama to a close for us, temporarily at least, the plutonium would have to be surrendered to the d'Angelos as much as I dreaded that idea. I just wished there were a way for Hollinger to intervene before the final transfer to enemy hands took place, not only to save the world, but to prevent us from going to jail as well.

Margaret shuffled into the lobby, looking like she'd been wounded. She was pale, and when she sat down without a word, she squinted and massaged her temples. Reinhardt held out a bottle of water, but she waved it away. I couldn't imagine she'd be any help at all at our meeting, yet she needed to be there because she knew Nash, and could use their shared history to make this whole thing go more smoothly, or so I hoped. Together, we waited for someone only Margaret could recognize.

The clock ticked on. One o'clock and still we waited. He was late, very late, and that put all of us on edge.

Margaret had since accepted the water and cautiously sipped it, which seemed to brighten her somewhat.

Ransom and Renegade paced and looked out the windows for a man they'd only seen in photos from Renegade's having pulled Nash's ID from computer records.

Reinhardt checked his watch every few minutes.

I sat with Robert, trying to appear calm, though my nerves were jangled.

At 1:30 p.m., Reinhardt abruptly stood and went to the reception desk. "It appears I won't be needing the conference room I booked," he said.

The clerk frowned. "Which room was that, sir?"

"The Garden room, I think it was."

She typed on her computer. "I apologize, sir, but if I'd known it was you waiting in the lobby, I would have let you know immediately that your guest arrived. Quite some time ago, I'm afraid."

Reinhardt looked stunned, and I was equally surprised as were the others. How could Nash have gotten past us without our noticing? We had deliberately positioned ourselves in the front lobby to intercept him, and escort him personally to our meeting room. People did come and go, but no one bore traits even close to what we were expecting from his photo.

"And he's in the meeting room now?" Reinhardt asked.

"Yes, sir. He's been there for about..." she checked her watch. "Goodness. Close to an hour."

The manager called her over. "Excuse me, sir. Please let us know if you need anything else. And I do apologize for this." He smiled at her though I could see he was seething, by his wrinkled forehead and knitted eyebrows.

I was frustrated, too, because it seemed evident tht Nash had done this on purpose. But why? Did he want the upper hand? Of course, I didn't trust him; any friend of Felix's was an enemy of the Drakers. But that didn't matter now. We needed to get in there and meet him, face to face.

***

The meeting room was down on the lower floor of the hotel. We proceeded along a flight of steps to a lower lobby, then went down a hallway that led to several meeting rooms. About halfway down the hall to the right, one of the doors to a meeting room was open.

Ransom put his hand to his heart. For a split second, I wondered if he were praying or being patriotic but then I laughed at myself. He was checking for the Glock holstered just under his sports jacket.

Reinhardt, Renegade, and even Robert, seemed prepared in the same way. Damn, I thought with annoyance. I hated that I didn't have my gun. I felt vulnerable in a way I didn't like.

Nobody wanted to unnerve Nash by bolting in with guns in hand, so we moved in stealthily.

When we were within inches of the door, a man called out in a gruff caustic voice, "You're about as unnoticeable as a tank on an empty street. Get in here already if you want to talk. I've waited long enough."

Reinhardt stepped into the room and paused. He immediately tensed up and fixed his eyes on one spot in the room. He took one step, turning slightly to nod that we should follow.

We came in close behind Reinhardt, standing in a tight group, and stared at a man seated at the head of a long table. We stared at him, and he stared back with no expression on his face, but with tight, dark eyes that bore into each of us. I felt fear. Renegade had been right. I could already tell this Nash fellow was unusual, not at all what I had anticipated, though I wasn't sure what I'd expected. I only knew we couldn't trust him, and his demeanor wasn't making it any easier to try. The silent standoff was eerie.

Finally, Nash said, "Nice to meet you, too." He let out a grumbly laugh. He was a long, lean man with thinning brown hair that came down over his shoulders, and long teeth. His bony fingers were splayed out wide over the table.

Reinhardt didn't reply but came into the room and sat beside Nash. He was ready.

"Stop being so dramatic, Nash," Margaret said, her voice both scolding and affectionate. "This isn't the theater. We have some serious arrangements to look after."

I hadn't heard her speak to anyone this way before and stared at her.

"Hello, Margaret," Nash said, his voice equally as histrionic. He winked at her and plucked a folded piece of paper from the table and held it up.

It looked like the one Felix had given Margaret in the secret envelope.

Nash and Margaret looked at each other for maybe four or five seconds before he stood up and came over to her.

I almost laughed when I saw how he was dressed: tie-dyed tunic over a black Beatles T-shirt, frayed bell-bottom jeans, and aged, leather sandals. There was no way we could have missed him. He must have come in a back door. Or maybe this guy had time-warped straight into the conference room from the '60s.

He stood in front of Margaret and took both of her hands in his. "Sorry about Felix," Nash said. "I know he was a bastard, but he's still Oscar's dad." His condolences came across as sincere.

Margaret's eyes welled with tears as she nodded. "You have to help us get Oscar back. Please."

"How much do you know, Nash?" Robert asked.

Nash walked over, closed the door, then poured himself a coffee the hotel had put on a side table. "Nice setup, don't you think?" Nash said, "but I could sure appreciate something stronger…" His eyebrows went up impishly.

"Shut up, Nash," Hannah said curtly. "We need to focus here." She glared at him as she walked past him to the side table. She poured a coffee and brought it to Margaret who had already seated herself at the other end of the table from where Nash was.

He studied Hannah and Margaret for a moment as if he were sizing up their relationship.

"Hmm," Nash grunted and returned to his place at the head of the table. He sat and spread his arms to indicate that we should be seated, that the meeting could start now. The assured expression on his face indicated he intended to be in charge of the next move.

"Look here, Nash," Robert said. He had read the note Nash had flaunted earlier, and when he set it down, I saw it said only, Building 717. "I don't know where Building 717 is, but I'm certain you do, and that you know what's at stake here."

"It's at the Rocky Flats site about twenty miles from here," Nash said. "It's well-guarded and under the Department of Energy these days. During the Cold War, the Department of Defense was in full charge. Back in my day, that's where we manufactured our nuclear weapons. It's completely decommissioned now, of course. All the plutonium was moved to a secret site I'm not aware of. Even though it's been many years, Rocky Flats is still highly contaminated, very toxic, unsafe from both a health and security perspective."

Margaret spoke up. "Felix left me a sizeable amount of cash to get your help,"

Nash leaned back in his chair, looking pensive. He shrugged and snorted. "That's Felix," he said. "Divide and conquer. That was always his strategy. He knew I needed money, and..." He snorted. "Felix needed to make sure that you'd come through if he needed you to. There was never any limit to who he might pit against whom. He was willing to put his son in jeopardy. And... Margaret... he knew exactly how to get you to cooperate. Even now, we're all compromised. Either his debtors will come after us or the US government will."

What he'd said was true. I had to hand it to this guy. I wasn't sure if he was trying to get us to see him as a pawn right along with Margaret, or if he had a deception of his own in mind. I opted for caution. As far as I was concerned, he was as much of a threat as Mateo was.

"Surely," Nash said, "the Department of Defense is watching you. So you want me to believe we're going to pull this off without them knowing about it? And if we did pass it off to Felix's people, am I supposed to think you'd allow enemies of the state to build a bomb?"

Nash wasn't stupid. He was testing us to see if we had some kind of underhanded plan. I was certain he already had a plan of his own. I could feel it coming off of him like heat. The truth was we had no idea where Felix had hidden the plutonium, and even if we did, we had no plan as to how we might get it into Mateo's hands to secure Oscar's release. To pull this off, we would have to have the plutonium securely stashed in such a way that only our group knew the location. Nonetheless, it seemed obvious we needed to not reveal to Nash how completely unprepared we were.

Reinhardt leaned forward at the table. "What makes you think we'd tell you anything about the DoD? As for our enemies, no one said they wanted the nuclear material to build a bomb. We don't know what they intend to do with it. Your only role is to take us to Building 717 and show us where Felix and you hid the materials. Once the transaction is complete, you get your reward just like Felix promised."

Reinhardt's taking charge didn't seem to sit well with Nash whose smug grin disappeared. I could see the dynamics shift and that Nash, who considered himself the key player in all of this, wasn't enjoying being treated like an intermediary.

Nash got up from his chair and approached Reinhardt, breathing hard and staring him down. They were so close, their noses almost touched. Then he smiled. "It's not like we can just make a reservation to tour the place." He stepped away from Reinhardt. "But lucky for you, I have contacts who owe me a favor." His grin widened again along with his confidence as he went back and sat in his chair, enjoying a *gotcha* chuckle.

Reinhardt said, "Margaret suggested we might be able to trust you. But I can see you have motives of your own. In that case, Mr. Nash, we will make alternate arrangements that don't involve you."

Reinhardt got up from the table and walked to the door, stopping there and indicating with a wave that we should also leave.

"What about my money?" Nash said, his voice almost a whine. He looked imploringly at Margaret. "Come on, Margaret. Felix owes me."

"All we need is to be assured that the plutonium is there," Reinhardt said. "When Oscar and Margaret are reunited and safe, the d'Angelos will arrange what to do with the nuclear material themselves. If you do help us, and only after everything else has gone as planned, you will be paid."

We were all filing out of the room.

"Not so fast," Nash said.

Reinhardt called back to him from down the hall. "We'll meet you in the lobby in an hour. If you're not there, our arrangement is over."

We all left, leaving Nash to reconsider his deal.

It seemed clear. He needed the money, and badly. Why else would he help us sell nuclear material to probable terrorists? Or maybe that's just how disgruntled ex-spies vented their grievances.

Instead of going to the lobby, we went to Reinhardt's room. We didn't know what game Nash was playing, but clearly, he was trying to be in charge. Why, I wasn't so sure. We had waited long enough to meet Nash, and I knew we were all in agreement that he'd worn out his welcome with that stunt. This time, we'd make him wait. If Nash waited, it would solidly confirm just how desperate he was for money.

"Margaret," I said. "You know him. Will Nash help us?"

"He's a chronic gambler," Margaret said, "a problem Felix always had to deal with. I used to wonder why Felix tolerated him. It was a weakness our enemies could have easily exploited. Felix knew how problematic it was, so he kept Nash on U.S. soil most of the time. I asked him about that once. Felix just laughed. He said you never know when a weakness can turn into an opportunity. I see he found his opportunity." Margaret's eyes searched the room and came to rest on the mini bar fridge. She started to pace as she continued. "Don't let Nash's addictive behavior fool you though. I mean, sure, the idea of getting a windfall of cash is a great teaser for his gambling binges, but he is no pushover. He would double-cross us in a second." She shrugged affectionately. "It's just the way he is. Maybe it's the way gamblers are. Or maybe being around Felix… Well. Maybe it just rubs off."

She locked eyes with Reinhardt.

"That's why he won't get one cent until Oscar is safe," Reinhardt said. He had seen Margaret's discomfort, too, and returned a sympathetic smile at her. "We can set up a money transfer that he can access only after we input the password. But that only happens when the deal is done and that means that Oscar is back on American soil and the two of you are together."

That seemed to relax her. She drew a long raspy breath and folded her arms tight across her ample bosom as if to keep her body from breaking apart. "While Nash can get along without the niceties of life, money to him…" she paused, rolling the discomfort in her shoulders, "… is a lure just as strong as alcohol is to me." Perspiration was dotting her forehead. I knew she was in trouble.

Hannah came to her side and put her arm around her shoulder. "Let's get a coffee."

Hannah was pushing her gently toward the door trying to distract her when she said, "Damn it, Hannah. I've had more than enough coffee."

"OK," Hannah said. "Let's throw some donuts in for good measure.

Always does it for me." Hannah laughed as she slapped her curvy hips, trying to take the tension out of the moment as she continued a stronger push to the door. "We'll be back before we need to meet Nash in the lobby."

Everyone knew that Margaret was in good hands. With a firm grip on Margaret, Hannah guided her out into the hall, the door making a booming thud, like the sound of a faraway cannon, as it closed behind them.

I could feel the stress getting to me. "Well! Isn't this lovely," I burst out. "We're paying the ransom in radioactive material capable of killing us, we're surrendering it to people who will sell it to terrorists, we're committing an act of treason punishable by life in prison, and the people in charge of this whole operation are addicts who could screw everything up! Why wouldn't this plan go off flawlessly?"

The men stared at me. Rosalind had been buzzing with a fury in my head since we left the meeting room. So much so, her words came out directly through me again. Oh, Rosalind, I thought. Why aren't you here with us?

I am Ruby. I am. You know what to do.

I listened to her and felt her presence but I wasn't so sure she was right. I sat down on the bed, curled over, and put my hands over my face.

***

The situation was so dire and overwhelming, I didn't know what to feel. I was being tugged between my old me, who wanted to panic, and my Ruby self, who had learned how to find bravery through coping mechanisms I'd observed and learned from Rosalind.

Ransom sat down beside me and put his arm around me. At his warmth, his body beside mine, I wanted to melt into him, but then I felt vulnerable, a feeling I had learned from experience never ended well. And between Serge, whom I knew I'd never see again, and my unmatched feelings Ransom was toying with because he could, I didn't want any of it. I shoved him hard, and he nearly fell off the bed. I had enough to deal with.

He stumbled and caught himself and looked around at me, but not with anger, almost with understanding. I immediately regretted my tantrum but couldn't find the words to apologize either.

He seemed to understand and reached down to his duffle bag on the floor. "If you won't let me comfort you," Ransom said, opening it, "then maybe this will." He held out a gun with one hand and with his other hand, he reached for mine.

I was instantly delighted which both frightened and reassured me so I let him put the hard, cold weapon into my palm. I closed my fingers around it and he put his warm, strong hand beneath mine and gripped my closed palm. I felt myself surge into desire again and fought it. His closeness, his concern, his eyes on mine.

I shook my head and listened. *Make your own comfort, Ruby. Use it if you have to.* Rosalind's voice snapped me back to reality. She was right and that was the focus I needed. I was strong and powerful and unafraid and now I had the reinforcement I needed so I could be entirely self-sufficient. I slipped the piece into my jacket pocket.

Ransom watched me, wordlessly. He reached into the duffle again, pulled out a holster strap, and handed it to me.

"I suppose that's better," I said. I accepted the strap, put it on, and holstered the gun in it. Then I fastened the button on my jacket and stood to examine my image in the mirror near the door. "Yep. Better."

I turned to the room and got unanimous thumbs up from everyone, which cracked me up. I was happy for a release of tension because otherwise, it was thick in the room.

It didn't get much better as we waited in Reinhardt's room, the hour turning into an hour and a half. Hannah and Margaret hadn't returned, but we decided it was time to go to the lobby and try to intercept them there.

Maybe they'd gone to the coffee shop.

We left Reinhardt's room, watching the hallway closely.

I was glad I wasn't alone in my mistrust of Nash. For all we knew, he could be trying to ambush us, or find a way to retaliate because he thought we had found other means of checking out the Rocky Flats facility without him. I knew it was good to keep him off balance, but that came with different risks.

The hallway opened up to the lobby at an odd angle. We had a clear view of the lobby but no one there could see us. My heart sank when I noticed only two people out there. One was a woman in a blue business suit, sitting with her back to us. The other was a man dressed in a crisp military-green shirt with an embroidered logo on the pocket, and matching trousers. His hair was pulled back off his face in a low bun, which seemed strange for a military person. When he pulled up a sleeve to check his watch, I saw his fist tighten. He turned to view the reception desk but scanned the lobby area as if he were looking for someone.

Of course. It was Nash. When he turned and spied us coming in, his crooked smile, erupting over his now-clean-shaven face, sent shivers down my back. He had given himself a complete makeover, which confused me and reinforced what Margaret had warned us about: this guy could change strategy in an instant, and we wouldn't see it coming.

I kept my eyes fixed on him and though I didn't look at the others, I felt sure they were doing the same.

"You people have a bad habit of being late," Nash said. I'm sure his gruff voice was intended to be intimidating. He paused to see our reaction.

Try again, Hippie Man, I thought. Do you think we're intimidated by you? I had to hand it to this guy. He understood power relations well and was trying to get the upper hand again.

"Where's Margaret?" He cocked his head and looked at Reinhardt as though Reinhardt had forgotten part of his crew. Nash sniffed a reprimanding snigger.

"How lovely," Margaret said on cue as she and Hannah entered the lobby with large take-out coffees in their hands. "You missed me."

I almost laughed at the perfect timing.

"Well, well!" Nash said, looking at each one of us slowly. "Might be a bit tight in my van." Another titter fluttered under his breath. "But you remember that kind of silliness, don't you, Margaret? I remember getting twenty people into my VW bus once." Nash pointed to Margaret's coffee. "But we had ways of easing our claustrophobia." He pinched his thumb and index finger to his lips and blew out a long satisfying puff, smirking the whole time, and ended his charade with a wink.

"Nash, we don't have time for this," Hannah said. It was the second time she'd spoken to him like she clearly couldn't suffer his antics.

I hadn't ever seen this side of her before. I liked it.

"Or maybe you're already high? You do look kind of out of it." Hannah, with her hand on her hip, stepped in front of Margaret as a barrier between her and Nash's taunts.

I watched Nash's face and wondered if Hannah's move were a mistake. Strangely, it seemed to please him. He threw up both hands in a mock gesture of defense. "Yes, your highness. Now, can you lighten up? Otherwise my Rocky Flats security buddies are going to think you're up to more than just viewing the facility. I told them I had some dear old friends who wanted a private tour."

This game of who was in charge of whom was getting old. Every time Nash spoke, he tried to assert his command over us.

"Well it's nice you're nostalgic for piling into one car, but we'll drive separately," Renegade said, starting for the parking lot.

"But..." Nash stammered. He glared, the frown lines between his eyes deepened. That wasn't in his plans.

"You heard the man," Amos said, dangling his keys and following Renegade.

Nash slumped a little. "But the van would have been a hoot..." He grumbled inaudible comments as he followed behind.

When I saw his beloved van out in the parking lot, I nearly burst out laughing. It was an old Volkswagen van painted in flowers and smiley faces, its sides sporting many dents and scrapes like it was straight out of an action movie. I started to think Hannah was right and he'd smoked so much weed he wasn't able to think anymore. I'd seen enough stoned lab rats during my research hours at school to be able to identify the signs.

Renegade had already started the SUV and was holding the front passenger door open for Nash who, in his new outfit, up close resembled a security guard more than a military officer.

Nash sneered as he settled into the front seat and slammed the heavy door shut.

Amos and Hannah climbed nimbly into the back row while Reinhardt occupied the center.

I joined Ransom and Margaret in the second SUV that we'd rented in Denver. Renegade backed his SUV out of its parking spot and took the lead, driving onto the highway.

We followed.

I knew the Rocky Flats facility was only half an hour's drive away. We didn't talk. I'm not even sure we breathed, the tension was so thick. The air in the car felt like the minutes before a storm.

I was deep in my thoughts and only tacitly noticed the flat, bleak landscape going by. Apart from the mountains in the distance, the terrain was almost as if it had been laid bare by a nuclear blast of its own. I imagined mutant species of rodents, snakes and scorpions roaming menacingly over this stretch of godless land. There were few cars and no trees, only scraggly grasses and rocks on the flat land. The place was certainly appropriately named.

***

We followed Renegade down a lonely side road and slowed to a stop beside a decrepit guard station. Nash got out and was talking with a security guard dressed in the same uniform. I had to wonder why Nash had worn a security guard's uniform. He wasn't one of them, and their conversation seemed strained, almost like an argument. But then the guard paused. He looked down the road and stared at us in our vehicle, then cast an angry eye back at Nash. At first, I thought he was going to turn us away, but he re-entered the guard station. Nash went back to the car, and seconds later, the ten-foot gate was raised and Renegade drove through. I swallowed hard. We were here.

Inside the perimeter of the fence, only a few buildings remained within the once-massive compound. As we drove closer, I saw several foundations where buildings had once stood. I felt very uncomfortable being in a former munitions facility that had produced nuclear bombs.

We joggled and bounced along the dusty road pocked with holes and jagged cracks where scrub grass pushed through.

We approached a rectangular building at the end of the road. It was made entirely of concrete, like a bunker with one door for people at the far end and a larger metal shipping door beside. I wondered if this was it: the place from where the deadly material would be shipped. Then I wondered what nuclear materials even looked like.

We pulled up beside Renegade and sat for a moment not knowing whether to get out.

Nash was staring straight ahead, then suddenly he got out of the SUV and went up a set of cement steps to the door. He reached up to a small box mounted on the wall then punched in something on a small keypad.

The door opened.

He looked back at us and waved us over. When none of us moved, a crooked smile formed on his face. I figured he liked being in charge again, using our reluctance against us. He stepped through the doorway and disappeared inside. My stomach was in a knot so tight I thought I wouldn't be able to walk. Rosalind's buzz was so loud it made me dizzy. *Careful… careful… careful.* I wanted to slap at her. How on earth were we supposed to be careful in such a contaminated and cursed place? We followed and went inside the cool dark building.

Somehow, I had expected it to be littered with debris and mutant rats that would lunge at our throats but once Nash threw on several overhead lights, the dank space revealed a relatively clean and orderly laboratory.

I couldn't imagine the life of the person tasked with maintaining this place for so many years while everything else around the facility had gone derelict. How lonely a job that would be.

"Time to suit up," Nash said.

I don't know why this panicked me. Of course, we had to suit up. Plutonium was the most hazardous material in the world. Exposure was deadly.

Suddenly, the danger of where we were hit me with an even harder force and almost took my breath away. Growing up, I'd known about the danger of nuclear war. I used to have nightmares from the videos they showed us at school. People running for their lives. The skin lesions. The children. I bent over thinking I would vomit.

"Don't worry," Nash said. He was almost kind in his assurance. "Plutonium has to be ingested or enter the body through a cut or puncture in the skin. Either scenario us unlikely here. What we have to guard against is inhaling it, but our HAZMAT suits are equipped with breathing apparatuses so that won't happen either."

I nodded, unconvinced.

Nash studied me for a moment longer but said nothing.

"I don't see any protective equipment," I said. I couldn't move. We were now effectively hi prisoners in this building. If he wanted to kill us, he probably could very easily and no one would ever know what happened. For all I knew, there could be tons of dead people in this building already.

"It's on a lower level," Nash said.

He walked to the other side of the lab and opened a door.

In the quiet of this concrete bunker, the thud was so loud it sounded like an explosion.

I jumped.

Fear had made me lose feeling my legs. Somehow, my lifeless limbs moved me toward him. It was as if I were levitating. My heart was beating so loudly, I could barely hear Rosalind's cautionary buzz. I looked at Reinhardt and Ransom who moved cautiously behind me.

Nash left the door open as he thumped down the cement stairwell.

We followed in single file behind. The stairs stank of stale dried and contaminated concrete. I imagined the dust laden with microscopic radioactive particulates and remembered what Nash had said, that plutonium could be inhaled. I tried to hold my breath, but soon I started to get dizzy. I had to breathe but I was terrified that with every breath, I was taking in poison from the air.

Nash went down several levels of stairs until he clunked open another thick metal door with a 4 beside it.

I looked up. We seemed so deep below the surface, I began to shake, but I fought hard against it. We paused, not following him.

"If you want to see the stuff, you have to gear up," Nash said from inside, his voice direct and commanding.

One by one, we reluctantly entered. Inside, hanging in rows along the wall were yellow HAZMAT suits of thick rubber, paired with astronaut-type helmets with clear viewing shields, and heavy, black, rubber boots on the floor below.

Nash got his suit on quickly but left his headgear off to help each of us seal ourselves in and check that our oxygen supply was operational.

I was extremely heartened to see my oxygen tank was at FULL.

Once everyone was ready, he secured his hood and walked to the door at the far end of the room.

Another loud boom and he was in a different giant room lit up only by emergency lights on the vaulted ceiling. We were standing on a wide, cement platform railed off from a still and dark pool of water two stories below, that shimmered green from the lights.

I hugged the wall, feeling like I was on the edge of a precipice overlooking an alien pool of who-knew-what. This was the stuff of Sci-Fi movies, and yet that stale smell, the humid, rank stink of my suit, the sound of my breathing in my ears, and that creepy green light on whatever sludge we were looking at was so surreal, I almost forgot to be frightened. Almost. In the middle of the pool sat four dark metallic containers. That was it.

Nash pointed, his voice muffled. "There. That's what you're after. In the wrong hands, it's enough to blow mankind to kingdom come. That is if we're lucky. More likely we'd all be blown to hell because even God himself wouldn't be able to handle this stuff."

Eighteen

No one spoke much on our way back to the hotel. Reinhardt suggested we go to our rooms so we could rest. When we got into the lobby, I mumbled a quick goodbye and dashed up to my room. I felt infected, polluted, and so dirty with the experience of our day. The heavy plastic smell of the HAZMAT suit hung in my nose and I was sure it had permeated my skin, that radiation had leaked in despite the protective gear. I prickled as if it had entered my body like insects burrowing deep inside me. The image festered like something from a horror movie.

When I got inside the standard beige room, I locked the door, secured the safety chain, looked around for anything suspicious, then stripped off my clothes and turned on the shower until the water pummeled the tiles. I stepped in and let the water scald me. Then I scrubbed and rinsed several times.

I was prepared to remain there forever if not for Rosalind's gentle urging. *It's OK, Ruby. It's OK. You're strong. You will find the answer.* I finally turned off the water and stepped out, exhausted, my skin red, and my hair and body dripping water onto the floor mat.

The steamed-up mirror obscured my sodden image. I stood there wet and shivering not from cold but from terror and disbelief of where we had been and what we were about to do. I was so deep in my thoughts I didn't register the sound of knocking until it had gone on for some time.

"Ruby, are you all right?" It was Ransom. "Please answer so I know you're OK. What's going on with you?"

I pulled a towel off the rack in the bathroom and went to the door, hesitating and wondering whether to answer. I didn't trust myself to speak.

"Come on, Ruby. Answer me!"

I didn't think. I didn't want to think anymore. I unlatched the security chain with trembling fingers and opened the door. He stood in the hall, staring at me shivering with my wet hair hanging down over the towel.

Eyes gentle, he stepped inside, shut the door, reached for my hand, and pulled me toward him.

I let him.

He wrapped his arms around me and put his mouth to my neck.

His hot breath against my wet skin, his neck smelling sweet and spicy from his cologne, stirred a repressed longing, a hurt deeply buried within me. I pulled away and looked up into his face.

A strand of his chestnut-colored hair had fallen to his forehead and he hesitated, looking at me as if trying to figure out what was happening.

I brought my hands up under his untucked shirt, running them over his sculpted chest. "Ransom, I…"

He didn't wait for me to say anything. He looked at me with intense hunger and pushed me backward into the room.

I wanted him.

He pulled at the towel tucked around my chest and let it fall to the floor. "Oh," he said, as he took in my body. He grabbed my face in his hands and kissed me hard. "Ruby."

He broke away to whisper but I shook my head and tore at the buttons on his shirt, wanting his skin on mine. I unzipped his pants and pulled them down to his feet.

He kicked them off to the side, picked me up and threw me onto the bed where we clutched at each other. I wanted him more than I'd ever wanted anything. I arched to meet him and held on to him, over and over, the two of us like one, our hands, our legs, our mouths owning every inch of each other's body.

Afterward, we lay sweaty and breathless, not speaking. For a moment, I felt weak and wanted to kiss him again, to hold on to that feeling, but I felt suddenly like Rose was watching us and rolled away.

He sat up and put on his underwear and pants. He reached over and stroked my back. I turned to look at his face. His expression was tender and soft, still full of desire.

"It was always you," he said quietly.

Although I had ached to hear those exact words from him, they hurt. I knew it wasn't true. He had chosen Rose. Or maybe it was true. I didn't know what to think.

He kissed my neck softly, letting his lips linger over my skin. "Always you," he whispered. He got up, picked up his shirt, and left.

I wanted to scream, to throw a big fat childish tantrum. What the fuck did he mean by that? I grabbed a pillow and let loose into it. Was I his second choice? I raced back into the bathroom to scrub again. Only this time, a few tears mixed in and I knew I was washing away something I'd wanted for a long time.

I realized that my only clothes were still in a rumpled, contaminated heap on the bathroom floor. I picked up the towel again and tucked it around me before going to the closet.

I found the complimentary plastic laundry bag on the top shelf then gingerly picked up my clothes using only my index finger and thumb to drop them inside the plastic. I knotted the bag securely.

In a daze, I tried to think about what I could do about clothes, then remembered, with a flood of relief Hannah's clothes she'd brought me when they'd rescued me from the d'Angelos. I had at least had the presence of mind to tuck them into my bag, and I'd never been so happy to see a tourist T-shirt and baggy pants in all my life. I returned to the bathroom, showered again, and dried my hair before putting them on.

My contrived decontamination ritual had calmed me somewhat. Or else I was high from finally doing with Ransom what I'd wanted to do for so long. I couldn't tell. I felt like I was a perfect mixture of terror and desire, but that was a weird combination, making it so I didn't know what to do.

I wished I could go under the covers and hide in the room, but I knew I was supposed to regroup with Reinhardt and the others. There were still so many details to look after, and I knew those details would not be pleasant. Plus, now I'd gone and made things that much more complicated, but I couldn't deal with that now. The idea that we were soon to turn over nuclear material to enemies so they could destroy the Western world seemed slightly more important. I left my room to go find them in the lounge where I figured they'd be regrouping over lunch.

When I entered the lobby, I paused when I saw a man who looked familiar. I went into denial not being able to see his face, but his shape, body language, and tailored suit in a sea of jeans and cowboy hats betrayed him, and I quickly pressed myself against the wall. It was Vince d'Angelo. I wondered if he had seen me. I hurried into the lounge where, as I'd suspected, our group was sitting and chatting over cocktails.

"Are you OK, Ruby?" Robert asked. When he saw me, his smile dissolved. Robert always read a situation as easily as a doting parent could read a kid's book. He looked at me then glanced around the room.

I hurried to him and whispered, "I think I saw Vince d'Angelo in the lobby."

His eyebrows raised.

I shook my head. "No, I'm positive it was him. Did you see him?"

Robert snorted and shook his head. He stood and took a few steps away from the table. "I think I'll take a little walk," he announced, glancing at me as if to say, "have a seat. I'll handle this."

He left his cane by his chair and walked with an awkward gait to the lobby. I felt reassured. If anyone could spot someone watching for us, it would be Robert. Besides, he knew the d'Angelos well.

"Sit down, Ruby," Ransom said gently. He pulled out a chair for me and inched closer, so our hips touched.

It was awkward. I felt like what we'd just done was practically so obvious it could've been announced over the loudspeaker. I couldn't look at him, and I could tell he was avoiding my eyes as well.

"Want a sip?" he asked quietly, holding out his beer.

I took it wordlessly and drank down several swallows before handing it back, letting my eyes go anywhere but to his knee or his shoe. I looked around and that's when I noticed Nash sitting with Margaret, both of them with martinis in their hands. They seemed to be drunk but acting cordially.

"What's Nash doing here?" I asked, not minding that he was within earshot. It hadn't occurred to me until just now that he probably would stay close to us for as long as he was waiting for his payment.

"It seems he has a room here," Renegade said, rolling his eyes. "No wonder we didn't see him coming in from the parking lot."

"I'm thinking there may be a silver lining with Vince finding us," Reinhardt said. "It'll make it easier to arrange Oscar's release." He was thinking while he was talking, and his eyes were moving side to side as he did calculations in his head for how we could use this circumstance to our advantage.

"Nash," I said, raising my voice. "You have to keep your mouth shut and let us handle the exchange."

Nash didn't respond so Ransom called over even more loudly, "Did you hear that, Nash?"

Nash looked up confused, his expression both dazed and giddy.

Yep, he was several sheets to the wind. For that matter so was Margaret. My heart sank. These two had their issues, but we needed them. In this state, it was probably best to get them back to their respective rooms while we made contact with Vince.

Reinhardt motioned with a sideways nod of his head to Renegade who stood up and offered his hand to Margaret.

"Margaret," Renegade said. "It's been a long day. Let me help you to your room."

Margaret looked up and then at the rest of us. "I've got to stop doing this," she said, tears forming in her eyes. "Oscar deserves better." She stood up slowly, wobbled, and let Renegade catch her and take her back to her room.

"You too, Nash," Reinhardt said. "If you want your money, it's best you stay out of what we need to do next."

Nash squinted, then stood and followed Margaret and Renegade.

That left Amos, Hannah, Reinhardt, Ransom and me to wait for Robert to return.

We didn't have to wait long before two men strode in from the lobby. Robert walked with clumsy footsteps behind them. I had to marvel at how each time I saw him, his mobility was improved. Seeing Vince aiming for our table in the lounge made my stomach lurch, but at least I was flanked by Drakers who would keep him away from me.

A slimy grin formed on his thick face when he spotted me. He stopped right in front of my chair and reached for my hand, pulling it to his face as if he intended to kiss it. I yanked it back and stared at him, fantasizing about poking his eyes out.

"It's so good to see you, Ruby," Vince said. "My father tells me you parted from his hospitality without saying goodbye." He tsked as if scolding a child.

I smiled then feigned sympathy. "I believe he did the same to you, Vince." I paused. "I know, it hurts."

Vince was already caught off guard by my calling him out, and when Reinhardt commanded, "Have a seat, Mr. d'Angelo," he flinched. Yet another father figure telling him what to do.

He sat and flopped one leg over the other, trying to recover. "Please, call me Vince. After all, we're all friends, aren't we?"

I felt sorry for him. Vince's imitation of his father didn't quite meet the mark.

I detected a subtle smirk on Reinhardt's lips. "I don't think we should consider each other friends, Vince," he said, his lip curling.

Vince merely shrugged at the rebuff and re-crossed his legs. "So," he said, now glaring at the rest of us at the table. "I trust that your explorations here in Arvada and Rocky Flats have yielded some promise for things in which we both have a common interest?"

"That depends," Reinhardt said. He leaned back in his chair and studied Vince before speaking again. "Only if your father is still interested in an exchange. Whether or not we have what you are interested in is contingent upon that."

Vince's eyes went wide. In my limited dealings with him, it seemed he never did well with an authoritative challenge. Mateo had instilled that insecurity into his sons to keep them in line and now Reinhardt had minimized Vince's role as Mateo's representative to mere messenger boy.

"I am doing my father's business here," Vince said, pounding his chest. "I will decide when this so-called exchange will take place." He raised his head with authority.

Reinhardt fished the olive out of his martini and chewed it mindfully before depositing the toothpick on the cocktail napkin. "I'm afraid not, Vince," he said. "Tell Mateo that I will negotiate only with him. No offense, but every precaution must be exercised in this very critical matter. I want you to consult with him and report back to me as soon as possible." Reinhardt flicked the back of his hand to wave him away and turned back to us to resume our conversation, leaving Vince standing there looking foolish and ignored. He fumed. He shifted uneasily, his eyes darting around, clearly not sure what to do next. After a moment, he jerked his head in some semblance of a nod and left the lounge.

I could imagine the phone call. Mateo would not be gentle with the verbal lashing of his son.

"And tell Mateo to bring Oscar with him," Reinhardt called out after him, his voice echoing through the lounge. "Margaret is looking forward to a happy reunion with her son."

Vince paused, hunched his shoulders, and kept walking.

Reinhardt's meaning had been clear: Oscar was to be delivered safe and sound if the deal were going to go through.

***

I was pleased Reinhardt had asserted his authority over the situation, but while I reveled in that triumph momentarily, a feeling of unease pleaded with me to be cautious. Vince surely wasn't here alone. I looked around the lounge, suddenly distrusting everyone I saw. The hotel could have been crawling with Vince's accomplices, people working for Mateo. Margaret had cautioned us about Nash, but I knew he was only a small fraction of what didn't feel right in this place.

I *assumed* that Mateo had taken Francine and Luciano back to their villa in Corsica, but I was *certain* that once Vince explained what had happened here, and what our demands were, Mateo would arrange a hasty family trip to Colorado to show his bungling son how these matters were to be correctly handled. And I was *convinced* he would immediately arrange some extra persuasion that communicated we did not have as large a bargaining chip as we might have thought.

We waited until a few more men also left the lobby, accomplices or cronies, I assumed, before we made our way to Renegade's room. We needed to plan an unnoticeable exit and get out of this hotel as soon as possible.

On our way, I thought about Vince and how his father would lay into him, furthering his feelings of ineptitude. I could imagine him cowering and cringing at his father's words. I realized I was overly fascinated by Vince as a subject, for the same reason I'd been fascinated by Felix: each of them had a wounded ego that festered with fear and anger, and which made them both pathetic and inanely dangerous. So dangerous, in fact, that it was impossible to predict their next moves because the emotions that drove each, spurred them on to erratic behaviors. I knew what fear and uncertainty could do to your mind. I remembered case studies from my Psych classes detailing the unusual behaviors and coping mechanisms that resulted from those negative feelings about the self, and how unpredictable behavior evolved as confidence lessened. The subjects took on more environmental factors in an even stronger attempt to satisfy the outer forces rather than find resources from within. If only someone had loved Felix. He may not have turned out to be such a monster. I felt there was still hope for Vince, but he was at a tipping point.

"Robert," I said, "how many men do you think Vince has with him?"

Robert looked like he was feeling uneasy and the same went for the others. The lounge was filling up with other people, mostly men. Was it my imagination or were we being watched?

"Give me a second to hack into the hotel's registration," Renegade said. "We can assume that anyone who checked in around the same time as Vince belongs to his group." Renegade left the table to return to his room where he had left his laptop.

Two men got up from their bar stools and also left.

"I spotted at least three men in and around the lobby who appear to be on surveillance," Robert said. Robert took his cane into his hand as he scrutinized three more burly men at the bar.

"The lounge is only half full," Amos muttered, "but I feel like there have been a lot of eyes on our table. For some reason, they find us rather interesting."

Amos and Robert exchanged looks and shifted their gaze to the men at the bar without turning their heads.

The man at the end of the bar looked over his shoulder at us but quickly returned his focus to the back of the bar where he could still see us in the mirror behind the wine and liquor bottles.

My gut told me they'd been assigned to watch and perhaps listen to what happened at our table. I hoped that Renegade hadn't been followed to his room.

"Let's see what happens if we all leave," Ransom said.

He wrapped my arm around his and walked me out of the lounge. I hoped it looked innocuous to the others, but my body responded to his touch in a way I wished it hadn't. I cleared my throat and tried to keep my focus. Amos and Hannah also locked arms and left the lounge. Robert hobbled with his cane and Reinhardt followed.

We waited in the concealed alcove where dining room patrons waited before being seated at their tables.

Sure enough, less than a minute after we left, four men fanned out into the lobby to search for us, each going in a different direction: one out to the parking lot, another down the steps to the conference rooms, the third, down the hall to the first-floor rooms, and the last making circles around the lobby.

We waited until they were no longer in sight before we moved toward Renegade's room. It was clear we were no longer safe here at the hotel. We needed to gather Margaret and Nash and make a plan for a very discreet exit.

Hannah used the key card she had for Margaret's room to open the door. Margaret was on the bed, fully dressed and snoring. Hannah went over and gently shook her.

She pushed Hannah away. "Leave me alone," she slurred. "I need to sleep." I remembered what Reinhardt had said about her being able to work with truth serum in her veins and felt so sad at how far she'd fallen. This was not the same person.

"Margaret," Hannah said, her voice getting louder. "Vince has found us, and we need to leave. You have to get hold of yourself. Come on now. Quickly."

Margaret sat up abruptly as if the words had jolted her into sobriety. She stood up, but staggered.

We each took an arm to help guide her as we steered her across the hall to Renegade's room. Reinhardt had waited for us, holding the door open while he carefully surveyed the hall. Another door opened and Ransom pushed Nash out to join us. Once they were inside, we locked and bolted the door.

The room was crowded with all nine of us, two of which were pretty drunk and needing to sprawl out. Renegade and Robert were hunched over at the desk to look at the computer where Renegade had accessed the hotel's registration.

"Seven men," Renegade said, "registered when Vince did. We spotted six. One is probably with Vince. His room is on the second floor, the executive suite room 2243. The other check-ins are across the hall and adjacent to his."

"Will they know what rooms we're in?" I asked.

"Nope. I put malware in the hotel computers that will change the room numbers for every guest every few minutes."Renegade chuckled.

"But they'll be watching our vehicles," Reinhardt said, "plus any taxis or shuttles that come to the hotel. We won't be able to just drive away. Robert? How else can we get away from here?"

Robert shook his head to think, then slapped his legs. "We'll wait until after midnight when they think we're asleep, and leave out the back entrance. We'll have to run until we get out of the sight range of the hotel," he said. "When we're far enough down the road, we can arrange for taxis to take us back to Denver."

"But Robert," I said. "How are you going to manage?"

Robert was improving and able to walk short distances, but a long run would be beyond his ability.

"We'll take turns carrying him on our backs," Nash said.

We all stared at him.

"What?" he said defensively. "I may not look it, but I'm strong, and I'd bet you boys can handle him for a spell, too. There's a service station about half a mile down the road where we can arrange to have two rentals waiting for us." Nash pulled his cell phone from his pocket and pressed a quick dial button. Someone answered and he ordered the cars. "Hold on for a second." Grinning, he handed the phone to Reinhardt. "They need a credit card number."

Reinhardt frowned lightly but quickly ordered two new vehicles, holding the reservation under his initials RD.

All we had to do now was wait. It would be two hours before we'd make a run for it. At least that gave both Margaret and Nash time to sober up somewhat. We needed every one in top shape for our getaway.

Two hungover individuals and one whose legs were compromised seemed like an unlikely recipe for success.

***

At five minutes after midnight, we slipped silently down the hall, being watchful of any movement, or men scouting the common areas. We saw no one, not even the night clerk at the desk.

The lower level had doors that opened to a dimly lit employee parking area that had only two cars at the back. We opened the door and went outside into the night, staying close to the hotel wall as it ascended a slope to the west end of the hotel at the outermost end of the parking lot. The lot was empty at this end and by some stroke of luck also poorly illuminated.

"Hop on," Ransom said.

I took Robert's cane as he climbed onto Ransom's back.

"Oh, man, Robert. You're bigger than you look!" he laughed.

"Sorry, old friend. I'll think light thoughts," said Robert.

They scurried the two hundred feet to the highway. Once we were sure they had made it, we ran to join them. I paused to look back, but I didn't see anyone following.

Renegade took his turn carrying Robert then Ransom switched again.

Our pace was pretty good, all things considered, and twenty minutes later, we arrived at a garishly lit 7-Eleven. Two SUVs were parked off to the side, and the license plates matched those the car rental place had given us.

Reinhardt went inside and claimed the fobs. Through the storefront window, I watched him slip the clerk a bill. The man looked delighted, and I chuckled. Another happy customer courtesy of Reinhardt Draker!

Reinhardt left the store, threw one of the fobs to Renegade, we piled into the vehicles and drove off quickly toward Denver.

***

It was about 1 a.m. when we pulled into the hotel in Denver. The rustic wood-paneled lobby was empty.

Robert and Reinhardt approached the night clerk, gave him some money, and got another gleaming smile. My guess was it was another payoff that ensured our names wouldn't show on the register.

I was exhausted from the day's activity. In the morning we'd have to decide how to execute the rest of our plan but I was curious about what to do now. "How will Vince and Mateo know how to contact us, and how will we know if they've brought Oscar?" I asked.

"I left my cell number on a slip of paper on the desk," Reinhardt aid. "They'll find it and give it to Mateo. We won't stay in any one place too long. If we keep moving, naturally, they'll have a harder time finding us. We can refuse to talk to Mateo unless Margaret verifies that Oscar is with them. Only Nash has security clearance for Rocky Flats, so they'll comply with our demands, or not get what they're after. With all these delays, I'm sure Mateo's clients are losing patience."

I was drained by the time I lay down on the hotel bed, yet I kept ruminating over the various possible outcomes. I vaguely wondered, as I was drifting off, whether Ransom would come to me again, but the next thing I knew, I was being jolted awake. I heard other hotel guests talking and opening and shutting their doors. I thought about a shower and regretted that I didn't have any more spare clothes to save me from my tourist T-shirt which, by now, I never wanted to see again. I wished I'd been clever enough to order something and have it delivered before we'd dashed for it. How far I've fallen, I sighed, remembering how long I used to take to get ready for school, with meticulous mascara application and perfectly blow-dried hair. I checked the bathroom and celebrated all the little bottles of free stuff. At least I would be clean. I gathered up everything, showered, put my clothes back on, and went to Reinhardt's room.

Ransom answered the door. He smiled gently at me and brought me inside. I was surprised to see everyone already there.

"You look refreshed," Ransom said. "You must have slept well." He brushed a strand of hair from my face. "We've been talking for an hour already about the usual things people talk about over coffee. How we're going to stay out of jail while also staying alive and away from Mateo's wrath."

He chuckled, put his arm around me, and guided me to a table where breakfast foods were set out.

I wished I could have hugged him back, or maybe our encounter the other night was just a one-night affair, to be taken for what it was and forgotten. I studied his face.

He poured me a coffee and motioned to a chair.

"Ruby," Nash said, looking alert and ready. "I'll catch you up with the Cliffs Notes version. My contact at Rocky Flats—the man who argued with me yesterday—has agreed to let me take over his post while the deal goes down. Reinhardt has thrown some extra cash his way, which he's more than happy to accept. When Mateo calls us, and he will, we'll insist they bring Oscar to the site. One cask from the well will be extracted and put in the shipping bay. If he insists that one of his guys inspects it, and he verifies that it is 'hot' as they call it, then once Mateo is assured the shipment is valid, he'll release Oscar to us.

"Then, once Oscar is safely and securely with us, I'll use the code to open the shipping doors to load their special secured shipping receptacle onto the trailer. The crane will already be loaded. It will be a simple matter of putting the container into the cargo hold of the trailer. They will be out of there in less than ten minutes. As for getting it out of the country…" He chuckled ruefully and shook his head. "That's up to them, and good luck. What we care about is Margaret has Oscar, she pays me, Mateo fulfills his deal with the terrorists, and everyone goes home happy. In the meantime, while we wait for Mateo to contact us, we keep on the move so his hit-men don't use us as target practice, which I wouldn't put past the guy since he wants to make sure we know he's the alpha dog in this exchange."

"How long before you think we'll hear from him?" I asked.

"The wheels are already in motion," Reinhardt said. "We just have to wait. Who knows? Maybe twenty-four hours? I'd guess he'll first try to settle things his way."

"You mean he'll try to kill everyone who isn't directly connected to the shipment," I said flatly.

"That's why we have to stay ahead of him," Ransom said. He tried to stroke my cheek. He was being attentive to me in a way that wasn't sitting well. I wasn't a child who needed soothing. I needed a greater reassurance that his gestures weren't an arrogant man's way of showing the world that he'd conquered me. That he had reinvested at some deeper level. Ransom's smile faded and he looked away.

I knew I was acting just like a child, but I'd had enough of insincere gestures. I needed something deeper than that.

"So what is on the agenda for today?" I asked. I refilled my coffee cup and tore into a bagel from the breakfast tray to give myself something else to focus on.

"If it takes a couple of days," said Renegade, "we'll just keep going from one hotel to the next. The faster we move, the harder it'll be to find us. I'll decide where at the last moment and react to our situation as it evolves."

So that was it. We would run just like we had the summer before when Felix was pursuing us. We'd run like we were being chased by a pack of wolves, only these wolves had guns and we were the target.

Nineteen

THE HOTEL FELT LIKE A MINEFIELD as we walked from our rooms to our cars. Being constantly on guard for Vince and his men had a way of making me see everyone in a suspicious light. The married couple at the elevator didn't smile and the frowns on their faces made me think they had more than an argument to settle. Their overcoats could easily have concealed weapons, and their bags, bombs. I pretended to straighten the lapel on my jacket, letting the back of my hand brush past the bulk of the gun holstered there. When they got in the elevator, and we let them go ahead alone, their faces softened. They probably just needed some alone time. I felt bad for suspecting them.

But that one instance didn't stop me from seeing danger in everyone else. In the lobby, I watched a man sitting in a leather chair. Was he really reading the newspaper he held up in front of his face? It appeared to me that he was peering over it every few minutes as if he were searching for someone in the lobby. I suppose he could have been watching for a business colleague or friend or wife or lover, but Rosalind had always said, assume guilt and trust your instincts. Rosalind wasn't hissing at me this morning, yet I still felt her with me, cautioning me.

Finally, the man stood, folded the paper, and left. As we passed each other on the way to the rotating door at the entrance, I watched him out of the corner of my eye. I felt his eyes on me also. Was he following us? Was he messaging someone else as to where we were at this very moment? As we made our way to our vehicles, I glanced back to see if he'd followed, but the doorway was empty and clear.

Reinhardt, Robert, Nash, Hannah and Amos got into their SUV while Margaret and I took the back seat of the other, and Ransom and Renegade went upfront. Ransom pulled out onto the busy Denver street, following Reinhardt's lead, and headed to the outskirts of the city where Robert had booked our next accommodation.

Unlike Reinhardt, who preferred more upscale hotels, Robert seemed to favor shabby out-of-the-way retreats. He explained that a ten-unit motel was small enough to keep track of all the guests and made it easy to spot anything unusual. Robert had told me that it had a small diner attached that served home-cooked meals. A restaurant was not a home, but we'd been eating so sporadically, the thought of whatever was home-cooked sounded wonderful. I thought back to the kindly proprietor at the Springfield Motor Inn the summer before, and what a great cook she was. My mouth watered at the memory of her pie. I had to laugh at myself. I'd had that meal right before Felix kidnapped me. Funny that now I fixated on that pie.

The SUV was eerily quiet as we maintained the in-town speed limit. I'm sure Ransom figured there was no point in speeding and getting extra unwanted attention.

I strained my neck to look out at the passing traffic as we drove. A light-blue Ford sedan caught my attention. It had been behind us for several city blocks, and two men dressed in black suits and gaudy shirts with ties sat in the front. I tried to remain calm, reassuring myself that this was a common highway leading into downtown Denver.

The city street was crowded with morning traffic and the ramp to the highway about half a mile ahead. But five minutes later, when we turned onto the freeway and the Ford did the same, now only two vehicles behind us, I turned and snapped a picture with my phone.

"I think we're being followed," I said. "That blue Ford has been on us ever since we pulled out of the hotel parking."

"I've had my eye on it, too," Ransom said.

Renegade nodded while checking the back window, acknowledging the same. "I know all about those two clowns," he said. "We can handle them."

We drove on for several more miles before Reinhardt pulled off the freeway onto a county road. We followed Reinhardt and the Ford followed us, though it had fallen back and separated itself from us by several car lengths. Well out of the city by now, Reinhardt pulled off the county road into a ten-unit motel.

Reinhardt and everyone in his car must have noticed the Ford as well because for several moments, no one moved, expecting the worst. We would have needed to make a run for it had it pulled in behind us, but then, as if life just decided to take a different path, the Ford drove on by.

I exhaled. I wasn't completely convinced it was a coincidence and they were normal people. Maybe they didn't pull up because they wanted to keep their cover for longer, but I was glad they didn't come after us for a confrontation.

We all stepped out of our cars.

"Yikes," I said aloud. The motor inn's parking lot was cracked and full of holes. The office and diner were on the west end and the rooms were in a straight row running off to the right. Attempts at landscaping included sand and rocks. "Nice choice," I said to Robert and winked.

"I know, I know," laughed Robert, "but practically speaking it's quiet and easy to see who else might share our same fine discriminating taste in accommodation." He grinned and winked back at me.

I understood completely what Robert meant. At present, we were the only guests. Any other cars or people who came in would be easy for us to keep a close eye on. Robert's taking charge reassured me. This was the Robert we knew and loved, the man who was always in command of every detail. Although the feeling of being followed and watched didn't release its grip on me, somehow, knowing that Robert was returning to his old self, even if he still had a way to go physically, was extremely comforting.

Robert limped to the reception area where he engaged in cordial conversation with the pert woman behind the desk. He pulled out a wallet and paid her in cash. The woman handed him four keys. Robert smiled winningly back at the woman and returned to us. He handed a key to Amos for him and Hannah, and gave one to me.

"You and Margaret can have the room between us," he said.

I wondered what it would be like to share a room with Margaret and tried not to feel disappointed I wasn't going to share with Ransom, though, naturally, that would have been impossible. It wasn't like we wanted to advertise whatever was happening. Or happened. Or what might never happen again. I didn't want to think about it anymore. My brain hurt.

"Ransom, Renegade," Robert said, "I'm bunking with you. Nash? You and Reinhardt will take the room on the end."

We all left and settled ourselves in.

I held back for a moment as I scanned the front of the motel. It was empty. Then I looked out to the road where not a single car went by. A hot wind swept dust over the asphalt. It looked like not only were we the only guests in the motel, it looked like we were alone in the world.

I followed Margaret into the room, and when I got inside, I had to pause to adjust to the smell. Someone had gone to town with a floral air freshener and my eyes were watering, possibly also from the décor, which was a celebration of plaid: plaid curtains, plaid bedspreads on the two double beds, and plaid upholstery on the chair and recliner. And not one of the plaids matched.

Margaret was pulling out drawers and checking corners. She cursed and fell back onto the second bed, huffing loudly. "What are we supposed to do now?"

I looked at her, feeling sisterly affection. "Let's get some air."

"And head to the diner." She looked hopeful and rushed to the door.

"Margaret," I said. My tone sounded reprimanding to me. I guess my Rosalind personality was rising. I told myself, Tone it down. Margaret hasn't had an easy life. I will—or rather *we* will—keep her from ordering something she ought not order. I giggled inwardly at my personality disorder.

"For coffee," Margaret said flatly. She was already out the door and clipping across the parking lot at a spry pace. I was surprised at her energy when she had a mission.

I hurried to catch up to her, and as we walked past the reception office, I heard a car pull up, its tires crunching on the loose gravel. Margaret was already in the diner. I was still outside and glanced over my shoulder. My heart stopped and my eyes went wide. It was the light-blue Ford. I prayed they didn't see me.

I ran into the diner to warn Margaret. "We were followed," I said. "We need to get back to the rooms to warn the others."

Margaret looked guiltily startled and annoyed. The young waitress had just brought her a bottle of Heineken at the bar.

We looked around the diner for an alternate exit but saw none.

"Where's the ladies' room?" I asked.

The waitress pointed to a narrow hall between the diner and the adjacent reception office. I pulled Margaret by the arm, hoping we'd also find an exit there. The hall dead-ended and we were trapped in the diner. I ran back to the counter.

"Is there a back way out of here?"

The waitress looked around to see what might be causing me to freak out.

"The beer is five dollars," she said slowly like a question.

I went into my secret jacket pocket where I'd learned to stash a variety of bills of different currencies, just in case. I handed her a twenty.

"Just ten back," I said. "Look." I lowered my voice. "An old boy-friend is stalking me, and my mother and I want to avoid him. I have a restraining order against him and everything." I tried to drum up some tears, which I was able to do because I was legitimately frightened.

That seemed to convince her. She nodded with a look of understanding. "You can go out through the kitchen," she said, holding the swinging door to the kitchen open for us. "It goes out to the back."

Margaret and I ran through the kitchen and out the back. We slid quietly yet quickly along the rear of the motel rooms, dropping below each of the back side's windows so we wouldn't be seen in case anyone had checked into these rooms, anyone like the two men I was sure were sent to kill us.

We headed for Reinhardt and Nash's room. We peered around the side to the front door. The way was clear so we ran for Reinhardt's door and knocked as quietly and frantically as possible until Nash answered, looking confused.

I pushed him out of the way, as did Margaret, who actually knocked him over before she slammed the door shut again.

"Reinhardt," I said. My heart was thumping. "We have to get out of here. The light-blue Ford is here. I'll bet the two men are at the reception desk."

Reinhardt sprang into action before I'd finished the last sentence. He grabbed for his gun that he had stowed within his jacket. Nash had the door open a crack and was peeking through. He had a firm grip on his Glock using both of his hands to steady it and ensure an accurate aim. I pulled my gun out as well and lined up behind the two of them at the door. If these thugs were coming for us, we'd give them one hell of a fight.

"I see two hulky types with gaudy shirts and ties coming our way," Nash said. "I know they're up to no good, but I don't see any weapons."

Nash pulled back from the door to allow Reinhardt to have a look.

"No." Reinhardt's voice was taut. "They've stopped at Hannah and Amos's room."

"Oh no," I said. "They don't know they're in danger. I came here first."

Nash burst out of our doorway, shooting wildly into the air to distract our assailants. Immediately after discharging his gun, he rolled and somersaulted, disappearing around the side of the motel for cover.

I knew the gunshots would warn Hannah and Amos that something was going on.

But it all happened so fast. By opening fire, Nash had initiated a gunfight.

The men, whoever they were, must have seen Nash.

One of them came around the corner. He reached into his jacket, pulled out a pistol, and popped off several gunshots in Nash's direction. The other man pulled an object from his pocket, kicked open Amos and Hannah's door with one mighty strike, pulled a pin, and threw what I realized was a grenade inside the room.

I screamed, "No!" as the two of them sprinted back to their waiting Ford. I pushed past Reinhardt and began to run toward Amos and Hannah's room when a blast shattered the air and shook the motel.

I fell to the ground clutching my ears. When I realized I wasn't dead, I looked up and saw billowing smoke, fire and debris pouring from Hannah and Amos's room. Tires screeched behind me, and I turned around to see the Ford skidding and shooting gravel and loose pavement back at what remained of the Denver Highway Motor Inn as it escaped.

"Hannah! Amos!" I screamed over the din.

Ransom, Renegade and Robert ran to me. Ransom helped me up and clutched me to him. He was shaking.

"We have to go in there!" I yelled.

But the smoke and fire were dense and impenetrable. I screamed their names, but no one answered. "No, no, no." I was crying now, my heart pounding.

"I'm going in," Ransom said, unwrapping my arms from his waist.

"I'm right behind you," Renegade said.

Without hesitation, they were both inside of the fiery room, out of sight, swallowed by smoke and flames.

Reinhardt was on his phone calling 9-1-1.

The lady from the reception desk, the owner, ran to join us. She was screaming and swearing, not knowing whether to be terrified or angry.

"Oh my God," she yelled. "Oh my God. What the hell is happening?" She was hysterical with her arms waving madly over her head, pacing and spinning and calling out.

I was too gripped by my terror to pay attention to her. I feared even more because Ransom and Renegade had run into the inferno where the smoke would have choked out the oxygen in the room. It seemed like forever. Why weren't they coming out?

I screamed out. "Ransom... Ransom." Of course, I wanted to call all their names, but somehow the only name I could say was Ransom's. I had buried and denied my feelings, I had been fearing my feelings, but on the brink of possibly losing him, they all poured from me like a broken dam. I couldn't lose him like I'd lost my real family in the fire. I hated that it took him maybe dying for me to admit I loved him, I wanted him, and I wanted him to want me, too.

My hysteria was taking over. I was screaming that loudly as if hoping my voice would keep them alive. I was getting ready to run in after them when Reinhardt and Nash caught me.

"They're in there. They're in there," I pleaded.

But they had me in such a tight grip, I couldn't break away.

My throat burned with the smoke and the strain of my repeated screams. My collar was wet from tears that streamed down my cheeks. I looked pleadingly to Reinhardt. "Please, let me go."

Reinhardt's face was tortured with pain as well, his face wet with tears, too, as he gripped me tightly, both of us shaking.

"Ruby, honey," Reinhardt said, his voice barely recognizable. "There's nothing we can do. Nothing." Horrified, we could only watch the door.

I became aware of sirens in the distance when another burst of chaos split the air. A crash like the motel was coming down on itself came from the burning building, sparks flying like fireworks lighting up the air dulled by smoke and debris.

Just as Hannah and Amos's room was about to collapse onto itself, two blackened figures ruptured through what was left of the front door, each carrying a body over his shoulders.

Our hearts leaped as we ran to help guide them to a spot a safe distance from the fire.

There, amid this tragic scene, two motionless bodies lay on the broken pavement and two other bodies crouched beside them desperately trying to breathe fresh air into their lungs.

The world began to move in slow motion as lights flashed and the commanding voices of emergency workers echoed around me.

Twenty

HANNAH AND AMOS WERE BROUGHT to the Denver Memorial Hospital burn ward in critical condition. Both had suffered multiple third-degree burns and significant respiratory damage. But they were alive. At least for now.

Ransom and Renegade had first-degree burns and were suffering from smoke inhalation, but they were responding well to treatment and the doctors told us they would probably be released in twenty-four hours. We'd have to find a safe place for them to recover. We couldn't rest easy leaving them in a public hospital where anyone could have access to them.

Reinhardt and Robert sat on their phones for over an hour. Robert was trying to line up somewhere for us to stay, and Reinhardt was looking into hiring private burn and respiratory medical specialists. He would make sure that Hannah and Amos got the best medical care possible.

Margaret was another matter. She hadn't had a drink for nearly a whole day, and her body was in the grip of withdrawal. We told her she could get help here at the hospital, but she declined. How could she be incapacitated by treatment while Oscar was held captive? Her discomfort would have to wait until Oscar was safe, regardless of what it cost her—or the safety of every American. She trembled as we provided her with coffee and more coffee, though what she desperately needed was a drink.

Nash was also acting strange. He paced like a caged tiger, skulking mysteriously, offering no comforting words as if he were detached from our pain, watching us, but still staying close.

I wondered why he hung around. This was the first time I got the sense that he had more of an agenda than just wanting money to pay off gambling debts. Several times, he walked away to be by himself. At a few points, when my curiosity got the better of me, I looked for him and found him on his phone, arguing with someone. I approached him once to see if I could find out who he was talking to, but he hung up abruptly.

Margaret was right. He couldn't be trusted. But we were stuck with him; he was the only one who could help us complete the exchange. I hoped he would come through and not turn on us at the last second.

While we waited to see how we could get everyone out of the hospital and into private care, Margaret and I stayed in the waiting room, leaving Reinhardt to consult with Amos and Hannah's doctors. Robert had left to check out a possible rental property, a house on the outskirts of town. Nash wasn't around. I figured he was making more phone calls in private. Who the hell was he talking to with such persistence?

But that was the least of my concern at the moment. Amid all of this, I was awash with thoughts of Ransom. I was scared and worried for Amos and Hannah, but I couldn't help it; my thoughts kept running back to him. I had been such an ass in the morning, acting like a spoiled child. Just a couple of nights prior we had made love, and he had said something I could have held on to, but instead, I wanted more commitment, more ardor, more something, and acted as if what we'd shared had been meaningless to me. Tears choked my throat when I thought about who I was. I was built up purely out of loss: my parents, my brother, my original me, and my life, and now I was looking at losing not only another chance at love but the person who I hoped loved me.

Reinhardt came in to give us an update. He looked weary, his olive skin pale under the white lights. "The doctors tell me that Hannah and Amos will likely be in critical condition for some time and have to stay in isolation. Which means we can't see them yet. But the boys are asking for you."

Reinhardt came over and held me in a tender hug. "Come on, Ruby. Let's go see your brothers."

Margaret croaked from across the room, "I'll stay here and hold down the fort." She was rocking back and forth in her chair, her arms wound tightly around her torso, her head bent toward her knees.

Reinhardt nodded and we left her to go see Ransom and Renegade.

My knees were wobbly as we walked down the corridor to their room.

I let Reinhardt go in first. He pushed open the door to their room and peered in. "You guys ready for some company?"

We shuffled in. I was happy to see they were both sitting up and awake, though both were hooked up to IVs with clear tubes snaking into their arms and noses. Both shifted uncomfortably to try and greet us.

Seeing Ransom like this, I was instantly flooded with the memory of when he'd been shot in Washington, taking bullets that were intended for me, and I nearly began to sob. I was relieved to see him conscious and alert.

He reached out his hand to me. "Come here," he mouthed.

I ran to him and threw my arms around him. He held me gently, which started even more tears.

"Hey," Renegade said. "What about me?"

I laughed and wiped my face and went to Renegade to hug him as well. "I'm so glad you're OK," I whispered.

"Amos and Hannah?" Ransom asked, uncertainty hanging in his voice.

"They're in the burn unit," Reinhardt said. "I'm flying in two specialists from Switzerland to take over their care. They'll be here in the morning."

That was when I looked up and saw that it was dark outside. I had lost all track of time.

Reinhardt's phone pinged. He pulled it from his pocket and read the message. "Robert has found a house rental for us. He's making sure it's secure and will be back here in half an hour to take us there. We need to get back to Margaret. I'm afraid she needs…" He shrugged and Ransom and Renegade nodded.

"Good," Ransom said. "Can you get a nurse to unhook me?" He began fidgeting with his IV line.

Reinhardt put his hand out to stop Ransom. "You two," he said sternly, "are here for the night. We'll be back in the morning and if the doctors clear you, then you can come with us. For now, you need to rest and recover. Ruby and I will look after Margaret."

Reinhardt started pushing me toward the door. I smiled and blew a kiss to both of them.

Out in the hallway, a man carrying flowers was wandering around as if he were looking for a patient but couldn't find the room. I went to ask Reinhardt whether this looked suspicious or not, but when we got to the waiting room, and I saw Margaret and Nash chatting away holding large Styrofoam cups with straws sticking out of the lids and a paper bag on the floor, I felt exasperated. Nash, thinking about his own interests, had gone out and bought a bottle of something to make sure she held it together long enough to make all the arrangements with the d'Angelos.

Reinhardt's eyes narrowed as he pointed to the bag.

Nash smirked and shrugged. "So when can we get out of here? Everyone seems stable for now, right?"

"Robert is on his way," Reinhardt said. "He has a place for us."

I nudged Reinhardt. Nash would be along for the ride, but I didn't think he needed to know where we were headed in case he planned to alert some of his secret contacts who could have been out to hurt us. He could see it when he got there.

Robert was taking longer to get back than he had thought, which made me even more nervous. There was nothing we could do but wait, pace, and keep checking the hallway and elevators for signs of him. The halls were fuller now with visitors, but at this hour, that didn't seem right. We were here keeping a watchful eye, and everything was calm, but still, I was relieved when he finally walked into the waiting room looking a little exasperated.

"Sorry," Robert said. "Bad traffic."

We left without further explanation. I was surprised he had taken our SUV and was driving again. He looked comfortable and so very much in command again as he sat contentedly in the driver's seat.

He maneuvered easily out into the heavy traffic of downtown Denver. We drove for almost an hour. Robert was right. The traffic was heavy.

Near the outskirts of the city, he turned onto a private road and stopped at a guardhouse in front of a gate. He put down the window and handed a card to a uniformed guard who examined it, handed it back, and opened the gate.

We drove down a street lined with expensive-looking houses. He turned a corner and came to another hut where a guard approached our SUV. The guard looked through the window and seemed to recognize Robert. He saluted and walked back to the hut and this gate opened to us as well. Robert drove in and stopped in front of a large modern two-story Spanish-style house.

All the military personnel was odd, I thought. Was this a military base? I didn't see any other evidence of that being so. Maybe the guy was just a saluter. At this point, I didn't think much of it because I was so busy looking at the opulent house.

"Robert, you've upgraded," I teased him.

He laughed.

Inside, a wide staircase in the center of the vaulted entryway divided the giant house in half. Downstairs to the left was a luxurious living room with a grand piano in front of a floor-to-ceiling window that looked out over a pool in the back. On the right was a rich cream-and-gold room with bookshelves and art. A dining area near a kitchen opened up behind the staircase. I doubted this place would have donuts. Remembering Amos and Hannah, I squeezed my eyes shut for a second to send them strength.

Robert was pointing us to head toward the dining room when a tiny woman in a maid's uniform greeted him warmly. "*Hola, Señor Robert,*" she said, smiling brightly. "I have food ready in the dining room for everyone."

Robert returned her smile and turned to us for introductions. "This is Señora Lopez," Robert said. "She's going to be our cook and house-keeper. Just ask her for anything you need."

"Maria please. Call me Maria." She laughed and gestured that we should all come inside.

After we finished the delicious meal of tamales, salad, and roast chicken, and Margaret had enjoyed several glasses of wine, we adjourned to the den where fat brown leather sofas were like magnets.

I was heading to the love seat to flop down when I spotted a giant globe on a stand. I went to it, wanting to see Corsica on the map.

Reinhardt closed the double doors. Everyone else was getting comfortable on the sofas when Reinhardt's phone rang. My heart skipped several beats. I hoped it wasn't the hospital.

Reinhardt looked at it and frowned. "What do you know," he said, "it's Mateo." He cleared his throat, put the phone on speaker, and answered the call. "This is Reinhardt Draker."

"Reinhardt," Mateo said. "I am so very sorry to hear of your family's... How shall I say...? Misfortune. I hear your friends are still in the hospital, fighting for their lives." He clucked his tongue. "I do hope you realize the danger you are in until you provide me with what I am owed."

Reinhardt clenched his teeth and moved closer to the phone that he had put on the desk. "If any more misfortune befalls my family, you can kiss your payment goodbye. Our deal is simple. You release Oscar, and we release the plutonium to your handlers. Why complicate the matter with messy... misfortunes. You're not doing yourself any favors."

Silence.

I didn't like the way this conversation was going. In my mind's eye, I could see Mateo's anger rising. He tolerated no one who dared challenge him.

Then Mateo spoke. "You are ready to turn over the materials?"

"All you had to do was call," Reinhardt said. "The ball has been in your court for some time. Does this mean *you* are ready?"

"If you mean do I have Oscar with me," Mateo said, "the answer is yes."

"Let me talk to him."

There was another long pause on the phone.

In the background, I heard Mateo say, "Go get him."

Several moments went by, and I started to wonder what was going on.

There was scuffling and a man began to talk. It didn't sound at all like the same person who'd been on the Skype call back at the Canadian compound. "Margaret," the man said. "I want to talk to Margaret."

"Oscar, is that you?" Margaret's eyes looked wild. "It doesn't sound like you."

I felt sorry for her.

"It's me," the man said, his voice cracking. "Mom, please! Get me out of—"

Mateo cut in abruptly. "There you go," he said. "You have your confirmation. Now when and where do we make the exchange?"

Reinhardt looked at Nash. I could see in his eyes that he didn't like relying on Nash, but that was the reality. Nash and his connection were the only ones who could get us into the facility at Rocky Flats.

Reinhardt motioned that Nash should answer.

Nash moved closer to the phone and spoke, enunciating clearly, "Tomorrow at noon at the Rocky Flats site. Have your movers at the west gate. Your shipment will be ready. We open the gates when we have Oscar safely in our hands."

"And whom am I talking to?" Mateo asked. His tone had shifted. He sounded both annoyed and surprised. Maybe he was caught off guard that the voice was not Reinhardt's.

"It's Felix's old friend, George Nash," said Reinhardt. "The one and the only person who can make this happen." Reinhardt leaned in more closely. "D'Angelo, if you're not there by five minutes after..." Reinhardt's voice growing dark and threatening, "... and if we don't see Oscar in plain view, the deal is off."

I panicked. Reinhardt was going too far but I didn't know how to let him know to stop. I leaped up and waved my hands and shook my head, but Reinhardt persisted.

"I need to hear you say it, d'Angelo." His voice boomed into the phone. "If you're late, we turn the matter over to the CIA."

Margaret gasped, and Robert gripped her mouth.

"You think you can threaten me?" Mateo yelled back. "Make sure you hold up your end of the bargain, or you will regret this." There was a click, and he was gone.

We all sat speechless for a moment.

"Fuck this. I'm getting a drink," Nash said, unfolding his lanky body from the sofa and leaving the room.

I figured he was going somewhere to make another private phone call. I looked at Reinhardt then shifted my eyes in Nash's direction. If he were about to warn someone about what was going down, we would want to know who that was. We gave him less than a minute then fanned out to look for him.

We heard him in the kitchen, murmuring to someone.

Reinhardt pushed the door open a crack.

Nash was leaning against the counter with his phone to his ear. "Tomorrow at noon," he said. "Have the one cask pulled and in the shipping bay. Leave the crane attached so they can load their truck and get out of there fast? A hostage is going to be released so nothing can go wrong."

Reinhardt tapped me on the shoulder and we tiptoed back to the den.

Robert was sitting alone. "Where's Margaret?" I asked.

"Maria took her upstairs," Robert said. "She's so on edge, she's more of a liability than an asset. I asked Maria to bring her more wine, which will ensure she'll both sleep and be too wrecked to come with us tomorrow. It's for the best."

"Nash made a phone call. He told someone about the time and the deal," I blurted out. "But we couldn't tell if it was his man at Rocky Flats. It sounded like it might be, but I still don't trust him. Why would he have been making all those secret calls at the hospital?"

"I wish Renegade were here," Robert said. "He'd be able to trace those calls."

I smiled sadly. "Renegade is magical, but his computer was destroyed at the motel. He's not that magical."

"Well, there's a computer here," Robert said, smiling like a fox. "Reinhardt? What do you think? Are they well enough?"

"The doctor was going to release them tomorrow," I said. I was pulled in two directions. I wanted them out of the hospital where I knew they weren't safe, but at the same time, the doctors were looking after them, and if anything went wrong…

"How much difference is twelve hours going to make?" Robert said. He pulled the fob from his pocket and started at a fast limp for the door.

***

I let Robert handle that end of things while I ruminated over Nash and what was going on with him. I wondered whether Nash merely appeared to have everything under control: the removal of the plutonium from the heavy water reservoir, the operation of the crane to take it to the shipping bay, a quick and flawless loading and exit from the facility.

It was such a complicated procedure, and for one person and his "contact"—some dubious insider who could easily be bought off, to be in charge of it—seemed very strange to me. Things were never straightforward, which, to my mind, meant something was fishy. I had too many questions popping around in my mind and I needed answers. I wished I could ask Nash outright: what the hell are you up to? But I worried he would get nervous and something would go wrong. It was best if he believed we trusted him.

Reinhardt seemed to be reading my mind. I could see he felt the same too. "It's just all too easy," I said woefully. "The head of a mafia drives up to a secret facility, Nash gets dangerous nuclear material onto a transport carrier, and they just drive away and leave us their hostage as payment in return? I'm sorry. I might be new at this, but this whole thing stinks. We're being led down a dark path, Reinhardt. It's definitely not going to go down that way."

I ran to the door to see if Nash was standing there the way Reinhardt and I had done to him. I hoped that when Renegade got here, he could tap into the phone records to give us information about who Nash had called and what he was really doing. But until Robert stole the boys from the hospital and got them back to this house, Reinhardt and I would have to keep tabs on Nash by ourselves.

It was near midnight when Robert returned with Ransom and Renegade. Seeing them walk in looking almost like their normal selves, if not a little tousled and underslept, made it clear why they'd been so fidgety at the hospital. Being confined to a hospital bed, stuck to oxygen and IV lines, must have felt like being handcuffed.

Nash came to the foyer to join our reunion but hung back with an artificial grin pasted on his face.

We Drakers had a sixth sense about people when their body language didn't synchronize with their motives, but Reinhardt and I pretended everything was fine. We were particularly cautious not to disclose the reason Renegade and Ransom had come here at this late hour instead of in the morning when they were scheduled to be discharged. I hoped he thought our purpose was to have their help with the exchange the next day.

After brief hugs and a quick assessment of how they were feeling, we all feigned fatigue, saying we should all get a good night's sleep to be ready and alert for the next day. After all, we could hardly run a computer search on Nash's phone calls with him standing there.

The boys caught on but my guess was Nash did, too. We went upstairs saying our goodnights on the way.

My room was extremely well-appointed with a pillow-top mattress and a duvet as fluffy as I'd ever seen, but I couldn't enjoy it knowing, in a few minutes, I'd be back to work. I sat and waited.

A soft rap on my door startled me and I nearly fell off the bed. I waited, my heart racing, and the person knocked again. I hurled myself to the door, flung it open, and was staring right into Ransom's face. I wanted to throw my arms around him and kiss him, but I froze.

He put one finger to his lips and reached for my hand and pulled me into the hall. We both scanned the hallway, and seeing no one, we made our way down the steps back to the den.

Renegade was already there, hunched over the computer with Reinhardt and Robert peering over his shoulders. Renegade's fingers clicked over the keyboard as he huffed with frustration. "I'm not finding a single thing," he said. "His phone records are tightly encrypted. I'll have to run a more-specialized decryption program. I just need to get into the SS7 network exchange, which should give me access to all his correspondence."

He got up, paced across the room, peeked out the door to look up the stairs and make sure Nash wasn't awake and watching, before gently shutting the door.

"No one puts this kind of encryption on their phone records. Ordinary people don't care and wouldn't even think about it. It appears that our Nash is no ordinary person." Renegade searched our faces to make sure we understood the seriousness of this.

Suddenly, my mistrust of Nash took on a whole new tenor. Never mind his motives; now I suspected he wasn't at all who he said he was, which also made Margaret suspicious because that meant she was playing along. Worse still, we were about to allow him to turn over bomb-making materials to a crime lord who would pass them along to who knows who.

"Once I hack into the right program," Renegade said. "It could still take a few hours for it to find a way past his security."He sighed. "You guys may as well go to bed. I'll stay here and try to get some rest on the sofa."

I could feel his frustration. Renegade didn't usually take long to find what he was looking for, but then he didn't have his specialized equipment or software that was in the control center at Fairhaven.

"I could stay with you for moral support?" I offered.

"Thanks, Ruby, but you're going to be much more helpful tomorrow on some sleep. I can handle this."

***

It was 6 a.m. when I awoke in a sweat, my heart pounding almost out of my chest. I tried to lie back down but I knew my night was over so I threw my clothes back on and crept downstairs to check Renegade's progress.

The room was dark except for the glow from the computer screen. I went around the back of the desk to have a look. SEARCHING FILES the message read. The software was running and still had found no entry.

I looked over at the sofa where Renegade was asleep. I nudged his shoulder. "Renegade," I whispered.

He jumped up, nearly knocking me over, and blindly scrambled over to the computer where he tripped on the chair and landed on his belly.

"The program is still searching." I reached down to help him up.

"Damn it," Renegade said, though I wasn't sure if he was exclaiming from having hurt himself, or from the program's not yet having found its way into Nash's phone records.

He picked himself up off the floor and limped to the computer where he opened up a dialogue box to try and program another way in. "How long before you guys have to leave for Rocky Flats?"

"It's about an hour from here," I said. "But Nash may want to leave earlier to make sure everything is in order. Let's see if we can get some coffee."

Renegade leaned back in his chair to stretch and cracked his neck. "That's a great idea."

He stood and followed me to the kitchen.

Twenty-One

WHEN WE GOT TO THE KITCHEN, Maria was already there, pulling a batch of heavenly-smelling scones out of the oven. She gave us a surprised smile when we came in. "Good morning, *Señor y Señorita*. You are awake so early. I have not made coffee yet." She wiped her hands on a towel and scurried over to the counter to put water in the coffee maker. "Sit, please. I will have it ready for you in a few minutes."

Renegade and I sat down on the stools at the island while Maria brought us mugs and milk and sugar before going back to the next batch of dough.

"I have to mix it while the butter is cold," she said. "You like to cook?"

"I would like to. I only need to be in one place for long enough," I laughed, and Renegade joined in. "Maria," I asked. "Do you know if anyone else is awake yet?"

"Only *Señor Nash*," she said. "But he say he not hungry and no coffee until later. *Por qué?*"

Renegade and I looked at each other before hopping off our stools.

"We'll be right back," I said as we made for the door.

Suddenly all the lights went out. Even with the pre-dawn gray glow seeping in from the window, the kitchen was too dark for us to see. We groped our way to the door, my heart heavy. If the power went out, the computer would've gone down too.

"No," wailed Renegade. "The program will have to start all over again."

When we were nearly at the den, the lights came on again. We ran to the desk, and sure enough, the screen was blank. I didn't have any proof, but I was sure it was Nash's doing. He'd probably flipped the breaker switches, which disabled Renegade's program. My stomach knotted.

"I've restarted it, Ruby, but we won't have any answers before you guys leave today," Renegade said. His hands were clenched, and his nostrils were flaring.

I looked around for Nash, sure I'd find him lurking close by, but except for us and Maria, the house was quiet.

Maria came to the den looking puzzled and worried. "The coffee is ready. If you like, I can bring it in here."

"That's OK, Maria," Renegade said. "We'll come back to the kitchen."

A short ten minutes later, Nash came down the stairs, whistling.

Bastard, I thought. No wonder he was cheerful. His moody disposition from the night before had lifted, probably because we had no way to implicate him now. I wasn't sure who he was involved with, but whoever it was would remain a secret even while we depended on him to carry out the plutonium transfer to Mateo.

Not long afterward, Margaret came down to the kitchen. I was surprised to see her up so early, but I soon realized she hadn't yet gone to sleep. She looked like a zombie minus the skin lesions.

Maria turned back from the oven where she was popping the last tray of scones in. When she saw Margaret trying to crawl onto a counter stool, she paused. "*Ay, dios mia,*" she murmured. She poured Margaret a mug of coffee and slid it over to her.

Margaret bent over to sip. "Ouch," she said numbly, tried again, then smoothly bypassed her mug and vomited onto the floor. She moaned and tried to wipe her mouth with her sleeve but missed. It looked like she wouldn't be going anywhere.

Maria waved her hands at us to go out. "Is OK. I take her back to bed. Come, *Señora*. I will get you cleaned up and some aspirin."

She led Margaret back up the stairs to her room, passing Reinhardt and Ransom on the stairway. They hugged the wall so the women could pass and came into the kitchen, stopping short of the purple mess on the floor.

"Oh, man," Ransom said, holding his nose.

Now at least they knew what happened with Margaret, but since they probably didn't know about the power interruption, I filled them in.

"It's been an exciting morning. We had a power outage," I said, glaring at Nash. "Renegade had to restart the search program."

Nash didn't make any move at what I was saying or try to save face by asking "what search program?" I guessed he figured, at this point, it no longer mattered. "We should leave here by ten a.m.," he said. "I want to be there long before d'Angelo comes on the scene. Plutonium is nasty stuff. You don't handle it right, and…" He let a slow smile spread out over his face. "Let's not discuss that part and just say it's not pretty."

Everyone stared at him. I knew today would be a crap-shoot. I had no idea what to expect. But at this point in the game, what choice did we have?

At 10 a.m. , Reinhardt, Robert, Nash and I piled into the SUV. Nash didn't ask why Ransom and Renegade were staying behind, but Robert slipped it in that they were still under the weather and needed to keep quiet. Nash didn't seem to care. They were going to continue to try and access Nash's phone records, but Renegade was going to have to figure out a more expedient way. Reinhardt had his cell handy if they found anything out.

As we drove in, I realized how much I hated the desolate terrain in this town. It looked the way I felt: like we were about to unleash an apocalypse. The closer we got to Rocky Flats, the heavier the responsibility weighed on me. Why wasn't Rosalind whispering advice?

Although I felt alone and abandoned as I watched the back of Nash's head in the driver's seat, a resolve awakened in me. Whatever he was up to, I'd foil his deception. There, Rosalind! I thought. I'm not letting him get away with this. I'm going to stop him and this jerk, Mateo. I felt for my gun. It was there if I needed it, and I'd use it if I had to.

When we arrived, the site seemed too quiet. The last time we'd come here, the security guard had stepped out of his hut long before we reached the gate. The two other squad cars we'd seen the last time on patrol also were not around. Already something was not right. I could tell Nash noticed it, too, by how he was shifting uneasily in his seat.

When we got to the security hut, he barked, "Stay in the car." He drew his pistol and got out of the car. He walked to the hut, hesitated, then kicked the door open, with his gun pointed from shoulder level. We followed with our guns drawn in case he needed cover.

Before we reached him, Nash had lowered his gun. Robert and Reinhardt stepped up close and looked in, shaking their heads in disbelief.

"What? What's happening," I asked from behind.

The men let me see for myself. On the floor, the security guard lay in a pool of blood, dead from a gunshot wound to the heart.

Nash stepped out of the vicinity of the guard hut and scoured the landscape, letting his eyes linger over the roads and buildings beyond the gate. He raised his hand to find his phone in his shirt pocket but stopped when he realized we were staring at him. "I should check out the shipping bay," Nash said.

"I'll cover you," Reinhardt said. "Ruby, you and Robert stay here and keep an eye on the road and for Mateo."

"Shouldn't we phone the authorities?" I asked, looking at the body on the floor.

"Not yet," Nash said. He walked into the guard hut, carefully stepping around the blood, and pounded on a large red button on the control panel to lift the security gate.

The gate opened, and he and Reinhardt got back into the SUV and drove through in the direction of the building where the plutonium rested in its watery hold many stories below ground. I wondered who he had contacted to arrange extracting it and having the plutonium transferred to the shipping bay. Were they even safe being near it?

Time seemed to stand still in this desolate place. Even the wind had paused, and the air felt like the inside of a tomb, one that harbored an evil entity. It wasn't the plutonium in and of itself that was evil, but the people who coveted its power and the destruction that it could wreak on humankind.

Robert and I stood guard at the entrance, waiting for Mateo and his entourage to arrive. It was 11:45 a.m. and the bleakness of our task and our fear seemed to summon dark clouds. An eerie void hung heavily in the air. I looked at the man lying on the floor, with his eyes wide open and terrified. Was this Mateo's way of saying "don't mess with me"? I was sure he was setting up the scene to throw us off our game, unnerve us with dead bodies we'd now have to deal with.

I wasn't unnerved though. I was angry. And scared. And anxious. Nash and Reinhardt seemed to be taking a very long time. "How long should it take them?"

Robert looked at his watch. "It's only been ten minutes."

He had barely finished his sentence when we saw the SUV driving back from the loading dock. They got out of the car and returned to us in the hut.

"The shipment is in place," Nash said. "All the handlers will have to do is input a numeric code into the access terminal at the main door to Building 717, and the robots will use the automated sensor system built into the floor to push the cask onto the trailer. No one has to touch anything. They can simply pull away from the dock, close the cargo doors, and drive away. But without the code, they get nothing. And no Oscar? No code." Nash looked smug, as if he thought nothing could go wrong.

"Who makes the first move?" I asked. "Mateo is no fool. If he gives us Oscar, we could still leave him without the code. No," I shook my head. "Mateo won't let that happen. And on the other side, if we give him the code, he'll have what he wants and could just drive off without holding up his end of the bargain."

"It will be a delicate dance of nerves," Nash said. His left cheek twitched.

I couldn't help but smile. I was glad to see the tension was finally getting to him. That was good. It meant he wasn't entirely trying to ruin us. "First we demand Oscar's release."

A *ping* came from Reinhardt's phone, interrupting Nash.

Reinhardt reached into his pocket and looked at the display. Shock formed on his face before the lines turned to anger. He held the display up for Nash to see. "CIA?" Reinhardt sputtered. "Nash. All this time you've been working with the CIA?"

Nash squirmed. His expression softened as he tried to explain. "It was the only way we could keep Mateo from knowing we at the DoD and CIA were onto him. We kept him busy tracking you guys down. We've known about Felix's hidden stash. We intercepted Margaret's envelope and kept the information."

He started to say something else, but suddenly the silence that enveloped the morning burst into a loud frenzy of wind and whapping blades. Two large choppers on their descent were stirring up the dust into a giant cloud.

We ran inside the guard shed, our backs against the wall so as not to disturb the evidence at our feet.

It was only seconds before a dozen or so men in dark coveralls had us surrounded in the hut, their automatic weapons held high. We were trapped and vastly outnumbered.

"Yours?" Robert hissed.

Nash made a sour face and shook his head. "No," he said resignedly. "This is completely d'Angelo's doing."

He stepped forward to confront the gunman at the head of the pack. "If you hurt any one of us, you don't get the loading code. Mateo won't be very happy with you if he doesn't get what he came for."

The lead man grunted and continued his threatening posture, but after several moments of a standoff, he had no choice but to move outside in retreat.

He lowered his weapon and stepped to the back of the group. He took out his phone and mumbled into it. "Move the carrier in. We're secured at the site." A few minutes later, an all-black tractor-trailer rolled up the road in a cloud of dust. It pulled up and stopped at the gate.

The driver rolled down his window and shouted, "Where do I move the rig to load?"

One of Mateo's men nudged Nash with the tip of his automatic rifle.

Nash stumbled, then turned around, his face bright with satisfaction. "Not a chance," he said. "Oscar Worchenski gets released before we do a single thing." He folded his arms over his chest. His pleasant expression turned dark and he stared at the gunman defiantly.

The man lowered his gun and pulled out his phone again. "They want the hostage."

I hated all this cat and mouse. We'd already been very clear about how this would work and I didn't like that Mateo was trying to change the rules.

The man listened for a few seconds then cast a menacing glance at Nash before he put the phone back in his pocket and leaned back against the door. He folded his arms around his gun and looked at the sky. The wind whistled through the barren landscape. In the silence, I became more and more nervous.

After several minutes, I saw what looked like a dust storm in the distance, but when it came closer, I realized it was a car. A black limo with tinted windows emerged and came to a stop in front of us.

The back passenger door opened. I held my breath. The hulking figure who got out was Vince. He took his sweet time as he ambled over to the group of us in the guard hut, a haughty smile on his face.

"You guys really are thick," said Nash angrily. "Is there a language barrier?" He raised his voice, enunciating each word. "We get Oscar or there is no deal. You need the shipping door number and the release code to load the material. But nothing happens until we have Oscar."

Vince shrugged. "There has been a change of plans." He dropped his creepy smile. "Do you think you're in a position to make demands? I could easily have all of you killed." He pointed around to the small army of men. "I am in charge here. Not you."

To his credit, Nash stood firm and stepped closer to Vince. "No Oscar. No deal. Your father knows our terms."

Vince kept up his firm expression but he hunched down just a bit.

He couldn't fool us. He was just a tool. And not a very good one.

I would have felt bad for him, but at this moment, I wasn't allying myself with anyone who was on Mateo's side, even if by the accident of being his family.

The limousine door opened again on the passenger side and Mateo stepped out. He turned in a circle, his hands on his hips, and slowly pretended to check out the area. He looked over at Vince and cocked his head as if to ask, "what's taking so long?"

Mateo shook his head as he rounded the front of the limo and walked to the driver's window where he tapped twice.

There was a double click from the trunk.

Mateo snorted at his son who seemed to be staring him down. He pointed with his chin toward the trunk and glared at his son.

Vince did not move.

Mateo's face darkened, his eyes flaring with rage, his lips drawn tight with disgust. "Do as I say," Mateo said as he strode toward his son.

With each step, Vince cowered a bit more until finally he turned and lifted the trunk lid. He reached inside and hefted out a person by pulling him out under his arms.

We saw a head, then his arms tied together in front of him, and finally one leg as he clumsily tried to get over the rise in the trunk.

Vince twisted the man by the torso to pull him out and then the man fell to the ground.

Vince jerked up the man's head by the chin and pointed angrily.

Then he pulled out his pistol from inside his jacket and pointed it into the man's back.

"Move," Vince said and the two of them marched over to the hut, the man in front dragging his feet to resist Vince.

The man, breathless, and with his eyes open wide, stood before us, searching our faces. He yanked away from Vince's hold. "Where is Margaret?" he demanded. "I want to know she's all right." His features made me cringe. He was so like his father. The man in front of us was unmistakably Oscar, the son of Felix Szabo.

Vince shoved Oscar into the guard hut. He stumbled on the blood and came to stand beside Reinhardt, Robert and Nash.

For the briefest of moments, I felt relief. After all, we had him. We did what we'd set out to do.

Then Vince lunged forward and grabbed me by the arm, his gun pointed tight to my neck. He yanked me out of the hut and started pulling me toward Mateo.

"Now give us the code, or your Ruby here…" Vince stroked my cheek with his pistol. "… becomes our new guest. Again." He gave out a delighted series of snorts that sounded like the bray of a jackass.

I was really confused. Now the Drakers would have to get me back before giving the code. What were these people thinking? They didn't need me!

"Get her into the limo," Mateo said.

Vince gave his father another grunt but pushed me into the back seat, leaving the door open.

My heart was thumping loudly. I had expected a double-cross but not this. Could Reinhardt, Nash and Robert talk them into releasing me as well? I waited, wondering what the Drakers would do next.

"We will release your Ruby after the cargo carrier is loaded and far away from here," Mateo said.

I wanted to shout something, anything, but my heart was in my throat, and my ability to speak was as much a hostage as I was.

"Nash," Robert said, "give him the code."

Reinhardt and Robert stepped toward Nash, giving him a threatening look.

Nash stood firm. His agenda was not ours. We knew that now. "If you hold Ruby, then we want your son. We trade again when the truck is leaving."

Mateo laughed and Nash looked unsettled.

Mateo motioned to the gunmen to take Vince. "Here. You can have him."

Vince's expression went slack, and his mouth hung open. He kept his eyes down the whole time Reinhardt was handcuffing him to the chair in the hut.

Nash was all business. "Have the transport drive to Building 717 and back up to Shipping Door A. When your driver gets there, he needs to pick up the phone at the main entrance. I will give him the code he needs to punch into the keypad. Then he pounded his fist on the red release button and the gate opened.

Mateo signaled for the truck to drive through.

We watched as the specialized carrier turned and backed into the intended dock. Moments later the driver walked up the four cement steps to the door we had used to enter the facility a few days earlier. He looked around as if uncertain but then picked up the phone. The wall-mounted phone rang in the guard hut and Nash picked it up, his eyes on the security monitors.

"Lift the keypad latch," Nash said. "Now punch in this code: 1991-17-FX-999."

The driver did as he was told, his forehead creased with concentration.

The shipping door lifted.

Nash was focused on the next monitor whose camera was trained on the automated crane.

The crane went through the loading sequence: first lifting a black metal canister into another metal container painted bright red, then into a wooden crate where it attached a fitted lid, and then placing the shipment onto an AGV which slowly moved into the trailer's cargo hold.

Looking shaken, the driver climbed back into the cab, pulled out a short distance from the dock, stopped, got out of his cab, and walked to the back end of the trailer where he went through a long process of closing and sealing the cargo doors. He returned to the cab and drove back to us at the gate. There, he rolled down his window and waited for Mateo's clearance.

Mateo put a phone to his ear and held up his finger. He muttered into the phone before returning it to his jacket. He waved the driver to head out onto the road. When the black eighteen-wheeler pulled slowly away, I had the feeling it was the devil on its way back to hell.

Through the back windows of the limo, I watched the truck disappear. Once it was out of sight, well on its way to their rendezvous point, Mateo reached his hand inside to help me out again. I had no idea what would happen next, but amid all my fears, all I could think about was how soft his hand was.

"Ruby. That went very well. I am a man of my word. You may go." He smiled and kissed my hand before gently guiding it toward Reinhardt's. Mateo turned and went back to the limo.

"Father," Vince said. "What about me?"

Without turning around, Mateo flipped his hand backward in the air and kept walking.

Nash released Vince with a rough shove in Mateo's direction.

Vince tripped and fell onto his knees to the floor of the hut. His face looked feral, his breath vicious.

One of the gunmen let out a snicker.

"You don't laugh at me!" Vince screamed. He grabbed his automatic weapon and jumped to a standing position, weapon poised, looking enraged and lost.

He ran out of the hut, shooting at the car, riddling the limo—and his father—with bullets.

Mateo's body contorted from the force of the shots. He glanced at his son with horror on his face before falling into the dirt, blood oozing onto the sand. Mateo's men scurried to tear the weapon away from Vince, and to help Mateo.

Then three more helicopters appeared and rapidly descended. The first landed a short distance from the hut.

I cried out as dirt and gravel bit into my eyes and face. When I could see again, the dust was thickly covering one of the choppers that had landed.

The door opened and Hollinger jumped to the ground in a Kevlar vest, an assault rifle held high.

Two more men jumped down.

I froze. It was Renegade and Ransom, also armed and in bulletproof gear.

The other helicopters landed and there were men and the sound of rifles and shouting overtaking everything.

Hollinger crouched low and ran into the hut. He went straight to Robert. I watched his lips as he spoke. "You did the right thing, Robert. We'll take it from here."

I froze. Robert? What?

Hollinger looked at each of us, his eyes settling on Oscar, who looked exhausted and suspicious and frightened.

"I don't have to ask who you are," Hollinger said, reaching out to shake Oscar's hand. "I'm glad you're OK." Hollinger shook his head as he grasped the hand of the son of his enemy. He turned at the sound of another set of whapping blades from a helicopter.

One of Hollinger's men shouted, "Sir, they're getting away."

I looked over to the limo. Vince was no longer there. Nor was Mateo's body. "Aren't your guys going after them?"

Hollinger looked at Robert and Nash, the three of them shaking their heads. "Let's get out of here," Hollinger said. "I'll debrief you back at the house."

Twenty-Two

LOOKING WORRIED, MARIA GREETED HOLLINGER at the door. "Major Hollinger," she said. "I am happy to see you. Everything is secure here. It went OK?"

"Thank you, Maria. Everything went very well," said Hollinger, shouldering off his jacket. "Can you bring Margaret Warren to the den, please? We'll debrief in there."

Maria nodded and went upstairs as we followed Hollinger to the den.

I could hear Margaret thumping down the staircase before she appeared at the den's door. I hadn't ever heard her move so quickly.

"Oscar?" she said as she came through the door. "Do you have him? Is he all right?" She squinted and searched the room for her son.

Oscar stood up from his chair in the corner and they stared at each other without moving. Curious, I thought.

"Hello, Mom," Oscar finally said. "I guess I have to thank you for saving my life." He managed a faint smile but still didn't move to embrace her.

"You have no idea what I've gone through," Margaret said. She was smiling but also did not approach her son. Their tentative standoff revealed a relationship made up of hurt and walls. After a moment, Margaret walked over and looked closely at him before she took the upholstered chair next to him.

Hollinger cleared his throat. "I would imagine you all want to know what's going on."

No one spoke, waiting for Hollinger to dive in. I was trying to adjust to the idea that the DoD and the CIA had been in on this the whole time, but I wasn't adjusting well. I was tired, strung out, and getting angry.

"Let me see," I snapped. "You were on the scene of a nuclear heist and had government troops who outnumbered Mateo and his dozen or so men and they all got away, including Vince and his father, though I'm not sure if Mateo is dead or not. And to add to the game—which you seem to have had no problem with starting in the first place—dangerous plutonium that terrorists will make into a bomb probably intended for an American target is now out of the country, something you'd said we would go to prison for. Yes, I'd say we'd like to know what the hell is going on."

Hollinger came over and awkwardly took my elbow. "Ruby," he said. "That's exactly how it was supposed to happen. Let me explain." He found a chair and perched on it. He was excited by how all of this had gone down.

I just wished I knew what the "this" was.

"After Felix escaped from Washington last summer, we learned that he was doing business with a Corsican crime family. It seemed they had given him millions of dollars in exchange for weapons. Not just guns and ammo but..." He paused and nodded as if we would all say it together. "... enough plutonium to make several nuclear bombs. Right.

"As you know, the d'Angelos had a customer. A terrorist faction who would pay whatever he asked for the plutonium. So, being a business-minded fellow, naturally, he said he'd sell it to them. Mateo, however, soon figured out that Felix was insane and knowing the odds were against someone like Felix..." He chuckled mirthlessly. "He demanded Felix come up with some insurance in case Felix were killed during all of his dangerous dealings, which of course he was. Felix had no problem finding such insurance. He left a letter that would be delivered to Margaret should he be killed, telling Mateo to kidnap Oscar and hold him for whatever ransom he decided. Mateo was fine with this arrangement. Knowing how strong a mother's bond was with her son, he felt confident giving Felix his money, which helped him pursue you and attack Fairhaven.

"Anyway." He looked at Oscar, who was staring into his lap. "Oscar found the letter among his belongings after he learned Felix was dead. For his protection, we put him under video surveillance while he was working at the Archives and also in his apartment. That's how we knew about the letter. We got hold of the letter and learned about the plutonium's location but made sure to leave just enough information in the package for Margaret to involve the Drakers for help. But of course, in the interim, Oscar was kidnapped."

"Damn it, Hollinger," Reinhardt said. "You knew all along Robert was alive!"

Hollinger put out his hands. "No, I didn't. Not until Margaret came looking for the letter after Oscar's kidnapping."

"After the raid on the farmhouse," Margaret said, "where I was believed to have been killed in the helicopter crash, I tried to find out what was done with the bodies. Imagine my surprise when I found Robert in the hospital in New York. Then when I got Felix's letter and found out that Oscar had been kidnapped, I knew I needed help to get him back. At first, I didn't think I could go to Hollinger. If Mateo were to find out I'd gone to the authorities, they'd have killed Oscar for sure. So after Robert started to get better, we devised a plan to bring you here to help us find the plutonium, since that pivotal information was missing from the information in the package Felix left me." She glared at Hollinger. "You caused me a lot of pain," she said flatly.

"I'm sorry," interjected Robert softly. "It was a matter of national security. I couldn't let you know about me until the time was right."

Hollinger nodded. "And things then spun out of my control when

Mateo kidnapped Robert, holding him hostage until he got Margaret to reveal where Felix had hidden the plutonium."

"After Robert was taken," said Margaret. "I had no choice left but to call Hollinger and let him know exactly what was at stake. So to keep everyone alive, we, the DoD and the CIA pretended we had no clue. That the Drakers were part of Felix's scheme. That together we'd make the payoff. And even now, as far as they're concerned, everything worked as planned."

"OK, fine," I said. "But did you forget you just gave plutonium to terrorists?"

"We have intelligence everywhere in Corsica," Hollinger said brightly, leaning back in his chair. "As soon as the party comes forward to claim their purchase, we'll move agents into wherever they're based and take them and their facility out. Letting them get fairly far in will give them a feeling of security, which will cause them to let down their guard. This is the only way we can get to them. We have it all under control."

Right, I thought. Although Hollinger seemed to have come through for us this time, I wasn't assured that he had "everything under control" given how he'd misjudged the situation last time and cost Rosalind and Rose their lives.

My heart pinched at the thought of Rosalind. I missed her desperately right now. I needed her. Apart from Amos and Hannah, who had a long road of recovery ahead of them, we were all at least alive. We had Robert back with us and Margaret had Oscar. Soon we could all head home, back to Fairhaven. But Rosalind would never be with us again.

I wanted to be warmer toward Hollinger for handling this, but I was now feeling grief pool up in my body and kept to my chair until after he'd left.

The others, as if they knew what was happening, left me alone.

Except for Ransom. He turned, paused, and slowly came to me. He bent down to meet my eyes and wound his fingers in mine. He put his mouth to my ear. "You know what you need?"

I looked up at him, my cheeks wet. I rubbed them. "What?"

He grinned. "A donut."

I laughed.

Now that things were settled, we piled into the SUVs to go visit Amos and Hannah. The specialists Reinhardt had brought in were already deftly handling their care. The two had undergone surgery for the most severe of their burns and the surgery had gone very well. When we arrived at the hospital, one of the doctors met us. She was chic with angular hair and dressed in black slacks and stilettos with silver heels. Rosalind would've approved, I thought, feeling better.

"They're in stable condition," said the doctor, smiling. "They're awake and have even made a few jokes. Any long-term damage will be minimal. Once they're fully healed, they'll respond well to plastic surgery." She looked at Reinhardt knowingly.

I stared at her. Was she present when they changed my face? When I had become Ruby? I waited to feel odd or disoriented seeing someone who would have known me as my former self, but I didn't feel anything. I loved who I used to be, but now it was more with a sisterly affection for someone I used to know, not with a longing to be her again. I was Ruby Draker now. And I was with my family.

Alice, Norm and Roscoe showed up at the hospital, too, creating a happy cacophony of noise and greetings and love.

After we hugged Alice and Norm and gave them an overview of what had happened, they dashed down the hall to see Amos and Hannah.

When Roscoe came in for his hug, he didn't walk, he bounded, nearly knocking me over. Seeing him taller, ganglier, more adult, yet with fear still in his eyes for his not having known what was happening to the rest of us, I was instantly a mess, crying all over him, and he all over me.

It was such a relief to be together again and weep away the tension and fear from the last several weeks. We had come through so much. As soon as Hannah and Amos were up and able to fly, we would all return to Fairhaven, to the protection of our own home. I knew that Drakers courted trouble—I'd learned to accept that—but for now, all that mattered was that we were fine, and whatever the future might bring, we could take it. We were Drakers. We would handle whatever came our way, together.

Acknowledgments

WRITING A NOVEL IS A LONG AND GRUELING TASK. This being my first literary work wasn't accomplished without assistance. Very special thanks go out to Jenna Kalinsky, my writing coach and editor. Jenna, you helped me accomplish a dream that I'd been harboring for most of my life. You also made me realize that writing is a passion for me. Thank you for holding my hand every step of the way.

I also want to thank my daughter Tiffany Eby Ferrie for beta reading several drafts. She caught all those errors that writers don't see. Thank you.

A special thank you to Sherrill Wark of Crowe Creations, my publisher, advisor, and trusted friend. You have made this publication everything it was meant to be. Thank you.

And never to be forgotten, I thank my late husband, Paul Stephen Scott, for the support and encouragement he gave me during the whole process. I hold him in my heart and miss him.

About the Author

IN ALL THE YEARS MARIANNE SCOTT worked in business, she never knew she had a flair for storytelling. Being tangled in the day-to-day challenges of meeting deadlines, dollar targets, and ever tighter delivery expectations left little time or energy for creativity. Yet at her core, she always felt something there. She didn't know how to name it, this yearning, that grew inside her with every passing year.

At work, Marianne would jokingly threaten to write a "tell-all" about her colleagues, exposing the difficult personalities and the stressful foibles of the fast-paced manufacturing industry, but in fact, she found herself more interested in letting her imagination run with stories of conspiracy, forbidden affairs, corporate espionage and other sundry misdoings.

Once she left the corporate world, instead of penning non-fiction tales, she gave herself over to her imagined worlds. Her truest pleasure, amusement, and release soon came from turning the ordinary into the extraordinary. From this, *Reinhardt*, *Finding Ruby Draker*, and *Shadows in the Aftermath* were born.